CHRISTOPHER KLOEBLE

THE MUSEUM OF THE WORLD

A NOVEL

Translated from the German by

REKHA KAMATH RAJAN

HarperCollins *Publishers* India

First published in English in India by HarperCollins *Publishers* 2022
4th Floor, Tower A, Building No 10, DLF Cyber City,
DLF Phase II, Gurugram, Haryana – 122002
www.harpercollins.co.in

2 4 6 8 10 9 7 5 3 1

P-ISBN: 978-93-5629-387-8
E-ISBN: 978-93-5629-388-5

Typeset in 11/14.7 Adobe Caslon Pro at
Manipal Technologies Limited, Manipal

Printed and bound at
Thomson Press (India) Ltd

This book is produced from independently certified FSC® paper
to ensure responsible forest management.

For my father

'Among all the things I have been instrumental in doing, your expedition remains one of the most important. It will gladden me even on my deathbed.'

Alexander von Humboldt,
in his letter to the Brothers Schlagintweit

'The task namely is to follow the trail of the Brothers Schlagintweit … and of so many other famous travellers.'

Jules Verne,
In Search of the Castaways

'I wish the Schlagintweits had never come to India.'

Bartholomew from Bombay

CONTENTS

From 1854 till 1857, at the end of the Little Ice Age and shortly before the outbreak of the first Indian War of Independence, the Bavarian brothers Hermann, Adolph and Robert Schlagintweit travelled through India and High Asia. Endorsed by the world-renowned scientist Alexander von Humboldt, and with the mandate of the East India Company that ruled over large parts of the subcontinent, the three scientists embarked on a broad range of explorations. Only two of them returned to Germany. It was one of the most expensive and elaborate expeditions of the modern era. The brothers set a record for climbing heights, penetrated unexplored regions, carried out espionage, collected almost 40,000 objects and gained, as they themselves liked to boast, remarkable insights into many fields of science.

They would never have been able to achieve all this without the help of the numerous people who accompanied them.

One of them was an orphan boy from Bombay.

PART I

Bombay
1854

Remarkable Object No. 1

THE MUSEUM OF THE WORLD

My name is Bartholomew, I am at least twelve years old and today, on 20 October 1854, I have founded India's first museum. I call it the Museum of the World. Smitaben says it should be called the Museum of Wretchedness. But what does a cook from Gujarat really know about such things? I do not want to write anything bad about her (even if she cannot read), but time and again she surprises me with how little she understands – in more than one regard. After over ten years in Bombay, she can barely speak a word of Marathi or Hindi. Without my help no one in the Glass House would know what she has cooked for us and Smitaben would not be able to tell the sabzi-wallah what vegetables she needs. When he arrives with his cart in front of our gate early in the morning, she has long been up and about cleaning one of the many windows that give St. Helena its sobriquet. Smitaben is always the first to get up and I am not sure whether she sleeps at all. In the evenings when the lights are put out in the dormitories, we can hear her downstairs in the kitchen scrubbing the pots and chasing the cockroaches. She does not have a family; at any rate, not a real one. All the orphans call her Maasi. Her hair is white, not grey like that of other maasis, but white like the dough of the Portuguese pão that she sometimes bakes for us. Smitaben knows a thing or two about taste. I prefer her salty-sweet handvo to almost all, no, to all of Bombay's dishes. Unfortunately, her other senses are not as well-developed. She has spent so much of her life looking at ordinary things that she does not see what is remarkable. How silly of me not to have thought of that! Smitaben's reaction to India's first museum matched her rustic nature. She gave me a smack on the back of my head, which did not hurt, and disappeared again into her territory, the kitchen.

I WENT OUTSIDE to show Devinder the museum. Devinder is our gardener. He comes from Punjab. Although he is not a Sikh, he allows his hair to grow. All over, he once whispered to me. He claims that to cut one's hair, or indeed to shave, means to lack in any masculinity whatsoever. I claim that Devinder is too lazy and too poor to visit a barber. The first is clearly indicated by the condition of the plants all around the Glass House: the palms bend as if they were bowing down to the sun, the grass has crept back into the earth and the mogra flowers wither away before they have fully blossomed. Still, Father Fuchs does not have the heart to dismiss Devinder. That is how I know that Devinder is poor. Because Father Fuchs is overly friendly to everyone he considers poor. He must be one of the friendliest people in Bombay.

BUT I WANTED to talk about Devinder. Even without Father Fuchs, I would know that Devinder is poor. Everyone I know is poor. We possess nothing more than the clothes on our backs and our hope. Hope that one day we will not be rich perhaps, but at least less poor. For there is only one kind of rich but many forms of poor. The problem, however, is that hope can be a demonic possession. Devinder is literally possessed by it. This should not be surprising since he lives with his grandmother and his parents, and his wife and her parents, and his children in a chawl in Blacktown. There they share one room. They sleep, they eat and increase their numbers on the one and the same mat. Devinder's family dies far more slowly than it grows. A chair hangs on a long, rusty nail in the wall of the room. The chair is only brought down for visitors. Respectable visitors like Father Fuchs. Some years ago, Devinder found the chair in a bay and rescued it from the salt water. The Parsis, Banias, Portuguese and, naturally, the Vickys[1] can afford to throw their properties into the sea. Their pieces of furniture outnumber their family members by far.

DEVINDER IS PROBABLY not lazy at all, just tired. His strength is taken up in keeping his hope alive. He does this best behind the garden shed in the shade of the Ficus tree. Buddha attained wisdom under such a tree; Devinder, on the other hand, inhales hope. He does that, like most of us, by sleeping. Especially in the afternoon hours, when the humid air of Bombay presses all the air from the body like Smitaben extracting the juice from a ripe imli.

THE OBJECTS IN my museum had shifted while being transported to the garden. Before waking Devinder up I had to arrange them again. Then I nudged him with my foot.

Devinder asked me not to disturb him.

I promised him that he had never seen anything like my museum.

This tempted him. In contrast to Smitaben, Devinder still has a hunger for the remarkable. He rubbed his eyes.

I carefully placed the museum down near him. Devinder blinked a few times, looked at it, then at me, then again at it and finally again at me.

I asked him what he saw.

An old wooden box, he said.

A display area, I said, and asked him what he saw in it.

Garbage, he said.

---

1 Father Fuchs says that the English call everything and everyone in India as it pleases them. Therefore, it is only fair that I call them what I please.

My collection, I said.

You collect garbage, he asked?

I did not want to give up so soon.

My collection is a holistic one, I said.

He looked at me blankly. I said: Holistic means concerning the whole. It is built on the idea that everything relates to everything else. Every object, however useless it may appear to be, is remarkable in its own way and can help us to understand the world.

Even a stone?

Especially a stone.

He smiled through his thick beard.

This puts me in the tradition of Humboldt, I said.

He wanted to know what a Humboldt is.

The greatest scientist of our times!

The greatest scientist of our times collects garbage?

Now that was a bit too much for me. I picked up my museum and left.

There was something else I had not considered. In order to recognize something remarkable, one needed not only hunger but a certain keenness of the eye.

I CARRIED THE museum to the paper room. The walls, floors, shelves and the table there are covered by so many layers of scrolls and despatches and letters that the room appears to be made of paper. This is where the *Lord of Existence* sits. That is the meaning of Hormazd's name, which he tells everyone. It is also fitting because he is responsible for the finances of the Glass House. Unlike Smitaben or Devinder, Hormazd can read and write. As a Parsi he was fed with numbers and letters while still in the womb. On good days Hormazd reads out to me from the *Bombay Times* about what is happening in the world. On bad days he drinks too much Pale Ale and spends the night in the paper room because, as he always says, he has had an *elaborate debate* with his wife. After such elaborate debates he often has a black eye and his topi sits crookedly on his head. Smitaben has told me what these debates are about. Although Hormazd is the least poor person I know (he lives in the Fort and not in Blacktown), he lacks something fundamental: offspring. Hormazd and his wife lack something that Devinder has in surplus. Why? Because of Hormazd, says his wife. Because of his wife, says Hormazd. Because of his false belief, say Devinder and Smitaben. Devinder and Smitaben seldom agree on anything, but on this one thing they agree: Hormazd would have had children long ago if he had been born a Hindu. I say, the solution is staring Hormazd in the face. After all, he works in an orphanage. But others have also thought about this. Some children are exceptionally friendly to him; they bring him a chickoo, ask questions about Zoroastrianism as if they were interested in it. They do not understand that he will never adopt one of us. A Parsi only takes Parsis into his family (in case there are any Parsi orphans; I have never encountered one). A Hindu, Muslim or Christian would not act differently. That is the problem with India, says Father Fuchs. A thousand different bricks do not want to be used for the same building. And yet, together they could create a palace!

When I opened the door to the paper room, there was a draught and the many loose papers rustled. This is how, I imagine, autumn must sound in the country Father Fuchs comes from. A season that we do not have. In Bombay, the high summer changes with the monsoon into a summer in which it rains from above and below before it retreats a little at the end of the year. Soon after that it begins to burn again with its full strength.

The air was hot and stagnant in the paper room. Pieces of cloth hung in front of the open window. They were stiff and dry. Hormazd had not dipped them into water for a long time.

I put the museum down next to the table at which he sat. His bloodshot eyes were open, but I had to wake him too. When he is busy calculating, the numbers clog his head.

I tapped him on the shoulder.

Not now, he said.

But he always says that. It means try a little harder so that I know you are worth my time.

Hormazd Sir?

Hormazd Sir is busy, he said.

His breath smelt of Pale Ale, but his speech was not slurred, and his gaze was clear.

You are an educated person, are you not? I asked.

Hormazd grunted and put the columns aside.

The only educated person far and wide, he said. What do you want?

I have founded India's first museum.

Have you indeed?

It is called the Museum of the World.

And where is this museum with the modest name?

I showed it to him.

Hormazd examined it thoroughly.

After a while he said: That entire museum is you. It is a picture without being a picture.

I nodded.

But, he asked, why should it interest anyone?

The British Museum, I said.

Hormazd raised an eyebrow wearily.

The British Museum is a museum in London, I said.

I know that, he said impatiently.

Father Fuchs visited it once, I said.

Hormazd rolled his eyes. Of course, Father Fuchs. What ideas has he put into your head this time? Don't you have any friends?

I have Father Fuchs.

That is not the same.

No, it's better! Father Fuchs says the British Museum is a temple. And he says the Vickys …

Vickys? he asked.

The Victorians.

You mean the English?

Yes, precisely, the Vickys. Their temple reminds them of who they are: A people that rules over half the world!

I think they know that even without a temple.

Maybe. But we in India, we need one.

We already have too many of those.

But we don't have one like this! We don't know who we are. That is why we let the Vickys tell us who we should be.

Says Father Fuchs, said Hormazd.

Yes! If we want to be free, we must remember who we are. We all need a museum. And this here, I pointed to the museum, this here is me.

Hormazd pressed his lips together, nodded, bent over his columns again and, using both index fingers, searched for a way through the labyrinth of numbers.

Do you like it? I asked.

The index fingers became still. He turned to me again.

Bartholomew, if I may give you some advice. You will never be free. You are an orphan. Even worse, an ambitious orphan! If you aren't careful, your life will be a series of disappointments. Someone like you does not found museums. Someone like you should be thankful if he does not perish as a child.

I PICKED UP the museum, thanked him for the advice, which rankled me almost physically, and set out for the chapel to wait for the man who always plants the best ideas in my head. During the day Father Fuchs is often in Blacktown. Despite the heat in which even the flies don't leave the shade, he walks from chawl to chawl and offers the residents his help. He is a great admirer of Hildegard von Bingen, and his knowledge of herbal medicine is considered second to none. But he can seldom use it in Bombay, for he lacks the herbs. But he is interested in our healing methods. This earns him a great deal of respect. Most of the firangi, especially the Vickys, avoid the bazaars. They believe that by sending their servants they can protect themselves from the most neutral judge on all seven islands: cholera. (As though the servants only bring back the shopping from the bazaars!) Father Fuchs, on the other hand, is delighted when on his explorations in Blacktown he discovers an oil that prevents teeth from rotting, or a powder that aids digestion. I think that Father Fuchs would have made an excellent scientist. If God had not discovered him before science did.

In the corridor the Others came towards me. Forty-seven orphans live in the Glass House and I know each one of them by name, but the Others as a designation for them is quite adequate.

We come from all four corners of the country. One would assume that we are all different. But I have learnt that one orphan is often like every other orphan. For instance, they only talk to me if necessary. Basically, therefore, never. Except for those evenings when we play cricket and they all yell at me. As soon as the heat abates a little, but there is still enough light to see the ball, we gather on the Esplanade and form two groups. I am always selected third-last as a team member. Only Aloisius who is blind and Francis who is left-handed and, of all things, doesn't have a left arm, come after me, even though I am not much better than them.

Technically, my agility should balance out my incompetence as a batsman. The problem is that my body does not obey me in such situations. When it is my turn to step up, my legs refuse to carry me onto the field, my head is locked in place and my arms hang uselessly from my shoulders. In the end, the team I am in always loses.

Only the dare is more agonizing!

Since April, Bori Bunder has the first railway station in all of Asia. The Vickys built it to transport their goods and their puffed-up egos. The dare consists in crawling between the wheels and over the tracks as soon as the train starts moving. Even Francis has managed to do it (he lost his arm before he came to us). I just cannot. Every time I face the rumbling, squealing giant droning in a deep bass tone, my strength deserts me and I cannot move because I know what will happen if I do. I see it clearly before me. And I not only see it. In such moments, I literally feel the iron wheels slice through my body as if through ghee.

The Others call me Bartholo-mouse, spit into my dal or dribble onion juice in my eyes when I am sleeping. If I want to be left in peace, I must remain unseen. I make myself even smaller than I am, sit in the last row during class, occupy the bed under the slope of the roof at the window with the lightning-like crack and, on the whole, avoid looking at them.

For a long time, I did not know why the Others are like that. I looked for answers in my reflection. That was not an easy thing to do. Bombay's puddles cannot be relied upon; sometimes they draw me rounder than Smitaben and sometimes as skinny as a street child from Blacktown. And the sea doesn't go to any trouble at all, it only sketches an indistinct cloud.

The only mirror that tells the truth is in Father Fuchs's room. It shows me the smallest at least twelve-year-old that I know. The colour of my skin changes with the seasons; in the burning summer I look like a fisherman from Bandra and in the monsoon like an overprotected Bengali son who seldom leaves the house. Father Fuchs says that my eyes are the colour of amber. I have never seen amber, but the light in it is said to glow like the Battliwalas' bottles in the evening sun.

The more often and the more carefully I looked at myself, the clearer it became to me what bothers the Others. It has nothing to do with how I look. Yet, the answer lies in the mirror.

Father Fuchs.

Once when he found me examining myself, he reminded me of the fate of Narcissus. I replied like a wiseacre that my father was most certainly not a river-god, otherwise I would have known how to swim.

Most of what I know I have learnt from Father Fuchs. He even taught me about my name (and gave it to me). Before me there were only two other Bartholomews in India. The first one preached here. He was an apostle and Jesus called him the man without falsehood. The second, Bartholomew Ziegenbalg, lived in the Danish colony of Tranquebar in the previous century. Before him there had never been a German missionary in India. He was also an orphan and a remarkable man. Most firangi force us to learn their language. But Ziegenbalg taught his tongue Tamil! He also built schools and a children's home. I bear his name with pride. Even though I prefer my gods to his God. I feel sorry for the Christians that they have only one. What a sad family!

Some of the missionaries get angry when I share such thoughts with them. Not Father Fuchs. He says he is sure I will find the path to enlightenment. We always speak to each other in German. The Others, none of whom have mastered the language as well as I have, say that is why I talk like an old man. But I don't want to talk like a child anyway. After class, when the Others run out as if the school is on fire, I stay back for a while and talk to Father Fuchs. He gifts me many strange words, some even in Bavarian. That is the language one speaks where Father Fuchs comes from. When he talks about Bavaria, he sounds sad and happy. He says his native country is without mangoes or the sea, and its people are like the Punjabis: honourable and self-assured and hearty but blessed with far less hair.

This is also a rather accurate description of Father Fuchs. Moreover, he has a smile that never leaves his face. I only have to think of it and it no longer matters that the dare petrifies me. His smile is like Smitaben's cooking. If one has to go without it for too long, one becomes weak, tired, sad, angry. Father Fuchs's smile is not broad, and neither is it particularly beautiful. But it is an honest smile; it offers more hope than a snooze in the shade of the Ficus tree.

He often gifts me his smile, in the mirror and also otherwise.

The Others do not fail to notice this.

WHEN I LEFT the paper room and encountered them in the corridor, I pressed against the wall like a lizard and tried to melt into it. But the museum attracted their attention. They formed a crescent around me.

One Other asked what I was carrying.

Garbage, I said and avoided their gaze. They mustn't know that I owned something. Otherwise they would take it away from me.

Liar! another Other shouted.

A third Other said: Devinder said that is supposed to be a museum, the first in all of India!

All the Others laughed. They grabbed the museum and broke the objects. I could not stop them. My body would not obey me. After they had destroyed most of it, they seemed to get bored. They turned away.

Just then one of them saw that I had set about carrying away the remains of the museum. They followed me outside. I ran away. I am faster than they are. But the museum was too heavy. They caught up with me, snatched it out of my arms and trampled all over it. Again, I could do nothing about it. One Other brought a piece of hot coal he had stolen from the istry-wallah. He used it to set a few dry champa leaves alight and threw them into the museum. It began to burn at once. The Others waited for my reaction. They looked at me hungrily. I concentrated on not letting even one teardrop fall from my eyes. It did not take long for them to leave me alone. Still, I did not put the fire out. I knew the Others would set it ablaze again if I did so. The Museum of the World disintegrated into its smallest parts before my eyes. The smoke tasted acrid.

THE SUN HAD long set, and evening mass was over when Father Fuchs came to me. The Others had had a wash and lay in their beds stuffed with Smitaben's pav bhaji.[2] I was still sitting in front of the ashes which were cold and grey like old bird-shit.

Father Fuchs announced himself with his wheezing cough. Father Fuchs's cough is one of the most splendid sounds of Bombay. When he coughs, the Others don't bother me. When he coughs, I can fall asleep easily and wake up quickly. When he coughs, I know that I will soon know a little more.

He came and stood near me and covered his mouth with his Bavarian handkerchief. It is embroidered with red roses. I have never seen such perfect roses. The roses in the bazaars of Blacktown look like shrivelled-up corals. The ones on Father Fuchs's handkerchief never wither. In fact, they blossom afresh with his blood when he coughs. That is good, says Father Fuchs, if it all comes out. But Smitaben says it can't be good, so much is not supposed to come out.

He asked what the matter was.

I founded a museum, I said, just as we had discussed.

Where, he wanted to know.

I pointed to the ashes.

A moment passed. I was grateful that he did not ask how this heap could be my museum.

That is India's first museum, he said.

That was India's first museum, I said.

He asked for a tour of the museum.

It has been burnt down, I said.

But not in your head, right? They can never burn what is in your head.

No, I said, they cannot.

Then show it to me, he said, and closed his eyes. Lead me through your museum.

I hesitated.

---

2 Smitaben insists that she invented it. Even if by now it has been copied, as she says, in every squalid kitchen in Bombay.

I am waiting, he said.

So I began with the handvo.

It was, I said, and Father Fuchs said: It is.

It is, I said, happiness that can be eaten. But only a rustic maasi from Gujarat knows the secret of how to make it with ghee, dal, masala, and patience.

Then there was … is a tiffin box. But not just any tiffin box! It is no longer used to keep food. A lazy or tired gardener mislaid this specimen during the monsoon, so that it is now coated with a thick layer of rust and can never be opened again. And yet, it feeds everyone who shakes it with something, namely with hope, because it clicks and clacks most delightfully.

Then there is a scroll. Thanks to the air in Bombay, it is as supple as algae; it smells of Pale Ale and the group of inked numbers on it is faint. But when one looks at it long enough, one can see in it almost anything the heart desires: children, wealth, a museum.

Then there are some smaller and exceedingly small objects that were collected on the street; they were thrown away or forgotten like orphans. It is difficult to decide what purpose they serve, but they have the right to a place in the museum like all other objects.

Then there is the wooden cross that was gifted to a certain orphan when he came to live in the Glass House. Every day it reminds him of the place he calls home and of the person he learns so much from.

And then … then there is an empty space; there would have been something there if the Vickys had not come to India and if my parents would still be alive.

When I finished, Father Fuchs did not move for a long time as if he were me trying to execute the dare. Then he opened his eyes and clapped. He clapped so loud and so long that the Others looked out of the window and stabbed me with their looks.

Congratulations, said Father Fuchs, your whole museum is a remarkable object.

He rushed into the house and fetched a mango, our favourite fruit. The season is long over, but Father Fuchs had been able to find a few last ones in Mazagaon, home of the country's sweetest mangoes. He cut it in half with a knife, took out the seed and laid it aside almost tenderly. Then he scored a lattice design into the flesh of the fruit on each half, upended it and handed one to me. We bit into it at the same time, slurped and chewed. Juice ran over my chin. The taste of a ripe mango is as good as the sound of Father Fuchs's cough!

After we had nibbled away the last of the fruit from the skin and licked our fingers, he asked: What is the name of the museum?

I told him.

He looked up at the night sky; the moon was white and round like a fresh idli.

A good choice, he said, and yet … isn't there something missing?

What? I asked.

Father Fuchs smiled as he always smiles when he is putting an idea into my head.

What? I asked again.

He offered me a deal. If I were to go to bed immediately, he would reveal the perfect name before breakfast.

I didn't have to think long about it.

Now I am lying in the dormitory wishing that morning would come.

Writing helps. That way time passes more quickly. Father Fuchs has given me a small book. He says that it is the best place for my museum. I can collect everything I want in it: the heaviest, most expensive and most dangerous objects of the continent, and even invisible things such as feelings, dreams and memories. If I make an effort, he says, if I try really hard, it can even become a museum for all of us Indians. The pages are whiter than the moon tonight; I will fill them like a proper scientist with many remarkable objects.

No. 1 is the Museum of the World.

Outside, in the corridors, the echo of Father Fuchs's cough resounds. I hear it clearly even though the Others are being noisy.

Bartholo-mouse, they call out repeatedly, Bartholo-mouse!

But I don't pay any mind to it.

My name is Bartholomew, I am at least twelve years old and today, on 20 October 1854, I have founded India's first museum.

Remarkable Object No. 2

THE BAMBOO CANE

On the morning after I had made the opening entry in my notebook, I was the first in the dormitory to jump out of bed. On other days I would have tried to hold on to the night with closed eyes. Not that day. I felt hope growing in me as if I were breathing it in.

I slipped into my kurta that smelt of a charred museum and ran out of the dormitory.

Father Holbein, who supervised us, called out my name. At first threateningly, then angrily. He emphasized each syllable; it sounded as if he were chanting a prayer.

Bar-tho-lo-mew!

While calling out, he raised his bamboo cane which he always carries with him. It is the extension of his hands. Even the strongest among the Others do not defy him. His cane knows every sensitive part of our bodies.

Despite this, I did not stop. I was aware of the consequences. Five blows at least.

But a perfect name was worth it.

I BRAKED IN the corridor in front of Father Fuchs's room, gasped for air and knocked.

There was no reply.

I tried again. It was only then that it struck me. Something was different. I listened. In the distance two cannon shots announced the weekly arrival of the packet ship; a macaque lounged on a girder above me; at the main door the sabzi-wallah and Smitaben argued about whether the amrut were rotten or ripe; Father Holbein drew nearer in his chappals with his shuffling gait.

An ordinary morning in the Glass House.

Except …

The cough. It was missing. Had Father Fuchs forgotten about our deal and already left for Blacktown?

I pushed open the door to his room.

He was not there. In order to be certain, I even looked into the mirror.

Suddenly, Father Holbein was on me. With his thumb and forefinger, he grabbed the skin under my chin and dragged me behind him. I fought back the pain and asked about Father Fuchs. He did not say anything. Which does not surprise me. Father Holbein prefers to speak through his cane.

In the dormitory he let go of me and ordered me to take off my kurta.

I obeyed.

On all fours, he said. His voice did not sound harsh; rather as if he were giving me directions, as if he wanted to help me.

My hands looked for support on the stone floor and I made sure my knees were not resting on anything sharp. Then, I humped my back as he had asked, so that the skin on it was stretched.

Father Holbein did not hit me at once. First, he waited, till there was silence in the dormitory. Out of the corner of my eyes I could see the bare, dirty feet of the Others. I was fine with that. At least I would not have to endure their looks.

The first blow felt like the cut of a sharp knife. With each subsequent blow the pain pierced deeper into my back and flowed like boiling water in all directions. I concentrated on counting the blows. But Father Holbein's blows did not have a regular rhythm. He composed his blows wilfully, took breaks that lasted a few seconds or an entire minute. The unexpectedness of the pain was part of his punishment.

My counting got mixed up. Every time when I thought he was finished, he hit me again. When I had given up and was prepared for many more blows, Father Holbein took a step back. No one in the dormitory moved. The only noise was from my snuffling.

Father Holbein told me to have a wash and turned to the Others again.

I got up slowly. Each movement felt like another blow. Gradually, the voices of the Others returned.

When I let the water flow over my back, it turned pink at my feet. Father Fuchs will treat the wounds with an ointment, I thought. As soon as he returns, he will take care of me.

In the dining room I was not given any breakfast. Father Holbein's punishment had not ended. I had to stand in the corner and watch the Others eat. Some of them deliberately licked the khichri slowly from their fingers. I inhaled its fragrance and told myself that it alone would fill me. My back was on fire, as if I had lain down in one of Smitaben's large hot pans.

Father Fuchs was missing at the adults' table.

After morning mass, I went to Smitaben and asked her about Father Fuchs. She turned around with a frightened look and pushed me out of the kitchen with both hands. The anklets on her feet jingled nervously.

Father Holbein had given her clear instructions. He knew how well we understand each other, namely in a language that he cannot even begin to master.

In the garden, Devinder was hoeing the earth in the vegetable patch unusually vigorously. Drops of sweat hung like glittering stones in his beard. I asked if he could tell me something about Father Fuchs's whereabouts. He pretended not to understand me. I tried in Hindi and Punjabi, and with sign language. I pointed to the window of Father Fuchs's room. But Devinder simply continued to dig the sandy earth.

The door to the paper room was open. With his eyes to the ground, Hormazd stalked the room like a stork. When he found what he was looking for, he snapped it up and the paper wriggled in his hand like a hapless fish.

Before I could say anything, he shook his head and imitated someone swinging a cane.

I left the room.

In the corridor I heard a throat being cleared behind me. It was Hormazd. He pressed a finger to his chapped lips and held out a note for me. It read: *The Lord of Existence does not take orders from a 'hollow leg' (Hohlbein).* He handed me a white cloth that had been tied to make a pouch. Inside were mutton tikkas. I am not particularly fond of mutton, but these tikkas smelt like a delicious plant. I put a piece in my mouth. It tasted buttery and pungent. I swallowed it hungrily almost without chewing.

Hormazd's lips formed a curve. (He is not very practised at smiling.)

I hurried away so that I would not be late for class. But I wanted to first gobble up the tikkas behind the garden shed.

It never came to that. As I was running through the doorway, my foot caught on something and I fell down the stairs. My shoulder caught the impact of the fall, but my back felt as if it had snapped. Some Others laughed; they had placed a trip cord there.

One of them asked what was in the pouch.

One Other shouted: A museum!

All of them found it very funny.

They took the pouch, opened it and looked at me in surprise wondering where I could have got the tikkas, but also in wonder at the gift they were getting.

First, they stuffed their mouths with it. Then they shouted for Father Holbein.

SINCE THEN, FIVE days have passed. Today is the first day I feel strong enough to write. I still cannot get up. This time Father Holbein chose my feet and the hollows of my knees.

Smitaben changes the bandages in the mornings and evenings. While doing this she deliberately bends over me in such a way that I cannot see the wounds. Yet, I know they are there. And *how* I know! The pain reminds me of them. I try taking shallow breaths and moving as little as possible, so that the pain does not get worse. Sometimes I find I have to cry when Smitaben comes, even though I do not want to cry. Then she looks at me as if she would like to say a friendly word.

But no one is allowed to talk to me.

Father Holbein has also chalked a line around my bed. Only two people are allowed to cross it: Smitaben and he. When I ask him where Father Fuchs is, he raises the cane. It is still shining as if it has never been used.

That is what I like about bamboo. Even if one cuts it, or uproots it, or bends it, it lives on proudly for a long time. If I want to find out what has happened to Father Fuchs, I have to be as strong as bamboo.

Remarkable Object No. 3

THE BAVARIAN HANDKERCHIEF

Today three white men came to the orphanage. But none of them was Father Fuchs. Father Holbein showed them around. He steered them through the kitchen and the paper room, the school, the garden and the chapel. I followed them furtively. (Since a few days I can walk again, although I am only allowed to cross the chalked line to go to the latrine.) I maintained a distance so Father Holbein could not see me. That is why I could not hear what they were talking about. Father Holbein also introduced the men to Smitaben, Devinder and Hormazd. But they talked only to Hormazd. I presume because he is the only one who knows English. Father Holbein waved his cane around the entire time. That kept the Others away. Even though they crowded behind hedges and doors to observe the visitors.

THE VISITORS' ATTIRE was exceedingly ugly and unserviceable; trousers and shirts and a multitude of buttons constricted their bodies, not allowing the air to touch their skins. Their faces were almost as red as Smitaben's bindi.

But these men presented an unusual sight even for firangi. I especially noticed three things:

1. The way they walked. They took large steps as though they had to cover as much distance as possible as quickly

as possible. A Bombayite is more careful. He places his feet closely one behind the other because he knows that a careless step can land him in an unpleasant place. Moreover, the men's steps reminded me of the steps Devinder takes when he measures out an area of the garden.

2. Their faces. They looked like three versions of the same man. The youngest wore a hat with a broad brim and had pointy ears which stuck out like a bat's. He was not much older than I. I cannot describe his look other than to say it was directed inwards. His somewhat more mature version, the man in the middle, on the other hand, allowed his glance to wander around merrily and his cheeks puffed up while breathing. The oldest, in turn, cultivated a tuft of hair on his upper lip which flounced around like a nervous animal when he talked. And he talked a lot!
3. Their effect on Father Holbein. In the presence of these men, he swung the cane around in the air as if it were not a feared instrument but a brush with which he painted cheerful pictures. He stumbled several times in his chappals because he was paying attention to the men while walking and not to the ground. He was also practising several kinds of smiles: attentive, pleased, hopeful, charming. I never knew that Father Holbein could smile like that.

By the time he led the men into the dormitory I had already hurried ahead and returned to my bed.

They came directly to me.

Is that him? asked Tufty.

Father Holbein nodded.

He is very small, said Chubby Cheeks.

Bat came closer and looked me over.

Say something, Father Holbein demanded.

In which language? I asked in German.

Father Holbein laughed and pointed the cane at me. See? he said to the men.

How many languages do you speak? asked Tufty.

Why do you want to know? I asked.

Father Holbein put his cane on my shoulder.

Answer, he said.

I am proficient in Hindi and English and German and Gujarati and Punjabi and Marathi. My Persian leaves much to be desired. But, instead, I am at present learning Bavarian.

Bavarian! Chubby Cheeks burst out.

We are from Bavaria, Tufty said.

Do you know Father Fuchs? I asked.

We were in contact with him.

Do you know where he is?

No, he replied, unfortunately not.

Say something in Bavarian, Chubby Cheeks demanded.

I said: *Kruzifix*!

Tufty clapped his hands.

Very good! he called out.

Bat smiled.

Chubby Cheeks looked at me with narrowed eyes.

I am not convinced, he said.

We could try him out, said Tufty.

An excellent idea! said Father Holbein. Would you like to take him with you at once?

Tufty looked at his younger versions. They nodded.

Why not, he said.

Then it is decided, said Father Holbein, and pointed his cane at the tip of my nose. Have a bath and get dressed!

Where are we going? I asked.

You will find out soon enough, Chubby Cheeks replied.

You should be happy that you are allowed to serve these gentlemen, said Father Holbein.

I am not a servant, I retorted.

Chubby Cheeks wanted to say something, but Tufty beat him to it.

Who are you then? he asked.

I am Bartholomew, I said.

One of the twelve apostles, he said.

I know, I said.

Hermann Schlagintweit, he said, and held out his hand.

I shook his hand firmly so that he could feel my strength.

Hermann Schlagintweit's hand was rougher than Devinder's. Unusual for a firangi. He pointed first to Chubby Cheeks, then to Bat.

These are Adolph and Robert Schlagintweit, he said, my brothers. We are on a research expedition.

You are scientists? What are you studying?

Hermann, Chubby Cheeks-Adolph said, food is served.

Right, said Hermann, but why don't you join us?

He has already eaten, said Father Holbein, and nudged the brothers towards the exit.

I could do with some more, I said.

Father Holbein's hand tightened around his cane. But Hermann had already put an arm around me and was talking.

He did not stop talking the whole evening. And so, I learnt that the brothers wanted to travel for three years through India and the elevated plateau in Central Asia to conduct scientific investigations. First, however, they would stay in Bombay for a few weeks to study the city and make arrangements for their expedition.

We were sitting in the dining room at the adults' table where no child has ever sat. I could not see the Others, but I could sense that they were observing us. Smitaben dished up enough food for an entire ship's crew. I stuffed myself with handvo while Hermann filled us up with words. It seemed as if he had to use all the words that Robert saved up. Robert continued to be silent. (Perhaps he does not have a voice.) Adolph, on the other hand, smacked his lips instead of talking. And Father Holbein blew copiously on every spoon of dal before he put it in his mouth. In all the years with us he has still not understood that dal only tastes good when it is eaten steaming hot.

Hermann reported that he and his brothers were already taking … had taken Hindi lessons. From a Muslim whom Adolph called a Musalman and Hermann a Munshi. They had come to an agreement with him on what in their view was an *overly generous payment*. How generous, they did not say. I presume, therefore: not very generous. When it was time to pay him, the Munshi suddenly demanded the sum agreed upon for each of them individually. (Naturally! said Father Holbein, indignantly.) The brothers refused. Vehemently! Hermann emphasized. On the following day, when they were returning from measuring the groundwater, they experienced, as he said, an *Indian peculiarity*: a chaprasi handed them a judicial summons. The Munshi had sued them, and they had to appear before the Court of Petty Sessions. Although there are many more Indians than firangi in Bombay, the court is presided over alternately by a European and an Indian judge. If you were to ask me, only every fourth or fifth judge should be European. The firangi should consider themselves lucky that they even have judges at all in our country. Do Indian judges preside over courts in London? The brothers, at any rate, were assigned to a Parsi. (Naturally, Father Holbein again.) But to their surprise, they were found not guilty. (Naturally! I almost called out. *We* are not as biased as *they* are – and moreover, the Parsis are known to have a weakness for the West.)

This experience, said Hermann, made us realize that it would be advisable to hire a brilliant translator rather than a cunning teacher.

He fell silent for the first time and looked at me. Lassi dripped from his tuft of hair like paint from a brush.

How old are you? he asked.

At least twelve years old, I replied.

Not very old.

Old enough, said Adolph. At his age we were climbing the Alps on our own.

Not quite on our own, said Hermann.

He would not be alone either, replied Adolph.

They both stared at each other as Father Fuchs and Father Holbein sometimes do when one wants to smile and the other wants to use his cane.

The dining room became quiet.

I used the opportunity to inform them that I could not help them.

Father Holbein put his spoon down and seized the cutlery next to it, his cane: You will do what they ask.

I cannot do that, I said, and asked myself which part of my body would now become acquainted with the cane.

Adolph burst out laughing: You are one hell of a dog!

I am not a dog, I said.

It's just a figure of speech in Bavarian, said Hermann.

What does it mean? I asked.

That one cannot trust you, said Adolph, and turned to his brothers. Let it be Hermann. Don't forget the boy was raised by Jesuits.

I beg your pardon, said Father Holbein.

Adolph did not pay heed to him and continued talking: What will we do with someone like him? He will only cause trouble.

Hermann licked his fingers. (I was very taken with the fact that he had made the effort to eat with his hands.)

Will you cause us trouble? he asked me.

Three brothers and a Father waited for my reply.

Most probably, I said.

Father Holbein gasped, Adolph chuckled, and Robert pulled his hat further down his face.

He is coming with us, said Hermann to Father Holbein.

Adolph said: Hermann!

Hermann said: Adolph!

Father Holbein said: Splendid!

Robert said nothing.

And I said: That is not possible! I have to be here when Father Fuchs returns!

Only a few days, said Hermann, at the most a few weeks.

Weeks! I exclaimed.

Be thankful, Father Holbein said to me, you will get to know a side of Bombay that you have never seen.

Then they sent me to fetch my things.

In the dormitory I stuffed my notebook and the second kurta I possessed into a bag.

An Other asked: They are taking you with them?

He sounded confused. Something like this had never happened. Many of the Others observed me sceptically from their beds.

On the way back to the dining room I stopped in Father Fuchs's room. I tore a page from the notebook and wrote:

Dear Father Fuchs,

You have to help me. The Brothers Schlagintweit have taken me.

Bartholomew.

When I was clamping the page to the upper end of the mattress, I saw it. The Bavarian handkerchief with the red roses was lying under the bed. I picked it up, shook off the dust and pocketed it.

Today is my first night in Bombay which I am not spending in the Glass House. But maybe that is a good thing. Father Fuchs would never leave his handkerchief behind without good reason. He deliberately placed it there as a secret message for me. Something has happened to him. He wants me to look for him. Father Fuchs must be somewhere in Bombay. And I will find him.

Remarkable Objects

Nos. 4 & 5 & 6 & 7 & 8 & 9 & 10

NOT A PROPER DIYA
ICE WITHOUT BUBBLES
BOMBAY DUCK
THE PICTURE MACHINE
THE TASTE OF NAKEDNESS
THE ISLAND OF THE GODS
A KHANA

I will never find Father Fuchs! November, the best month in a Bombay year, has passed and I cannot forgive it even if it caressed me with a cool, but not cold, breeze and lulled me to sleep with warm, but not hot, air; let me have my first taste of ice and showed me a picture machine; even if it let me almost fly, ride on a boat and taste nakedness, I cannot forgive it. Henceforth, I will call it the worst month of the year.

It began when I moved in with the Schlagintweits. I did not want to serve them. But I could not go back to the Glass House, and the brothers were my best chance to find Father Fuchs. They constantly profess to be interested in all the depths and heights of India. This gave me what I now know was a demonic hope. In Bombay one always knows someone, who knows someone, who knows someone. Every Bombayite drags an invisible net behind them in which large fish from the Fort and puny fish from Blacktown get caught. If I went around with the Schlagintweits I would stumble on Father Fuchs's net sooner or later, I thought.

Unfortunately, on an average, only every fourth Bavarian is pleasant. I learnt this during my time with the brothers. However, each one of them is unpleasant in his own particular way. They have nothing in common with Father Fuchs. Apart from the fact that they are also from Bavaria.

They were staying with a consul.

I asked them why they did not want to move into one of the two Parsi hotels in the Fort.

Adolph ignored me. Robert too, perhaps. His silence can mean approval or disapproval – he mostly leaves the choice to his counterpart.

But Hermann replied that they were not fitting accommodations. The location of the hotels in the Fort did not suit them. They would rather be closer to other Europeans.

What kind of scientists are these, who travel thousands of kilometres only to arrive at the place from where they had left?

The consul's residence is to the west of the Fort. The Glass House would easily fit into it at least twice over. But what is even more impressive than the residence itself is the air around it. There is so much place there, so much nothing to inhale, to run through and to look right up to the sky. In Blacktown, every place is something. The garden which surrounds the consul's residence is so large that he can ride in it on a black horse imported from Australia, because the Indian ones are apparently inferior and Arabian ones are presently not in fashion. Each Schlagintweit had his own room in the residence. For each one there was a bed in which half of Devinder's family could have slept comfortably. Hermann was delighted with the chunam[3] and carefully observed the embellishments that were made by the, as he calls them, natives. He likes to appear scientific. Adolph, on the other hand, deplored the lack of any kind of oil paintings.[4] He likes to appear artistic.

I was accommodated in an attic room which I did not have to share with anyone. I have never not shared. It seemed wrong to me. I had a bed, a washbowl, many hooks for my few things and a window from which I could see the Colaba lighthouse. It towers into the sky like a giant candle and is said to be hundred and fifty feet high. (The Vickys' feet, however, are not just sickly white, but they are also small because they are always laced in, which hinders their growth.) If I could have climbed it and could have operated the light, my search would not have lasted long.

A smaller candle was on the windowsill, and it was placed on a metal plate. Next to it some matches. A light entirely for me alone. What was I supposed to do with so much light? Sometimes I lit the candle in broad daylight and held my hand over it till I could not hold out any more. The pain was not pain because it felt good; the stronger it was, the more awake I felt. On Diwali I let the candle burn all night. Naturally, it could not replace a proper diya. Despite that, it could perhaps lead Father Fuchs to me. Just as the diyas led Rama and Sita home.

EVERY MORNING AND every evening I took out Father Fuchs's handkerchief. It reminded me of my goal, my mission. Only a few of my tears were on it. They could hardly be seen.

---

3 The humidity in Bombay is no friend of European wallpaper, that is why many firangi have the walls of their houses trimmed with quicklime.

4 Bombay humidity, as mentioned.

I SPENT THE first days of the worst month of the year at Hermann's side. His communicativeness made translation difficult. He flushed so many words through my head! To these I had to attach my own words without him noticing. I had to thread my questions about Father Fuchs into every conversation. I made all of Bombay shake its head. No one had seen Father Fuchs, no one remembered him. But I did not give up. Soon, Hermann was known on the street as the firangi who was looking for a Jesuit. Only Hermann was not aware of it.

AT THE END of the day I would feel sated. I had never before heard and spoken so much. All at the same time! Bombayites prefer speaking to not-speaking. Especially when one does not have time. But Hermann was the merciless king of talk. In the bazaars, even the Banias and the Jains ran away from us because he hardly let them speak. And what is a merchant without his words?

WHEN HERMANN IS not talking, he is writing. In his notebook. He uses a pencil that he has either stolen or borrowed. It has *Faber* written on it. Hermann fills his pages faster than I do. I have often asked him what exactly it is that he is writing. He did not tell me, not once. I found that suspicious and decided to find out the answer for myself. Maybe this way I would get a clue about Father Fuchs.

FOR DAYS I was unable to get anywhere near the notebook. Hermann always carried it in his breast pocket and watched over it like Smitaben over a ripening papaya. But, towards the end of my first week with the Schlagintweits, an opportunity arose.

In the evening, the brothers drank gin with Consul Ventz on his baramahda (wrongly called *veranda* by the firangi).

The gin had been sent to the consul directly from London, supplied by an acquaintance called Charles Tanqueray. The drinks were cooled by ice. I had never seen ice before in my life.

I asked whether I may be allowed to taste a piece.

Consul Ventz turned to me; his nose had the same reddish tint as Hormazd's.

You want to taste bubble-free ice from the lakes of North America?

I nodded.

Indians! he exclaimed to the brothers and laughed. This ice has not travelled all around the southern tip of Africa in order to land in your mouth!

With a crunching sound he chewed the ice and held out his empty glass to the servant who immediately began to make a fresh drink.

When I looked at the brothers, Adolph ignored me. Hermann was dozing. Robert blinked – or perhaps it was more of a wink. At any rate, he finished his drink and put the glass down next to his wicker chair, even pushing it a little away from himself. The ice in the glass sparkled.

While the consul complained that there were no decent apples in India, I moved towards the glass without attracting attention, snatched the ice in a favourable moment and let it disappear in my mouth. First it tasted pungent and bitter, the gin. Then, however, a salty chill filled my mouth; it flowed down my throat and rose into my head. I would never have imagined that something so cold could be so pleasant! I sucked on it carefully so that the ice would melt slowly. Only when it had become a thin slice on my tongue I bit on it, and it broke deliciously into small pieces. For one moment – and just for a brief one – I was glad that the Schlagintweits had recruited me. I would have loved to tell Smitaben about it. I asked myself, not for the first time, how she and all the others, except the Others, were doing.

Where I was now standing, I was only two steps away from Hermann. His notebook was in the right pocket of his waistcoat which he had hung over the backrest of an armchair. Since he was not talking, he must have dozed off. I pulled the notebook carefully out of the pocket and went away.

Bartholomew! someone called. At first, I did not recognize Robert's voice because he uses it so rarely; it has a confident ring to it and does not mesh with the bat-ears and smooth cheeks.

I stopped.

What have you got there? he asked.

Nothing, I said.

Then put this nothing back from where you took it.

Indians! Consul Ventz mumbled into his gin. It's their nature, they simply cannot help it.

I only wanted to borrow it, I said in my defence. To read it.

He can read? Consul Ventz lifted his ungainly body into an upright position. Where did you find this specimen? I demand a demonstration, immediately!

Adolph gestured invitingly.

I should read?

Hermann has nothing against it, said Adolph and grinned.

Robert jabbed his shoulder.

I opened the notebook at a random page. Hermann's handwriting was childish, but I could decipher it despite the exaggerated flourishes.

I read: *What can be said commonly in favour of all races in India is that even on streets that are so densely packed during a large part of the day as the ones in Bombay are, scuffles and dangerous hustling are rare; however, there is also no great ambition to finish a lot of work in a short time.*

How true! said Consul Ventz and told me to continue reading.

I scanned through a few paragraphs and looked for a suitable passage.

The first impression, I read, *that a newly arrived person gets of the behaviour of Europeans towards the natives is not a very satisfactory one; the Europeans seem to greatly overestimate themselves in regard to the Indian Hindus and Musalmans.*

Surely that is not written there! said Consul Ventz. He got up, looked for balance, found it, took the book from me and studied the page.

It really is! he called out. Mr Schlagintweit!

Hermann stirred.

Hermann Schlagintweit! blustered Consul Ventz and emptied his glass in one go.

Hermann looked up at him.

You are here to study India, he said. What is the meaning of these biases against your own people?

Adolph and Robert smirked.

It would be better if you left science to the scientists, said Hermann, our research demands a holistic approach.

Holistic? asked Ventz.

Holistic means concerning the whole, I said.

All four of them looked at me as if they had never seen me before.

I know that! shouted Ventz. Do you think I don't know that? Of course, I know that!

Hermann took the notebook from him. It is late, he said, I will take my leave.

Come, he said to me as he went into the house. I followed him.

In the library, which smelt musty like the paper room, Hermann pointed a finger at me.

How do you know what holistic means?

Father Fuchs, I said.

It is remarkable how much he could teach you.

I also had a part in it.

Hermann smoothed down his moustache.

I can understand why he means so much to you. Without him you would be just one of the many natives.

Would you help me find him?

You should forget him. We will soon be travelling on, to Madras. Your skills are very useful. I have decided that you will accompany us.

I cannot go to Madras!

The decision is not yours to make.

What disturbed me the most was how unemotionally he spoke. I searched for words that would hit him hard and shot out: You are an unsavoury person!

Be that as it may, he said and held out his notebook to me. For you. I can teach you more than a man of God.

I did not move, and so he placed the notebook on the armrest of a chair and left me alone.

I made a promise to myself: Under no circumstances would I go with the brothers to Madras. I would rather run away and find refuge in the lanes of Blacktown.

IN THIS NIGHT I used an entire candle and a lot of moonlight after that. My fingers turned silvery from leafing through Hermann's notebook. The Schlagintweit noted down everything: observations, measurements, thoughts. Some things I did not understand. *Periodic changes* and *magnetic observations* and *absolute intensity determinations*.

Above all, the Schlagintweit had a fondness for numbers. How could I have lived at least twelve years in Bombay and not known that the surface of the city measured fifty-five square kilometres? In his notes, Malabar Hill was fifty-eight metres high. These figures represented my country. How is it that he knew something about it which I did not? It seemed to me as if he were taking possession of Bombay in this way. By subordinating places I had always known to his numerical system, he was taking them away from me. They now belonged to him. The population figure was the most horrifying. *A little over 2 million*, he had noted. Could that be true? Who had counted them? I imagined all Bombayites standing in a long line to be counted. An unheard-of event! Not one of us can keep still longer than a newborn. And yet Hermann had arrived at this result. And so, I did not find Father Fuchs in the notebook, rather his opposite:

fear. How was I supposed to locate him among more than two million people?

Several days went by. I often had to accompany Hermann to the offices in the governor's palace. He was making arrangements there for the onward journey. And so, I got to know a part of the city I had never set foot in before. An Indian orphan is not allowed to enter buildings in which there are more firangi than anywhere else in Bombay. But even so, I already knew a few things about what goes on in these buildings. Father Fuchs criticizes the Vickys for it more severely than anyone else, and he puts this criticism in letters to the superiors. He ends most of these letters with the words of Karl Marx:[5] *At all events, we may safely expect to see, at a more or less remote period, the regeneration of that great and interesting country.*

But the superiors never reply to Father Fuchs.

The higher posts in the offices are filled only by Europeans. They are hired by the East India Company, which some say is more powerful than the Crown. Most of the clerks, most of the *lower placed* clerks, are Indo-Europeans. Their fathers are Europeans, their mothers from India, Persia and so forth. It is never the other way around, but if it does happen to be that way, the child of such a union does not live long. The Indo-Europeans belong neither to us nor to them. Many stand out on account of their good looks, and they often wear a dark alpaca jacket, but never a white calico jacket like the Europeans. Father Fuchs says it is almost as if they wished to avoid more of the white that they had inherited from their fathers.

Hermann was soon given a taste of how different the races and castes in the offices are. Time and again he had to postpone his work because the offices were closed on the days of religious festivals.[6] By

---

5 A German who reflects a lot on the poor and the rich.

6 Some more figures from Hermann's notebook: 11 for Europeans, 15 for Hindus, 6 for Muslims, 13 each for the Jews and the two castes of Parsis.

the middle of November, it was already clear that they would not be able to leave before December.

Moreover, the officials work at their own leisurely pace. Once I heard one of them snap at his colleague: don't show off with your efficiency, you are making the rest of us look bad!

I did not need to translate that for Hermann, he had already understood it. I watched how he wrote in his notebook: *Reminded of Fryer's description of Bombay. 'The people that live here are a Mixture of most of the Neighbouring Countries, most of them Fugitives and Vagabonds, no account being taken here of them: Others perhaps invited hither (and of them a great number) by the Liberty granted them in their several Religions; which are here solemnized with Variety of Fopperies (a Toleration consistent enough with the Rules of Gain), [...]'*

Once, when Hermann and I were again asked to wait, we sat down on one of the wooden benches, the numerous scratches on which were a reminder of the sufferings of our predecessors. Hermann swore. At least I think it was an expletive, even if I did not know the expression, because he hit his knee hard while saying it.

Was that Bavarian? I asked.

Yes, he cried, stood up, puffed and panted, and sat down again.

I know what a twine is, I said, and *Himme* probably means sky – but what is an *O-asch*?

A backside, said Hermann.

What do the sky, a backside and twine have to do with one another?

Am I the *Encyclopaedia Britannica*?

I think not.

More than seventy holidays! With his fidgety backside he inflicted a few more scars on the wooden bench. And this climate on top of that! It acts like a soporific!

I am sorry that everything is going so slowly, I lied.

Even in the offices I used every conversation to ask about Father Fuchs. And in my free time I explored all the places which I knew that he regularly frequented: the sandbanks, Mazagaon and Bori Bunder, the bazaars of Blacktown, the harbour, and a Portuguese bakery in the Fort.

It didn't help. Father Fuchs was still missing.

That is why every day that was lost for the Schlagintweits was time gained for me. And so it did indeed transpire that I made the occasional *mistake* while translating. 'In a moment' quickly became 'later' and 'today' became 'tomorrow'. I never went so far as to make a 'yes' into a 'no'; even with their limited Hindi vocabulary, the brothers would have seen through that. But here and there I allowed the mention of an urgently required document to disappear in the flow of language. Or I transformed the precise instructions given by an official into diffuse statements which sometimes drove Hermann to such desperation that he broke off the proceedings and postponed them to another time.

I would have been able to continue with this strategy successfully for weeks.

Had it not been for Lord Elphinstone.

Lord Elphinstone is not just one person. He is several people rolled into one. Most Bombayites know him as the governor of Bombay. But many also call him The Nose. The most obvious reason for this stands out in every portrait of his. The second and equally important reason: He has repeatedly been able to sniff out the insurgents who act against the Vickys and the East India Company and has thwarted their plans. The third reason is more of a claim. Some say he is a phenomenal lover because he once seduced the incorruptible Queen Victoria.[7] That is why Victoria's mother is said to have sent him off to India, far beyond Victoria's reach, who was then quickly married off to a German nobleman.

---

7 The Others say that she enjoys horse riding and so Lord Elphinstone, as captain of the Queen's Guard, had an easy job of it.

Until now, I had only seen Lord Elphinstone from afar. That changed in the worst month of the year.

At dusk, I accompanied the brothers to the harbour. There we boarded Lord Elphinstone's yacht. During the past few weeks, the Schlagintweits had made friends with the Vickys. I had not been present at any of their meetings because they did not require my services for conversations in English (even though Lord Elphinstone speaks with a Scottish accent). But this time Hermann insisted that I come along.

Our brother needs his audience, Adolph told Robert loudly so that Hermann could hear him. Both smirked. The eldest brother ignored them.

When we cast off, we were not the only ones. Other ships spread out in the harbour. The Bandar boats had short masts and square sails that Adolph oddly enough called *Latin* sail. The Europeans faced the cool flow of air from the sea. They appeared relieved to be escaping the mainland, even if only for a few minutes. Most of the passengers turned towards the expanse of the ocean. Not I. How Bombay shone! The ivory-coloured houses and behind them the peaks of the Western Ghats. I had never been so far away from the city. I cannot remember the time before Father Fuchs brought me to Bombay. I had always been a part of the city, and the city had always been a part of me. Now, on the yacht, I felt as if I were cutting myself off from the city. I felt it very clearly indeed: I became queasy and had to hold on tightly to the railing.

Ever been on a boat before? Adolph asked me.

I shook my head. It was impossible to talk.

Seasick, he said, it will pass.

It did not pass.

When Lord Elphinstone received us at the back of the yacht which had been equipped with jalousies for Europeans afraid of the sun, I threw up at his feet.

After that I felt better.

Lord Elphinstone seemed unfazed. Other Vickys would have thrown me overboard. This one looked me over stony-faced while two agitated servants wiped up the half-digested jalebis.

Ek bilkul siddha tar milna itna hi mushkil hai jaise ek bilkul siddha admi,[8] he said.

He speaks Hindi! I exclaimed to the brothers.

That much we understand, said Adolph.

I had never met a Vicky who could say more than a few words in Hindi.

How else would I find out what the natives are thinking, said Lord Elphinstone, this time in English. You Indians learn our language in order to speak with us, but you continue to think in your language. Usually, you even think …

He stopped, raised a hand to his mouth. A servant approached with a bronze goblet. Lord Elphinstone waved him away and began again: Usually, you even think very loudly.

At the entrance to the harbour, our boat sailed around a network of stakes that were pushed into the mud for catching fish.

I think very softly, I said.

Are you sure?

In the silence that ensued, the sound of waves rose and filled my head. The nausea slowly returned.

Bombay duck, Lord Elphinstone continued in English to me, has always fascinated me. It is eaten dried and is extremely popular with the natives. Even though it stinks horridly like the socks of an infantryman. Yet, one should not underestimate it because it is accepted by most castes and religions despite their arbitrary laws about food. Bombay duck is a versatile creature.

Lord Elphinstone did not blink, like a lizard.

---

8 This proverb is naturally only used in regions of India where the fan palms grow (and Hindi is spoken).

I asked Mr Schlagintweit to bring you today so that I can see the boy for myself who …

He again stopped and raised a hand to his mouth. This time he coughed. I knew this cough. It pulled at my heartstrings.

Lord Elphinstone bent over the goblet held out by the servant and spat into it.

Do you sometimes cough up blood, Sir? I asked.

Bartholomew! shouted Hermann.

For the first time something stirred in Lord Elphinstone's face. Even though I could not say exactly what.

He cleared his throat: A boy who makes a fool of even my best officials. I was told that you take great liberties while translating. My officials needed a long time to see through your game. For that I salute you.

He clapped once. Waited. Clapped again.

Before he could continue, he was overcome by a fit of coughing whose familiar sound transported me back to the Glass House.

When Lord Elphinstone recovered his breath again, he turned to the Schlagintweits: I recommend lashes of the whip. But, gentlemen, be moderate! He is quite delicate.

He then withdrew with the Schlagintweits. I made my way along the railing. The sun had disappeared suddenly, and the sea spread out in the gathering dusk. I had to, I wanted to escape. The water was only a leap away. Bombay was in the direction from which a muezzin called out for the evening prayer and gaslights glowed like restless stars in the night sky. Really not so far away – and yet, very far away for a boy who could not swim. In the monsoon I had waded through knee-high slush, and to cool down on hot afternoons I had sat on a sandbank near Blacktown where the water came up to my bellybutton. But not once had I jumped into the sea like Father Fuchs who swam out fearlessly every few days, always paddling backwards and calling out to me: Come, Bartholomew, come, it is your sea, it will carry you, come!

Maybe this was the moment to obey his call. The sea waited for me, it slapped impatiently against the boat.

And what did I do? I turned into stone just like I did in the face of the moving wagons in Bori Bunder and held on so firmly to the railing that its rusted edge cut into my hand.

When we returned, the Schlagintweits locked me up in my attic room. On the way home, I had tried to explain my sabotage. They did not say a word in my presence. Even Hermann was silent. When they left me alone, I rolled up into a ball on the mattress and wished I was back in the Glass House, even in a Glass House without Father Fuchs.

Were lashes of the whip more painful than blows of the cane?

The voices of the brothers below penetrated through the floor. I could not understand what was being said. The wood between us lent a strange accent to their words. Hermann was particularly loud, but I still could not understand him; that evening, he rambled on even more than a priest being asked for advice by a pretty believer. In between, there was Adolph's resounding laughter which eclipsed his words. Robert, on the other hand, was the only one who spoke in a measured voice, but then, only seldom.

It was he who came to me late in the night.

What were you talking about? I asked.

Morals and integrity, he said.

And about my punishment?

We took a vote.

Were you for me? I asked.

I abstained.

But Hermann could not have been for me.

He was not.

Adolph voted for me?

Robert nodded.

Why?

You will have to ask him that yourself.

And? How many do I get?

Robert knitted his brow.

Lashes of the whip, I said.

Go to sleep now, he said, while closing the door behind him. We are leaving before sunrise.

Nobody can sleep when they are told to do so. I had already learnt that in the Glass House. I lit the candle for Father Fuchs and moved it near the window. My hopefulness celebrated Diwali every day. But in the end, a candle is only a candle and not a diya. The dried-up brownish blood on the handkerchief made the cloth stiff like a papad. Did Lord Elphinstone also have a handkerchief like this? He had the same cough as Father Fuchs. Had they perhaps passed it on to each other? Or had they both been infected in the same place?

When Robert woke me up and we left the house, it was so early that some may have said it was very late.

I asked where we were going. But Robert used his words only for the four porters who were hauling massive wooden boxes behind us. Every few metres he prompted me to warn them to be careful. When I said once that they had understood this by now, he took off his hat and looked at me so insistently that I was prepared for a blow. I apologized and reminded the porters to handle the boxes gently.

It was still dark. There was so much moisture in the air that it felt as if we were walking through a light rain. In these hours, Bombay gave off the strongest smell of rancid oil and algae and ash and farts and heeng. As though the city opened its pores at night and discarded everything that had been fed into it during the day.

I soon realized that we were going to Malabar Hill. The sun had long been up when we reached the place that Robert had in mind. From there we had an unimpeded view of the Fort. Steamships and sailboats were anchored in the harbour. A multitude of Indian skiffs weaved through them to unload the ships like the smallest members of a herd.

Robert ordered the boxes to be opened. When the porters had done so and seen the contents, they shrank back, but step by step they moved closer to them again. Robert forbade them to touch the contents and shooed them away. They sat down together close by and let the sun dry their sweat. Robert took out parts made of metal and of smooth wood and began assembling them. Out of these parts there rose an apparatus such as I had never seen before. It resembled a caterpillar that Devinder had once found in the garden and which the Others had cut into pieces. But Robert's caterpillar had only one glass eye and it stood on long, thin legs. The entire time I wanted to ask him what it was, but the process and Robert's grave precision cast their spell on me. When he seemed to be ready, he looked up at the sky and smiled.

Does my punishment begin now? I asked.

What begins now, he said, is a new scientific epoch.

He pointed to the apparatus.

Isn't it lovely?

I nodded, even though I found it hideous.

This is a Voigtländer.

Aha, I said.

It will give us the latest insights. I will use it to take pictures of the people and the country.

A picture machine?

Yes, he laughed. So to say.

Will you also take a picture of me?

Why should I do that?

No one has ever taken a picture of me.

Almost nothing here has ever been photographed, he said. We are the first Germans with photography equipment in India!

Robert had never before said so much in my presence. He touched his picture machine gently and trustingly like a rider touches his camel before it has to carry him far. Once, he put his head under a black cloth. Presumably, he was looking for protection from the sun. Shortly thereafter, he dismantled the picture machine again.

Is the picture ready? I asked. Can I see it?

Robert shook his head.

I saw clouds gathering on the horizon and felt an ominous breeze.

We should hurry, I said. It will rain soon.

Robert pointed to the sun and the expanse of blue sky above us. You will certainly not become a meteorologist, he said.

I do not know what a meteorologist is, but for at least twelve years I have been reading this sky, and I am telling you there will be heavy rain.

Robert did not allow himself to be rushed. He had again transformed into his silent self.

On the way back, he appeared to be relaxed, indeed even cheerful. He kept changing his pace. Several times he doffed his hat while greeting people, whether they were coolies or Vickys in scarlet uniforms.

Along the way he admitted that he had thought about my punishment and would support Hermann's suggestion. As soon as the brothers left Bombay, I would return to the Glass House.

You will not be allowed to accompany us to Madras, he said. I am sorry.

I hung my head. That way he could not see my smile. How happy I was! Father Fuchs would not be found in Madras but in Bombay.

Above us the clouds multiplied as if they were swelling out of a hole in the blue expanse. All of a sudden, they overran the sun. The wind jostled us from all directions. The porters were finding it difficult to hang on to the boxes. Robert shouted at them in English, and I translated his panic into Marathi: The firangi is afraid of water.

The porters grinned at this which caused Robert to shout at them even more. Lightning and thunder set in, and the gap between them kept becoming shorter. The rain hit us as suddenly as a blow from Father Holbein. Robert looked for shelter under a palm tree. He told us to follow him. We refused. When the first coconuts crashed to the ground near him, he fled into the open where we were standing. The entire time he did not even once take his eyes off the boxes. He looked as if he feared for his life.

After a few moments, the storm passed. The green of the plants was now intense, they positively glowed.

Robert immediately examined the contents of the boxes. It seemed that the picture machine had not suffered any damage. When our eyes met, he looked away.

It was the first time that a firangi had avoided my look.

Later, on the same day, I had barely caught up on some sleep when Adolph woke me up. We took a hackney cab to the Esplanade. I had not known how quickly one could get around in Bombay! The smells of the city had no time to linger in my nose, and the wind tousled my hair like Smitaben would in a good mood.

Flying cannot be much better.

This time I did not ask the Schlagintweit where we were headed. It did not interest me. I would soon be leaving the strange affairs of these Bavarians behind me.

Men in small groups squatted together on the withered grass of the Esplanade playing cards. Scrawny vendors offered refreshments: sugarcane and sitaphal. It seemed a long time ago that I had failed in cricket here. I looked around for the Others. It would have been nice if they had seen me. None of us ever travel by hackney cab – except the brave ones who dare to come up quietly from behind, jump up and travel along secretly till the coachman sees and chases them away.

Adolph held out a glass bottle with a brownish liquid: Drink!

I did not know whether it was a friendly invitation or an order, but because I was thirsty anyway, I took a mouthful. At first the drink tasted sweetish and of vanilla, then it singed my throat and filled my stomach with a strange warmth.

It will be on the market in a few days, he said. They call it Old Monk. A funny name for a rum, don't you think?

That is rum?

Don't tell me you have never had rum!

I have never had rum.

It seems as if today is a special day, not only for me.

What do you mean?

Bart …

My name is Bartholomew.

Bart, I would like to offer you a deal: you will not tell my brothers where we are going and your dasturi[9] for that is that I will help you find Father Fuchs.

You want to help me?

Don't be so suspicious, young man!

No one had ever called me that before. It felt like a compliment and an insult rolled into one. I was not sure whether I could trust this Bavarian. Not even his brothers could trust him completely. In their presence he had told Consul Ventz that Robert hums like a bee while sleeping and that as a young man Hermann always put his hand inside his shirt like Napoleon, only lower. And now Adolph had something planned behind their backs. No, I should not trust him. But he was the only Schlagintweit who had offered to help me.

Where are we going, I said rather than asked.

To a secret place.

A place you should not go to, Sir?

Possibly, he said, and his eyes gleamed.

---

9 It was only later that I realized how casually Adolph had used one of our words. He is adapting faster to his new environment than his brothers.

What happens in this place?

Before he could reply, another hackney cab drawn by two white horses pulled up beside ours. The coachman was a Sikh. He was wearing a turban of sea-green and his imposing stature reminded me, as almost all Sikhs do, of my own not so imposing stature. He asked Adolph in Punjabi whether he was Alphonso. He was probably thinking of *Alphonso mangoes*. I replied, this is *Adolph* Schlagintweit. That seemed to confuse the Sikh. Which is why I added: Yes, he is Alphonso. It is generally advisable to give a Sikh what he wants. On hearing this he produced two white cloths with which he covered our eyes: his beard smelt of til oil and his breath of buffalo meat.

We rode, I think, towards the south. The sea breeze blew for a long time from our right. Bombay's voices grew louder, and I thought that we were moving in the direction of the Fort. Then we were making our way more against the wind and deeper into the silence. I would have bet a box of mangoes from Mazagaon that we were heading towards a place in Malabar.

The hackney cab stopped, and the Sikh warned us not to take off our blindfolds. He lifted me, and perhaps also Adolph, from the hackney cab.

A gentle male voice requested us in Marathi to take his arm. I told Adolph.

The arm was covered in a cloth softer than the feathers of the hens whose heads Smitaben chops off in the garden.

We were led forward slowly. The gentle voice warned us about a low passageway and a flight of stairs with thirteen steps and about a fur mat with a tiger's head. Finally, we entered a stuffy room in which we were greeted by a thick warmth that can only come from many candles and torches. Our blindfolds were taken off. We were in a room smaller than Devinder's. The carpet was the colour of Father Fuchs's roses. The wooden walls had no pictures, there was no furniture except for an armchair.

The gentle voice belonged to a good-looking man in a white calico jacket. He must surely serve an influential person. Men with dark skin like his seldom wear such a jacket. On him it stood out particularly. Not only because of the contrast of colours, but also because of the way he wore it. He breathed from deep within his chest which rose and fell like a second skin.

While bowing down to the Schlagintweit he stuck his backside in my direction. He disapproved of my presence. Because he acted as if I was not present. I am sure I reminded him too much of the colour of his skin and of the fact that he needed a small orphan boy as a translator.

He introduced himself as Nrupal.

I introduced him as Nobody. I, too, could act as if he were not present.

He adjusted the armchair for Adolph, and the Schlagintweit sat down.

What is this place? I asked, and Nobody told Adolph that his servant should be quiet.

I did not translate that.

Adolph asked what Nobody had said.

That you should be quiet, I said.

Nobody glared at me and then turned away. On a tray he brought Adolph a glass of whisky without bubble-free ice.

Would you also like some? the Schlagintweit asked me.

I did not want any, but I still took a small sip because I knew that Nobody would be shocked. What gentleman shares his drink with his translator!

The whisky burned in my throat.

Nobody spoke softly into Adolph's ear. He wanted to make it difficult for me to grasp his words.

Evidently, he did not know how sharp an orphan's hearing is because he must always be on his guard.

The gopis are ready, I translated.

I was surprised that Adolph did not ask what a gopi is.

A gopi is a cowherd, I explained.

Adolph said he knew that.

Nobody stepped up to the wooden wall and opened a metal aperture. Adolph bent forward and looked through it.

I asked him what he was looking at.

Not now, Adolph snapped.

Nobody smiled complacently. He began to talk with his lips so close to Adolph's ear that they almost touched it. His words followed one another quickly like ants. Did Nobody think that I would then be out of my depth? Through Hermann I was well prepared for such situations.

I summarized: the gopis want to serve only Krishna. They do this through their boundless love. In return, Krishna gives each of them his undivided attention. Their devotion is rewarded by entry into his kingdom. It is the highest form of bliss.

The story is well known. I do not know why Nobody was telling it to Adolph. The Schlagintweit did not seem particularly interested. He did not ask any questions. After a while, he leaned back and blinked. Nobody appeared to be satisfied.

Adolph asked me if I wanted to risk a look.

I wanted to.

As I went closer to the aperture, Nobody blocked my path.

But Adolph harrumphed, and Nobody stepped aside.

On the other side of the wall was a room. I could not make out exactly how big it was, because it was lit only by a few candelabras. It was laid out with several cushions and carpets. Women were sitting on them. Their eyes were open, but they did not move, like dolls. When I realized that they were only wearing transparent saris, I turned away.

I had never before seen naked women. I had never seen naked men either, except Father Fuchs in a lungi and the sadhus who washed themselves in the talao of Blacktown (although a frizzy coat of blackish-grey hair covered their bodies). The Others, who waylay girls in the bazaars and give them betel nuts (or pelt them with these), outdo each other in descriptions of female nudity which do not even come close to what I had seen this evening. This nakedness was more terrifying than bamboo canes or train coaches or two million people.

Nobody closed the metal aperture and said: the maharajas are descendants of Krishna. When a gopi unites with them, she is sure to be reborn.

I have never heard that part of the story, I objected.

Translate, he said, without looking at me.

What does *to unite* mean?

Two become one, said Nobody.

It did not make any sense. Hormazd would have shaken his head.

Adolph asked when the maharaja would come.

A maharaja is coming, Sir? I asked first him and then Nobody.

Maybe, but maybe also not, he said. The gopis always await the appearance of Krishna's descendants.

Is it true, asked Adolph, that the gopis even drink the dirty water with which a descendant of Krishna washes himself after an orgy?

What is an orgy? I asked Adolph.

He pondered and then said: A … fruitful celebration.

Nobody listened attentively to my translation, but only his ear pointed in my direction.

That and even more can become true, he said.

Adolph asked him what he meant.

Nobody asked a stupid question. He wants to know, I said to Adolph, whether you are a descendant of Krishna.

I believe he knows the answer, said the Schlagintweit.

That is a stupid question, I translated.

Krishna manifests himself in many mortals, said Nobody. There are ways to call him, even just for the night.

Adolph looked through the aperture once more.

For a dasturi, said Nobody.

I looked at Adolph and waited for his reply.

Were you born in Bombay? Adolph asked me on the way home when the Sikh drove us back to the Esplanade and the night air was swirling around our heads. We were again wearing blindfolds, but I had a clear picture of the women before my eyes. Till today, this memory tastes of rum.

No, I replied. But Father Fuchs says Bombay was born in me.

Adolph's laughter came from deep within his body.

Sir, why did you not want to be Krishna's descendant? I asked.

Although I cared nothing for this or any other Schlagintweit, I was glad that he had decided against it. No Bavarian should pretend to be a maharaja. Not even for a night.

Bombay is like a museum, Adolph said. One should see and study everything but not touch anything at all costs.

Bombay is like a museum, I whispered to myself. That was the first sensible thing a Schlagintweit had said.

What a presentation! Adolph exclaimed. The beautiful and the ugly in such close proximity. My brother – you know which one – says culture is rare in India. That is not my opinion. One experiences it in unusual places.

He laid a finger on his lips.

But Bart …

Bartholomew.

Bart, not a word about this to my brothers!

Schlagintweit, Sir? Will we now look for Father Fuchs?

Even better, he said. I will find him.

He sounded so confident. A part of me, a small foreign part, wanted to believe him.

The worst month of the year became longer and ate into December. Father Fuchs had not been found. Robert occasionally used my services. But I did not see Adolph again in that time. And Hermann only once: when he, Robert and I set out for Gharapuri.

On the journey in the Bandar boat my seasickness returned. This time I succeeded in not throwing up at a governor's feet, only at those of a small gull. I was excited. I had never before visited the gods on the island.

At the quay, we were received by a Munshi with an orange beard, who constantly sneezed as if he were inhaling chilli powder, and by a deformed stone elephant because of which the firangi call this island Elephanta. Father Fuchs says, as soon as the Vickys leave India, the island will get its real name again.

The Munshi led us through the caves. He had been doing this job for many years. Too many. His listlessness made his words sluggish and pulled down the corners of his mouth. I translated his descriptions which did not go beyond what we could see with our own eyes: stone, old, big, very big. With a half-raised arm, he pointed to the large Shiva statue and murmured: god.

Hermann eyed me suspiciously while I translated. For every word he probed deeper to find out if that was exactly what the Munshi had said.

The brothers started measuring. Hermann strained to note everything down, as if by doing so he could smash the rock.

He thought it was remarkable that the caves had been cut from the rock with bare hands. However, he felt the proportions of the body in various sculptures were very faulty. At least, he said, they had taken the trouble to place the columns of solid stone parallel to one another and equidistant from each other.

He sounded like Devinder scolding his youngest child because he still cannot walk. (His son is eight months old.)

Can't you see how beautiful it is?

Hermann turned in my direction. It seemed that I had said that aloud.

Beauty is not a scientific category, he replied. Someone who insists only on beauty will never improve his reason.

But someone who does not see beauty, Sir, will never know what is ugly, I retorted.

A short burst of laughter came from Robert who had gone deeper into the cave. The echo resonated like the laughter of many Schlagintweits. The Munshi looked at Hermann as if he were waiting for a signal to join in the laughter.

The look Hermann gave him was clear. The Munshi only sneezed.

You have spent too much time with my brother, said the Schlagintweit.

I will spend even more time with him, I said.

I venture to doubt that.

You can ask him.

Adolph has already left. A few days ago.

When will he come back?

Why should he? asked Hermann.

He will find Father Fuchs for me.

Adolph is already on the way to Madras.

That is not possible, I said.

Hermann buried himself in his notebook again.

I ran to Robert. That is not possible! I said to him.

Robert opened his mouth, drew a breath, and closed his mouth.

On the return trip I was so nauseous I could not even throw up.

Back in my attic room, I lit the candle. I wanted to set the whole house on fire. Then the world would be free of two Schlagintweits – but also of the founder of the first Indian museum. And the liar would have escaped.

I pressed Father Fuchs's handkerchief to my nose. It did not smell of him any more and of his smile, but of the sweat of my hands and of the dirt in my pocket. I held it above the candle. For a long time, the flame acted coy. When it finally bit into the Bavarian material, I let the handkerchief fall and stamped out the flame. Now at least, it smelt of the evening when I had last seen him.

On the worst day of the worst month the most famous Parsi in Bombay came to visit the Schlagintweits. Sir Jamsetjee Jeejeebhoy is an opium merchant and the first Indian to be knighted by the Vickys. He owns more shops and residences and businesses than most of the firangi. He sat in Consul Ventz's garden with Hermann and Robert and they were eating ice cream from the only Parsi confectionery in Bombay. (I used to often go to Rustomji Framji's shop to look through the window and imagine how exquisite[10] something must taste which is said to be sweeter than sugarcane and colder than Father Holbein's glance.) At first, I did not recognize Jeejeebhoy. I had never seen a picture of him, and his appearance resembled that of every other rich Parsi: a lot of jewellery on his hands and ears and chest, pointed shoes, a kurta tied at the side and a shining, dark fur topi. But his assistant provided the decisive clue. Everyone in Bombay knows that one of Jeejeebhoy's closest associates is a Chinese man.

I was not called out to them – for an ally of the Vickys the brothers do not need a translator – and so I could only observe them through the window. Jeejeebhoy sat upright and attentive in his armchair; he radiated warmth like Smitaben and he seemed to be smiling, but I could not be sure about that because of his moustache. His Chinaman stood behind him without moving. He was covered in a robe that came down to his feet and it was deep blue in colour like Hormazd's ink. I could not make out very clearly because of the distance, but his eyes seemed to be moving constantly as if he were expecting an attack at any minute. Robert showed Jeejeebhoy

---

10 It is said that Framji mixes a little opium in his ice cream to make it even more irresistible. But that is probably a rumour spread by the only other confectioner in Bombay, a firangi.

his picture machine which he seemed to find boring. I could see it because the Parsi began playing with the rings on his finger and from the way he kept looking at his Chinaman for help. Hermann was not much better. He jotted down notes and talked, talked and jotted down notes. Jeejeebhoy fanned himself with the flat of his hand as if he were warding off the many words like mosquitoes.

Shortly after the group had left the garden, the Chinaman returned and waved in my direction. I was sure he did not mean me. But he waved again, this time with both arms. I opened the window.

We do not have much time, he called out softly in Gujarati. Come to Battliwala today after sunset.

Why? I called back.

He was almost whispering, but I could have also read what he said from his lips: Father Fuchs.

THE BATTLIWALA is located in the heart of Blacktown. Houses in this area proliferate like a garden for which Devinder is responsible. Every day new baramahdas sprout up and crooked eaves grow. I know it sounds absurd, but I believe that the many languages here make the buildings grow. Urdu, Hindi, Gujarati, Marathi, Marwari fall like rain on Blacktown and make it flourish. I have always felt at ease there. Every language gives me another home. And all of them together give me the confidence to know that the Vickys will soon go away. They will never be able to plant their English over our innumerable languages.

On the worst day of the worst month, however, I did not have the time to listen to the tongues of Blacktown. I ran down the streets and the lanes. In Munich, my progress would have been faster. They have pavements there, Father Fuchs had told me. Only a few scattered people would be walking on them, and even they would be moving in straight lines. Blacktown's lanes are messy. I avoided bullock carts and washerwomen and sadhus and hackney cabs and hens and monks and an ear-cleaner.

The Chinaman was waiting in front of the shop.

Battliwala was Jeejeebhoy's father-in-law. After he died, Jeejeebhoy took over his glass-bottle business. Everyone in Bombay knows the story. Most of us are very proud of the fact that a rich Parsi like him continues to run a modest shop in our neighbourhood.

Follow me, said the Chinaman, this time in Hindi, and set off.

Do you know where Father Fuchs is?

He did not reply and lengthened his stride. We crossed a bazaar. A shopkeeper was touting his Bombay duck; a coppersmith was stacking his dishes and tumblers one on top of the other as if he were trying to set a record; in front of another shop a Parsi was lining up English sauces, his assistant was chewing chunam and amusing himself with the toys rather than arranging them; another salesman offered soap with a picture on the wrapping showing a black boy turning white after using it.

We turned into a narrow lane barely three times wider than me and tried not to step into the stinking trickle that snaked through it. Its source was not far away: a popular latrine in the area under whose seats there were neither pits nor pans, only baskets with holes.

I stopped and asked him if this was an ambush.

The Chinaman turned to me and covered his nose with his hand. He did not seem pleased.

Interesting, he said. An arrogant orphan boy. One does not get to see that every day. Do you really think someone like you is worth an ambush?

Before I could respond to that, he continued talking: Sir Jamsetjee Jeejeebhoy and Mr Adolph Schlagintweit had – he searched for the right word – business with one another. Mr Adolph Schlagintweit requested us to find the Father for you. And now come.

He hurried on.

Had I been wrong about Adolph? The unknown small part of me made my heart thump.

We reached a place where a banyan tree grew in competition with the houses surrounding it. I would have been glad to come across Father Fuchs here.

The Chinaman knocked on a door adorned with artistic trimmings. I know these kinds of doors in Blacktown. Father Fuchs told me that they had once even been shown at a world exhibition in Paris.

Another Chinaman opened the door. He was one of the fattest persons I had ever seen. Even an Australian stallion could not have carried him. He was cleaning his teeth with a betel nut. We stepped inside. When he bowed to Jeejeebhoy's assistant, I felt he might topple.

A bluish haze swallowed us. It smelt strange. Someone like me who has grown up in Bombay knows all of its smells. This one seemed to be familiar, yet I did not know from where.

The Chinamen exchanged a few words in Chinese.

Then Jeejeebhoy's assistant tapped me roughly on the shoulder.

Haven't you understood? he asked, this time in Marathi.

I don't speak Chinese.

And you claim to be a translator? he said in English, followed by something in Chinese.

The fat Chinaman's laugh sounded like that of a girl.

Can I speak with Jeejeebhoy? I asked in German to prove that no one knows all languages.

Jeejeebhoy's assistant replied in German: *Sir* Jamsetjee Jeejeebhoy has more important things to do!

At least his accent was more pronounced than mine.

He told me in Hindi that Father Fuchs had last been seen in this place.

Go! he told me. Look for him!

I went deeper into the cellar and the haze. The room extended into the darkness; the city retreated in the distance. On both sides, men lay on mats and moved, if at all, very slowly, as if they were underwater. Here and there a flame sparked briefly when they lit up their chillums.

I now realized where I was: in a khana. Father Holbein had forbidden us to visit such an, as he called it, *opium den*, because the Glass House had lost one of its best servants, Om Prakash, in this kind of hell. Hormazd had advised me against visiting such a place because, statistically speaking, 99 of 100 opium smokers, he says, are worth even less than a Bania's word. Devinder recommended drinking alcohol rather than going to such a place because opium, he says, makes you infertile. Smitaben banned me from going to such a place because, she says, it drives children into addiction. Only Father Fuchs had never said that I should not enter a khana.

Therefore, I could go to such a place.

I wandered through the room and looked for Father Fuchs. I had to take care not to stumble over one of the men. Most of them were Muslims. It was possible that Father Fuchs had been seen here. On his visits to Blacktown, he helps the weakest and the poorest. Many of the men in this khana looked wrinkled and tired, as if they could only find happiness in sleep.

The smell – I now knew why it seemed so familiar. Father Fuchs brought it in his clothes and enfolded me in it every time we met.

I walked across the room in vain. I went on a second round and allowed myself more time. Then I tried it a third time. After that, a fourth time, just to be sure.

Finally, I went back to the Chinamen and shook my head.

Jeejeebhoy's assistant pointed to the fat Chinaman: He says the Father was a good customer, he came almost daily.

He was not a customer, I said. He helped the sick.

The assistant clapped his hands as if to awaken me from an opium sleep: The Father was a customer – a sick customer!

The fat Chinaman said something, the assistant translated: Only here he found relief for his cough.

Father Fuchs smoked?

I had not addressed the words to the two men. I brought out the Bavarian handkerchief.

The fat Chinaman immediately pointed to it and said: Fuchs.

Again, they spoke to one another in Chinese. This time, however, Jeejeebhoy's assistant raised his voice; he seemed to be angry. When the fat Chinaman added something, the assistant slapped him. The fat Chinaman hung his head.

The assistant dragged me towards the door. We stepped out. Blacktown's air had never before seemed so clean. I discovered a crow in the branches of the banyan tree. Its feathers were blacker than the night sky.

The assistant's eyes no longer flitted back and forth; he looked at me directly and asked to be forgiven. He had not been given all the information. His smile was strained as if it cost him a great deal of effort. And then he told me where Father Fuchs was. I wish he had spoken in Chinese. Because I understood every single word.

I WILL NEVER find Father Fuchs, that is certain. I will forget what Jeejeebhoy's assistant has told me and I will never return to the Glass House. I will never curse Father Holbein for concealing Father Fuchs's fate from me, and I will not get caned for it. The Others will not laugh at me, and Smitaben will not hug me, and Devinder will not invite me home, and Hormazd will not offer me Pale Ale. I will convince the Schlagintweits that they need a brilliant translator and I will leave Bombay with them and so leave behind everything that reminds me of Father Fuchs. I will travel to every corner of India. I will continue with the Museum of the World so that we Indians can remember who we are. And I will not enter the cemetery behind the Glass House and not look for the grave and not cry.

I will never find Father Fuchs!

PART II

The Route to Madras 1854–55

Remarkable Object No. 11

A COMPLETELY STRAIGHT TAR

I write my words in a pool of light. I write one word, sometimes one more, almost never a third, because then I have to shift my book a little so that the pool of light again falls on a blank space on the paper. The pool of light is my eye for everything on the inside and the outside. Smitaben gouged out the hole in the side of the wooden box for me. Since we left Bombay I have been living in the wooden box. It is like my old home: there is very little space, it has a penetrating smell, I am hurled around by forces stronger than myself and I can do very little about all of it.

The Vickys are buried in such wooden boxes. But I will never allow myself to be buried. When does one know that one is really dead? What if one is already buried in the earth and still alive? I, at any rate, want to burn when my time comes. One is only guaranteed to die if one burns, says Smitaben. I completely agree with her. One is only reborn if one burns, says Devinder. That is probably also true. (But there are so many places and so many creatures that I have never encountered someone I knew in his earlier life.) Hormazd does not believe in burning. He says it desecrates the fire. I have never thought about how the fire feels about all Hindus forcing it to eat them. Maybe the fire does not like the taste. Hormazd says that fire should be treated with respect. That is why the Zoroastrians never use firearms and never put out a fire. But Hormazd also does not wish to be buried in the earth. He wishes to be laid on the grills high up in the Towers of Silence in Bombay. There, the birds of prey should devour him till his bones fall down through the grills. If, however, there is no choice, says Hormazd, if he is not in Bombay when he dies, then he would prefer that dogs gnaw off his bones. He has already told me that several times since we left Bombay. He says this as clearly and as distinctly as possible into the hole in the wooden box. He is afraid that he will be burnt or buried, because he is the only Parsi working for the Schlagintweits. Each time I tell him not to worry. He will not die. He will return to Bombay and have many children with his wife. His reply to this is: Yes, and you Bartholomew, you will open India's first museum.

For someone whose faith is so strong, Hormazd does not have a lot of faith. Apart from me, only Father Fuchs believed … believes that I will establish India's first museum. Even three Bavarian brothers will not keep me from doing it. No. In fact, they will help me. Even if they do not know this as yet.

On the morning after the night in which I had run away to meet Jeejeebhoy's assistant in Blacktown, I had gone to them and begged them to take me with them on their expedition.

They did not let me enter Consul Ventz's house just as they did not let my words enter their ears. They asked the guards to escort me to the street and to never let me in again. When I asked for an explanation, Hermann crowned the worst month with an Indian saying: *It is just as difficult to find an absolutely straight tar as it is to find a completely honest man.*

The fact that he said *tar* and not *palm* made it especially bad. Had his Hindi improved so much in the meantime? Or had they already found a new brilliant translator?

I sat down on the side of the road in front of Consul Ventz's house near a wall that leaned against its shade and kept my eyes trained on the entrance. They needed me. Surely, they would understand that soon and come get me.

With each passing hour I felt my pride melt away.

I was surprised that I was not hungry. I had had my last meal the evening before. In my stomach were the remains of a time to which I could never return, a time in the Glass House with Father Fuchs and with an appetite. The world had continued to turn and now every grain of sand at my feet seemed to be different. I had to remind myself about who I was and where I came from. I had to continue the Museum of the World as Father Fuchs had wanted me to, and for this I had to accompany the brothers on their journey. Only in this way would I see India as no orphan before me has.

When the sun was already so low that its rays pushed the wall even more to the side, Smitaben appeared in front of the gate of Consul Ventz's house. She entered it before I could attract her attention. It was not long before she came out again. I ran to her at once.

She called out my name as only Smitaben can and she hugged me, enveloping me in her irresistible kitchen fragrance. The world had continued to turn, but a few things had not changed.

The Schlagintweits have recruited Smitaben. She will accompany the brothers on their expedition and cook for them. The maasi is not the only one the Bavarians have employed. Hormazd and Devinder also have to leave the Glass House behind and accompany the Schlagintweits regardless of their own wishes.

But you are not a slave? I asked, just to be sure.

Father Fuchs had told me that the Vickys had abolished slavery.

No, I am not a slave, she said.

But Maasi, what are you then?

I am a cook.

Yes, but you are not being allowed to stay in Bombay which is your home.

No, I am not being allowed to.

And you have to obey them?

Yes, I do.

And you will be punished if you don't obey them?

Yes, I will be.

Doesn't one then call someone like you a slave?

Smitaben thought about this and rubbed at a dried-up blob of sauce on her clothes.

No, she said suddenly, because they are paying me.

She was correct. I had never heard of slaves receiving a wage. If someone was being paid, it meant he was free.

Take me with you, Maasi.

She looked at me as if I had asked her to slaughter a cow.

Before she could object, I told her why I would never find Father Fuchs. She only nodded and embraced me once again in her fragrance.

On 31 December 1854 we left Bombay on a steamer. I was now no longer a translator; I was smuggled goods. Smitaben had hidden me in a nailed-down wooden box in which she was transporting 'the most important, most fragile kitchenware'. She said that to everyone who came near the wooden box.

I pressed my face to the hole. The sea breeze tickled the hairs on my nose. For a brief while I smelt the sea, but soon after I smelt only the sour remnants of the time to which I could never return. I had tried to spit these out in a corner of the wooden box. They flowed back to me as if they were missing their container. My clothes soaked them up, and I soon smelt like them. The pool of light was almost a pool of shadows. Other boxes had been piled up in front of the hole. The floor vibrated. It was not a seaman or slave toiling away below me, but a machine, a metallic heart. Till now I had only seen steamships in the harbour and from afar. Now I was being borne away by this beast that was lifeless and yet so alive. It surely weighed more than any buffalo. Yet, it transported us quickly through the water. I heard it puffing.

After a few hours everything was reloaded. In the pool of light, I could make out a smaller boat. The porters handled Smitaben's most important, most fragile kitchenware as if they were unimportant, robust kitchen things. I struck my head often and bit my tongue once so badly that it bled.

We are in Ulva, Smitaben whispered to me.

Can I come out? I asked, although I knew it was still too soon.

Patience, she said.

The hours passed. The sour stink was so strong that I had to suck in air from the pool of light, and this air was cool and fresh, not like in Bombay where everything one breathes in has already been breathed in by many others.

It was night when we reached Panvél. Hormazd knocked on my box, told me that Smitaben was busy and pushed some aloo-rotis through the hole.

I devoured them. The taste transported me back to the Glass House. I asked myself whether I would ever see it again and told myself that there was nothing left to see there.

I will not survive this, said Hormazd. He sounded tired.

What? I asked.

This journey. I have never before left Bombay.

Neither have I, I said.

I wish my wife were here.

I had never heard him say that before. If that was what he wished for, he must really be feeling bad.

My bones are not strong enough and my feet are too flat for the journey, said Hormazd.

You will get used to it, I said.

How I would have loved to use my feet! They lay around uselessly in the wooden box.

You mean, said Hormazd, one gets used to dying?

You are not going to die, I said.

We all die all the time, he replied. Some faster, some more slowly.

You are not at all old, I said.

I am too old, and you are not old enough.

Will I also not survive this? I asked.

It would surprise me, he said.

I was silent, because I did not want to be caged in the box with even more thoughts of this kind.

Hormazd was missing his best friends, his numbers. Without them he had to talk to himself. Someone who talks too much with himself soon believes everything. Father Fuchs had warned me against it. He says that is why he loves Bombay. The voices of the city prevent one from hearing only one's own voice. Now, after a day or more inside the wooden box, I understood for the first time what he meant. I would have even preferred a room full of Others to this creaking, stinking, dark and tiny space.

Before sunrise, I heard Hermann's voice. He was giving orders about which objects the coolies should transport. Devinder was also one of the coolies. The sternness in Hermann's voice clearly indicated that the coolies would be bearing not only the load, but, more than that, a great responsibility. Barometers, chronometers, geothermometers. I do not know what these things are. But they must be very valuable, because he emphasized that. He emphasized it often. A friendly voice translated his words flawlessly into Hindi.

I decided not to like the owner of this voice.

We continued on. In the light of the moon I saw mango trees. They had more leaves than the ones in Bombay. I could not smell them. But it helped to imagine how good they must smell.

There was a lot of traffic on the road although dawn had not yet come. We overtook oxcarts, walked through villages where lights were already burning in the houses. The first rays of the sun showed me parts of a mountain range that looked like the stairs of a giant. The Western Ghats.

Shortly after our train stopped for a rest, an eye with bushy eyebrows darkened the pool of light. Devinder.

Smitaben has sent me, he said, and passed me a banana through the hole.

Where are we? I asked.

Chauk, he said.

Where is that?

I have never been to Chauk.

What are we doing here?

Waiting, for the camels.

Am I allowed to come out?

I don't know.

And Smitaben?

Should I ask her?

Yes, yes!

He disappeared and came back after a few minutes.

And? I asked.

What, and? he said.

Did you ask her?

Yes, he said.

And what did she say?

This was followed by a familiar silence: the noise of Devinder thinking.

Devinder?

Yes?

You didn't ask her, did you?

No, he said, I did not.

Could you then go back again and ask her?

He disappeared again, but this time he did not come back.

I watched for him, peeping in all directions through my hole. I only saw coolies massaging their feet and a bungalow with the

Schlagintweits in front of it. Hermann was staring at his pocket watch. Robert was sitting in the shade and had pulled his hat down on his forehead.

Devinder came back.

I can't find her, he said.

She has to be somewhere.

I can't find her, he repeated.

I am not surprised that he is a gardener. His mind moves at the rate plants grow.

You have to help me, I said. Open the box.

We should wait for Smitaben, he said.

I cannot, I said.

Only an hour, he said.

By then it will be too late, I said. I have eaten a lot.

I too, he said.

I am trying to say that my stomach is full. Do you understand?

He blinked, blinked again and then his eye widened.

Oh, he said.

Let me out, I said.

Do it inside, he said.

Here? That is not possible. Do you know how cramped it is in here?

No, I don't know.

Would you want to sit in a box with your own waste?

Devinder looked around and began to tamper with the lid.

The friendly voice that had translated for Hermann called out to him in Hindi: What are you doing there? That box contains important, fragile kitchenware. Go away!

And Devinder went away at once.

I waited for a moment and then pushed against the lid. It did not move an inch. I went down on my knees and braced my back against it. I could not manage to let in even a sliver of light. My full stomach and I were prisoners. Should I call out to the Schlagintweits and reveal myself to them? I decided against that. We had not travelled far enough. They would send me back to Bombay at once.

I WOKE UP and did not know when I had fallen asleep and how much time had passed. The hole was covered with camel hair. I was being carried somewhere smoothly and more gently than by the coolies. A nasty smell emanated from my clothes. What I had been able to prevent while awake had happened while I was asleep. I pulled out the Bavarian handkerchief and stuffed it in my nose. Even that hardly helped.

I did not dare to knock against the wooden box.

And so, I sat in the dark in my own waste. Father Fuchs had told me that people purged their bowels when they died. Maybe I was dead, maybe I only did not know it as yet.

We stopped. My box was lowered to the ground. I immediately pressed my nose to the pool of light. Only then did I allow my eyes to get some light and I saw Hermann hanging on a not very straight tar; his arms and legs were wrapped around the trunk of the palm as if it were the mast of a sinking boat. He tried several times to push up the rope with which he was tied to the palm. He was not able to do that. Some coolies exchanged glances. I could see that they were suppressing their laughter. They were afraid of the firangi's reaction.

Wouldn't you like to come down again? Robert called out to him. He circled the palm with his head tilted back.

I did not climb the palm in order to come down, said Hermann.

Why did you do it then?

I will scale its summit.

It is not a mountain, said Robert.

Exactly! It is only a monocotyledon.

How long do you think this ascent will take? Robert asked.

It cannot be that difficult, said Hermann, his head as red as a beetroot.

Try again tomorrow.

And lose a whole day? Never!

We have not come to India to climb palms, said Robert.

There, dear brother, I have to contradict you. That is exactly why we have come to India. This palm tree is no less significant than the Sagarmatha.

The Sagarmatha is unique, said Robert. It has never been conquered.

We cannot be sure about that. And that is probably also true about this palm.

You could try another palm.

You know I cannot do that. If I accept defeat today, then it makes no difference how many palms I scale tomorrow. I will always be the person who was not able to succeed at what he had undertaken.

It is only a palm, Hermann.

Exactly, Robert.

Shall we pitch camp?

Hermann pulled on the rope without replying.

We will pitch camp, said Robert and plodded away.

The brothers urgently need a brilliant translator. A translator can be helpful even if two people speak the same language. In this situation I would have successfully mediated between Hermann, Robert and the tar.

Instead, I had to wait.

Smitaben did not come. Hormazd did not come. Devinder did not come. Hermann continued to hang on the palm. When dusk fell, his brother sought him out again and called his name.

Hermann acted as if he were not Hermann.

I can understand him. The Schlagintweit had climbed too far up to give up, and he had not climbed far enough to be satisfied. He had only one choice: to remain hanging.

THIS MORNING, HOWEVER, Hermann is the first on his horse. Only the moon and I know what happened in the night.

An obstinate fly has joined me. It flies against the walls of the wooden box. In between, it takes a break. It lands on my book and rubs its feet. Over and over. I catch it in my hands, and it buzzes nervously. Leave me in peace, I whisper to it, and nothing will happen. I release it like a good Jain and continue writing. The friendly voice calls out something; its owner is standing directly in front of the pool of light. I have to be very quiet now. I breathe through my mouth and write softly.

The fly lands in my

Remarkable Object No. 12

THE KINGDOM OF EVIL

It is difficult to be quiet when a fly is creeping up your nose.

Someone prised open the cover of the wooden box and daylight blinded me. The friendly voice ordered me to stand up. That was difficult. My legs trembled, as if they had forgotten what they were meant to do. I fell down. The friendly voice called two coolies who carried me in the wooden box. I still could not see anything. The light was so strong, it felt as if I were looking directly into the sun. But I could hear the porters, who were all talking agitatedly at the same time because they had never seen anyone who was so dirty and who stank so infernally. They called me a rakshas.

I am not a rakshas, I called out in Hindi. My name is Bartholomew, and I am an orphan boy from Bombay!

This only served to confirm their impression. Only a devious rakshas would pretend to be an orphan boy. Even though I could not see it, I was certain that they kept their distance from me. I might breathe fire or put a curse on them.

What is a rakshas? asked one of the two shadows who were now in front of me. It was Hermann. This was an opportunity to prove my worth as a translator and an expert on all things Indian.

A demon, the friendly voice said in English before I could answer.

A demon, I said in German to demonstrate my superiority.

We understood him, replied Hermann in English. What are you doing here?

I am a brilliant translator, I said.

And unreliable and dishonest and too young, said Hermann.

And arrogant, Robert added.

My eyes slowly accustomed themselves to the light. I looked around. Neither Smitaben nor Devinder or Hormazd were anywhere to be seen.

You have to take me with you, I said to the Schlagintweits, please!

Hermann and Robert exchanged looks. I saw their thoughts fluttering through the air. I had to win over some for myself.

I will do everything you ask of me, I said. Everything! I will not be unreliable and dishonest and too young. Please don't send me back to Bombay!

THEY ARE GOING to send me back to Bombay. On a ship. As soon as we reach Madras.

Bombay is like a mother who does not know what she would do without her children. She does not want to let me go.

But I do not belong to her family any more. I have time till we reach Madras to prove to the Schlagintweits that I belong to them. Because what is a caravan other than a family? All its members are bound together whether they want it or not; they harm and help each other; they cannot stand each other for long stretches and still have to get along with one another.

Hermann and Robert are the heads. I asked them why they had not sailed to Madras, for that would have been faster. Robert looked at me as if I were someone who did not even know in which direction the sun rises. And Hermann replied that their journey was not a question of speed. The main objective was to capture the continent in its entirety. He and his brothers were mainly here because of the mountain ranges in the north, but one could not study heights without also plumbing the depths.

You mean, I asked, you only know what mountains are when you have seen what are not mountains?

I could see that Hermann was suppressing a smile.

Except for what Hermann and Robert say to each other, everything they say is translated by Eleazar, the friendly voice. He also supervises me. I am only allowed to go so far that he can still catch me by the ear in one second. It is as if we were bound together by an invisible rope. I always go where Eleazar goes. And he is constantly in motion, a little like the disloyal fly. His blood urges him on; he is a Bania from Cochin. I know that from Hermann; he talked with Eleazar about it. The Banias are often spice traders, they travel more than other castes, make friends everywhere and are normally called Aggarwal or Gupta. Eleazar is a Jewish name.[11] I asked the Bania why he had a Jewish name, but Eleazar only said it was the perfect name for him. When I asked how that was possible, he replied: I might tell you that one day.

Eleazar's skin is darker than mine becomes in a burning summer. That means he is probably very good at what he does. If his skin were lighter, he would not be so good. The army of the Vickys in Bombay assigned the Bania to the Schlagintweits. I think the brothers recruited him because they needed a replacement for their brilliant translator. Eleazar not only has a friendly voice, but he is also very friendly. It is horrible how friendly he is. Eleazar's friendliness allows him to say the most unfriendly things. In the past few days, he has used many names for me. Except for my actual name. I am a pest, a beast, a harami, a rakshas. Because he is friendly, I swallow each name even though it tastes foul. Because he is friendly, he is well-liked by the members of the train. He treats everyone with respect, whether Muslim, Hindu, Christian or Hormazd. The

---

11 That is the name of a Jewish merchant in Bombay who works for the famous David Sassoon and who distributes chapatis to the poor once a week in Blacktown.

Schlagintweits are also teaching him how to use their instruments. And because I am always bound to Eleazar, they are also teaching me something. I am not as shallow-brained as most of the people in the train and would not call every instrument a compass. I can distinguish between barometer and thermometer and chronometer and clinometer and magnetometer and sextant. And by now, I also know what is measured with each of them and how it is done.

Eleazar also copies maps for the Schlagintweits and operates their gadgets. (Except for the picture machine. Robert does not allow even Hermann to touch it.) Eleazar also teaches the brothers a little Hindi every day. Which is not a very clever thing to do. As soon as the brothers have learnt enough words, they will not need him any more.

I pointed this out to him, but I am not sure that he heard me. Although I am always near him, it feels as if he were very far away. His friendliness is like a splendid sherwani. I think, a completely different person is under it, and that Eleazar does not show this person to anyone. He says a lot to me, but he does not talk to me. I should get out of the way, I should hold something for him, I should fetch something for him, I should not move. He would have preferred it if I did not have a head. He can make use of my hands and feet. My eyes, my mouth and my ears bother him. He never responds to questions and he never asks me anything.

ELEAZAR RECEIVES ALL his orders from the Schlagintweits. Or from the leader of the caravan. The makadam always holds the end of his beard in one hand and the camel-whip in the other. But he is no Father Holbein. He seldom uses his whip. For that his camels love him. When he is particularly pleased with them, he tickles them on the nose with his beard which sometimes makes them sneeze, spreading their mucus on his face. This makes him laugh, a vibrant, generous laugh. Even Robert has to smile. I have seen the makadam use his whip only once, namely on one of his herders who was being too rough with a camel.

Twenty camels are accompanying our train along with the twelve people who look after them. The Schlagintweits ride on horses. Eleazar could do the same, but his horse mostly carries an empty saddle. Eleazar moves around a lot on foot. In this way he is on par with the members of the caravan. They therefore believe he is one of them; they pay attention to what he says and seldom contradict him. Hermann does not know this trick. When he sits on his horse and looks down, on Eleazar or on someone else, I can see that he feels bigger than them. He seems to forget that he is sitting on a horse and that everyone, at some time or the other, has to get down from his horse.

Each horse is assigned to a ghora-wallah. And then there is also the ghas-wallah who ensures that there is always enough hay.

Another important member of our caravan family: the khansaman. Hermann calls him a butler, even though he is clearly a khansaman. He is responsible for order among the servants. He too rides on a horse and never gets down when talking to one of the servants. Although he is a little shorter than Hermann, the khansaman looks down on him. I seldom hear him saying 'Sir'. When the Schlagintweits are not around, he makes fun of them and their studies. He says that he is better than the firangi at everything. I asked him why he then only speaks Hindi. He replied that he does not wish to speak anything else. The khansaman masters the art of lying as little as he does other languages. He claims that if he did not have to work so much in the sun he would be as white as a firangi. He also claims that he is not afraid of firangi. But he blinks every time one of the Schlagintweits calls him. Instead, he treats the servants worse than the makadam treats his camels. But he is not very imaginative in this. If the khalasis do not pitch the tents quickly enough, he threatens to dismiss them. If the torchbearers pretend to have forgotten that they also have to do the dishes in the kitchen, he threatens to dismiss them. When the dhobi does not wash the clothes properly, the chowkidars fall asleep while on guard-duty or the bihishti does not fetch enough water, he threatens … he is, as mentioned, not very inventive. All the servants appease him by touching his feet, where he is particularly ticklish. However, he seems to enjoy it.

Now I MUST report what happened to my old family.

Devinder was replaced. At every station, the Schlagintweits substitute the old porters with new ones. An Indian body cannot withstand the firangi's load for very long. The backs of the coolies bend like bamboo in a storm. Devinder is by now already on the way back to Bombay. I asked why the Schlagintweits had not sent me back with him. That would have been irresponsible, Hermann had said; I am, after all, only a child. He does not understand that in my head I am more of a grown-up than Devinder. It is doubtful whether the Punjabi will find his way home alone. India is huge and Devinder sometimes loses his way when coming to the Glass House. At least that is what he says when Father Holbein reprimands him for coming too late or for not appearing at all.

Hormazd too will not be part of the caravan for very long. At least that is what he says. Even though he has fever, I do not think he will die soon. When people are close to death, as I have seen often enough in Blacktown, they become very quiet. They hardly talk, especially not about death, so that it does not find them. But Hormazd talks all the time about dying. Naturally, I could be wrong. I have never seen a Parsi die. Hormazd says, since his death is imminent, evil spirits are gathering nearby. He has appointed me as his death guard. I would prefer to be a translator. But Eleazar has ordered me to look after Hormazd.

We need the Parsi. He can handle money and figures, he had said. You will fulfil his every wish.

Therefore, I am a death guard. I brush the flies away from him because they, as he says, carry the ghosts of corpses within them which could catch him. I rub him down with cow-urine and give it to him to drink. I bring a dog to Hormazd's bedside, so that the dog can stare at him for a long time. The dog will lead Hormazd after he has died. But I have to ensure that the shadow of the dog does not fall on Hormazd. Shadows belong to the kingdom of evil.

THE ONLY PERSON who will stay, and who wishes to stay with the caravan for a long time, is Smitaben. She achieves wonders. That is what the firangi says, Smitaben tells me. She cannot tell the difference between Hermann and Robert. That is why I do not know which firangi she means. White men all look the same to her. But she likes the Schlagintweits a great deal more than the Jesuits in the Glass House.

Every evening, Smitaben leaves in advance with the coolies and most of the camels in order to use the cool hours to get ahead. The rest of the train follows in the early-morning hours. We always arrive in a camp in which the pots are already boiling. Our train requires many different pots. Some eat meat but not pork, and if they eat pork, they do not eat beef. Most of them can only agree on chicken. But many do not eat meat at all. Some do not eat even onions and potatoes. The only thing everyone eats is dal. However, only in theory. Smitaben's dal is excellent, despite which some Hindus refuse to eat it. They consider her caste to be too low, and they prefer to do their own cooking. This leads to considerable delays in the Schlagintweit's schedule which invariably upsets Hermann. It is this state of things, he grumbles, that shows us how important the spread of Christianity is!

On one such occasion I also heard Hermann telling Robert that he prefers Hindus or Muslims as servants because, on account of their faith, they would not eat everything. He was not so much in favour of Indian Christians; they would endanger the meat supply of the train.

Anyway, Smitaben is grateful to the Schlagintweits for taking her on their journey. I would have thought that an old woman like her would not last long. But with each passing day, Smitaben looks younger. I discovered black streaks in her white hair. They were not there before. I would like to ask her if she misses Bombay. But I do not ask, because I know she would say she misses Bombay, because she knows that is what I would like to hear. I do not wish to miss Bombay. I want to be happy that I am not in Bombay. But I miss Bombay. I had a family there and I always knew where my place was.

Now I spend most of my time at Eleazar's side and in Hormazd's kingdom of evil. But I really only know where my place is when I am writing.

Eleazar has often watched me doing this. I could feel his curiosity.

Then, on the morning before we reached Poona, he accosted me and pointed to my book.

What are you writing? Finally he asked me something.

India's first museum.

A museum isn't a text, it is a place one goes to.

Father Fuchs says one can also go to a text.

Eleazar considered this.

Father Fuchs is not stupid, he said and gave me a friendly smile, but a different kind of friendly than usual. This friendliness came more from inside him and even reached his eyes.

Where is Father Fuchs? Eleazar asked.

Why did he have to ask me that?

I will never find him, I said.

Eleazar squatted a little so that we were on the same level. He was about to say something, but then he closed his mouth and nodded.

I used the opportunity to ask him something which I had been thinking about. Why was Hermann so adamant about climbing the palm?

That is a tradition with the firangi.

Climbing?

Eleazar looked around, made sure that no one was listening to us and said: They always want to be the first to have climbed something.

Is it very different if one is the second to climb it?

I believe not.

How do they know that someone has not climbed it before them?

They do not know that.

But, I said, how can they then say they were the first?

He replied: By saying they are the first, they become the first.

By saying it, it is like that.

What a wonderful formula!

By saying it, it is like that!

Maybe this works for everyone, not only for the firangi.

And I am not simply content with saying something. I even write it down. Then no one can say later that I never said it.

Remarkable Object No. 13

A LIST OF THINGS THAT WILL COME TO BE

1. The train will become my new family. (I lost my family once already and found a new one in the Glass House. There are many families and one only has to look for the right one.)

2. Devinder will find his way back to his family in Bombay on his own.

3. Hormazd will recover, and I will no longer be his death guard and the kingdom of evil will retreat from under our feet.

4. The Schlagintweits need help which only I can give them, and when I give it to them, they will finally understand how important I am for their research, and they will apologize to me and ask me to accompany them on their entire journey, to which I will reply that I need to think about it, even though that is not necessary, and I have mentally already agreed.

5. The Vickys return to where they came from.

6. They take the Others with them.

7. And Father Holbein.

8. I return home after many years of travel with the Schlagintweits and have written a museum about all of India; together the pages are almost as heavy as I am, and these pages will free the Indians and I will enter the Glass House and Father Fuchs will be there, because the Father Fuchs they buried was a different Father Fuchs. And my Father Fuchs hugs me, reveals the perfect name for the museum and coughs joy into my heart.

Remarkable Object No. 14

ADOLPH SCHLAGINTWEIT

We arrived in Poona on 4 January. It seemed as if we had been on the road for weeks. But we had only spent four days on the Grand Trunk Roads. Four days. The greater a journey is, the slower the passage of time. Has anyone studied that? I have never travelled before. Except once when Father Fuchs brought me to Bombay, but I was too small then and slept most of the time in his arms.

Now, I do not sleep most of the time and move laboriously through time as if through the sludgy lanes of Blacktown in the monsoon.

Adolph joined us in Poona. When I heard this, I urged Eleazar to introduce himself to Adolph. But Eleazar had other things to do first. Several hours passed before he went to Adolph.

Eleazar bowed to Adolph, and the Schlagintweit told him not to do that. I greeted him so cheerfully as I had not greeted any Schlagintweit for a long time. I was sure he would intercede on my behalf to make the train my new family.

But Adolph did not return my greeting. He did not even look at me.

It is I, Sir, I said in my best German.

Adolph did not react and instead asked Eleazar what he knew about Poona.

Too much, it seemed. Eleazar told him about the resistance of the Marathas to the Vickys, who had conquered the region only in 1818. Eleazar gushed about the quality of local jewellery as if he had a relative who dealt in bracelets and ornaments for the hair. There is a well-known sanatorium and a garrison square as well as numerous bungalows, and even a church and a school for the firangi who retreat to nearby Mahabaleshwar in the summer months, because in the cool air up there, it is easier to grumble about the hot air down here.

When I could no longer endure Eleazar's explanations, I called out again in German: Don't you remember me?

Adolph looked at me for the first time.

What is he saying? Eleazar asked Adolph in English.

The Schlagintweit laughed.

Who is here whose translator? he said.

You, harami, Eleazar said to me in Hindi and not in a very friendly tone, shut up!

You helped me, Sir, I said to Adolph in German, you sent Jeejeebhoy's Chinaman to me.

Adolph looked at me without any expression on his face as if he did not speak German.

So that I find Father Fuchs, I added.

The Schlagintweit turned to Eleazar again: Don't all young Indians look alike?

Eleazar nodded and continued with his report about Poona.

Was I not far too small to resemble everyone else? Not even my shortcomings could be counted upon!

I wanted to run to Smitaben and ask her to say my name so that I could be transformed from any random young Indian into Bartholomew. But I knew that Eleazar would have stopped me from leaving, and so I stayed by his side and trained my most piercing gaze on Adolph's fat face.

THE SCHLAGINTWEITS CONTINUE to delay our onward journey because they are interested in everything. Even in muck. On 5

January they asked peasants to show them how flat discs are formed from soft cow-dung and pressed against the walls of the houses to dry. The dung discs are used as fuel, even for cooking. Hermann told the other Schlagintweits that in Graubünden[12] sheep-dung is used for the same purpose.

The khansaman called out to some servants that he would gladly sell his unique dung to the firangi.

The braver servants laughed, the timider ones looked down to hide their grins.

Hermann asked Eleazar what the khansaman had said.

Eleazar translated flawlessly.

Hermann called out to the khansaman to come over to him.

The man began to pick at his clothes as if they were suddenly too tight.

Hermann took a muhar out of his coin pouch. Since it is the only gold coin minted by the Vickys, I have just seen it a few times. I would have loved to know how heavy fifteen rupees feel in my hand.

The khansaman looked at the coin the way a dog would look at a fresh chicken leg.

Hermann narrated (and Eleazar translated) that he had heard about a raja who, before he died, was prompted by Brahmins to weigh himself and his two wives against rupees. The raja's weight was equivalent to four thousand, that of his two healthy wives ten thousand rupees. The total weight was given to the Brahmins in minted coins. Hermann said, he, the khansaman, was not a raja and, moreover, as far as Hermann knew, not close to death. But as a scientist he had the greatest interest in unique dung. Hermann announced that he would weigh it against muhars and pay them to the khansaman. However, the khansaman would have to give him a sample on the spot.

The khansaman smiled as if Hermann were joking.

The Schlagintweit's expression was stony.

---

12 A place or a country in the mountains they call the Alps.

The khansaman's smile shrivelled up.

Thank you, Sir, rather not, Sir, he said.

Hermann jingled the coins in the pouch.

What now, he said, I would have really liked to have some of this excellent dung.

The khansaman went down on his knees and touched Hermann's feet.

The latter took a step back and said: Stand up!

The khansaman obeyed the order like a frail man.

Adolph said: Hermann, he has learnt his lesson.

Has he? Hermann asked Eleazar, and the translator in turn asked the khansaman.

He nodded several times.

One more example of such audacity and we will look for a new butler, said Hermann.

When the Schlagintweits allowed the khansaman to leave, he digested his humiliation as all men do: he humiliated others. The servants who had laughed at his joke had one arm tied back; the servants who had not laughed at his joke had both arms tied to their backs.

Hermann asked his brothers how they thought Humboldt would have dealt with such a situation, and Adolph assumed: differently.

Do you know Humboldt? I asked.

Eleazar pulled my ear.

The three Schlagintweits looked at me.

Do *you* know Humboldt? Adolph asked.

He is the greatest scientist of our times!

The Schlagintweits exchanged looks. Even Robert seemed to be on the verge of saying something.

Before I could ask anything more, Eleazar pulled my ear so hard that I felt a sharp prick in my head, and he only let go when we were far enough from the Schlagintweits. They, in the meantime, had already turned back to the cow-dung cakes on the peasants' huts.

THAT NIGHT WAS colder than all previous nights. In Bombay, the warm air is often enough as a cover, but on the vast plains of South India the cold descends on travellers like robbers in the dark. My blanket barely protected me from it. The Schlagintweits were again resting in a bungalow. So far, they have only had to spend one single night in a tent. Should they not, as true scientists, sleep out in the open so that they do not miss the chance to see how one freezes here?

Someone nudged me. It was Adolph. He was holding a torch: a stick with cotton rags tied to one end onto which lamp-oil is fed from a gourd.

Alexander von Humboldt, he said. You know who he is?

I could have told him that Father Fuchs idolizes Humboldt because he[13] goes to faraway places and exposes himself to danger in order to study the world; that Father Fuchs always calls Humboldt a second Columbus; that he sometimes takes Humboldt's *Kosmos* from the library of the orphanage and reads out passages to me, so reverently as if it were the Bible; that he regards Humboldt next to the father in heaven as his most important father; that, in fact, he instilled in me more love and appreciation for Humboldt than for perfectly ripe mangoes.

But I did not say anything and merely nodded. I had the impression that Adolph did not want to know any details.

He looked at me, handed me the torch and indicated that I should follow him. I was tired, but also curious. Moreover, the fire warmed my face and hands.

He sat down on a chair behind the bungalow and spread out a drawing on his lap.

More light, he said.

---

13 In contrast to a scientist like Friedrich Max Mueller who, as Father Fuchs sometimes rants, did not ship his backside to India even once.

I came closer. With a charcoal stick he added some trees to a mountain range.

Do these mountains really exist? I asked.

Naturally, he said, without looking up. I travelled along them recently.

But are these trees also there? Or do they exist only in your head, Sir?

This time he looked up briefly.

Both, he said. I memorized them.

You memorized each leaf?

Yes, he said.

Each individual leaf? I asked in astonishment.

Each individual one.

But, Sir, how can you then no longer know who I am? I said.

He put down the charcoal stick.

Oh, he said, I do know that, Bart.

When he said my almost correct name, the torch almost fell out of my hand.

Sir?

Adolph continued to draw in silence.

Have you met Humboldt, Sir?

Quiet now, he said, I have to concentrate.

I AM NOW no longer a death guard. (Although Hormazd continues to maintain that he has fever, Smitaben says it is only the South Indian sun and his homesickness.) Since four days I have my own place in the caravan: I am a torchbearer. And not just any torchbearer. Every night, while Hermann writes, and Robert lovingly cleans his picture machine like the makadam cleans the coat of his camels, I guide Adolph's hand. I hold the kingdom of evil at bay for him too. He refines drawings that have been done in broad strokes during the day. I have to be careful. The more I keep still, the less still he is. Adolph does not like the sound of his own voice as much as Hermann, but considerably more than Robert. And he answers many of my questions. People[14] like it when they are asked who they are and what they are doing and what they think. I learnt that from Father Fuchs, the most popular man in all of Bombay. People are pleased that someone wants to see them, because although we cannot see ourselves most of the time, we live as if we were carrying a mirror in front of our heads.

Adolph's mirror is particularly large.

Am I not remarkable? he says sometimes.

You are a very remarkable object, Sir, I reply.

I do not say it to make fun of him, I also do not say it because it is true. I say it because he needs it. Of all the Schlagintweits Adolph may be the loudest and the heaviest; he may laugh more than Father Fuchs coughs and drink more than Hormazd – but that is only the Adolph he likes to show to the world.

I encounter the real Adolph who is invisible to many when I am alone with him and he talks about himself. He draws with his charcoal crayon and his voice. This voice purrs like the stray cats who loiter in the garden of the Glass House because Devinder feeds them (although Smitaben has forbidden it). Adolph reflects for longer than is usual about his answer to a question. Sometimes he corrects himself, sometimes he says, I do not know. Adolph would never say that in the light of day. I believe he likes that I listen to him. We only speak German with each other; no one else in the train would be able to understand him. Except his brothers. But they are busy with other things. They have no time for their older/younger brother. He will still be there when they return home.

---

14 Except for Eleazar. He is as closed as South Indian villages which protect themselves from strangers with a wall of cacti plants.

Remarkable Object No. 15

A TRUE LOVE

Most of the things Adolph told me are not very remarkable. For almost a week I had to listen to stories about his childhood in Bavaria and how much he enjoyed the private classes with an artist who I mention here only because his name sounds like heart or Delhi in Hindi: Dillis.

But then, the night before we reached Anapur, Adolph spoke for the first time about his true love.

In school, Hermann was the second-best in class. Because even in his free time his head was buried in books. Only one boy was better: Adolph. Even though he never willingly devoted himself to books in his free time. He preferred girls.

These girls, however, did not keep him away for long from his true love. He discovered it on a hike through the Alps with Hermann. From that day on he could not stop thinking about her.

Geography.

Adolph says the earth is home and school to humans. It determines our existence. A person who can identify the earth, whether it is made up of sand, cow-dung, or a fresh potato field, understands the world. *The mother of all existence* – this is what the Schlagintweit calls geography. When he talks about it, the humour vanishes from his eyes. He radiates a calm and a tenderness which I have observed in Hermann and Robert when they are carrying out their research. And in Father Fuchs when he finds herbs in the bazaar that are otherwise only available in Baghdad, Bukhara, or Samarkand.

Adolph says, because he shares his true love with his older brother, it makes this love even greater.

I know what he means. I shared a lot with Father Fuchs. And now that I have everything just for myself, it has become smaller.

Remarkable Object No. 16

THE SILVER HAIR

Alexander von Humboldt is the father of the Schlagintweits!

Adolph says he will never forget the day when they met him for the first time. And I will never forget the night when Adolph told me about this day. On the way from Anapur to Kaladghi we had pitched camp early because the sun in South India suddenly disappears behind the horizon. The nights were darker than the hours in the garden shed in which Father Holbein sometimes locked me or one of the Others as punishment. I had to hold the torch so close to Adolph and his drawing that invariably a strand of his hair would get singed. That smelt awful, like the khansaman's feet. Adolph would then harrumph, and I would move back a little till he beckoned me over again and the whole thing started once more. And so, I danced back and forth between the night and Adolph.

Then he said: It was on 24 June 1849.

ON THIS DAY, the Schlagintweits met Humboldt for the first time. After their doctorate they had moved to Berlin, the hub of their true love. For years, Hermann and Adolph had studied Humboldt's writings; now they would finally meet the author.

At first glance, Adolph said, Humboldt seemed to be like every other old man, bowed down by time. It was only his eyes that belied the rest of his appearance. A childlike curiosity shone in them.

Humboldt impressed the brothers especially because he did not make them feel who he was. He showed an interest in their studies of the Alps and, after the meeting, he gifted them a copy of his volumes on Central Asia with the words: *This is a work in which, in my opinion, I have presented more new insights than in any other book.*

In the weeks after their first meeting, the brothers met with Humboldt as often as possible. They had always known, said Adolph, that they wanted to become travelling researchers, but the travelling researchers Schlagintweit were only born thanks to Humboldt. And so, he became their second father. Hermann and Adolph wrote a book about their travels in the Alps and dedicated it to him.

When they presented the book to him, he spent a long time reading the dedication. Not because he was moved or disappointed. This was the moment in which he arrived at a decision: he would bequeath his wishes to the Schlagintweits.

At least that is what Adolph claims. Humboldt, he says, had long wished to undertake an expedition to India. Because he assumes that extraordinary scientific knowledge is waiting to be discovered, especially in the mountain regions. But the supposedly honourable East India Company did not react to his requests even once. His fame was not enough for them to grant permission for such an undertaking. On his expedition in America he criticized the Spaniards, said Adolph. The Vickys want to spare themselves criticism from the greatest scientist of our times. He never got a direct refusal. The Company avoids any kind of furore and prefers to let things play out by themselves. With great success. In the meantime, Humboldt is over eighty years old. Too old to embark on such a journey.

BUT THE ENGLISH, said Adolph, did not reckon with three remarkable brothers from Bavaria.

A dark-blue hue bloomed in the air of South India. The night was almost over. My shoulders ached from holding the torch, and its heat had made my mouth dry. But I did not want to go to sleep. As long as the sun had not risen and the Schlagintweit continued talking, Alexander von Humboldt would stay with us.

What happened next, Sir? I asked.

Adolph looked up at the sky.

It is late, he said.

Not that late, Sir.

He looked at me.

You look as if the torch were holding you.

It is very light, Sir.

Give it to me, he said.

Carry on with your drawing, Sir.

Give it here!

I hesitated, whereupon he stretched his hand out for it.

I handed it to him.

Sit down!

I beg your pardon, Sir?

You should sit down.

I sat down on the ground and smiled, and he pretended not to have seen.

Together with Humboldt the Schlagintweits developed a strategy. The brothers went to London.[15] Humboldt established many contacts for them there to the most powerful white men in

---

15 There is no place I know more about even if I have not been there. In London, the East India Company reigns over a place where many of its members have never been: the Indian territories. In many irate hours, Father Fuchs would rant about a Company administering a realm that is ever greater than their arrogance. The Company alone decides who can enter this realm. Not only that. The Company raises taxes, enters into contracts between Indian states and other countries, and has at its disposal an army of more than two hundred thousand sepoys (who

the world. These personalities, as Adolph snidely referred to them, all wore high shirt collars which the Schlagintweit calls chokers. The pointed corners of these collars were coloured pink from port wine. In the offices, the brothers were received by the personalities and their stiff look-alikes: large portraits in which they looked past the observer. The polite cordiality of the personalities often misled the brothers into speaking openly. Only with time they understood the need to be more circumspect. Scaling the high social circles in London was, they found, more difficult that scaling the Zugspitze.

When they returned to Berlin, however, they were hopeful. The meetings had gone well and most of the personalities had hardly any objections to an India-journey. In their language this meant that the Schlagintweits had won them over as patrons.

Humboldt gained an audience with the king of Prussia. On this occasion, he promoted the idea of an expedition in the Himalayas financed by Prussia and brought a glow to the cheeks of William IV. The king's interest was kindled. But the minister of education promptly doused the flames. Because he loathes Humboldt. This is why I loathe the minister from now on. This pagal criticizes a holistic method in research. He does not understand that everything is connected with everything else. The proof of that reached the Schlagintweits a few weeks later when luck came to their aid.

Captain Charles M. Elliot had died.

Now who is that? asked Smitaben.

It was late afternoon, and she was walking around between giant pots in which I would have fit twice over. They had been set up far from each other so that nothing from one pot landed in another one. The fragrance of at least five religions rose from them. A coolie

---

are actually called sepahis, Persian for infantry soldiers, which is too complicated for the lazy tongues of the Vickys).

stood in front of each pot stirring the contents with a metre-long wooden paddle.

Paddle faster! Smitaben ordered some of them. Others were warned: Paddle more evenly! With more feeling!

After arriving in the camp, I had immediately asked Eleazar for permission to be an extra pair of hands and feet for Smitaben, had hurried to her and had begun, even more verbose than Hermann, to report on my discoveries of the previous night.

Even though I had not slept a wink, I was not tired. The last time I had felt so wide awake had been when I had introduced the Museum of the World to Father Fuchs. I had to share the news with someone. And although she is not a very good listener and understands less than Hormazd, at least she does not brush everything I say aside as insignificant in the face of death.

Charles M. Elliot was a captain; he was in charge of the magnetic tests, I said.

Hmm, said Smitaben.

Do you know what a magnetic test is?

Should I know? she asked, took away the wooden paddle from a sleepy coolie, hit him against the head with one end, poked around in the dal with the other and showed him the speed at which he had to stir.

Naturally, Maasi! I said, you are a part of it.

Smitaben burst out laughing.

No one told me that! Magnetic, she said, as if she had just tasted an unfamiliar ingredient, what is that?

Magnetism, I said, is a force that exists everywhere around us, but which we cannot see.

But how do we know then, she asked, that it is there?

How do you know that the wind is there?

I can see it.

You cannot see the wind, Maasi.

Of course, I can – in the sand and in the tents and in the makadam's beard.

You can only see the force it exercises on everything. You cannot see the wind itself.

Smitaben thought about it.

I can feel it, she said.

With special instruments magnetism can be measured and made visible. The firangi are carrying out such measurements in the whole world. They are working on a map that will always tell them where they are.

Can't they, asked the sleepy coolie, just ask someone?

Smitaben hit him on the head again with the wooden paddle.

Would you tell a firangi which is the right way?

The coolie thought about this.

You would not, she said, and handed the wooden paddle back to him.

When Charles M. Elliot died, I said to Smitaben, the Angrez needed a replacement for him. That is why the Schlagintweits are here.

She went to one of the rice sacks, cut it open, took out a few grains of rice and studied them in her hand like the Schlagintweits study the soil. Then she nodded, grabbed the whole sack and poured its contents into a pot of boiling water.

She was so old, older than all the others in the train, and yet she became stronger every day, perhaps even younger.

So, the firangi are here, she said, to draw a map of something that is invisible.

Yes, I said, and then immediately: No. Not only. They are also carrying out many other tests. They are studying geography, meteorology, vegetation, ethnology—

Bartholomew! she interrupted me and smacked her forehead. One more word like that and you will land in the pot!

I fell silent.

Smitaben tied up her hair in order not to lose any of her new black hair to the pots.

Where have you learnt all these terrible words? she asked.

Adolph gave them to me.

An Angrez?

No, Adolph is a Bavarian.

Smitaben's expression told me she had not understood.

The one who likes to eat, I said.

Ah! The healthy boy.

For a Gujarati, a man of Adolph's girth is just that – a healthy boy.

Do you like him? she asked.

I like what he tells me, I replied.

Smitaben went down on her knees. Which she seldom does because her knees are rusty like the hinges of the cellar door in the Glass House that always stays open a bit. She looked at me seriously.

Be careful, she said. For the firangi you are just another Indian. They will soon leave and forget us. They are not like Father Fuchs.

No one is like Father Fuchs, I wanted to retort. But I kept quiet. Father Fuchs is like the wind. When I say his name, I can feel him even though I cannot see him. And the feeling is so good, it is sad.

Smitaben is right. Yet I cannot stop myself from thinking how much Adolph and I have in common. We do not like the Vickys. We have a scientific mission and both of us have a second father who has taught us a lot. And we have both lost our first father.

The old Schlagintweit died one month before the brothers left for India. He was a famous eye-specialist who was also allowed to operate on the dancer Lola Montez.[16]

Adolph talked about his death in the same tone of voice he used to ask his horse to gallop or to praise Smitaben's cooking. He conceals something behind this tone, and I think I know what it is.

---

16 For her, Adolph says, Ludwig I, King of Bavaria, even gave up his throne.

I know this feeling, Sir, I said.

What feeling?

When one can never find one's father again. I am sure you are happy that you could travel so far away from home.

That I am, he said. But it has nothing to do with my father.

You are not sad, Sir?

You are the first to ask me that.

And are you?

Adolph poked his forefinger with the charcoal stick.

No, he said. No, to be honest, I don't think so.

I know why: Because he has another father. And this one is waiting for him. More than that, he is at his side.

Last night Adolph showed me a letter.

Of all the things we have brought on our journey this is the most important. Humboldt wrote it.

I took one hand away from the torch and reached out for the letter.

Adolph took a step back.

You must handle it very carefully, he said.

I promise, Sir.

He took the torch from me.

Careful, he repeated, and handed me the letter.

Now Adolph guided my eyes with light.

The letter was written on 4 September 1854 and addressed to Hermann & Adolph Schlagintweit. (What did Robert make of that?) The lines were slanted and moved from a lower point on the left to a higher point on the right as if they had lost their balance. Humboldt's eyes may contain the curiosity of a child's eyes but not their keenness. At first glance, I could barely decipher the handwriting. It reminded me of Father Fuchs's handwriting, fine and small and somehow friendly. The longer I stared at the letters, the more the sentences began to form.

In this night when I wrote 4 long, warm and artful letters for you, my kind, precious friends, I did not have the time to send you one word of love, of remembrance, of my heartfelt esteem and of eternal farewell. Among all the things I have been instrumental in doing, your expedition remains one of the most important. It will gladden me even on my deathbed. You will enjoy what has constantly fired my imagination in the time between my return from Mexico and my Siberian journey. May you be well!

I READ THE letter once, twice, three times, four times, five times. It was so exquisite that I could not stop stuffing myself with his words. And yet, what he said was not that important. The fact that this letter had been written by the greatest scientist of our times tasted sweeter than any mango from Mazagaon.

Then something caught my eye.

Sir? I said. Did you see that?

Adolph looked shocked, as if I had discovered a tear in the paper.

I pointed to one of the folds in the letter. A strand of silver hair was stuck in it.

Adolph looked at it.

Obviously not mine, he said.

And your brothers also do not have silver hair.

Not as far as I know.

Sir, could it be his?

Humboldt?

I nodded.

Possibly, he said.

What if that is not by chance? I said.

You mean Humboldt pulled out a hair and placed it there?

I nodded again.

Why would he do that?

But, Sir, you said that he always wanted to come to India. He has been able to do it now with this strand of hair. Even if it is a very small part of him.

Adolph looked at me. And then he said something he has never said before: Bartholomew.

Adolph took the letter from me, took out the strand of hair and put the letter back into his breast pocket. Then he held out his open palm to me on which the strand of hair that had perhaps grown on Humboldt's head shone like a silver thread.

For me, Sir?

Take it before the wind snatches it away.

I picked it up with my thumb and forefinger. This was the second moment in which I was happy to have met the Schlagintweits. And it lasted much longer than the first one.

What does one say now? asked Adolph.

I don't know, Sir.

Indians! he said to himself and then to me: Thank you.

For what, Sir?

No, you should thank me.

I said: Thank you.

Do you have a place, he asked, where you can keep it?

Naturally, I cannot be sure. It could be the hair from the head of a butler, a servant, a post office clerk, or a curious person. But if I have learnt something from Father Fuchs it is this: There are no coincidences. Father Fuchs actually had three fathers: the husband of his mother, God and science. The last two particularly taught him how much everything is connected, even if we cannot see it often. But sometimes we are reminded of it.

I keep the strand of silver hair in the Bavarian handkerchief.

Both once belonged to second fathers, and their children are now travelling together through India.

Remarkable Objects
Nos. 17 & 18 & 19 & 20

FLYING FISH
ALI THE CAMEL
A SADRA
STRONG RED PEPPER
OR
WEAK FIRANGI

The train is my new family. Most of the members do not love each other and do not resemble each other and do not speak the same language; they do not even know that the train is a family and that they belong to it (I asked them). But that is exactly what constitutes a family: if you are a part of it, you are a part of it. Regardless of who you are.

In this family, I sleep very little. At night I am Adolph's torchbearer and during the day Eleazar's hands and feet. The khansaman, who Hermann still calls butler, calls me a slave.

The khansaman's mind is as small as a grain of masoor dal. He does not even know that the Vickys abolished slavery long ago. This fact and the British Museum are their only remarkable achievements.

Obviously, I am not a slave. Would a slave, if he is tired, sometimes be allowed to ride behind Adolph on his horse? Would a slave lean his head on the back of a Schlagintweit? Would a slave, who then falls into such a deep sleep that he falls down, bring an entire train to a halt? Would a slave be picked up by Adolph and placed on his horse? Would a slave ride on the Schlagintweit's horse while the Schlagintweit walks beside it?

His gift was very generous. I repeat every day *what one says*. Smitaben advises me to throw away this very small part of Humboldt. Bad energy sits in hair, that is why a Hindu's head is shaved a few months after birth. But Alexander von Humboldt is not a Hindu, and neither is he a child.

I have made it a habit to take out the Bavarian handkerchief every time the Muslims roll out their janamazes to pray. To make sure the hair is still there. I look at it closely like the Schlagintweits look at their instruments when they measure magnetism. I hold it firmly with two fingers so that it does not fly away. Seeing it fills me with confidence that I am on the right path. The Schlagintweit's compass always points to the north, the Muslims' janamaz to Mecca. I have Humboldt's hair. There is good energy in it. Before sunrise and at noon when the sun has passed its zenith, in the late afternoon, after sunset and before midnight, it shines like the lifesaving thread with which Father Fuchs once sewed the wound on my arm.[17]

No one will believe me, but when I forget to take out the hair, it reminds me to do so. I feel it then, really, I feel it distinctly through the handkerchief. Naturally, a hair cannot be a family member, but it is a part of a person without whom none of us would be travelling. Humboldt is the father of the train, and the hair is Humboldt. That is why I must guard it carefully.

---

17 For my ninth birthday the Others gifted me a tattoo. But without ink, instead with a piece of broken glass. Only the scar under Smitaben's navel is longer.

I ALMOST LOST it. And my life.

Before sunrise, we reached a river in the Krishna valley which fed some cotton fields around it. There was neither a ferry nor a bridge on its banks and so we had to wait for dawn.

The Schlagintweits wait differently from the rest of the train. They do not rest much, and they eat faster than all the others. Their arms are always moving, so it seems as if they have many arms like Shiva in the portrait in his temple. Perhaps the Schlagintweits rest so differently because they know they will not be in India for long. Three years here, says Hermann, are like three months in Bavaria.

With the help of the torchbearers, but without me, the brothers measured the temperature on the riverbank, of the water, the mud and of the dry places. From his horse the khansaman said something to the coolies which I could not hear because I was standing too far away. It must have been something disrespectful. As if by command, the coolies laughed. None of them want their arms tied to their backs again.

Soon the sun showed us that the river was very wide. In some places it flowed faster than in others.

Adolph began talking in an unusual voice like a pandit praying.

And see, the curtain rises on the horizon! The day dreams that the night is gone. The crimson lips that lay closed, breathe out, half open, sweet breaths. Suddenly, the eye flashes and, like God, with a leap, the day begins its regal flight.

Goethe? asked Hermann.

Adolph shook his head.

Eichendorff? asked Robert.

Adolph shook his head again.

Schiller? I asked.

The Schlagintweits looked at me as if I had insulted both their fathers.

Father Fuchs's favourite poet, I said.

Adolph shook his head slowly.

Mörike, he said.

Flying fish jumped out of the water, landed on rocks and in the mud, hopped and dived back into the river. How was it possible that such simple beings could swim and even fly while I was unable to do either?

It was obvious that Robert wished he could have set up his picture machine within a few moments to catch the fish.

A little later, when the caravan prepared to cross the river, some porters hesitated.

It cannot be very deep, the khansaman called out to them, the rainy period is long past.

But the river was deep enough that the water reached the shoulders of the shorter ones and came up to my forehead. Adolph helped me onto the horse. The water soon rose up to the saddle. I clung on to the Schlagintweit. Our horse had difficulty keeping its balance. It buckled sideways. We plunged down. I remembered the Bavarian handkerchief and let go of Adolph. The water must not be allowed to steal it. The river swept me along. I held the handkerchief firmly in my fist as if it could carry me like a piece of wood. I screamed. But only air bubbles came out.

The next thing I remember are the worry lines on Eleazar's forehead. I lay wet in the mud, and he was bent over me.

Am I alive? I asked.

Just about, he said. That was an impressive act of stupidity. Why didn't you hold on to Mr Schlagintweit?

I opened my fist and the handkerchief and scrutinized it in the light.

It was still there.

Eleazar looked at it.

What is that? he asked.

A strand of hair, I said.

It is more than that, isn't it?

I did not tell him. He would have laughed at me.

Eleazar stood up.

I hope that your life is worth it – for which incidentally you should thank the makadam. Without his whip you would be fish food. Flying-fish food.

My ankle was swollen. A flesh wound extended like a red band around my leg. For at least twelve years I had learnt that the birch is my enemy. And now a whip had saved me.

I hobbled to the makadam and touched his feet gratefully. He helped me to my feet. I did not expect him to say anything. He mostly talks only with his camels. Maybe because they cannot answer back.

When I turned away, he said: It is dangerous not to know who one is.

There was a tremor in his voice like Hormazd's voice when he has had too much Pale Ale. However, the makadam did not smell of rum but of wet animal coat. Drops of water hung in his beard along with remnants of a smile.

I know who I am, I said to him.

That is Ali, he said, pointing to one of his camels.

Ali did not deign to look at us.

If Ali would try to be a horse, the makadam said, that would be the end of him. No horse would accept him. And he would lose his place among the camels. He would be on his own.

Ali, I said, can cope with being on his own. One should not judge him too quickly. Who knows, maybe he is a better horse.

Hormazd had observed the incident. I learnt from him that the khansaman had immediately rushed to help Adolph. With his horse he had pulled the Schlagintweit from the shallows.

He could have saved you, said Hormazd, he had enough time to do it. But he did not.

Perhaps he could not see me, Sir. It all happened so quickly.

I could see you, said Hormazd. Although I was standing on the bank.

Far away, Sir.

With a little distance one sees more clearly.

He is not a murderer.

Not yet.

He only envies me.

He envies *you*?

He would like to be like me, he would like to understand as much as I do. And he thinks I want to take his place in the train.

Hormazd laughed.

You are even more conceited than I thought! That will be your ruin. Watch yourself!

I do not like him either, I said, but he is not out to kill me.

It seems you like him.

I?

You spend entire nights with him.

It was only then that I understood.

You don't mean the khansaman at all, I said.

Hormazd cast a quick glance at Adolph who was putting on a dry shirt.

For him you are just another Indian.

He says my eyes shine with curiosity like Humboldt's eyes.

That did not seem to impress Hormazd.

The Schlagintweit is certainly not a murderer, I said firmly.

Don't forget he is a firangi who is working for the Angrez.

And we work for him.

You almost died, Bartholomew.

We all die, all the time, I said.

Touché, he said.

I DID NOT ask him what that meant. French is the only language I do not want to learn. Something about it sounds false. When someone speaks French, I cannot believe him. That is why I also never use a French word. I even prefer English. Hormazd knows that. Sometimes he purposely annoys me with his French. But at this moment it did not matter; I was glad to hear it. His French proved that he was feeling better.

Ever since his fever subsided Hormazd is dying more slowly. He is missing his wife a lot, says Smitaben, because he often, very often, talks about how happy he is without her.

He chases away his loneliness with work. Just like in the Glass House he is the Lord of Existence, he looks after the finances of the train. His new duties include grumbling about the conditions for money on a journey. He grumbles about the fact that gold is almost never used anywhere, and that the train therefore has to carry a lot of silver. He grumbles that every region uses a different system of weights and measures, which unnecessarily complicates every transaction. He grumbles that most of the rupees are minted carelessly, that the stamp is overly large and the writing incomplete. He especially grumbles that this does not safeguard against counterfeit money. He grumbles softly that the Schlagintweits do not even know what one lakh is. He grumbles when he comes across copper coins with a Chinese imprint in which a square hole is punched out in the middle; and he also grumbles that the Chinese pretend as if the only reason for this is so that the coins can be strung in a practical manner onto a leather band and carried; and he grumbles even more that in this way they save a large amount of copper in each coin. He always grumbles that most of the members of the caravan do not want to be paid till we reach a city so that they can send their wages home, which means that Hormazd is responsible for the safekeeping of their wages. The only thing he does not grumble about is that in many places, the Schlagintweits receive large sums of money from the government which need to be accounted for only later. And he grumbles that this journey will lead us all to the grave.

You should wear a sadra, he told me.

A sadra? I asked.

He showed me the cotton smock under his shirt.

For protection against evil spirits, he said.

The Schlagintweit is only a human, I said.

That is why, said Hormazd, we Parsis earlier also wore mail shirts.

Would he? I asked myself that evening when I held the torch for Adolph again. Would the Schlagintweit not use these hands, which copied South India for him and always drew it a little more beautiful than it is in reality, would he not use them to catch me and pull me out of the water?

Most of the members of the train do not know Adolph well. Except Robert and Hermann. However, I do not know them well enough to judge whether they are lying. The only person who can give me an answer is Adolph. But not with words. If I ask him, he will give me a reply that he would like to hear himself saying in his big mirror. I will only know the truth if I am in danger again.

That will probably happen soon.

I went to the khansaman and told him I did not want to take his place in the train, that such misunderstandings sometimes occur, that we can both travel with the Schlagintweits and that this family is large enough for the both of us.

The khansaman bared the teeth still left in his mouth and spat in my face.

When I am with Adolph, he watches me closely as if I were a hyena that has wandered into the camp. As soon as I speak German, he narrows his eyes as if he would be able to understand me if he looked closely. I am careful about taking Humboldt's hair out only when the khansaman is distracted. Whenever I have been riding with Adolph for a long time, or have been talking to him, the khansaman calls me and asks me to do something. I should wash his feet or clean his boots or groom his horse. The khansaman is not clever, but he is also not so stupid as to attack me in front of Eleazar or the Schlagintweits. But I have grown up with the Others and sense when someone is waiting for an opportunity to hurt me.

In Mudhal, the Schlagintweits received an invitation from the raja to a feast. They discussed it with Eleazar in their bungalow. I positioned myself between the Bania and Adolph, which was the safest place. The khansaman, who was leaning against the door a little further away, did not take his eyes off me.

What does the raja expect from this? Hermann asked.

Mudhal is a small, independent territory, said Eleazar. Many states in this region were annexed by the English.

Conquered, I said.

Adolph laughed. Hermann and Robert did not react. They had become used to my presence by now. Eleazar pinched me on the shoulder and the khansaman fired a salvo of hatred at me.

The old raja died a few weeks ago, said Eleazar. His son wishes to establish good relations.

With whom? asked Hermann. We are not English.

Can one expect the natives to understand such differences? asked Adolph.

You are the first Europeans here since his father's death, said Eleazar.

We do not have time for festivities, said Hermann, who, of all the Schlagintweits, has the most different way of waiting.

I have already accepted the invitation, said Adolph.

Hermann stared at Adolph who stared back. Robert stared at the floor and Eleazar stared at the air between the brothers.

Without consulting us first, said Hermann.

You don't have to go, said Adolph. Robert and I will represent you.

If Hermann had not been wheezing so much, one would have heard everyone's heart beating. It was suddenly very quiet.

Again, the brothers stared at each other.

But this time Adolph started laughing. The tension was released, and everyone joined in the laughter, even the khansaman and Eleazar. Only I did not laugh. Even if I wanted to feel as Adolph did, I did not want to feel the same as the khansaman.

Sirs, I asked the brothers, can I accompany you?

Eleazar prodded me from behind.

The Schlagintweits exchanged a glance.

I have never been to a raja's feast, I said.

Oh, then it is high time, said Adolph.

You are responsible for him, Hermann told Adolph.

He will behave himself, said Adolph, isn't that right?

I will, Sir! Thank you, Sir!

Joy blinded me. When I ran out of the bungalow, I did not see the khansaman's foot. I stumbled and fell into the dirt. The khansaman caught hold of me and dug his hands into my skin. He made me stand up and tore out my hair on the pretext of removing dust.

He whispered to me in Hindi: Careful, rakshas!

An elephant was sent to fetch us. The Schlagintweits, Eleazar and I sat on the haudah and were carried to the feast. The khansaman followed us on his horse. He abhorred the fact that he had to look up to me. I waved to him. That was the only good thing about this ride. I had never before sat on an elephant. This will be the last time. The rocking movement is similar to that of a ship. I had to take care not to expel my last meal too early.

There was a dance performance at the feast.

A tamasha, Eleazar explained to the Schlagintweits.

I call that a spectacle with noise and without content, said Hermann.

A pity, said Adolph, I had hoped for a darbar.

Eleazar looked at him in surprise. I know what he was thinking. Although the Schlagintweits came to India at the same time, Adolph already seems to have been here much longer.

The feast was not what I had imagined a raja's feast would be.

All the rooms were conspicuously empty, as if somebody had sold or stolen the furniture. I heard Hermann asking Robert whether he had noticed how dirty the costumes of the natives were.

I do not believe they were wearing costumes. But it was true that many of them smelt as bad as an orphan boy confined to a wooden box.

And the food! One could hardly call it that. There was only paan. A trick that I knew from weddings of the poor in Bombay. The effect of betel nut in paan is said to be a little like opium, only much weaker, and it drives away hunger, at least for a little while.

Along with it we were served fragrant water with a few drops of oil swimming on the surface. Hermann emptied the glass in one gulp. Eleazar whispered something in his ear which I could not understand because of the tamasha, and he showed him what the water was meant for: to wet one's hands.

Even the raja was not how a raja was meant to be. When Adolph and Robert introduced themselves to him, they took me with them, and I had to translate. At the most, the raja was as old as I. He talked incessantly. Adolph soon lost interest. With good cause. Nothing the raja said was remarkable. The raja wanted to establish relations with the Schlagintweits through words. He had little else to offer. I felt sorry for him. We were the same age and had both lost our fathers. But he now had to be a father to his family.

The English are cutting off his ties to the neighbouring states, said Adolph; they want to force him to surrender his territory to the Crown. I would be surprised if he did not give in soon.

Should I translate that, Sir? I asked.

What do you think?

So, I told the raja what I thought. It is very honourable, Hukum, that you have not surrendered your territory to the Angrez.

The raja gave a weak nod. He did not seem particularly proud of that fact.

Robert put paan in his mouth, swallowed and began to cough. He gasped for air, his eyes popped out, his face became red. His brothers rushed to his side. Robert grasped his throat; his hat fell down. His cough was hard and deep, much uglier than that of Father Fuchs. Adolph put his fingers in his brother's mouth and rummaged around in it. He pulled his hand out again and looked around. Robert writhed on the floor. His cough became a rattle. Hermann held his head. The khansaman said the firangi were too weak for strong red pepper. Some of the raja's servants smirked to suppress a grin. The music continued to play. Adolph told me that his hand was too big. He did not have to say anything else. I put my hand in Robert's mouth, found the paan and pulled it out of his throat. Robert took a deep breath as if he were sucking in a scream. Hermann stroked his head, Adolph kissed him on the lips and helped him up. Robert caught his breath again and put on his hat. He could not look anyone in the face.

Soon afterwards, we returned to the camp. Adolph brought Robert something to drink, sat down with him at a campfire and stroked his back like the makadam strokes the necks of his camels.

Hermann called Eleazar and the khansaman to the bungalow. All the other servants were told to go away. Eleazar told me to wait at the door. He did not forbid me from listening at it.

Ask him, said Hermann to Eleazar, what he said.

Eleazar asked the khansaman in Hindi.

The khansaman was silent.

At the feast, Hermann said, when my brother was in danger of choking, he said something.

Eleazar translated.

The khansaman claimed he could not remember.

Something fell to the floor in the bungalow.

My patience is at an end, Hermann said loudly.

I don't know what the firangi means, the khansaman said to Eleazar.

Eleazar translated, the khansaman's memory is full of holes.

I knocked on the door.

Eleazar opened it.

Behind him, a chair was lying on the floor.

Before I could be sent away, I called out: I know what he said!

The khansaman does not know a word of German, but *that* he understood.

Don't believe the rakshas! he said to Hermann.

But no one translated that.

I am listening, said Hermann.

He, the khansaman and Eleazar, all looked at me.

He said: firangi are too weak for strong red pepper.

I said it first in German and then in Hindi. I wanted the khansaman to know that I had defeated him. He would not be a part of this family for long.

The khansaman sprang towards me. Eleazar stepped between us. He only narrowly managed to stop him from getting hold of me.

You are dead! the khansaman called out. You don't know it yet, rakshas, but you are already dead!

Eleazar, the friendly one, asked him to calm down. There has been a misunderstanding, he said.

He said it also to Hermann.

I did not know what he meant.

Eleazar pushed the khansaman far away from me and told him to stay calm. Nothing was lost as yet.

The khansaman looked as if he had been holding his breath for too long.

The Bania then turned to Hermann. The boy is mistaken, Sir. I was also present and, as you know, my memory can be relied upon. Actually, the khansaman said the following: The red pepper is too strong.

He also said it in German and in Hindi.

The khansaman nodded several times.

Hermann turned to me.

No! I said, no, that is not what he said!

The Schlagintweit looked in turn at me and at the khansaman. He picked up the chair and sat down.

Are you sure, Eleazar?

He is lying, I said.

Hermann ordered me to be quiet.

Absolutely, Sir! said Eleazar. It was a mistake. Don't take it amiss. How should he know better? He is only a small harami.

I AM NOW waiting for the khansaman. He will come for me at night, I am sure he will come. That is why I dare not sleep. The museum keeps me awake. I move the pencil slowly; it whispers my words onto the paper. In this way I can hear the khansaman when he sneaks up.

I wish I were wearing a mail shirt. Or at least a sadra.

No one will help me. Adolph is taking care of Robert. Smitaben, Hormazd and the makadam have already left with the other half of the train. And Eleazar?

I asked him why he had given a wrong translation.

He gave a friendly harrumph (only he can do that), pulled my ear and claimed that his translations were never wrong.

But I know what I had heard.

You are protecting him, I said to Eleazar, when he told me to go to sleep.

Something flared up in his eyes. In this second, I saw a bit of the Eleazar that is otherwise well-hidden. Even if I cannot exactly say what I had seen.

I will not let myself be deceived. Father Fuchs taught me that one cannot, need not or should not translate only from one language into another. Even when we speak the same language, there is always a lot to be translated. Sometimes because we use words carelessly, sometimes because we do not listen properly and sometimes because we are talking with someone who can handle words the way Smitaben handles spices, Hormazd numbers or the makadam his whip. Eleazar is someone like that.

One thing is certain. He will not help me.

But I do not need him. I am not afraid of the khansaman. I have been attacked often and I am still here. In the Glass House, I was locked in every night with the Others. When they put the head of a chicken on my mattress or hung me from the window or wet my sheet with their sour, warm juice, I could not run away from them. And now in South India, which offers me a thousand places to hide, I will not run away.

I belong to this family. Even though I have not yet found my right place in it. I am happy to be a torchbearer for Adolph. But I am not a torchbearer. The Schlagintweits and all the servants, and naturally the khansaman, and unfortunately also Eleazar and Hormazd and even Smitaben think I am less because I am small. They do not understand what Father Fuchs understood: precisely because I am small, I have more of everything else.

The khansaman is only the khansaman. I will defeat him tonight and I will not die.

Because one says it, it is so.

Remarkable Object No. 21

PSITTACIDAE

Every morning, the khansaman kills parrots. Hermann says they belong to the family of Psittacidae. They sit in the trees and squawk only when the sun rises. Someone who sleeps under one of these trees cannot miss the morning. Instead of looking for another place, the khansaman always lies down under such a tree and gets angry afterwards that he is rudely awakened by the *damned totas* as he calls them. He fails to see that the parrots will never understand why they should not screech. The khansaman then takes his rifle, which is so big that he could shoot a Bengal tiger with it, and shoots some of the parrots. But he does not collect their yellowish-green feathers and does not roast their bodies. He leaves them lying in the dust and steps on them. The snapping sound is softer, but also louder than the rifle shots. It appears as if the khansaman wants to be bothered by the parrots so that he can kill them. His revenge is the call for the whole train to wake up.

On the morning after the raja's feast, however, another shot woke everyone up. Even the parrots. Although the shot was not meant for them. They squawked but did not need to fall from the branches. One of them flew over me and shat on my right hand. I believe he was thanking me.

Father Fuchs says one is a different person in every language one speaks. That means, the more languages one speaks, the more persons one is. When I speak Farsi, I am someone who sings loudly and proudly, even if no one is listening. In Hindi, I am like my body: small, more agile, the fastest. In English, I am the least myself, which is both good and bad. And in German, I am Father Fuchs, but I am also Father Holbein. I cannot be the one without the other. The Fathers always have remarkable ideas. Even if I do not like some of them. They feel like nightmares from which I do not want to wake up.

It was just such an idea that I needed on the evening after the feast. I was waiting for the khansaman. He would come for me. I knew it as I always knew that the Others would come for me when Father Fuchs had praised me in their presence. When the last members of the train had wrapped themselves up in their covers and the campfires had died down, I saw him. With his rifle he tapped the shoulders of some servants and cursed when he saw they were not me. In this way, he wandered around the camp. With every disappointment his curses got louder. Once, he was on the verge of shooting the bihishti because the latter had buried his face deep in his cover and would not wake up. For the stupid khansaman this was proof that he had found me. He trained his rifle on the bihishti and called him a rakshas. The bihishti, however, was not going to put up with that. He threw off his cover, cursed the khansaman and so escaped death.

I was sitting on the branches of a tree among the parrots, watching our enemy. I cannot swim or fly, but I can climb. When the khansaman finally gave up and lay down to sleep, I climbed down and crept to the bungalow. Robert, who usually prefers a ceiling over his head, was sleeping outside next to Adolph who prefers the sky over his head. Robert was breathing silently; Adolph, on the other hand, was snoring, as if to compensate for his brother's silence. I bent down above him. If he were to wake up, I would say that I wanted to wake him up. In his breast pocket I found what I was looking for. I went away with Humboldt's letter and looked for the khansaman. As I had expected, he was sleeping under the tree with the most parrots in it. His rifle lay beside him. I unfolded the letter silently. When Humboldt wrote it in Berlin, he would never have thought that his message would reach a khansaman in Mudhal. I pictured how the Schlagintweits would find the torn-up letter of their second father in the khansaman's pocket and would finally banish him from the train. I admit, it was not a very sophisticated plan. But it was a plan that would work.

Hermann says, in meteorology the measurement of rain is expressed in a unit of length by marking how high a column of water would be if it could be collected without loss by evaporation in an open receptacle with vertical sides. If one were to similarly measure the things that the khansaman had said or done to displease the Schlagintweits, one would have a very high column.

Humboldt would bring about the end of the khansaman in the train. It was the perfect solution.

But I could not destroy the letter. Before that I had to read it at least once more. After all, they were the words of Alexander von Humboldt!

Among all the things I have been instrumental in doing, your expedition remains one of the most important. One of the most important.

My kind, precious friends. Kind.

One word of love, of remembrance, of my heartfelt esteem and of eternal farewell. Love, heartfelt esteem, eternal farewell.

May you be well.

Eternal farewell.

When I tore the paper, the noise was as terrible as the snapping sound when the khansaman steps on the parrots. I quickly stuffed the remains of the letter into his pocket. Now I only had to fetch the Schlagintweits.

Then, a parrot screeched. The khansaman opened his eyes, grabbed his rifle, and hit at me. I tried to avoid the blow, lost my balance, and fell on my chest. The khansaman got up and struck me on the back with the butt of the rifle. I curled up and begged for forgiveness. He kicked me. I saw that some servants in the camp were awake. Their eyes turned in our direction. They did not say anything, they did not move. I cried out for help. They closed their eyes and turned away. The khansaman aimed the rifle at my face. I held my hands out as if I could catch the bullet with them. I did not ask for forgiveness any more. The khansaman smiled, and I thought I had never seen him so happy.

Put down the rifle.

Robert approached the khansaman from behind. He had both arms outstretched as if he wanted to catch a butterfly.

I translated for the Schlagintweit.

But the khansaman did not put the rifle down.

Robert called out: the rifle! Put it down!

The Schlagintweit stopped. He did not even blink and looked as calm as he did when working with the picture machine. At any rate, Robert wanted to prevent something worse. That is what his composure said. One did not need a translator to understand that.

Only, the khansaman did not see him. He called me a rakshas.

I reminded him that he would be convicted, whereupon he reminded me that at least I would be dead before that.

This made me think of Hormazd's words.

You too will die, I said to the khansaman, who immediately tightened his hold on the rifle, while I continued talking and described the very dangerous rifle that Robert had aimed at him.

I was not lying. I was only translating his future for him.

The khansaman made a move to turn around, and I quickly pointed out that Robert would shoot his head off if he moved.

The khansaman did not turn around. Robert, who was only a few feet away from him, asked him what was going on here. But I could now no longer translate for the Schlagintweit.

The khansaman said that the firangi did not have any rifles, upon which I informed him about Robert's machine and that he could also shoot with it.

He has never shot anything till now, said the khansaman.

It is too valuable for simple animals, I said. He captures entire mountains and cities with it!

That impressed the khansaman. Now I had him. I told him that I did not want to die and that I did not want him to die. That was not a lie. I liked this man as little as Father Holbein. But I did not wish death upon him.

The khansaman thought about this, then he lowered his rifle and asked me not to curse his children.

A shot rang out and the parrots flew up. They squawked so loudly that they woke up the sun.

The khansaman fell down. His foot was torn to shreds. Robert grabbed his rifle. Suddenly, Adolph was there; he held his own rifle in one hand and, with the other, he hugged Robert.

Adolph said, in the dark he had not been able to aim properly. Robert asked him, a little superfluously, what he had done. Adolph replied that he had only wanted to protect his little brother. I know that he meant Robert. But could it be that he also meant me a little? After all, whether intentionally or not, he had saved me.

I still did not move. The khansaman screamed and held on to the stump at the end of his leg. It looked like the burnt end of a torch. No one would now kiss this foot.

The camp awakened, and so many voices were calling out at the same time that even a brilliant translator would not have been able to understand them. Hermann arrived on the scene and ordered Eleazar to have someone treat the khansaman's wound. I remembered the khansaman's last words and asked Eleazar if he really had children.

The Bania did not reply. He was busy establishing order in the camp.

The khansaman writhed on the ground in pain. A part of Humboldt's letter fell out of his pocket. The Schlagintweits recognized it. Hermann picked it up and showed it to his brothers. They were speaking so softly to one another that I could not hear them. I was surprised at how calm they were. Not one of them cursed or threatened the khansaman. Hermann asked him in a chilly voice like Father Holbein's what he was doing with the letter, and Eleazar translated. The khansaman claimed he had never seen this paper before. Hermann squatted. He looked like a hunter beside a dying animal. I could not see any emotion in his face. He demanded that the khansaman tell him the truth. The khansaman looked at me and away again. He admitted to having stolen the paper. Eleazar did not translate that. He asked the khansaman instead whether he had understood correctly, and the khansaman nodded. Eleazar still did not translate. He pointed out to the khansaman that he could not even read. The khansaman pounded his pain into the ground with his fist and fell silent. Only then did Eleazar translate. Hermann nodded and called me over. I moved for the first time since the khansaman had aimed his rifle at me. Each step cost strength. Hermann questioned me about the events of the night and I told him my (slightly altered) remarkable idea. After I had observed the khansaman's thievery, I had followed him, and he had attacked me when I confronted him. The khansaman could not contradict me. He did not understand German. Despite that, I would have expected him to say something against me. But he did not even look at me. Robert confirmed my statement. The brothers turned away and continued their discussion. I used the opportunity and approached the khansaman. He moved back at once. I wanted to tell him I was sorry. I did not know that he had children, that someone like him had children. But I knew that with his shot Adolph had not only struck the khansaman but also his entire family. The khansaman would never be able to walk properly again. And a khansaman who cannot walk properly is no khansaman.

Spare me, rakshas!

The khansaman closed his eyes and began to pray softly. It was only then that I understood. Father Fuchs says most people pray out of fear. No one has ever been afraid of me. It should have been a bad feeling. But it was not. I looked around and noticed that many coolies were watching me like the khansaman was. They saw something in me that I myself have never seen despite all the time spent in front of Father Fuchs's mirror.

The only ones who did not look at me differently were Eleazar and the Schlagintweits.

They agreed that the events of the past night would not be mentioned in their travel account in order not to alienate the Vickys. The Company, said Hermann, could assume that they had lost control over the expedition. The Schlagintweits named Eleazar their new khansaman. He pointed out that he was only a translator. But none of the brothers responded to that.

Because one says it, it is so, I whispered to Eleazar.

The Bania pulled my ear so hard that I could follow the rest of the conversation only with my other ear.

What do we do with him? Robert asked his brothers and looked at the khansaman on whose bandage the wound bloomed red like the roses on Father Fuchs's handkerchief.

He has to be punished, Adolph said.

Does he have to be? said Hermann.

We should treat him like every other member of the train, said Adolph.

But he is not like every other member, said Hermann.

What do you mean by that?

You know what I mean.

Adolph was silent, so Hermann said what he wanted to say.

He is a native, Adolph, what can one expect from him?

I expect the same from him as I do from you, said Adolph.

The native has very little in common with us, said Hermann.

That is yet to be proved, said Adolph.

Do you still maintain that his race is no different from ours? Just look at him! He has lost all control. He would have almost shot someone.

We do not know that for certain, said Adolph.

Someone? asked Robert.

Hermann blew air out of his nose. Naturally, I was on Adolph's side. He was the only Schlagintweit who had always been on my side.

How does it go? said Hermann. *In hot countries man matures earlier in all aspects, but he does not achieve the perfection of the temperate zones.*

Oh, Hermann, said Adolph.

Hermann was not happy to hear his name. He paid his brother back, now no longer in a chilly voice, by calling him a *Depp*.[18]

The white race …

Hermann! Adolph said sharply, and his brother fell silent. Both of them looked at Eleazar and me. Then they moved away and continued their discussion in low voices.

Robert told Eleazar to carry out some not very urgent tasks. The Bania dragged me with him.

As we were going away, he asked me in his as yet most unfriendly tone what I had done.

I was silent. I cannot trust any man who hides the truth about himself from everyone. I would have loved to know why the Bania has a Jewish name! Then I would know for sure who he really is.

Eleazar looked me over.

They always succeed in setting us against each other, he said. In this way we forget our real enemy.

Again, something flickered in his eyes.

I wanted to ask him who he meant by the enemy.

---

18 Bavarian for pagal.

But Eleazar was Eleazar again. He squatted, smiled politely, beat the dust from my clothes and told me to go and wash away the night. Before doing that, I watched how the Schlagintweits buried Humboldt's tattered letter in the middle of the triangle they formed. Emotions that had been concealed so far now surfaced. Robert studied the cloudless sky which appeared to be more interesting than the funeral. (So that is what he thinks of the fact that the letter was addressed only to Hermann and Adolph!) Hermann, on the other hand, repeatedly ran his hand over his face as if to wipe away his anger. And Adolph did not cry like someone who wanted to cry.

In Bellaris, where we have been for the last three nights, the brothers handed the khansaman over to the authorities.

The khansaman should thank the gods, said many in the train. He did not show any respect for the Schlagintweits, he always spoke ill of them behind their backs, he robbed them and almost committed murder. For that he only paid with his foot, his honour and his job. Truly, the khansaman should thank the gods!

But the gods have little to do with it. If the khansaman had been serving in a regiment of the Vickys, he would have been tied in front of a canon for his treachery.

I say the khansaman should in fact thank the Schlagintweits.

Adolph and Hermann do not say anything about all of this. Since that morning, they are not talking to each other. They could not agree on whether the khansaman should be punished and so they left the decision to others.

Robert now talks more than both of them together because, like a human pigeon, he has to carry messages from one older brother to the other older brother. The last messages were about travelling on separately. So, the khansaman divides our family even though he is no longer a part of it. I believe now more than ever that the Schlagintweits urgently need a brilliant translator so that they understand each other.

Eleazar cannot take on this task. He is the new khansaman, but the old Eleazar. He says that he will never be able to replace the khansaman. I am glad that he has taken on this position, and I would like to be happy that I defeated the khansaman. (The makadam says he would never have imagined that Ali the camel would win the contest.) But I cannot be happy. I think about his children and hope there are only two.

I say to myself that it is good for our family that he no longer exists.

Hormazd says the khansaman will die in a prison cell, the gunshot wound will fester, and the body will destroy itself.

Smitaben says with great self-confidence, as if she could personally attest to it, that the khansaman will be reborn as a worm. Because in his earlier life he was a tota. (Or a parrot. Or a Psittacidae.) That is why he always slept near them.

She did not say why he then shot at them. But she did not have to. I understood it. Sometimes one just shoots at one's family.

Remarkable Objects Nos. 22 & 23

THE KOH-I-NOOR
THE LEAF OF A FAN PALM

Every family breaks up at some point. Adolph Schlagintweit has yet to learn that. It is impossible for a family not to break up. This is also true for the Schlagintweits. After Bellaris, Adolph took a different route from that of his brothers. Smitaben, Hormazd, Eleazar and most of the train accompanied Hermann and Robert to Bangalore. I and a few coolies who called me rakshas and avoided me, travelled with Adolph via Bangapilli and Kadapa to the diamond districts. We explored some of the quarries. It is so hot in there, as if the summer had been locked up in a small space. The workers are completely naked to ensure they do not steal any diamonds. Their skin and even the white of their eyes have taken on the colour of the reddish stone. After their shift, even their stool is strictly controlled.

Adolph ran his hands over the red stone walls. He was now surrounded by his true love, geography, or, as he would say, *the mother of all existence.* The Schlagintweit said, although the mountains in the north were the main object of research of this expedition, the diamond districts alone had made the overland route to Madras worthwhile.

I asked myself whether the Koh-i-Noor had been born in South India. No one knows exactly where it came from. A few years ago, the Vickys of the East India Company presented it to their queen, even though neither it nor India belongs to them. They even had it cut to make it shine more brightly. That is typical for the Vickys. Only because they are not able to see a fire, they make it bigger. Father Fuchs says, when India gains its freedom, the Koh-i-Noor will return to the Peacock Throne and shine for Indian eyes.

Unique things, said Adolph as he brushed the red from his hands, are only born under great pressure.

He did not, I believe, say that to me.

Earlier it was assumed that diamonds were found only at lower latitudes. But as we know from Humboldt's reports, discoveries in the Urals have refuted that theory.

He also did not say that to me, but as if he were talking to someone who knows what an ural is. Someone like Hermann or Robert.

Do you miss your brothers, Sir? I asked him.

I would have liked to explore this region with them, he said.

Will your family break up?

He laughed, but the laugh did not sound like a full laugh. The red earth swallowed most of it.

My family, he said, is held together by something stronger than any physical force.

Even stronger than the Koh-i-Noor?

Considerably stronger.

You don't mean love, Sir?

That's exactly what I mean.

Hormazd says, love is not much better than a Bania's promise. He is right. My first family broke up even though we loved each other a lot. I know almost nothing about my parents. I do not know what they looked like and what they preferred, rajma or chana or masoor dal. I do not know how long my mother's hair or how thick my father's beard was. I do not know from which part of the country or from which caste they were. I do not know if I had siblings. If I have siblings. I do not know if my parents could read or write, and I do not know if they knew that they would die earlier than one has to. I do not even know in which language they spoke to each other apart from the language for which one needs no words and from which I was born. That is the only thing that I know, that I know for certain. I grew for nine months inside my mother, even if it was not much, and in this time, I learnt the first language of my life. It was taught to me by my mother and father. Both went to a lot of trouble to ensure that I learnt it. Perhaps they sensed that we did not have much time. I already knew it well when I came into the world. I loved them and they loved me.

And yet, our family broke up.

Love cannot protect a family, I said to Adolph.

He said: the love of natives is not so deep.

Are you a native, Sir?

Adolph grinned the way he grins when I say something he does not expect.

A native of Bavaria, he said.

How do you then know, Sir, how deep the love of Indians is?

He answered with a question: Do you have brothers?

I have the Others. Father Fuchs says I should regard them as brothers. But that is very difficult.

Then they are not real brothers. You will recognize true brothers by their love.

I did not know whether I should tell the Schlagintweit that his brothers probably did not love him very much. Otherwise, they would not have taken a different route.

I believe you are a good brother, I said, to cheer him up.

Thank you, he said, I believe so too.

Sir?

Yes, Bartholomew?

I like how he says my name. Most people do not take any time for it and slide over it carelessly. Adolph emphasizes every single syllable.

Do you think, I asked, that someone can be your brother even if he is not related to you?

Adolph grinned the way he grins when I say something he expects.

I do, actually, he said.

I also grinned.

Since our departure from Bombay, the buildings in South India had looked timid. The houses in the villages were low, earthen-coloured, and mostly surrounded by a wall that did not allow for any interesting vantage point. But on the journey with Adolph this has changed. The walls of the houses are painted with the same bright red stripes with which the gods in the temples are lined. They look as solemn as I feel because I am travelling with the best Schlagintweit.

When Adolph was sketching the houses, I pointed out the roofs to him. They were made of cane and reed.

Adolph tapped me on the head with the flat of his hand.

The coast cannot be very far away! he said.

I nodded.

Where are we going when we reach Madras? I asked.

My brothers and I will be taking a steamer to Calcutta.

My brothers and I.

I liked the sound of that.

We needed eighteen days to reach Madras. During this time, I was no longer Eleazar's hands and feet; I was also not a death guard and, although I continued to light the way for Adolph's hand at night, I was also not a torchbearer any more. I was his new brother. The train had taken me in as a family member. Even if many people in the train did not speak with this family member because they still thought I was a rakshas.

At nights I dreamed of nameless distant places that I would travel to, where languages were spoken which only a few outsiders had ever heard. I was confident that I would complete the Museum of the World. As Father Fuchs had wanted.

I am so thankful to him for all his knowledge. Especially about the most useful tree in India, which I found helpful on this leg of the journey. Smitaben's replacement, a skinny coolie, cooked as if he did not have a tongue. I introduced Adolph to the fruit of the date palm. But not only this. I roasted the fruit of the areca palm for us and cooked its shoots and enjoyed them together with Adolph's praise. In a village, I negotiated with a farmer with my hands and feet since I did not yet know any Tamil and bought a jug of toddy from him which Adolph finished in one night. The next day he told me to get more of the same. He had long since finished his supply of Old Monk. I persuaded him to leave a little of the fermented palm juice. What remained was not much, but enough to boil it down and make sugar from it. Adolph dipped his finger in the syrup, licked it and called out: Sakradi![19] I believe it was then that Adolph really saw how valuable I would be as a translator to him and his brothers. I not only translate words, but also the country. One day, when I saw the fan palm which Father Fuchs appreciates the most, I asked Adolph to stop the train. Only a short while ago no one would have listened to me. Now Adolph did not hesitate to give the order to stop. I cut the leaves of the palm into narrow strips with a knife and scratched Adolph's name into the soft surface. It was as easy as writing on paper. This time the Schlagintweit was so thrilled that he did not even call out to his God. He took the knife from me and wrote my name next to his. Then he gave the leaf to me.

I folded it and put it near Humboldt's hair.

On this night it rained for the first and only time on the route to Madras. Adolph packed his drawings away, took off his shirt, stood

---

19 Bavarian for god.

in the rain and put out his tongue. He drank water from the air. The coolies watched him suspiciously. I went to him and also put out my tongue. I probably looked like a rakshas. But that did not bother me. If this is what the life of a rakshas was, I was happy to be one. Every drop of rain tasted salty and yet sweeter than palm syrup.

On 18 February 1855, we reached Madras. Hermann had already arrived a few days ago. Adolph and I have not yet met him or Smitaben and the others.

The Schlagintweits are staying with the lieutenant governor. I was given a bed in his palace next to Eleazar in a servant's room that is almost as big as the dormitory in the Glass House. Adolph says that the extent and density of population in Madras surpasses that of Prussia. Despite this, the rich people in this presidency have more space than in Bombay. (The poor here also live in Blacktown and have just as little space.) The Mount Road, which leads from the Fort to the military station St. Thomas, is like a long chain strung with many villas. The rich people walk along this road in a peculiar manner: they stroll slowly as long as they are in the shade of a tree and faster as soon as they are in the sun. This makes their movement jerky. The roads are much more solid here than in Bombay, their stones more reliable. Perhaps that is because they have more practice in carrying out their job. Since there are no solid stones in the region, the stones of old houses are stripped off and carried away by prisoners to be used for building the roads. Even the air in Madras is different from the air in Bombay. The smell of the sea or of the city is not as intense. The city produces less sound, but some sounds stand out more clearly. Especially the ringing of church bells. They feed the ears of Christians of whom there are many more here.

The most important place in Madras is the promenade. Every evening the rich people of the city gather there and walk along the sea like ants at the edge of a pool of water. I entered the promenade for the first time before daybreak on 19 February. The city was bathed in the cool colours of dawn. Adolph and I had arranged to meet there to watch a rare horse race. Because I did not spot him immediately in the crowd, I went in search of him. I was looking forward to sharing this experience with my brother.

The sound of the sea thrust its way into all conversations. It is a language everyone understands and almost all like. Couples in love, families, gurus, Parsis, Muslims, Christians, old people, young people, rich and poor people, firangi and Indians, listen to the sea. I have always had little use for this commonplace swish of water. I prefer Hindi, German, Marathi. Even English. A lot of that buzzed around in the air on this early morning. There was an excitement all around; the Madrassis were more talkative than Hermann on a good day. They paid me no heed. For them, a brown boy was invisible. The advantage of that was that I could listen to them undisturbed. Some women pointed the tips of their noses at the riders and called them gentlemen. I did not waste any time explaining that most of them were only Vickys. One of the riders was darker than the others; his mother must be Indian. The women did not point at him that often. Which was just as conspicuous as if they had called out his name. A Vicky, whose cheeks were even smoother than mine, complained that this Indo-European should not be allowed into the Madras Club. Another Vicky, whose burnt skin had taken on the same colour as his uniform, said that was because of the lack of members. The times in which Madras had been the most remarkable English settlement were long gone. Both of them agreed it was necessary to have a port. That would again give Madras greater importance. And they could remain among themselves in the club.

The horse race began. But I had no eyes for it. I had to find Adolph first. I scrabbled through the crowd and the shouts and thundering of hooves. For a short while, the sea became silent. I looked out for

Adolph, for his broad shoulders, his self-confident stance and his alert look which he has in common with Father Fuchs.

I could not find him.

When the sun rose, the horse race ended. The crowd dispersed, the rich Madrassis made their way home to rest during the heat of the day. The smell of the sea battled with the smell of the horses and their manure. I ran once more up and down the promenade to make sure that Adolph was not waiting for me somewhere. Then I left.

When I returned to the lieutenant governor's palace, Adolph and Hermann were sitting together in one of the living rooms. I approached them from behind; they had not yet seen me. A large punkah hung from the ceiling. It was operated by a servant who stood in an adjacent serving room and pulled smoothly on a rope that was linked with the punkah through a hole in the wall. The air that was fanned made Hermann's moustache quiver. I crept closer to the brothers to understand what they were talking about. Adolph said he had found out something and showed Hermann a leaf of the fan palm. He cut it into strips and then wrote both their names on it. Hermann held the leaf against the light. Their names lit up green. Then they clinked their crystal glasses and drank up. It was only now that I recognized the smell of palm wine which hung in the room. Adolph did not mention my name even once.

Bartholomew, Adolph said cheerfully, when he saw me. Where were you?

At the horse race, I said.

And? he asked. How was it?

Unique, I said in the hope that it would hurt him.

Excellent, he said. We too have good news. Hermann has found a ship for you.

Sir?

You can go back to Bombay.

I thought we were taking a steamer to Calcutta, I said.

Adolph shook his head slowly.

You said your brothers and you were taking a steamer to Calcutta.

The Schlagintweits exchanged looks.

Did you think I meant you? asked Adolph.

Hermann smirked and Adolph laughed out loudly. Even if their ways of dealing with the world were very different, it was clear: they were brothers.

Remarkable Object No. 24

A SHARK

On 28 June 1851 Hermann completed his habilitation[20] and was hired by the university in Berlin. Adolph wanted to follow suit. He did not allow himself to be distracted by girls, wrote a thesis on geological work in the Alps, but failed.

That, says Adolph, was because of Weiss, a professor in Berlin who wrote a negative report. He insulted Adolph by praising him: for his physical constitution. Weiss suggested that he was more of a mountaineer than a scientist.

Hermann was on the scene immediately. After the setback, he convinced Adolph to go mountain climbing with him in a country with the implausible name of Switzerland.

There too they failed. They had to turn back just a few metres short of the main peak of the Monte Rosa massif. It would have been the first ascent. Adolph says that to his surprise this failure felt good. Because they had failed together. Since their childhood, the brothers had competed with each other – for the love of their mother, their father, a teacher, or a lady. One of them always won, often Adolph.

---

20 Adolph says that this is a kind of licence given to pass on one's knowledge to others. And he also says, ever since he met me, he has the impression that in India this licence is already given at birth.

This time both had lost.

Two victors rob each other of the sweetness of victory, said Adolph, but two losers console each other.

Adolph wrote another thesis, this time about his observations in the Monte Rosa. But it did not contain the most important thing he had learnt: that he had rediscovered his love for his brother there.

Adolph's second attempt was also unsuccessful.

Again, Weiss was responsible.

Hermann arrived on the scene again. Together they travelled to the Alps and scaled the Zugspitze.

This success was, as it happens, not that sweet, says Adolph. But it did give him the confidence to try a third time. Not in Berlin, however, but in his homeland Bavaria where there was greater appreciation for his research. Adolph was appointed adjunct professor.

He would never have reached this peak without Hermann, says Adolph.

WHEN ADOLPH HAD told me this story some weeks earlier, I had not written it down. It had not seemed remarkable to me then. But it came to my mind immediately when I saw the brothers sitting together happily under the swish of the punkah drinking palm wine.

You can recognize true brothers through their love, Adolph had said. I now saw this love. But it was not meant for me.

I LEFT THE palace of the lieutenant governor and ran to the edge of the city. When I reached the promenade, I took out the leaf of the fan palm. It was withered. But one could still read Adolph's and my name.

I crumpled up the leaf and threw it into the sea.

But the water did not want it; it washed the letters back at my feet.

I picked up the leaf and hurled it as far out as I could.

Again, the sea gave it back to me.

I noticed then that a coolie nearby was watching me. He walked back and forth on a wooden beam bringing up buckets filled with water. Madras gets its water from a complex of wells called Seven Wells. Many such square cisterns are found dispersed throughout the city. The only thing that kept the coolie from falling in were pliant rods that ran on both sides of the wooden beam and which he held on to.

Every family breaks up at some point of time, I said to him.

The coolie stopped walking and the buckets stopped.

I cannot disappoint Father Fuchs, I said. But how am I supposed to continue?

The coolie blinked.

I do not need a steamer to reach Calcutta, I said to him. If I follow the coast to the north, I will get there. In some weeks. Or months? In a year?

The coolie cocked his head.

Or I could threaten Adolph, I said. He would definitely not like me to tell his brothers about the forbidden place he visited in Bombay.

The coolie did not move.

Right, I said. Who will his brothers believe? Him or me?

The coolie again began walking back and forth.

I do not think he understood German.

I wish, I said to him, the Schlagintweits had never come to India. They are like the Vickys. Every time one of them comes to our country, someone dies. And we cannot do anything about it.

That is not true, said a friendly voice.

I turned around. Eleazar was sitting on a rock with his legs crossed.

How long have you been here?

Long enough, he said. If you really want to remain with the train, I can arrange that.

He stood up and kneeled down beside me.

However, it has its price, he said. You will be in my debt.

For the first time I had the impression that I was talking to the real Eleazar. He meant every word he said. I did not have to translate anything.

It is your only chance, he said. Think about it.

Then he left me alone with the sea and with the coolie.

I STAYED ON the promenade till well into the night and thought about Eleazar's offer. Countless glowing insects swarmed around the trees and bushes after sunset. If only Father Fuchs had been with me! He would have told me their names; he would have advised me.

The insects formed a glimmering cloud that hovered along the sea. They were an unreliable starry sky. For a few moments they radiated brightly and almost blindingly till the glow suddenly disappeared plunging the promenade into absolute darkness. This was repeated every few seconds. It reminded me of the lighthouse in Colaba. I asked myself what the insects were trying to communicate through this and whether their signal was actually being received.

2 MARCH 1855 was the day of our departure. *The Bengal*, a propellor steamer belonging to the Company, was anchored miles away from the shore. Even though the sea was calmer than on an ordinary day on Bombay's coast. The surf in Madras is too dangerous. Masulas were used to help cover the distance, boats made of wooden boards held together only with ropes so that they do not break on impact. But even the almost twenty oarsmen of the masulas did not dare to come too close to the shallow shore. Laskars, the seamen of the Company, carried the Schlagintweit's equipment to the masulas. Hermann and Robert had themselves transported on the shoulders of the laskars. Adolph was the only brother who insisted on striding to the masulas without any help. Similarly, Smitaben, Hormazd, Eleazar, I and a

few new members of the train waded through the water which soon reached up to my chest. With each wave I swallowed a lot of it.

A cry from the masulas brought everyone to a halt. Hermann wanted to know the reason, and Eleazar pointed to a place in the water not far from us. Some of the laskars seemed to be alarmed. They walked on but quickened their pace. At first, I could not see anything. Then I saw a fin.

Sharks, said Adolph and prepared to lift me onto his shoulders.

I resisted. I did not want to be carried by someone like him.

Adolph laughed, wished me luck, and carried on.

I followed him with my eyes. Eleazar had convinced him and his brothers to take me with them as a translator. I do not know how he had managed it. Adolph treats me as if nothing had happened. As if we were a family. But I have learnt my lesson. A firangi, whether a Vicky or a Bavarian, and an Indian will never belong to the same family. Father Fuchs is not an exception. For me he is more Indian than anything else.

The calls to hurry came again from the masulas. The fins were gliding towards us. Hormazd sprinted forward; I have never seen him move so quickly. The laskars thrust their bodies with all their strength through the water. One of them dropped the crate he was carrying and swam back to the shore. Hermann cursed in Bavarian; Robert worried in silence. Adolph lifted the crate onto his back and caught up with them. Eleazar continued walking steadily while looking around him attentively. Smitaben took her time as if she knew that her time had not yet come. And I? I stood still. A shadow came towards me. I felt the movement in the water. It was so close that I only needed to stretch my hand out to touch it. I was afraid. The fear came from a place deep within me and threatened to take hold of me. But I did not let it. I did not let it. It was no longer as strong as with the dare in Bori Bunder. And I was no longer an orphan boy. I was a translator for the scientists Schlagintweit on the way to Calcutta.

PART III

Calcutta 1855

Remarkable Object No. 25

ROBERT SCHLAGINTWEIT

The voyage lasted three days. My only memory of it is the sea, every second, every minute always the same horrible sea into which I spewed everything that was in me. Considering that the Schlagintweits love the earth so much they travel a lot with boats and ships.

ON 5 MARCH 1855, we reached the roadstead of Calcutta. As we pulled into the estuary of the Ganges–Brahmaputra delta, many passengers thronged the deck. We were welcomed only by bushes and by the trunks of trees that had washed up to the tips of the islands. I realized only a little later that the tree-trunks were actually crocodiles. They glided into the water and tore up a corpse that had been committed to the holy river. Some passengers screamed; others masked their shock behind a cackling laugh. Robert, who was standing beside me, pulled his hat down over his face as if he were ashamed of the other firangi.

As we approached the berth – it is called Garden Reach – the number of, I must admit, imposing ships and even more imposing buildings increased. In the distance the Vickys' flag floundered on the dome of the governor-general's palace.

There is a reason why Calcutta is called the city of palaces. Whether all cities in Europe looked like this? I asked myself but not

Robert who wasn't supposed to think that I was impressed. Bengal is the largest of the three presidencies belonging to the Vickys and is based in Calcutta. I do not know what exactly I had anticipated – more ugliness? I especially liked the ghats along the shore. In Bombay, the sea surrounds the islands of the city. In Calcutta, the city is not afraid of the sea; it enters into a union with it. The many steps beckon invitingly to visitors and water alike. There is a give and take. Smaller ships dock at the ghats; at others, people bathe in the river or servants wash thalis.

Most of the passengers, who are from Europe, leaned out over the guardrail, pointed to different buildings, talked all at once and appeared to be pleasantly surprised. Not Robert. His eyes reflected the passing shore.

Since his sight seems to me to be keener than that of his brothers, I asked him what he was seeing.

The same as you, he said.

I was not so sure about that.

Don't you like the city, Sir?

It is not a question of taste, he said. Travel accounts easily make mistakes by only praising everything without any gain for the portrayal as such.

You don't like it then?

An unbiased look is very important if we want to know the character of the place. That is why photography is of such immeasurable service to our studies.

And don't forget your brother's drawings, I said.

Yes, well, he said. A machine can have an unbiased gaze. Not a human being.

Not even your brothers?

Not even they, he said. After all, they are here.

But how are they supposed to look at something if they are not there?

Only then did Robert turn to me. I did not like him looking at me directly.

Every object of a scientific study changes when it is observed, he said. India can only be described objectively by someone who has never been here.

But that is impossible! I said.

Indeed! By being here we change India. And so, India becomes a place it would not have been if we had not come here.

That is true, I said. Very true!

Robert smiled and turned to the shore again.

Then he said: I should have thanked you a long time ago.

For what, Sir?

You saved my life. If you had not taken out the paan … what a deplorable death that would have been!

It was strange to hear him talking about his death. I never thought that a Schlagintweit can die. Yes, I think about the end every day. I often ask myself in the morning which member of our train will no longer be with us in the evening.

But in my head it was always, till now, an Indian.

Remarkable Object No. 26

DROP OF FLESH

Calcutta is like a beautiful Vicky. I do not want to look at her and yet I cannot stop myself. There is no Blacktown here. The commingling of Indians and Europeans is greater than I have ever experienced. Naturally, Calcutta is an Indian city. But whenever I traverse its streets and lanes, I lose the feeling that I am in India. But it also does not feel as if I had suddenly landed in Europe. Rather, it seems as if I were in a new eerie place. It gives me nightmares in which there are no Indians and Europeans any more, but only human beings who speak the same language and who do not know how different they really are.

When the Schlagintweits and Eleazar do not need my help, I roam around the city. After months on the Grand Trunk Roads the many voices and smells are refreshing. It awakens a longing for Bombay in me. And for Father Fuchs. I would love to walk around the large Government House with him and tell him that Duke Wellington, who the French liked even less than the Indians, had commissioned it to be built. Together with Father Fuchs I would admire the Town Hall, the colleges, the Martinière, and I would point out to him that even the most splendid building of the Vickys is clearly not immune to the Indian rains. I would take a buggy with him and follow the road along the Hooghly River. We would be moving at the same speed as the river and some corpses in it. We would vie with one another to present our observations: the wheel of a dilapidated coach that resembles an oval rather than a circle; the impractical, rustling costumes (yes, costumes) of the Vickys when they go to the opera; the massive fronds with which runners, who accompany carriages, ward off horseflies; the weapons of a Powinda camel-driver from Kabul; the ramrod-straight backs of the vice-governor's bodyguard; the smoking oil lamps. At the end of such an excursion Father Fuchs and I would sit down at one of the many stepwells whose surface is as smooth as a mirror, and we would see ourselves in it, only him and me.

Instead, I am a blurred reflection with the Schlagintweits on the polished tables of the Vickys. As in Bombay, we spend hours in the offices. One of the most important ones is the Great Trigonometrical Survey. But its superintendent, Sir George Everest, is presently not in Calcutta. The brothers could use his help. They are in a hurry to leave Calcutta and complete their study of the Indian plains before the monsoon and the worst of the summer heat. They are eager to study the heights, the heart of their expedition and of their true love.

Governor-General James Broun-Ramsay is helping them. Soon after we arrived, he received the Schlagintweits. Eleazar and I accompanied them. Before the meeting Hermann took me aside and drummed it into me to keep my mouth shut. Otherwise, I would lose my place in the train for good.

I was surprised that the brothers were actually taking me along. They did not need me for a conversation in English. I think Hermann was testing me, and I believe he was hoping I would fail.

Even before I met James Broun-Ramsay for the first time I did not like him. He had never replied to any of the letters in which Father Fuchs criticized the policies and conquering expeditions and laws of the Vickys.

How I would have loved to take James Broun-Ramsay to task, to rebuke him and demand a detailed reply.

But I could not allow any words to pass my lips. I had sworn that to myself. I now finally belonged to the train. And it was important not to endanger that.

When receiving us in his study James Broun-Ramsay stood up, but he did not come around from his table which was dark and massive like an oxcart. He stretched out his sinewy hand. Hermann rushed to it at once and took hold of it. Robert and Adolph followed his example. James Broun-Ramsay did something with his lips that was probably meant to be a smile and sank back into his chair. His movements were slow, like those of an old man, but they appeared to be fake, as if he wished to lull his counterpart into a false sense of security. His nose can compete with that of Lord Elphinstone. The tip of his nose is bent down; it looks like a drop of flesh. His eyes only move horizontally, from left to right to left. He never looks up or down, as if he were not able to do it. So, he did not notice me. I believe he did not even know I was there. When I wanted to sit down on one of the four chairs in front of his table, Eleazar pulled me by the hair and pointed me to a place near the door. Then he sat down next to the Schlagintweits.

Hermann thanked James Broun-Ramsay for his time.

Although no one had asked him, James Broun-Ramsay mentioned that he worked long and hard, to be exact, every day from half past eight in the morning till half past five in the evening.

Sometimes, I even miss lunch, he said.

His voice was calm and firm. It did not become louder even when the noises of Calcutta drowned it out. That is why the Schlagintweits, Eleazar and I were bent towards him most of the time.

Is that true, I wanted to say, that you miss lunch? How noble of you!

But I kept my mouth shut.

Hermann and Robert nodded; Adolph coughed as if he had to swallow a piece of raw mutton. Eleazar sat in friendly silence.

James Broun-Ramsay said that he even rode untiringly despite his weak back.

I wanted to ask James Broun-Ramsay to live for one day as Devinder or Smitaben or Bartholomew and walk through the city barefoot.

But I kept my mouth shut.

I focussed my eyes on the map of India behind him. Large patches on it were red. Red like the tunics of the Vickys.

When the Schlagintweits congratulated James Broun-Ramsay on his military conquests, he asked the brothers whether they wanted to hear him.

The brothers exchanged looks. I think they did not know who or what James Broun-Ramsay meant.

But of course! Hermann said.

You don't have to, said James Broun-Ramsay.

If it is no trouble, said Hermann.

Not at all, said James Broun-Ramsay, I am happy to say such a wonderful sentence.

Then, said Hermann, we would love to hear it.

James Broun-Ramsay cleared his throat and we all leaned forward.

Unwarned by precedent, he said, uninfluenced by example, the Sikh nation has called for war; and on my words, sirs, war they shall have and with a vengeance.

On no account will I translate this far from wonderful sentence into German. It is not worth it. James Broun-Ramsay uttered it at the beginning of the Anglo-Sikh War. The conquest of the Punjab is regarded as one of his great successes.

But your achievements are no less worthy, said James Broun-Ramsay and pointed to a book with a brown-red-golden cover that lay on the table.

It was the first volume of Alexander von Humboldt's *Kosmos*.

Similar-looking smiles appeared on the faces of the Schlagintweits, as if James Broun-Ramsay had named a mountain after them.

You know German? asked Hermann.

The corners of James Broun-Ramsay's mouth twitched.

You overestimate me, he said. The important parts were translated for me. Congratulations! You managed to enter the work of a great scientist.

I wondered what he was talking about.

It was only our journey in the Alps, said Hermann, who did not sound as modest as he wanted to.

From my place near the door, I looked at the backs of the Schlagintweits' heads. I was impressed. Humboldt had immortalized the Schlagintweits in his book.

Impressive, said James Broun-Ramsay in the same tone in which he said everything else.

I was filled with disgust. I did not want to share any feeling with someone like him.

How unfortunate, said James Broun-Ramsay, that Humboldt himself cannot lead the expedition. I would have loved to meet him.

Yes, it is unfortunate, said Adolph.

It is also unfortunate that the Company never replied to any of his requests, I wanted to say.

But I kept my mouth shut.

In any case, the Company is very grateful for your efforts, said James Broun-Ramsay. The promotion of the sciences has the highest priority for us. We are confident that your studies will contribute greatly to the furtherance of knowledge.

I thought of Father Fuchs's word: *The damned Company does not consume knowledge to feed it to others but uses it to become more powerful!*

But I kept my mouth shut.

Later, after the Schlagintweits had discussed all their business matters with James Broun-Ramsay there was a pause in the conversation. It was time to leave. But the Schlagintweits did not stand up. It took me a moment to understand what they were waiting for. James Broun-Ramsay had to dismiss them. Anything else would have been impolite.

He said: Ah!

A few seconds passed before he continued.

Father Fuchs, he said.

Again, there was a pause in which Hermann threw me a warning look, Adolph a curious look and Robert no look at all.

Do you know him? asked James Broun-Ramsay.

In passing, said Hermann.

You will leave India from Bombay, am I right?

Hermann nodded.

Since you are also from Bavaria, I have the vague hope that you might exert some influence on him. He is a very self-righteous, tenacious cleric.

He is the most popular man in all of Bombay, I wanted to say.

But I kept my mouth shut.

The Father should use his energy for his duties as a missionary rather than writing untenable letters of complaint.

For the first and only time, James Broun-Ramsay leaned forward towards the Schlagintweits.

He is not making any friends, he said.

What has he written? asked Adolph.

Hermann now threw a warning look in his direction.

That does not concern us, said Hermann.

Please! said James Broun-Ramsay. You have a right to know. After all, I asked for your help.

I was glad that Adolph had asked the question. Otherwise, I would have done it myself.

In his last letter, James Broun-Ramsay said while pulling on his drop of flesh as if he were storing memories in it, he expressed doubts about the Doctrine of Lapse. Can you imagine that?

Hermann shook his head. No! he said. Outrageous!

Evidently, he did not know this Doctrine, and neither did I.

What is it about? asked Adolph.

James Broun-Ramsay shook his head very quickly and stared at the Schlagintweit.

Surely you must have heard about it!

James Broun-Ramsay's voice had lost some of its firmness.

Adolph thought about his question.

No, he said, I am sorry.

James Broun-Ramsay leaned back, as if a beggar from Blacktown had breathed on him.

The Doctrine of Lapse is my modest stroke of genius, he said. It allows the Company to annex the state of an allied Indian prince if he does not have any progeny, or if he proves to be incompetent. I should add: particularly the latter is often the case.

The Schlagintweits, Eleazar and I remained silent.

Some people say that the Doctrine was developed by the Board of Directors. I have to contradict this in the strongest terms. It was my idea, mine alone. In this way we bring in primogeniture in an elegant way. We cannot allow the Indians to continue their archaic traditions. Where would we be if everyone can independently determine succession to the throne! The country must be reformed. Telegraph masts, a proper rail network, roads. Civilization! This Father Fuchs is dreaming if he thinks the Indians can do this without our help. He has lived here far too long. This disastrous climate! In the long run it destroys even the sharpest mind. I would not be surprised if, in the meantime, the poor man thinks he is an Indian.

At this point James Broun-Ramsay laughed for so long till the Schlagintweits, first Hermann, then Robert and, finally, Adolph, joined in the laughter.

I clenched my fist and took a step forward to beat the laughter out of the governor-general.

But Eleazar caught hold of my hand. And I interlaced my fingers with his and held on tightly.

Remarkable Object No. 27

THE EGG-DANCER

I told myself: Do not listen to the anger. It cannot force you to do something. Father Fuchs would have been proud of you. Bury the anger deep inside of you.

But three voices called out to it.

The first belonged to Hermann. Immediately after the meeting with James Broun-Ramsay he remarked on how well it had gone off.

Anger made me want to contradict him. It reminded me of Hermann's obsequiousness. It told me that he had treated the Vicky like a king. He would do anything for him.

The second voice belonged to Adolph. He called the Vicky a forward-looking man.

There, anger got the better of me briefly and I asked him what he meant by forward-looking.

He is thinking of the future, said Adolph.

I know what forward-looking means, I said.

Adolph looked at me in surprise. Anger had slipped into my words.

Sir, I added, in order to hide it.

He nodded.

Adolph only pretends not to like the Vickys, anger said. He does not realize that he envies every Vicky because he would actually like to be one himself. But there is no way in hell I will explain that to him. I was not hired to translate Adolph Schlagintweit to Adolph Schlagintweit.

The third voice belonged to Robert. Rather, it did not belong to Robert. Because, unlike his brothers, his silence called out the anger. He should finally raise his voice and not always follow his brothers like a slave. As things stand, he will only be remembered as the younger brother of Hermann and Adolph. The brother who was also in India. The brother whose name no one remembers.

Anger wanted me to catch hold of him and shake him up. Did he always have to wear this hat! It was far too warm for it. And it was not raining. The hat is only a place to hide. He can peep out from under it and hide his face. Stop that! anger demanded. It urged me to tear the hat off his head and stamp on it.

Again, it was Eleazar who saved me from the anger. He told me to come with him. I hesitated. Anger bound me to the Schlagintweits. But Eleazar cut me off from it. He dragged me away by the ear.

We went to the northern part of Calcutta. There are more Bengalis here than anywhere else in the city. We encountered some of them on the way. I envy them for their white linen, I do not envy them for their haste. The Bengalis always seem to be running away from something or running after something. They are swift, delicate, wavering people who never feel completely safe wherever they are.

Eleazar led me to a spot bathed in the last of the evening light. A woman was dancing, surrounded by a small crowd of onlookers. On her head she had a circlet from which threads hung down. Her movements were careful and fluid. She repeatedly put her hand into a basket and took out a raw egg each time, which she tied to one of the threads. Soon, more than twenty eggs were hanging from her head while she moved her body in circles in a way that the eggs did not bump against one another. Only by maintaining the correct speed could she avoid losing any of the eggs. And none of the onlookers.

You are allowed to cry, Eleazar said to me. There is no shame in it. We are amongst ourselves here.

And then, only then did I realize it. He was right, I wanted to cry. Because Father Fuchs was not here and because James Broun-Ramsay had done him an injustice. And because Father Fuchs is not sending any more letters to Calcutta. And because I will never know the perfect name for the museum. And because I cannot go back to the Glass House. And because I will never find Father Fuchs.

But my eyes remained dry.

I never cry in front of the Others. They can take everything away from me or laugh at me or do worse things, but they can never make me cry. Not that. Tears translate feelings. If one finds someone crying, one learns something about what is happening inside that person. Then one knows me and can do anything to me.

Do you know, asked Eleazar, how I convinced the Schlagintweits to make you part of the train?

I shook my head.

I told them the truth: that you are a far better translator than I am.

You did not!

I looked him deep in the eyes to find out whether he was lying. But I had to look away again, because in this way he could also see deep into my eyes.

My friend, I must now claim your debt.

Eleazar said that in Marathi. I was not aware that he knew Marathi. No one speaks Marathi in Calcutta.

After Calcutta, he said, the brothers will travel separately. I will accompany Hermann. You will travel with Adolph and Robert.

I know, I said.

The egg-dancer swung around like a jasmine blossom that is carried by the wind shortly before the monsoon arrives. The eggs flew just a few inches away from each other.

You will be a good translator. You will do what they ask of you so that they do not become suspicious.

The egg-dancer lost her balance. Some onlookers were startled.

She stretched her torso like a snake and circled rhythmically again. Her smirk revealed that the interruption was only an act for the amusement of her audience.

You will keep me informed about everything they do, Eleazar said.

He did not sound very friendly. I liked that. The friendly Bania was not really him. Maybe I was now standing across from the real Eleazar. I had to look into his eyes. They are darker than mine, but without any colour. I could not see anything in them, no lies, no truth.

Why do you want to know what the Schlagintweits do? I asked in Hindi. I had nothing to hide.

They serve the Angrez.

We do too, I said.

And that shall not be the case for much longer.

I noticed that during our conversation Eleazar had not hunkered down. He stood straight beside me and spoke with his head turned to the side as if I were as tall as he.

Who are you? I asked, although I knew that he would not give me a satisfactory answer.

An Indian, he said. Like you.

Eleazar read my look.

But you did not ask that, he said.

I waited for his reply.

Let us say, I am someone who will do anything so that India is free again.

Do you belong to the resistance? I whispered, this time also in Marathi. I did not want to be tied in front of a canon.

Eleazar laughed.

No. These amateurs? No.

Who do you work for then?

It is better for you, he said, if you don't know.

While dancing, the egg-dancer began to untie the eggs from the threads and put them back in the basket.

It would not be right to deceive the brothers, I said.

Why not? Are they loyal to you?

No, I said.

Are they your family?

No, certainly not.

What is stopping you then?

I thought about what Father Fuchs would have said. Finally, I decided to say: The Schlagintweits are Germans.

Germans, Angrez, Portuguese, Danes, French, Dutch, said Eleazar. What difference does that make?

The Germans do not have any colonies.

They would certainly like to have some.

No, Father Fuchs says that the Germans are committed more to the pen than the sword.

These scientists are only the vanguard of the Angrez, said Eleazar. Why do you think the Company supports their studies? They want to know how to conquer us and take our country from us.

That is not why the Schlagintweits are here. Humboldt sent them. He is the greatest scientist of our times.

And the greatest scientist of our times collaborates with the greatest empire of our times, he said.

I did not need the hair to remind me why I believe in Humboldt. But I still put my hand in my pocket and clasped the handkerchief. I felt better at once.

The Germans are not our enemies, I said. And I am not a traitor.

No, not a traitor, Eleazar said. A hero!

Father Fuchs would not have wanted it, I said.

I can believe that, he said. The question you must ask yourself is: why?

Because Father Fuchs is a good human being, I said.

Eleazar clapped his hands together.

Wrong, he said. Because he is one of them.

Father Fuchs, I said, champions the rights of Indians more than most Indians do.

Father Fuchs has fed you many lies.

That is not true!

This came out more loudly than I had intended.

The egg-dancer came to us. She handed me one of the eggs. It was still warm from her hand. Water dripped onto it. My tears. I did not know how long I had been crying. But now I could not stop.

The anger had disappeared. Eleazar had stolen it from me.

He looked at me hardfaced. However false his friendliness was, at this moment I wished it were back.

It would be better for you and everyone else if you do not tell anyone about our talk.

With this he went away.

I looked at the egg and asked myself if something was growing in it.

Remarkable Object No. 28

LORD GANESHA'S TRUE HEAD

My favourite god is Lord Ganesha. In Bombay I would always go to a shrine or temple dedicated to him if I needed to talk about something that even Father Fuchs would not understand. When I tell him things I am not supposed to say to anyone, Lord Ganesha does not betray my secrets. He listens to me attentively and never interrupts me, and although his infinite wisdom remains silent in his trunk, I always feel better after visiting him. But mainly I like going to him because he does not give me the feeling that I am speaking to a god. His parents radiate power and anger and strength. In front of Lord Shiva and Parvati I can only bow my head and whisper. Lord Ganesha, on the other hand, appears to be even more friendly than Father Fuchs. Sometimes I feel sorry for him. After all, almost no one, not even he, knows what he really looks like. Everyone is familiar with the story. When Lord Shiva found a stranger with his wife and cut off his head, he did not guess that it was their son. He sent servants to find the head, and they brought him an elephant's head. Shiva put it on him and wakened him to life again. But what happened to Lord Ganesha's real head? It has to be somewhere. Only his parents know what he really looks like. And even their memories must have faded with the centuries. I ask myself whether Lord Ganesha sometimes becomes sad when he looks into a mirror.

Would he not also like to have a nice face like Lord Shiva or Parvati? And how does he know that he is really who he is?

In Calcutta I go to his shrine every day if the Schlagintweits allow it. The nearest one is north of Bow Bazaar where many Indians live. The area reminds me of Bombay's Blacktown: smells flowing into each other, labyrinthine lanes, languages foreign even to me, shabby huts that grow faster than they fall. Only, none of it feels familiar. Is that because Calcutta is not Bombay? Or is it the influence of the firangi on me?

Each time I take a gift for Lord Ganesha. A few rupees from my wages, or a fresh marigold, or a stuffed egg like the ones the Bengalis love to eat. I told Lord Ganesha that I sometimes feel as if I were also carrying an alien head on my shoulders. I find it difficult to remember who I was. I still know everything; I can even read about it in the museum and yet I am no longer the boy who knew what is right and what is not.

Soon I will make a mistake.

One can only be free when one knows who one is, says Father Fuchs. And like all Indians, I will only know who I am when the Museum of the World has been completed. I can only do that as long as I remain in the train. But if I do not do what Eleazar wants, he will have me removed from the train. How am I then supposed to be free?

I push these thoughts into the farthest corner of my perhaps alien head and remind myself that I should forget to think about it. And I avoid Eleazar.

Even if I cannot escape him. Five days have passed since he called in the debt. Strangely enough, he has not mentioned it again. Why? Surely, he has not forgotten it. Eleazar is not someone who forgets something. I cannot betray him to the Schlagintweits because he has more influence with them than I do. And I cannot even let

Smitaben or Hormazd into it because he would harm them. Eleazar is someone like that.

I can only tell Lord Ganesha about him. But he keeps the solution to himself. Regardless of how often I beg him for it. He looks at me sleepily, points to me with his trunk and remains silent.

Remarkable Object No. 29

THE CHINAMAN

On 16 March, nine days after the conversation with Eleazar, I accompanied the Schlagintweits and Eleazar to the auction house Lawtie & Gould at Lal Dighi. Some of the grandest buildings of the Vickys are around this pond. Even I have never felt so small as I did in the face of these palaces. As I gazed at them one after the other, I realized that I had made a mistake. There is not just *one* realm. Another one exists in Calcutta. And naturally it belongs to the Vickys.

Despite its name, the pond is not red at all. The water shimmers clean. I am aware that one cannot tell if water is clean just by looking at it, but this water is clean. I am convinced of it. I would have liked to taste it. I am sure it is sweet. The Vickys have pressed the pond into a square shape and fenced it in. On a broad street beside it, coaches drawn by horses move on tracks. The Vickys call it the tram car. It crosses the city along precisely marked routes.[21] Street lamps bloom high and narrow like disciplined plants. Even the reflection of Writers' Building in the still waters of Lal Dighi submits to the

---

21 How can the Vickys plan so many years in advance where they would like to go? In doing so, all the paths that might suddenly open up remain closed to them. The tracks of the tram car determine their lives just like the constellations of the stars.

will of the Vickys and keeps as still as the Writers' Building itself. Each of the innumerable servants who accompany the white men and women holds the parasol so straight into the sky for them as if they expect terrible things to happen with any tilt.

The entire square radiates an order that I only know from the chapel in the Glass House. That used to have a calming effect on me. I respect the Vickys for the fact that they were able to create this order. Is that their vision for India? Do they want to bring this order into all countries? I do not know if I like that. But I also know that I do not not like it.

While we waited in front of the auction house, Hermann drummed it into me, like he did before every meeting, that I was to open my mouth only if I was asked.

I will have to exert myself so that he does not doubt my loyalty. His trust sprouts less than Devinder's plants.

Robert demonstrated his ability to repeat his elder brother's words without saying anything. He looked at me silently.

Only Adolph defended me.

Bartholomew can be relied upon, he said and tapped me on the head with the flat of his hand.

I let it pass. He continues to behave as if nothing had happened. At least he is not drawing in Calcutta. This means that I do not have to spend so much time with him. I do not particularly like any of the Schlagintweits, but him I particularly do not like. Especially when he treats me well. I know that it does not mean anything. I cried away my anger at the brothers while watching the egg-dancer. Disappointment has taken its place. It grows at a leisurely pace, but it is more difficult to remove it from my heart.

A one-horse carriage, which Adolph called a *brougham*, stopped in front of the auction house. I had never seen one like this before. It was closed like a box. Whoever was being transported in it, preferred to be locked in with his own smells. It must belong to a Vicky, I thought.

The gariwan jumped down from the carriage and helped two men to climb out. Sir Jamsetjee Jeejeebhoy and his Chinaman! The Schlagintweits greeted the Parsi warmly, as if they were old friends. Hermann and Robert grasped him by the shoulder and expressed their delight at meeting him again. Adolph embraced him like a brother.

Mr Maharaja! Jeejeebhoy cried out.

Adolph laughed and winked at me. I was sure then that the Parsi had provided the Schlagintweit access to the gopis in Bombay.

Hermann and Robert exchanged an irritated look before they entered the conversation again. All four spoke in English. Jeejeebhoy's fine and somehow sweet pronunciation emphasized the strong Bavarian accent of the Schlagintweits. Robert handed him a photograph.[22] Jeejeebhoy's eyes widened. I stood on tiptoe and tried to get a look at it. But I was too small. The Parsi laughed, making his stomach bounce, and thanked the Schlagintweits. Together they entered the auction house. When I wanted to follow them, Eleazar blocked my path.

Not we, he said, and exchanged a look with the Chinaman who, as in Bombay, wore a deep-blue robe.

I could have asked Eleazar why we had come if the Schlagintweits had not required our services. But then I would have had to talk to him. So, I remained silent.

The Chinaman's eyes moved constantly.

I greeted him with a nod.

He did not react to it.

Eleazar said something to him in Chinese, and Jeejeebhoy's assistant replied in Chinese.

I stared straight ahead as if I were not astonished that Eleazar spoke Chinese.

---

22 That is the name for the pictures one makes with his machine.

They continued talking. Once Eleazar pointed to me. His words sounded like a question.

The assistant's laugh sounded put on.

Eleazar again repeated the same words, none of which I could understand even when hearing them the second time.

The assistant took a step closer to Eleazar and looked around before whispering something.

Eleazar put on his friendliest smile and replied with a monosyllabic word.

Let us go, the assistant said to me in Hindi.

Where? I asked.

The assistant pushed me along in front of him. His hands were firm and bony.

I have to stay here, I said.

Don't resist, said Eleazar, you are making it unnecessarily difficult for us.

Who is *us*? I asked.

The Chinaman whistled for his gariwan, who came and opened the doors of the brougham.

Get in, said the assistant.

I did not get in.

What did he tell you? I asked and pointed to Eleazar. He cannot be trusted.

The assistant laughed, this time more boisterously and said something to Eleazar in Chinese. The Bania nodded and turned away.

The gariwan then grabbed me and put me in the carriage. I called out for help. But no one came. I was after all only a young Indian in a worn-out kurta.

Jeejeebhoy's assistant sat down opposite me and locked the door. He held out a cloth pouch to me.

Slip it on! he said.

No, I said in Hindi.

At once!

I said no in Marathi, then in English and then in German and even in Farsi.

The assistant slapped me. It hurt like Father Holbein's cane.

I slipped the bag over my head and the carriage rolled away.

Please don't harm me, I said.

Be silent! said the assistant.

Where are we going?

You will see.

I heard a smile in his words.

If you let me go, I said, I will not betray you.

He slapped me again.

I was silent.

There was a pleasant smell in the carriage. Like an aromatic fruit. The assistant smelt better than most people.

I thought about how I could escape from him. He was not significantly bigger or broader than I, but he was tough like the children who live in the blind alleys of Blacktown and armed with glass shards, pointed pieces of wood and the courage of the poorest of the poor, even attack merchants. He also had the gariwan. I had to wait for a suitable moment.

We travelled for a while. The voices of Calcutta increased, grew louder, deeper, more insistent. The screeching of the gulls interspersed itself into this clamour. A ship's bell revealed where we were even before the gariwan lifted me out of the carriage. The assistant again pushed me ahead. The smell of the river swooshed in my nose, a smell of much-loved, much-used water. The cloth pouch had slipped a little allowing me to see a dancing forest of masts. A dog growled and birds shrieked more agitatedly than South Indian totas. Calls came from all directions in Bengali and Hindi and English.

Careful, said the assistant, grabbed my arm and pulled me upwards.

We walked on a wooden plank.

Jump, he said. I hesitated and he pushed me.

I landed on my knees. Men laughed. The floor was wooden and greasy.

Stand up!

The assistant led me further away from the light. He pulled the pouch off my head. I was in a ship's cabin. The wood creaked in dissatisfaction. The assistant locked the door behind us. He took a lamp and pointed to a ladder that led deeper into the ship.

What are you planning to do with me? I asked.

Go, he said.

No, I said.

He lifted his hand to slap me.

This time I was faster; I evaded him.

You will obey, he said.

I am not a servant, I said.

The assistant, who was clearly a servant, pulled a face as if I had spit on him.

Still arrogant, he said.

Will I die a painful death? I asked.

Creases formed on his shaved head like waves in a puddle.

The ship suddenly rocked, and I supported myself against the wall. The Chinaman barely shifted his weight and did not even have to lift his feet.

How should I know that? he said.

Am I not here to die?

Die! he said and put down the lamp. We have more important things to do today.

You are not going to kill me? I asked.

The Chinaman looked at me sternly.

Who do you think I am?

Jeejeebhoy's assistant, I said.

Sir Jamsetjee Jeejeebhoy's assistant, he said. If we had wanted you to die, we would not have dealt with it ourselves.

That is good to know, I said.

We were both speaking German. Perhaps that is why I relaxed a little, perhaps also because the Chinaman now climbed down the stairs before me.

A hundred, possibly two hundred, boxes were stored in the ship's hold.

Do you know what is in them? he asked me.

How should I know? I replied.

The Chinaman looked at me intently.

That is when I noticed the smell. I did not have to open the boxes. The smell revealed their contents, even though it was much finer than in the khana. But it was unmistakeable. For me it was Father Fuchs's fragrance.

Opium, I said.

He is right, you are special, he said. The boxes contain not only opium but also the downfall of one culture and the rise of another.

I wanted to see that with my own eyes. I went to one of the boxes and opened it. There were cakes inside. White, square cakes covered with petals.

If you are clever, he said, you will never touch it.

Where did the boxes come from? I asked.

They were bought at an auction. At Lawtie & Gould.

By *Sir* Jamsetjee Jeejeebhoy?

The Chinaman nodded in satisfaction.

I thought he only did business in Bombay.

When he does business in Calcutta, it strengthens his position in Bombay.

I don't understand that, I said.

Thanks to Sir Jamsetjee Jeejeebhoy, Bombay is the new centre for the opium trade. In fact, without the opium trade, Bombay would just be a collection of provincial islands.

I don't believe that.

It is all the same to me what you believe. Bombay was not built on stone or earth but on opium.

Why are you telling me all this?

You and I, we have common friends, he said.

Eleazar? I said. He is not my friend.

He would disagree.

Freund! The word always tasted best for me in German, better than in Hindi or Marathi. But it is bitterer than the most bitter karela when I think of Eleazar along with it.

He has a present for you.

I don't want any presents from him.

It is a remarkable object, said the Chinaman. Eleazar told me about your museum.

Only I decide what is remarkable and what is not, I said. A present from him will never find its way into the museum.

The present is the truth about the most powerful flower in the world.

The most powerful flower in the world does not interest me, I lied.

The Chinaman rubbed the nape of his neck.

Nevertheless, I will give you the present, he said. After that you can decide what you want to do with it.

He pointed to one of the boxes.

Sit down! This could take a while.

I remained standing.

As you wish, he said, dusted off a box with his hand, sat down on it and began.

He had a strange way of telling a story. The Chinaman spoke about the most powerful flower in the world as if it were a person. I was reminded of the fairy tales of the Grimm Brothers which Father Fuchs sometimes tells me and the Others. I found it difficult not to listen. But I pretended as if I did. And I vowed to myself that on no account would I include the most powerful flower in the world in the museum.

Remarkable Object No. 30

THE MOST POWERFUL FLOWER IN THE WORLD

Jeejeebhoy's assistant says that the flower comes out into the light in Malwa. The humid, warm air lures it out. Indian hands distribute its seeds on Indian soil. But hands and soil were only allowed to begin their work after all the important Angrez, and all the Angrez who think they are important, have given permission.

Its blossom, says Jeejeebhoy's assistant, is whiter than a Brahmin's dhoti, whiter than fresh noodles from Canton, whiter than the fog in Hong Kong's harbour at the crack of dawn.

Previously, in a time before the Angrez, its relatives were at home in Assam and in other places in India. Indian hands there distributed only a few seeds on Indian soil. But they wiped down its juice with rags which were then boiled in water. The steam was inhaled only by Indians.

Today, in the times of the Angrez, its cultivation in Assam and other places in India is forbidden. The Angrez know exactly where they want the flower to grow and where not.

When the white of the flower fades, its second life begins. In the evenings Indian hands use a small implement that makes four parallel cuts in its head. Juice flows out of these cuts, thicker than blood. In the mornings, the juice is collected. This is repeated till there is no more juice left in the flower. The flower lives on in its juice, which quickly turns doughy. If the flower is of a poorer quality, Indian hands form round balls from it. These do not wander very far. They change hands in Indian bazaars and land up in a khana. There, they are smoked by Muslims and sometimes, secretly, by a coughing Jesuit.

But the juice of this flower from Malwa is of the best quality. Flat, square cakes are formed out of it and covered with petals. These cakes are stored in crates and brought to Bombay. The Angrez do not dirty their hands with transporting, reloading, or shipping; they only hold out open hands. They call it export duty. The opium merchants have to pay this. One of the most successful and famous ones is a Parsi. And what a Parsi he is! Sir Jeejeebhoy's career began as an accounting clerk on merchant vessels that plied between Bombay and China. He travelled this route four times. On the fourth and last voyage his ship, the *Brunswick*, had to surrender to the French.

A disaster for the owner of the *Brunswick*, a stroke of luck for Sir Jeejeebhoy. He met the resident physician, William Jardine. This was an important seed in the life of the Parsi. It grew into a friendship. And an economic power.

The flower leaves Bombay on Jeejeebhoy's *Good Success* or the *Shaw Kusroo* or the *Johnny* and sails to Hong Kong. A few years earlier it would have been handed over in Canton to Jardine Matheson & Company. But the Chinese emperor was not pleased about the fact that so many predecessors of the flower had killed millions of his subjects or had at least killed their will to live. The opium was therefore confiscated and destroyed in Canton. The Angrez did not like this. The most powerful men in the world obey the most powerful flower in the world; they depend on it. Not because they smoke it themselves, but because without the flower they cannot afford the porcelain, the silk and the tea from China. And in the country of the Angrez, the people do not want to live without porcelain, silk and tea from China. That is why the Angrez declared war on China. For free trade, they claimed. The Angrez won the war easily and got not only their free trade, but also Hong Kong.

After Bombay, this is the second city that could only prosper thanks to the most powerful flower in the world. The old friendship between Sir Jamsetjee Jeejeebhoy and William Jardine now thrives between these two cities. In Hong Kong, Jardine Matheson & Company ensures that the flower is smuggled to the remotest corners of the Chinese empire.

Wherever Chinese hands and noses and mouths receive it, its third life begins.

At the beginning it appears to be friendly. It soothes the mind and improves the flow of blood. That is why it is considered to be a companion, a helpmate in difficult times. And so, the last owners of the flower like to imbibe her often. With time, however, it takes root in the mind till the owner no longer understands his own language. No translator can help him. The most powerful flower in the world cannot be stopped. It is almost as if it were taking revenge for everything that was done to it. It buries itself deeper and deeper into its last owner as if into the soil of Malwa. But this time it does not emerge into the light. The flower blooms in his head; it blooms so painfully that its beauty takes him with it into the darkness.

Remarkable Object No. 31

MOBY DICK

I told myself: Do not listen to the anger. It cannot force you to do anything. Father Fuchs would have been proud of you. Bury the anger deep inside.

But the smell of opium, Father Fuchs's scent, called out to it. I could not get rid of it. It lingered in my kurta, my hair and my skin. I had spent too much time in the hold of Jeejeebhoy's ship and had taken in the story of the most powerful flower as well as its smell.

When the Chinaman had finished his story and placed the pouch over my head again, I asked him to take me to Consul Schiller. The Schlagintweits and the inner circle of the train are staying there. I had to talk to Hormazd. More than that, I needed Hormazd to tell me that the truth about the most powerful flower in the world was a lie. Because if it was not a lie, then Bombay and all of its residents, even Father Fuchs, had lied to me for at least twelve years.

I found Hormazd in the drawing room. He was sitting in an armchair reading a book and smiling cheerfully. A strange and an almost unpleasant sight. Since we arrived in Calcutta Hormazd is not doing much except sitting in the drawing room and reading. He is not even drinking Pale Ale! Hormazd does not leave the house and is cheating on his beloved numbers with letters. I have asked him several times whether he would like to see Calcutta with me. Hormazd prefers to stay in the drawing room. He says the city means nothing to him. He is safe in the drawing room. There he cannot contract any disease or be robbed, or worse still, develop an interest in Calcutta.

When Hormazd saw me, he called out: Bartholomew! I would like to have a word with you.

I would like to have many words with you, Sir, I said.

Anger throbbed in my chest.

He looked at me thoughtfully, far too thoughtfully for Hormazd. Usually, he does not yield to me. Something was wrong.

I told him, without mentioning the Chinaman, what I had learnt about the opium trade and asked him if it was all true.

Hormazd nodded at once.

Are you sure, Sir? Bombay is built on opium?

Absolutely sure.

Why did you never tell me?

You never asked about it.

You should have told me!

I think, he said, I am not the one you are angry at.

I remained silent. Because it was true, it made me even angrier.

Did you know, I asked, that Father Fuchs often went to a khana?

I suspected it, he said. His look. The smell. And the way he talked sometimes.

You should have helped him, I said.

It was my impression, he said, that the khana helped him.

Because of it I will never find him! I screamed.

Hormazd clapped his book shut. He stretched out a hand to me as if he wanted to hug me. But the Parsi is poor at translating what is in him. His hand did not know where to go. He touched my elbow with his fingertips and then coughed, so that he could free his hand from this awkward position and give it a job to do at his mouth.

I looked for the anger in me, but it had disappeared. In its place there was an empty feeling, emptier than fear. I wanted to be able to tell Hormazd what Eleazar was forcing me to do. The Parsi is cleverer than most men. Maybe even as clever as I am. He would definitely show me a way out.

Then Hormazd said: The Schlagintweits have found an acceptable replacement for me. I am going back to Bombay. My ship will sail in a few days. It is called *Good Fortune*. Can that be a coincidence?

He again had this unpleasant cheerful smile on his face.

You cannot go, I said.

Really?

He was amused.

Sir, no one can replace you.

I am aware of that, he said contentedly. And yet, it is time. I will tell you a secret: I miss my wife. Although I am fairly sure that she does not miss me, it does not matter. Maybe my missing her is enough for the both of us.

Do stay, Sir, I said.

Hormazd cast his eyes down and kept his hands occupied by playing with the rings on his fingers.

Would you like to come with me? he asked.

I cannot, I replied.

Let me speak with the firangi.

You can't do that!

Of course, I can! I will speak to them today.

Please don't do that! I said.

Hormazd's hands froze.

You are afraid, he said.

I did not want any harm to come to him. But I had to tell him what Eleazar was asking of me, I had to! When I began to tell him, the words flowed out like tears. I did not leave even the egg-dancer out.

Hormazd listened almost as attentively as Lord Ganesha. When I had finished, I looked at him and waited for the clever advice. The Parsi appeared to be sorting the thoughts out in his head as he does with numbers.

Finally, he moved his hands with a new sense of determination, and I thought: this time he will hug me. But he only picked up the book and handed it to me.

Do you know Moby Dick?

Sir?

Doesn't surprise me, he said. Not a remarkable success. But you should read it. It is about a bold hunt for a white whale. Very inspiring. It will take your mind off things.

And Eleazar? I asked. What should I tell Eleazar?

Hormazd put on his topi.

As far as I am concerned, you did not tell me anything.

But Sir!

He stood up and raised a hand in farewell. This time he was able to better translate what was in him: his hand trembled.

Forgive me, he said.

Then he left me alone with Moby Dick.

Remarkable Object No. 32

THE COURAGE ENGENDERED BY A COWARDLY PARSI

I do not need Hormazd. I will manage without him. Who is he after all? A Parsi who prefers to hunt a white whale in a drawing room rather than help me. I do not need someone like him, I tell Lord Ganesha.

And he does not contradict me.

Remarkable Object No. 33

TOGA VIRILIS

18 March. No one has sung the song with which Father Fuchs usually greets me on 18 March. I had to accompany Adolph first thing in the morning. He did not take a carriage. He is the only Schlagintweit who prefers his own feet to horses. Even when it makes his shoes dirty. Maybe even because of it. Each time he steps into the refuse on Calcutta's streets he does not curse like Hermann or make a coolie clean his boots immediately like Robert. He only laughs and swaggers on.

We turned into Nuncoo Jemadar's lane, past the shops of oyster sellers, milliners, undertakers, candlemakers, watchmakers, tattersalls, warehouses, butchers and wigmakers. Sadly, I could not study the shop windows. Adolph took large strides; he was in a hurry. I was surprised that he could find his way without help. Hermann and Robert do not venture out into the city without guides.

He asked me if I liked Calcutta.

Yes, Sir, I said.

I don't, he said. Too many Englishmen! And I miss our hours of drawing.

I don't, I would have liked to say.

A special honour will be bestowed on you today, he said. You will accompany us to a reception. Are you pleased?

Yes, I lied again.

We have to polish you up a little for that.

With these words he pushed open the door to a shop.

After you, Sir, he said and grinned.

I hesitated.

Adolph made a shooing gesture and I entered ahead of him. It was a tailor's shop used only by the firangi. Dark coloured fabrics were laid out; they shimmered like the sea at night. Buttons in all colours of eyes in Calcutta sparkled in a showcase. A broad man with childlike hands approached us. His skin was just light enough for him to be considered a firangi. It resembled mine in the monsoon-summer when I rarely go out. I knew at once that either his father, or more likely his mother, was Indian.

The bushy beard of the Indo-European duplicated his smile as he turned to Adolph.

What can I do for you, Sir? he asked in a very British English.

Adolph grabbed my shoulders and pushed me in front of the tailor.

Dress up the young man!

The tailor examined me and my old kurta the way Smitaben examines spoilt atta. His smile disappeared.

What do you mean, Sir?

Make him a Toga Virilis, Adolph said, enunciating his words while trying to suppress his Bavarian accent. And make it as quickly as possible! We need it this evening.

He is an Indian, Sir, said the tailor.

Well observed! said Adolph and winked at me.

We only fit out gentlemen here, said the tailor.

Excellent! said Adolph and laid an arm around me. Bartholomew is a gentleman of the highest order. How long will it take?

The tailor crossed his arms behind his back.

I fear, too long, he said.

Adolph remained silent.

It is a very busy day, the tailor added.

Adolph took a deep breath.

You can do nothing for us?

I am very sorry, Sir, said the tailor and smiled only with his beard.

I told myself: Do not listen to the anger. It cannot force you to do something. Father Fuchs would have been proud of you. Bury the anger deep inside you.

Adolph turned to me.

The governor-general will be disappointed, he said in English.

We are meeting the governor-general? I asked him.

No, he replied in German, but this little tailor does not know that.

The governor-general, Sir? asked the tailor and brought his arms forward.

You know him? asked Adolph.

Not personally, said the tailor.

A pity! A remarkable man.

That he is, said the tailor.

Adolph smacked the back of my head. Bartholomew here is one of his closest friends.

The tailor laughed out loudly.

Adolph looked at him gravely.

The tailor stopped laughing. He examined me once again.

Adolph said: Isn't that so, Bartholomew?

I looked at Adolph and then at the tailor and then again at Adolph who indicated a nod.

Yes, I said.

Even if I was not on Adolph's side, I was also not on the side of this little tailor.

He narrowed his eyes as if he were looking into the sun.

He, he said to Adolph while pointing at me, is supposed to be a close friend of the governor-general?

Ask him yourself, said Adolph and gestured invitingly.

The tailor plucked at his beard.

Is it true? he asked me.

Sir, Adolph added.

Sir, the tailor added.

Yes, I said.

What is your connection with him? the tailor asked.

Sir, I added.

The tailor did not react.

Adolph cleared his throat.

Sir, the tailor added.

I am a brilliant translator, I replied.

I can vouch for that, said Adolph. A busy day? Very unfortunate! We would have loved to tell the governor-general about your skills.

On hearing the word *skills,* the tailor's beard trembled.

Adolph opened the door.

Come, Bartholomew, I am sure we will find another place.

I just remembered …, said the tailor.

Yes? said Adolph.

I sincerely apologize, Sir! I was mistaken about the time.

Is that so? said Adolph.

Once again, the tailor's beard duplicated his smile.

The day is not as busy as I had assumed, he said.

Well, said Adolph, isn't that a happy coincidence?

The tailor fetched a measuring tape.

May I?

If you don't wish to disappoint the governor-general, said Adolph.

The tailor began at once. While taking my measurements he asked me to stand still, to stretch out my arms, to breathe in, to take a deep breath, not to hold my stomach in, to look straight ahead. And he added a Sir to each request.

Before Adolph left, he paid the tailor and gave him instructions about the pattern and the choice of fabric. Then he told me to come to Consul Schiller's house with the finished suit.

When we were alone, I said to the tailor in Hindi: You are an Indo-European.

He did not react.

Is your mother Indian or your father? I asked. Your mother, right?

I don't speak Hindi, he said in English. His Sir had left the shop with Adolph.

Why not?

I don't know the language, he said.

But Bengali!

Nor that either, he said.

Impossible! I said. A Bengali who doesn't speak Bengali!

I never said I am a Bengali, he said.

You are not a Vicky, I said.

A Victorian?

I was impressed that he understood immediately.

That is exactly what I am, he said.

You only speak English? Nothing else?

English is an extraordinary language and more than sufficient.

That is not true, I said. Those who speak only English, live only like one of them.

I agree with you there. And what a wonderful life it is!

But you are not one of them, I said.

I am an Englishman through and through.

An Englishman would just say: I am an Englishman.

You aren't one, so don't correct me.

You pluck the hair on your head, so that up there you look as bald as them.

I do nothing of the sort!

I am sure you never go out into the sun so that your skin doesn't turn brown.

I am, and will always be, white.

Do you practise your British accent in front of a mirror?

Be quiet!

What does your family have to say about it? Do they still talk to you? Or is it that you don't have a family and therefore want to belong to the Vickys?

That is when he cried out the most Bengali of all Bengali words: Chup!

The tailor hit his fist on the showcase. For a moment he did not move. Then he pulled out a bolt of fabric from the shelf and spread it out between our silence. I should have told him that there was no shame in being an Indian. But I let his whining scissors do the talking. His nails pricked me. Instead of words, he now used his small hands to move me around like a doll. His callused fingertips scratched.

I know what made me provoke him. But I will not think about it and certainly not write about it. Otherwise, it will become bigger.

IN THE EARLY evening, in Consul Schiller's house, the Schlagintweits called out to me. The carriage was at the door. But I was not yet dressed. The suit consisted of so many parts I did not know where to begin. My skin itched from the numerous attempts to bend the suit to my will, and I had used up all the expletives I knew.

Adolph entered my room without knocking. He looked at me and then at the suit, whose parts lay scattered on the bed. Wordlessly, he picked up one part and handed it to me. I was grateful that he did not laugh or even grin. He showed me the correct sequence, where I had to push the buttons through and how the tie had to be tied around my neck. When I was ready, he cocked his head and looked at me. He left the room and came back in a few seconds with an ivory comb which he ran through my hair. Although it pulled and was painful, I let it happen. Then Adolph stood back and looked at me again.

This time he nodded.

The suit was a tight fit. It, not I, seemed to dictate my movements. Strangely enough, I felt secure in it. I know it is not possible, but with the suit I was cleverer and stronger and a whole lot taller. Robert and Hermann applauded when they saw me coming down the stairs. I did not want to like it, but I did. A housemaid at Consul Schiller's lowered her eyes when I passed her. I did not want to like that either. But I did like it. In the carriage, on the way to the reception, Eleazar stared at me the whole time. He pressed his lips together in a smile so that no unfriendly words escaped. I liked that, and I also wanted it.

When we climbed out of the carriage, I asked Adolph: What does Toga Virilis mean?

Today is the eighteenth of March, he said. You are *at least* thirteen years old.

You know my birthday, Sir?

The Schlagintweit laughed out loud and patted me on the head.

A Toga Virilis, he said, is your goodbye to childhood. You are now a man.

THE FIRST BIRTHDAY gift I ever received came from Father Fuchs. He gave me my birth-day. Only my parents know the exact date. But, since no one can ask them, Father Fuchs says I was born on 18 March. That was the day on which he found me. Every year on 18 March, he and I go to the bazaar together, and I am allowed to choose something. I never choose anything that is big or expensive because I know it would disappoint Father Fuchs. He lays great store by moderation and humility. Mostly, I choose a candle. Or a marble. Or a soap that smells of sandalwood. The Others often take away my present. But they cannot take away these hours with Father Fuchs. The memory of that belongs to me forever.

I WILL ALSO remember the hours on 18 March 1855.

The house in which the reception took place is not actually a house. Or if it is a house, then Devinder's family does not live in a room, but in a box. We climbed up many steps to reach the entrance.

Some more steps awaited us there. Candles burnt from the ceiling and on the walls and on the tables. At night there was more light in these rooms than during the day in the open in Calcutta. And so, there were more shadows than guests moving through the house.

I soon felt very warm and wanted to loosen my tie. Adolph ordered me not to do it. To be a man apparently means having to perspire.

For once, Robert was not wearing a hat. Despite that, he held his head as if he were peeking out from under the brim. Hermann had combed his beard and shaved his cheeks. Adolph's hair shone and his suit concealed his stomach. This was not a new sight for me. Every second day in Calcutta the brothers are dressed like this. What kind of scientists are these who spend more time at receptions and festivities and dinners than in the remote regions they are supposed to study?

The walls of the house were painted white. I did not discover any colours even in the farthest corners. The paintings too seemed to be untouched by Calcutta's humidity. One of them depicted a grey-haired Vicky whose round stomach resembled the globe beside him, on which India was depicted only marginally bigger than the tiny island the Vickys call home.

A servant approached us. His skin was almost as dark as his suit. His eyes blazed mutely. He looked like one of the true natives of India. The firangi call us all natives. But most of our ancestors came to India at some point of time and settled down here. The ancestors of the servant had always been here. They are seldom drawn to the cities. They speak their own languages and live deep in the forests and the mountains. Earlier, Smitaben's, Hormazd's and Devinder's ancestors rousted them from there. Today they are driven away by the Vickys and their allies, or they are dressed up in a suit so that they can offer a tray with crystal glasses to Bavarian scientists at a reception.

Hermann and Robert took a glass each; Adolph took two. He handed me one. The light-yellow liquid in it bubbled, not like boiling water, but more like sizzling oil in Smitaben's pans.

What is this? I asked.

Try it, he said.

Do I have to?

Try it!

I took a sip and spat it out immediately. It tasted disgustingly bitter and horribly sour at the same time. The Schlagintweits laughed, clinked their glasses together and then drank. The sound was much nicer than the taste.

Why do you do that, Sir? I asked. The glasses could break.

You ask too many questions, said Adolph, and left us to join a group of women. In their wide skirts they looked like flowers standing on their heads. Adolph said only a few words and they giggled. His brothers watched him. Both were frowning. Hermann's frown was an expression of concern, while Robert's forehead reminded me of the envy of the Others when Father Fuchs spends time with me alone.

I am going out for a minute to get fresh … to get some air, Robert said and left me alone with Hermann.

It was only then I realized that Eleazar was no longer with us.

At the reception I found it difficult not to encounter myself. The house had innumerable mirrors. Some were fixed opposite one another so that the party was multiplied endlessly. I had never seen so many firangi gathered in one place.

Each one of the guests was white. Not as white as the walls, and sometimes in fact red, or at least pink, but not one of them was even a little brown like me.

It did not take long for one of the Vickys to notice this. Her shoulders were bare, and her dark-blond hair was tangled hopelessly.

May I? she asked Hermann.

Even before he could respond, she caught hold of my hair and pulled it.

So thick and firm! she said.

I moved away from her.

Does he belong to you? she asked Hermann.

I don't belong to anyone, I said.

Her eyes widened in surprise.

He speaks English!

She laid a hand on a bare spot under her throat.

Bartholomew is our translator, said Hermann and introduced himself. He began to talk about the scientific expedition, and soon started stringing his words closer together.

The Vicky interrupted him.

He knows more than one language?

She looked at me as Father Fuchs would look at a rare find in the bazaar.

Say something in Hindi, she told me.

I looked at Hermann, and he nodded.

You are not a remarkable woman, I said in Hindi.

She now pressed both hands on the bare spot.

Divine! she cried. And now something in German.

I again looked at Hermann. He nodded again.

And see! The curtain rises on the horizon, I said. The day dreams that the night has now gone.

What does it mean? she asked. What did he say?

Hermann stammered a few words in English.

I came to his help only after he asked me.

That is nice, she said. Where is it from?

From me, I said.

Bravo!

Before Hermann could object, some more women and even some gentlemen joined us. Over and over one of them asked me to say something in German, English, Hindi, or another language and, when necessary, to translate. It was followed each time by applause that echoed through the house and attracted even more spectators. At first, I was pleased that I could do something which no one there, except Eleazar, could do. But with each further sentence and each further translation something hardened in me, as if I had eaten too many gulab jamuns. My suit shrank, I gasped for air.

I excused myself and hurried outside to an empty balcony. There I loosened my collar, breathed in the night air and immediately felt better.

You look like one of them, a friendly voice said in Marathi.

He had followed me.

I am an Indian, I said in Marathi.

But you like yourself in your new … costume.

No, I lied.

Eleazar stood in the balcony door and screened out the light from the house.

So, you are now a man, he said. Has the man arrived at a decision yet?

His shadow was longer than all the others at the reception.

Why me? I said. Can't you ask someone else?

You speak many languages. You can read and write. I have seen with what seriousness and dedication you note things down in your little book. There is no one better for this task.

I warded off a mosquito.

You never thanked me for the present I gave you, he said.

The mosquito was persistent.

Opium, Eleazar said, is a poison. But not only for those who smoke it, like Father Fuchs. Also, for all those who engage in the business. Jeejeebhoy is betraying his own people in order to get rich.

The Chinaman regards you as his friend, I said.

He is my friend, said Eleazar.

Your friend is Jeejeebhoy's assistant!

I will explain that another time, said Eleazar. For now, you should rather ask yourself which side you are on. If you are not for us, then you are for them.

I am not for them, I said.

Then prove it. Help us.

It would not be right, I said.

But also, not wrong, he said.

Father Fuchs says, we Indians can only build a palace if we come together.

A wise man, said Eleazar.

But not like this, I continued. Father Fuchs would not approve of spying on German scientists. They are more for us than for them.

I caught the mosquito on my forehead. It had already drawn blood.

You are wrong, my friend. In so many different respects. You think your Father was a good man. But he kept many secrets from you besides the opium.

I was not sure the blood was mine.

I can find out for you who your parents were. Wouldn't you like to know more about them?

How do you know that?

You are an orphan. Every orphan wants that.

Eleazar pulled out a handkerchief. It was not embroidered and had holes in it.

Let me help you, he said.

He dabbed the blood from my forehead with the handkerchief.

He took his time.

Your loyalty to the Father is honourable, he said, even if it is misplaced. You still have six days to understand that. Then you go off with Adolph and Robert.

He said the last sentence so cordially, I almost believed him.

I hope you make the right decision.

When I entered the house again, Hermann had lost some of his audience. He tried to retain the rest with breathless sentences.

… good natural abilities, he said, but a European education is missing, which alone promotes the development of these abilities and which includes more than just schools; the circumstances of the family and the nation are just as important, and I know, respected ladies and gentlemen, what you are thinking, but one tends to overestimate those Indians who, despite their native clothes, have already learnt something about occidental ways in the offices; those who speak several Indian languages and have also learnt fairly good English are quite numerous, at least in port cities, but as soon as one tries to ask about an understanding of literature and solid knowledge of an average level, the impression is quite unsatisfactory.

At this point our eyes met.

With some rare exceptions, he added.

I told myself: Do not listen to the anger. It cannot force you to do something. Father Fuchs would have been proud of you. Bury the anger deep inside of you.

I walked on quickly. But I could not escape my reflection. I asked myself what Father Fuchs would have said to the boy in the suit who was now suddenly a man.

Where have you been?

Adolph straightened my collar.

Come!

We walked down a corridor at the end of which a servant stood at the entrance to a room from where the voices of men and fumes emerged. The servant helped Adolph out of his jacket and into a dark-green velvet jacket.

This smoking jacket, said Adolph, is inconvenient but necessary. After all, one cannot expect women to put up with the smell of smoke.

Before we entered the room, he bent down to my ear.

Don't let yourself be intimidated by these old dust bags, Bartholomew.

There were only men in the smoking room. Women were not allowed. There were also almost no mirrors. Many of the men greeted Adolph by name, clapped him on the back or nodded to him. Everyone seemed to know him, everyone wanted to be near him. Like the women earlier, they laughed readily at his jokes. I did not want to be, but I was flattered that the Schlagintweit introduced me as his brilliant translator. A firangi asked for a sample. Adolph tapped him on the chest and told him to improve his manners. The firangi fell silent and Adolph laughed so unreservedly that all those standing around joined in. Adolph told the firangi not to take offense, and I expected the firangi to berate him. But instead, he held out his hand to me and apologized.

Further inside the room and the fumes, a discussion had broken out between two men who stood facing each other with straight backs. Both spoke an English that only the Vickys can. Their mouths hardly opened; many words came out through the nose. They pulled fiercely on their pipes as if it were the only way to breathe. The men following the debate around them buzzed like a swarm of fat flies. One of the two men defended free trade and justified the war against China. A senior official of the Company, Adolph whispered to me. The second man criticized the opium trade. A captain of the Red Coats, the Schlagintweit whispered and sounded amused. The second man had just referred to the speech of a young politician called William Gladstone. He is supposed to have said that the war had been unjustified and a disgrace to England. The Company man drew on his pipe and replied: One could only laugh at that (which he did not do); even the great Duke of Wellington, the conqueror of Napoleon, had declared in the House of Lords that in his fifty years in public service he had not experienced a greater affront and injury to the English than in Canton. The captain jabbed the mouthpiece of his pipe at the Company man and cried: The British flag had degenerated into a pirate flag! The Company man then stuck his pipe towards the captain. I almost expected them to duel with their pipes. The Company man stated, the captain was wallowing in Gladstone's words, but the latter was only against the opium trade because his own sister indulged in laudanum.

I did not comprehend what I was seeing.

A Vicky who is against the Vickys?

If he is not on their side, is he then on ours?

Adolph went to stand between the two men, who then put their pipes in their mouths. He called them gentlemen several times, dear gentlemen. It sounded like a lavish compliment when he said it. They were not only gentlemen, but they were also his gentlemen, his dear gentlemen. They were compelled to listen to him and to relax. In his cheerful way Adolph said he had the impression that they could both use a little laudanum. The men around them laughed, and the two who had been arguing moved away from each other to fill their pipes as if that had been their intention all along.

What do you think about the matter? Adolph said loudly in English.

Only when several men looked at me, I realized that he had asked me.

I, Sir?

Adolph nodded.

I don't know anything about it, Sir.

Adolph now raised his voice so that he could be heard in the farthest corners of the smoking room.

This remarkable boy … pardon me, *man*, lost someone close to him to opium, am I right?

He looked at me.

I could not say anything, could not nod, I could only think: the Schlagintweit knew about it this whole time.

You, Bartholomew, undoubtedly have an important opinion on this matter, Adolph said. Come on, out with it!

The circle of buzzing firangi closed around me. They exhaled smoke which thickened and suddenly I was back in the khana. Only this time the fumes did not smell familiar; they were spicy like the smell of fried chillies. I wiped the moisture from my eyes. And then I saw him lying on the cushions. His hands rested on his chest; he did not move. Father Fuchs looked at me and now I was ashamed of my Toga Virilis. I wanted to explain it to him, and I wanted to tell him how much I missed him, especially today on 18 March, and that I would complete the Museum of the World for him, and that I had questions for him, so many questions, but before I could say a word to him, I saw from his eyes that he was no longer there.

I ran through the fumes and the buzzing of the men and Adolph's calls, out of the smoking room and faster than my reflection, down the stairs and out of the house.

On the street I slipped out of the jacket, opened my collar, and breathed properly for the first time in hours. And then I hummed the song with which Father Fuchs always greets me on my birthday: *Froh zu sein bedarf es wenig, und wer froh ist, ist ein König.*

It requires little to be happy, and one who is happy is a king.

The noise of the party spilled out from the house. I could barely hear my own voice.

I told myself: Do not listen to the anger. It cannot force you to do something. Father Fuchs would have been proud of you. Bury the anger deep inside of you.

Remarkable Object No. 34

A MEMORY OF SOMETHING ONE CANNOT KNOW

In the night of 18 March 1855, I received another gift. I dreamt that I know everything about my parents. What they looked like and where they lived, in which language they spoke to one another and what name they had given me.

But I was not allowed to keep the gift.

I only remember that I knew everything.

Remarkable Objects Nos. 35 & 36

SMITABEN ODOTI

19 March. Since I did not want to see Adolph, I went to the kitchen for breakfast. In the two weeks since our arrival in Calcutta Smitaben had taken over the kitchen like the Vickys take over an Indian princely state. Everyone cooks according to her instructions; no one dares to contradict her. A dark strand runs through Smitaben's hair like a precious ornament.

As I used to do in the Glass House, I squatted in a corner of the kitchen and waited for my breakfast while Smitaben whirled around like the egg-dancer, assigned tasks, tasted, corrected, rebuked, and never praised. Hardly any servant here understands her Gujarati but surprisingly she has learnt a little Bengali in the meantime. And if she lacks the words, she expresses herself very clearly with looks and blows.

She only paused when Adolph barged in, took a chickoo, bit into it and spat it out. Smitaben handed him a bowl with pieces of the peeled fruit. He shoved a handful into his mouth and, smacking his lips, asked me why I had run away the previous night. He did not wait for my reply and instead told me that it had indeed been a unique birthday.

I wanted to kick him in his fat stomach.

Yes, Sir, I said.

Adolph took the bowl with the pieces of chickoo and left.

Smitaben immediately resumed her kitchen-dance. But something was different. She did not pay as much attention to the servants and busied herself in preparing an elaborate dish. More than once she pushed away helping hands. She wanted to do it alone.

I enjoyed watching her. She is not a particularly beautiful woman and yet she is especially beautiful when she prepares a dish with love.

A little while later she called me, pushed a stool towards me and placed the finished handvo on the kitchen table. The steam rose from it in loops. The handvo was still too hot but I did not care. I burned my fingers when shoving some of it into my mouth and then burned my tongue. Naturally, it tasted better than everything else. But mainly, it tasted like a 18 March in the Glass House.

How could I forget your birthday! she cried and gave me a moist kiss on the cheek. Can you forgive me?

I nodded.

For that she kissed me once more. We ate the handvo together and Smitaben praised it saying it was unparalleled. How right she was!

Even after I had eaten my fill and was only eating so that the taste did not vanish, Smitaben said: Tell me!

I looked at her.

Smitaben was always a little cleverer than one assumed. However, she thinks with her heart, not with her head. I would have liked to tell her about Eleazar. But this time I did not indulge this wish. I want to protect her. I do not want to see her hands tremble. And I certainly do not want to risk hearing her say that I had not told her anything precisely because I had told her about it.

That is why I spoke of other things: You will be travelling on with Hermann, Maasi.

The one with the hair under his nose, she said and nodded happily, or so it seemed.

It surprised me that she remembered his name.

But I will be going with Adolph and Robert, I said.

Smitaben hugged me.

Only for a few months.

Months?

Maybe also a year.

A year!

Don't worry, she said, the Schlagtweins will take good care of us. We will meet again, sooner than you think.

Their name is Schlagintweit, I said.

That's what I said. Schlagtweins.

No, Maasi.

Say their name once again.

I repeated slowly: Schlag-int-weit.

Smitaben shook her head.

They are called Schlagtweins, she said. As their translator you should know that. You wouldn't want to disappoint the gentlemen.

You like them, I said.

And you don't? she asked.

They are firangi, I said. They will leave again soon and forget about us.

One doesn't forget Smitaben so easily!

Maasi, you said it yourself. *For them you are just another Indian.*

You must be mistaken. I would never talk such nonsense. Without the firangi I would not know that I am more than a cook.

What are you then?

A *brillant* cook.

She said *brillant* in German.

The Schlagintweits …, I said.

Schlagtweins, she corrected.

… said that you are a *brillant* cook?

She nodded, and I felt my chest tighten.

Smitaben bent forward to wipe my mouth with the back of her hand.

Do you know what *brillant* means?

I thought I did, I said.

A *brillant*, she said, is a very rare precious stone.

Smitaben smiled to herself when saying this. I tried to smile with her, but I was not very successful. I realized that from the way she looked at me. As if I had refused one of her dishes.

You still haven't told me what is troubling you, she said. Smitaben knows this face.

This time I came out with the truth: Do you think Father Fuchs was a good man?

The dark strand of hair fell into her face, but Smitaben did not push it back and looked at me for a long time without blinking. When I wanted to look away, she held my chin and saw the look in my eyes.

Do you know why I came to Bombay so many years ago?

I shook my head. She pushed her sari away from her hip and showed me a part of the smiling scar under her navel. Odoti, she said.

I have known Smitaben almost as long as I have known Father Fuchs. But I would not have thought that she is a remarkable object. Strictly speaking, she constitutes two remarkable objects: she and her daughter.

Smitaben said that when she was living in Gujarat, she had a good husband. When they were alone, she was allowed to call him by his name. And sometimes she did not even have to wait till he had eaten but was allowed to eat with him. When she became pregnant, everyone – his family, her family, all the families in the village – hoped it would be a boy. But it was a girl. Immediately after the child was born, her husband took it away to sell it to the Bhil tribe.

Smitaben accepted this because she knew her husband was a good man. At least that is what everyone in the village said. And since she had never had a husband before, she believed them.

Many weeks went by. Smitaben did not become pregnant again.

During Navratri, Durga appeared in Smitaben's dream and asked to know the name of her daughter. Smitaben could not fulfil the goddess's wish. She had not given her daughter a name because she had assumed that she had lost the child to the Bhil. But if Durga wanted to know her daughter's name, it meant that one day her daughter would leave the tribe and return to her real family. And then, Smitaben would recognize her from the name.

Smitaben opted for Odoti. The break of dawn was always her favourite part of the day. At the break of dawn everything is still possible, one never knows what surprises the day might bring.

To Smitaben's surprise her husband was not pleased that she had given their daughter a name. He hit her with a hot pan.

Her husband had hit her before. Just as most of the men in the village hit their wives and daughters, but never their mothers. Smitaben's husband was considered a good man because he rarely hit her, and only then when he was particularly tired after working in the fields. He always used an open hand, and the imprint generally faded away after one or two days.

This time, the pan burned marks in her skin forever.

Smitaben told his family, and his family said it was Smitaben's fault. She had driven him to it, and why was she not pregnant again?

Smitaben's family said the same thing.

So, she prayed to Durga. She invoked the goddess and sacrificed a chicken to her. If only she could give birth to a son, she would be able to see what a good man her husband really was.

Many weeks went by. Smitaben did not become pregnant.

In the meantime, she had become accustomed to the blows with the hot pan. It was not so bad if she treated the wounds immediately with herbs and reminded herself that her husband was a good man. Because he never hit her in the face.

Now he touched her more often than before. Always after he had hit her. She was sad that he did not do it otherwise. Smitaben missed the nights in which he had kissed her instead. But she was thankful, she was so thankful when he held her close after the beating. Even if it never lasted very long, she enjoyed this closeness and embraced her good husband for as long as he allowed it.

Many weeks went by. Smitaben did not become pregnant.

And then the day came when a hot pan was no longer enough. He cut her with a knife, scratched her skin. At first, Smitaben thought he was doing it because he did not want to cause her so much pain. The cuts burned less than the blows from the hot pan. But they bled. He always cut Smitaben in the same place under her navel. Each time he continued where he had stopped the previous time. Over the course of days, he painted a wound in her stomach. Smitaben bandaged it and took care not to make any sudden movements so that the skin did not tear open. But mainly, she had to ensure that no one saw the wound. Otherwise, his family and hers too would become very angry with her. How could she drive her good husband to such deeds!

He now rarely touched her.

On one night, he cut too deep. The wound bled profusely. Smitaben thought this was the last surprise of her life. She asked her husband something that she had not dared to ask in all these weeks: whether the Bhil were treating her Odoti well.

He looked at her in surprise and laughed. The good man told her that he had not sold their daughter because she had been too ugly and dark; it would only have brought misfortune to the family. He had been left with no other choice than to leave her far away in the desert.

When Smitaben heard this, she wanted to drown in her pain. Durga entered her. Before her husband could react, she took the knife from him, jabbed it into her stomach and cut open a larger wound than he had ever managed to do.

Her husband stumbled backwards, away from her. He cursed Smitaben for destroying his life; he would not help her any more.

Then he ran out of the hut.

Night became day. Although she shouted loudly for help, no one came. And so, Smitaben closed her eyes at the break of dawn and placed her hopes in her next life.

This life began a few days later in a Christian mission. But Smitaben had not been reborn; she was still Smitaben. She did not know how she came to be in the mission. The missionaries had found her unconscious in front of the gates in her blood-soaked sari. No one had to tell Smitaben that the village – her family, the family of her good husband, all families – had cast her out. Smitaben understood without being told.

One of the Christians took care of her most kind-heartedly. He treated her wound with the very tinctures she would have used herself.

Many weeks went by. Smitaben recovered her health.

When she wanted to leave the mission and begin her new life as a beggar, the Christian who had looked after her, ran behind her. He asked Smitaben to go with him to Bombay to work there in an orphanage.

No man had ever asked her for something. She wanted to agree at once. But Durga got into her head and warned her to choose the men in her life with greater care. That is why Smitaben asked the Christian whether she would have to believe in his God if she went with him. The Christian coughed into a handkerchief decorated with red flowers before he replied, she could bring as many gods as she wanted with her, everyone was welcome in St. Helena.

FATHER FUCHS WAS not a good man, Smitaben said to me. Good men cause misery!

We were still sitting in the kitchen and had finished most of the handvo. In the meantime, the other servants had begun to cut a mountain of gobi for lunch.

Do you know who else is not a good man? Smitaben asked and continued at once: The governor-general.

I was not sure what she meant.

He does a lot for us women, she said. He believes that only clever women can improve life for everyone.

How do you know what he believes?

He said it.

I have not heard anything of the kind, Maasi.

That does not surprise me. Men, whether young or old, don't hear such things. You can ask any woman on the street. They all know about it.[23]

Smitaben stuffed the rest of the handvo into her mouth and swallowed it without chewing.

He has even established schools for us. When my work with the Schlagtweins is over, I will go there and become a Female Doctor, so that I can help other women when they have a child, and no man is allowed near them.

And Bombay?

What about it?

You are not coming back, Maasi?

Silently, she embraced me, and I understood then that whenever she held me in her warm embrace all these years, she held not only me, but each time also Odoti.

---

23 I checked that. It is true that the Vicky with the drop of flesh really speaks up for women. Indian women! What does that make James Broun-Ramsay? Not such a not good man like Father Fuchs. But also, not such a good man like Smitaben's husband.

Remarkable Object No. 37

THE SCHLAGINTWEITS (BUT REALLY FATHER FUCHS)

Today, on 21 March 1855, three days before our departure, I have arrived at a decision. I know now what I will tell Eleazar.

I did not know it this morning when I wanted to get into the carriage and Adolph stopped me.

Alipur Jail is not a nice place, he said to his brothers. Bartholomew need not accompany us, we have Eleazar.

Hermann and Robert agreed.

Do not deny him his wish, Sir, the Bania said.

I did not know what he was talking about.

The young man wishes to see the truth with his own eyes, Eleazar said. He has a very enquiring mind and does not wish to miss out on any part of the country. Even a part like this. Am I right?

He and the Schlagintweits looked at me.

I had to nod.

Adolph clapped me on the head.

Then let us go! Next stop: Truth.

On the way Eleazar smiled as if he had already won me over for his ends. At the same time, more than ever, I felt Father Fuchs at my side. Smitaben had reminded me that he had always believed in me. Now I had to believe in Father Fuchs in order to find the right path. I doubted that the Bania would be able to find out anything about my parents. If that had been possible, Father Fuchs would have told me.

Eleazar was talking to the Schlagintweits, but I could not shake off the feeling that he was addressing me. They were speaking about the skeletons that a Doctor Webb, head of the Native Hospital in Calcutta, had made available to the Schlagintweits. Eleazar asked if it would be helpful for their research. The Bania sounded genuinely interested. But he has already shown too much of himself to me, and now I can translate his actions much better. He only asked the question because he already knew the answer and because he wanted me to hear it. Hermann began to talk readily. It turns out that it is very difficult to have corpses fished out of the water, he said. According to him it is a disastrous custom that Indians allow the dead to be carried away by a holy river. It is even more annoying that we place sick people on the riverbank with their feet in the water which most certainly contributes to their death. Also, wherever the bank is flat, the cadavers are washed in and out of the river, polluting the air.

Eleazar listened attentively. He was still smiling, but directly behind his smile I glimpsed his satisfaction. Because he saw that I had become angry.

A Doctor Mouat received us at the main entrance of the jail. He has published the first illustrated book on human anatomy in Urdu, said Hermann. I do not know if that is true; I only know: saying it makes it true. Among other things, Doctor Mouat is the Inspector of Jails. The hairs in his beard are as orderly as all his movements. His strides seem to be even more measured than those of the Schlagintweits; he is economical with his gestures. He clearly belongs to the Vickys who maintain order in Calcutta.

Doctor Mouat has placed three rooms at the disposal of the Schlagintweits to carry out their research. These contain nothing other than their instruments and material. Each of the doors has a heavy lock. The ceilings are low, and dirt climbs up all over the walls. The air is thick and hot. It carries the sounds of Calcutta from outside, the calls of a seller, neighing of horses, ringing of bells, the cries of seagulls. Even someone like me, who has hardly spent any time in jail, likes to hear these sounds. They help a person to imagine life in the city.

It reminds me of the many times when Father Holbein locked me up in the garden shed. But that was always only for a few days (and there at least I was safe from the Others). The prisoners spend years in the jail. Every thought that they admit swells up very quickly. It becomes so big that it does not fit in the jail with them. They must destroy it and throw it away, otherwise it will crush them. In order to endure the jail, they have to stop listening and thinking, they have to close themselves up completely.

I saw this immediately in the eyes of the first prisoner the Schlagintweits examined. His skin had a dark sheen like that of brinjals. He was naked except for a dirty piece of cloth covering his private parts. He had shackles around his ankles which were linked with ropes to an iron ring that encircled his waist. Two Bengali guards positioned him in front of Robert's picture machine. The prisoner immediately drew back. The guards again pushed him to the place Robert indicated. They spoke to the prisoner in Bengali, but he did not appear to understand them. He did not say anything. He tried several times to get away from the picture machine. Did he assume he was going to be shot? I told him that the firangi was only taking pictures and it would not hurt. He did not react at all; he was muter than Robert. I used every language I know, except German. The prisoner did not seem to hear me. He obeyed only when the guards hit him with their sticks on his bare thighs. But he did not stand straight. He leaned backwards as if he wanted to avoid his imminent death, but he pushed his head forward. A deep-seated fear was etched in his face, which also, however, displayed a remnant of curiosity. I asked Robert whether the prisoner knew what was being done with him. The Schlagintweit did not respond. The enthusiasm with which he operates his picture machine is otherwise hidden under his hat. He was now no longer Robert; he was the man behind the machine. I would have loved to take a picture of him and show it to him. Would he have recognized himself?

Hermann was already waiting in the next room. The prisoner had to lie down on a table. Again, he did not want to do as he was told. Although I knew that he did not understand me, I told him in Hindi that he should keep still, no one would do anything to harm him. He did not listen to me. Again, only the blows from the guards helped. The prisoner did not scream even once. He grimaced with each blow and seemed to take the pain in. The faces of the guards, however, contorted with the blows; they resembled fierce monkeys. The guards did not use their sticks like Father Holbein who speaks harshly but calmly with his cane. He prefers this language because it is generally more efficient. But the guards were using their sticks because it is the only language they really know. Hermann told them to stop, that was enough. I translated for him, although they surely understood even without my help why the Schlagintweit stretched out his arms and held them over the prisoner. The guards did not stop immediately. They hit the prisoner a few more times. That was their message for Hermann; only they knew when it was enough.

Hermann indicated that they should move away from the table. They acted as if they could not understand him. I translated his gesture. Only then did they comply, and Hermann pulled out a printed list. It was titled: MEASURINGS OF HUMAN RACES. Only four columns were already filled out. The prisoner's name was Nitu, he was male, fifty-three years old and belonged to the Gond tribe. I asked Hermann how he knew all this. Hermann said that this was what he had been told. Nitu? I said to the prisoner, and now he looked at me for the first time. Nitu can have many possible meanings in his language. Or perhaps Nitu is the name given to him in prison.

But I prefer Nitu to all the other words with which the guards cursed him and none of which I will mention here, because these men do not deserve the gift of language. After a brief examination Hermann wrote next to the 53 on the list: rather absurd. This man is much younger, he said. I have to agree with him. Wherever Nitu was free of scars, and around his eyes where Smitaben and Hormazd have the most wrinkles, his skin was as smooth as the upper surface of a banana leaf. Hermann said in German that he would now begin measuring, and he reached for a metal calliper. Although I was the only one present who knew German, I had the impression that he was not talking to me. He announced each measurement, this time in English, and entered it into the list:

Vertex to the beginning of the hairs on the forehead: 0.30.

Vertex to the orbit: 0166.

Vertex under the nose: 0202.

Antero-posterior diameter of the head: 0195.

Length of the mouth: 0054.

Length of the ear: 0065

Circumference round the calfs: 0322.

In this way Hermann filled twenty-five columns. Nitu resisted only when the Schlagintweit pressed the calliper deeper into his flesh. I asked him if that was necessary. Hermann explained that in anthropology the flesh is not as important as the bone, which is why he had to get as close to the bone as possible. Naturally, Nitu had a problem with that. He pushed away the Schlagintweit's instrument. Now Hermann turned to the guards and pointed to Nitu. They looked at him derisively. But that did not stop them from raining blows on Nitu again. Nitu had to decide what was more painful. In the end, he preferred to endure Hermann's callipers.

Afterwards, the Schlagintweit sent me with Nitu, the guards and the list to the third room. Adolph took the list from me, glanced at it briefly and put it aside. Nitu was told to lie down on the ground. Adolph wanted to put two small rolls of paper in his nose. Nitu resisted. The guards hit him. Adolph took the stick from one of them. They should stop doing that, he said to me, and I said it to them. The guards protested, and the one guard demanded to be given his stick back. Adolph threw the stick aside and told them to leave the room. I translated. The guards did not move. At once! Adolph barked at them. I did not need to translate that. They left. Adolph shook his head. Then he turned back to Nitu, held up the rolls of paper, put them in his own nose, closed his mouth and breathed demonstratively. Nitu observed him. After taking a few breaths Adolph removed the rolls of paper and brought them close to Nitu's nose. This time he kept still, and Adolph was able to fix them. The Schlagintweit began talking to Nitu in German. Strangely enough, Nitu seemed to understand this better than all the languages I had tried. I had not seen him so calm till now.

Nitu, I will now smear your face with oil, Adolph said, and did just that.

And now, Nitu, you must close your eyes, said Adolph, and ran a hand over his eyes, which Nitu closed.

Next, Nitu, I will spread a moist mass on your face with a spoon, he said, and smeared the white substance from Nitu's neck till his hairline and from one ear to the other.

Surely, no man had touched Nitu like this before. Did he even begin to understand what was happening? His fear must have been far greater than mine in Bori Bunder.

But Adolph made it tolerable.

The plaster will now become warm, Nitu, he said, that is how it should be. You only need to hold out for a little while and then it will be over.

Nitu's breaths came fast but evenly, and he did not move. Even when the cries of another prisoner came from the adjoining room.

We waited.

Adolph did not leave Nitu's side. Their breathing matched. And not only theirs. I found myself breathing in the same rhythm. Adolph thanked Nitu for his cooperation and told him that though he may not be aware of it, he belonged to an ethnic group that was not easily accessible. His face was useful for their research. And not only for that. Adolph told him about a place called Madame Tussauds in London where wax figures of extraordinary persons were displayed. Kings and popes, murderers and their victims, exotic peoples. Not even his brothers knew that on his last visit to London he had secretly explored the cabinet. If Hermann were not so vehemently opposed to it, Adolph said, then Nitu's cast could be admired by thousands there.

After half an hour the plaster had dried.

Nitu, I will now lift the cast, Adolph said, it could pull a little.

The Schlagintweit carefully lifted the hardened plaster and showed it to Nitu. That was the only time the prisoner allowed himself something resembling a smile. Then Adolph handed him a cloth and a bowl of fresh water so that Nitu could wash his face before the guards led him away.

THE SCHLAGINTWEITS ARCHIVED another twenty-four prisoners that day. I helped them do this, entered numbers in the lists, stirred plaster, explained the function of the picture machine. By the time we left the jail late in the evening I had already arrived at my decision. Now I was absolutely sure.

FATHER FUCHS PREPARES a racial type of every child in the Glass House,[24] paints it with one of the four shades of colour to depict the colour of the skin and adds it to the collection. Dozens of racial types from all parts of the country adorn the walls of the school in the Glass House. It is a museum of the faces of India. Some visitors

24 Father Fuchs learnt the technique to make these from the same Vicky in Bombay as did the Schlagintweits: the publisher of the *Bombay Times*, Doctor George Buist.

think they are death masks. But this is not true, because we use these masks to study the living. Father Fuchs says, racial types do not convey the expression of death, not even of sleep; they are more natural than photographic images, because they are not distorted by strong light or by the demand to keep absolutely still. They allow us to see racial differences in an objective manner. In this way we can understand better who we are.

He has fixed my racial type near the top in the school, almost as high up as the cross above the entrance, so that my face hovers above the faces of the Others.

I will never forget how Father Fuchs made it. It was my tenth birthday. (In the years before it would not have been sensible to make a cast when the face of a young child is not yet fully ready.) Father Fuchs applied the plaster, and although he had warned me, I suddenly thought I would suffocate. So, he took my hand, held it firmly and breathed loudly to give me a rhythm. And he talked to me. I no longer know what he said, but that was not important. What was far more important was the sound of his voice and his cough and the number of times he said my name. Father Fuchs guided me through these dark minutes as if through a tunnel; he remained by my side till I came out at the other end and was allowed to admire my cast.

Every object of a scientific study changes when it is viewed, Robert had said.

But, as I now know, the object also does something to the viewer.

When I saw Adolph with Nitu, I was there again, it was my tenth birthday again. It was not that I remembered it, and I also did not picture it, no, I *was* in the Glass House and I could see how Father Fuchs spread the plaster on my face, how carefully he went about it, how I began to fidget, how he laid a hand on my chest, despite which I did not calm down, how compassion showed in his eyes, how he took hold of my hand, pressed it and bent forward so that his head was directly next to mine, and how he showed me how to breathe and I imitated him and my body gradually relaxed.

Adolph translated all that for me; he allowed me to see what I could never have seen without him. This was the third moment in which I was happy to have met the Schlagintweits. And the moment still lingers.

Because I have now finally understood that although I will never find Father Fuchs, I do not need to look for him as long as I am travelling with the Schlagintweits. For far too long I did not want to see what they have shown me all this time: Father Fuchs lives more strongly in their vicinity than anywhere else – less in that of Robert, more in that of Hermann and most in that of Adolph. And even though they are not doing it for me, and I cannot bear them on many, on most, days, I am grateful to them for this. I will never belong to their family – that was the stupid wish of a stupid boy – and they will surely leave me behind at the end of their expedition. But there is still time until then. During this time, I want to be with Hermann, Robert and Adolph as much as possible. And with Father Fuchs. I cannot betray them.

That is what I will tell Eleazar.

Remarkable Object No. 38

HORMAZD'S DAKHMA

I now have to do something which makes my pen as heavy as my heart. I will give Hormazd a dakhma. He needs one urgently, and I am the only one who can help him.

Before I could seek out Eleazar I found a message in my room in Consul Schiller's house.

Meet. Immediately. At Lal Dighi.

It was written in Farsi. Hormazd's signature was smudged.

This was unusual, indeed terrible, for the pedantic Parsi and surprised me almost as much as the message itself. I thought he and his cowardice had long since boarded a ship for Bombay.

I hurried at once to Lal Dighi. He will be surprised to hear, I thought, that I will not be working for Eleazar against the Schlagintweits.

When I reached the pond, it was already dark. The shimmering water was no longer clean. It formed a black hole in the city. The lanterns did not illuminate it. Their light looked like burnt-up shadows.

I spotted Hormazd at once. The way he was sitting bent at the water reminded me of a painting in the Glass House in which Saint Christopher, in the same posture, is carrying the Christ Child across the river.

I said his name.

Hormazd did not turn around.

What are you doing here? Go away!

But, Sir, your message.

What message? he said.

I held it out to him.

He skimmed through it. The glow of a lantern fell on his face. I have never seen so little fear in his eyes. It made me afraid.

It is not from me, he said.

Apart from Hormazd and myself I only know one person in Calcutta who knows Farsi and who can write.

Why does he want me to be here? I asked Hormazd.

The Parsi sat up. The topi fell from his head. I held it out to him. He did not take it. His arms were clasped around his body as if to prevent it from falling apart.

Evil spirits are gathering nearby, he said.

It had become quiet around Lal Dighi. Most of the officials had long since left the Writers' Building. Only solitary carriages dashed past.

I do not like places where the bustle of the day is missing at night. One cannot trust such places.

I wanted to ask Hormazd to leave Lal Dighi with me, but I only held on to his topi with both hands.

With difficulty, Hormazd shuffled closer to the pond. In the semi-darkness he stretched out a long arm, and I saw the impossible. Even before he touched the water, drops fell from him into the pond. More and more. They took their time. Hormazd observed them. His hand did not tremble.

What is the matter with you, Sir? I asked.

Hormazd turned to me.

Bartholomew. Do not allow them to bury or cremate me.

Why do you say that, Sir?

He tried to grab my collar, missed, and grabbed my elbow.

Promise me!

I promised him.

Hormazd let go of me and hugged himself again.

I wanted to help you, he said.

What do you mean, Sir?

I wanted to protect you from him.

That is when I noticed he had left a red mark on my kurta.

You are bleeding, Sir!

Hormazd said: At least now the name is apt: Lal Dighi.

He sank down to one side. It was only now that I saw that his sadra was in tatters and drenched in blood.

The topi fell from my hand and rolled into the pond.

You need a doctor, Sir!

Why? I know what is going to happen now.

Maybe that is why there was no fear in his eyes. Because he knew it for the first time in his life.

Who was it? I asked. Who did this?

Hormazd raised his head.

Is the sun coming up? he asked.

Sir?

He pointed to one of the lanterns.

Is that the sun?

I nodded.

Good, he said. I am feeling cold. Its fire will warm me.

Hormazd smiled an improbable smile.

I STAYED WITH him till the real sun rose. With it came two Bengalis. I wanted to stop them when they lifted Hormazd's limp body. I fought with them. The men simply pushed me aside. I told them he would have to be bathed, wrapped in white sheets, carried through the city on an iron bier and that he should on no account be cremated or buried. But my words bounced off them, just like I had. I followed them to a nearby ghat. There they threw him into the Hooghly river and went away. The current carried his body away. My eyes followed him for a long time, and I did not cry, because I did not want to unnecessarily make it difficult for him. In the hereafter of the Parsis the tears of relatives and friends come together to form a river which he must cross.

Birds of prey will not devour Hormazd's body, and his bones will not fall down through the grill on the Towers of Silence. But despite this he has a good burial ground. His dakhma is part of the museum. His soul lives here. No one can take this dakhma away from Hormazd. As long as this museum exists, his soul is free.

Remarkable Object No. 39

THE FRIENDLY VOICE

22 March 1855.

Last night I could not sleep. For hours I thought about what I should do, and I kept telling myself: Do not listen to the anger. It cannot force you to do something. Father Fuchs would have been proud of you. Bury the anger deep inside of you.

But I want to listen to the anger. I breathed it in all night like black air. Nothing else seems to be right.

Hormazd did not deserve such an end. Eleazar must pay for it. I will go to the Schlagintweits and

THESE LINES COULD be my last ones.

While I was writing, there was a knock on my door. It is Eleazar.

He is calling me.

Fortunately, the door is locked.

I remain silent. Perhaps he will go away if I do not respond.

He calls me again.

His friendly voice penetrates clearly through the wood as if there was no door. It reminds me of how I had heard him the first time. This room is so much larger than my hiding place was then, and yet it seems as if I were still sitting in a box unable to influence what happens to me.

He calls me again.

He should stop that. As always, he does not use my name, but I am not his boy or his friend.

I tell him that I know what he has done.

So, you are there, he says.

Eleazar sounds relieved.

He says, it was not his decision.

Naturally, he is lying.

He says: I liked Hormazd.

I want to tear open the door and hurt him for taking Hormazd's name.

Instead, I hold on firmly to the Bavarian handkerchief.

He says: The two of you left me with no choice. You should not have told Hormazd anything, and Hormazd should not have tried to do something.

I say: Hormazd did not do anything!

He says: Didn't the Parsi tell you?

Again, his voice is filled with satisfaction.

He says: He felt compelled to do something for you, almost as for a son. He swore he would report me to the authorities as a spy. I had to stop him.

(Thank you, Hormazd. You were always better than who you pretended to be.)

I say: Hormazd wanted to do the right thing.

He says: My friend, when will you finally understand that you are on the wrong side?

I say: Eleazar.

I try to transform his name into a word he does not wish to hear.

He says: For these firangi you are no more than a remarkable object. That is bad. But it is far worse that you do not see it.

I say: Eleazar.

He says: Too many of us are like you. The firangi have succeeded in making us believe in them more than we believe in ourselves. We have internalized their world order as the highest. We are flattered that we are allowed to bow before them. We are honoured that they impose their customs and their ghastly language on us. We are grateful that they do not kill us. All this will end soon. And you, you can contribute to it. It will happen with or without your help – and you know what I would prefer, my friend.

I call out: Eleazar!

Finally, he stops talking.

I will tell the Schlagintweits what you have done. I will tell them everything. You will hang for it.

Silence.

I listen.

I am not sure if he is still there.

Continued silence.

I am sorry, he says.

I say: It is too late for apologies.

You misunderstand me, he says. I am not apologizing for what has already happened.

His voice, although still friendly, has shifted; something is missing in it. It is as if he has destroyed a part of it.

He says: I am sorry for what happens next.

PART IV

In the Himalayas 1855

Remarkable Object No. 40

WHAT HAPPENS NEXT

Adolph said I have been unusually quiet of late, and he asked if everything was all right. I said yes. The following day he asked me again. And I said yes again.

I wish I could say no. I feel as if I were standing on the shore and Father Fuchs was calling out to me to join him in the sea. I want it too, I want to risk it, and yet it will never happen. Otherwise, something bad will transpire. Because even if I tell Adolph the truth, and even if he believes me, and even if he sends a messenger to his brother at once, and even if the messenger rides night and day, and even if Hermann believes what Adolph believes, Eleazar's knife will be faster and will turn Smitaben's scar into a final wound. He promised me that. And so, I say yes, each time.

Remarkable Objects

Nos. 41 & 42

MASTERS AND SERVANTS

Father Fuchs says he serves two masters. One of them very willingly, the other unwillingly. One is the Lord in heaven and the other the governor of Bombay.

For a long time, I maintained that I do not serve anyone. Now I understand: Everyone serves someone. And I actually serve many masters. Three of them unwillingly and the fourth not at all willingly.

Eleazar is travelling with Hermann through Assam while I accompany Robert and Adolph. The two brothers are transported each in their own palki. They lie on cushions, close the blinds if they want to be on their own, to read or eat, while three or four palki-bearers, men from the low caste of the Kahars, carry them over long distances, mostly at night because of the heat. More palki-bearers walk alongside so that they can alternate without stopping. Even more palki-bearers carry bamboo poles with the Schlagintweits' luggage, including their sensitive instruments, dangling on ropes at both ends. Robert shows it more than Adolph, but I can see that they do not have much faith in the palki-bearers. But they are more concerned about their barometers and theodolites than about themselves. It is also not unusual to hear the Schlagintweits groaning when the palki-bearers are changed at some station, especially when it happens in the middle of the night, because then they have to get up to pay them. Beyond the Grand Trunk Roads, the palkis are the fastest way to move. Even horses or camels would not be able to keep up on these dirt roads. The palki-bearers set the speed of the train. In order to maintain it – Adolph measured it at about 3.2 miles per hour – they emit short sounds. The heartbeat of the train.

Adolph says that he prefers palkis to all other modes of transport. I believe he likes to be surrounded by people at all times. He has often tested his ghastly Hindi on the palki-bearers – another thing they have to tolerate. When they did not react, he asked me what he was doing wrong. I told him: nothing, and did not let on that they do not speak Hindi.

Adolph often tells me to travel with him in his palki. Every time I want to refuse. Because, like most of the others in the train (except the native doctor, Harkishen, and the new khansaman, Mani Singh, who both travel in dhulis, in simpler servant palkis) I want to remain in touch with India and not float above it like the firangi. But I have to accept Adolph's invitation in order to protect Smitaben. She is travelling in the other train with Hermann. And with Eleazar. As long as I serve him nothing will happen to her. Previously, I was his hands and feet, now I am his eyes and ears.

Adolph is making it almost too easy for me. He speaks as openly with me as Hormazd did when he drank too much Pale Ale. Even though most of what the Schlagintweit says does not constitute any remarkable information. I have to sort it out for Eleazar. I am the translator of two masters.

Eleazar drummed it into me: What he wants to know most is where the Schlagintweits will take the train. And so, I worm travel plans out of Adolph and note them down in the museum. Then I tear out that page. Then it does not belong to the museum any more, but to something else which I would not like to give a name to. Sometimes, something in me struggles against it and I do not want to tear out the page or I want to write to Eleazar and tell him he is a dastardly dog. But then I think of what he said: Smitaben should not suffer the same fate as the Parsi. He said it as if she meant something to him. As if Hormazd meant something to him.

When we stop for a rest during the heat of the day, I take off the boots which Adolph gave me for the mountain hikes to come (and which are heavy, as if a Bible were tied to my feet) and stuff the folded page into the right boot, always the right one, as Eleazar told me to do. He joked: After all, it is only right what we do for our country. I sleep uneasily and briefly in the heat. Always, when I wake up, the page is no longer there. I do not know who else in the train is working for Eleazar. The Bania said, it is better this way. Then I cannot betray anyone if the enemy were to discover me. It cannot be any of the palki-bearers; they are changed too often. And naturally, it also cannot be the Schlagintweits. But there are enough suspects remaining.

One of them is Mr Monteiro, an Indo-Portuguese. The Schlagintweits have a lot of faith in him. After all, he is looking after their collection. And the brothers are collecting more objects than I can make a note of. As long as it can be transported, they take it along. Samples of earth, scrub and entire tree trunks. In exchange, they also leave something behind: the names of the objects. I especially like the names of the animals. Ganges-Crowned River Turtle and Greater Yellow-Naped Woodpecker and Black-Spined Toad and Rat Snake. The Schlagintweits collect them, and I collect the names. My vocabulary is growing every day. How I would have loved to share all these new words with Father Fuchs!

Many objects have to be preserved and packed for the long journey to Europe. Mr Monteiro is in charge of this. He is an alert man who likes to nod. He understands what the Schlagintweits want from him before they have even completed their sentences. Mr Monteiro is free to leave the train, to hurry ahead of it or to stay back for a few days in order to carry out his tasks in a field laboratory. A very useful feature if he is doubling up as a traitor.

Another suspect is Abdullah, a draughtsman and surveyor. I, too, have witnessed his remarkable abilities. Within minutes he can capture the scenery or the course of a river on paper, faster and almost as precisely as Adolph. Every time Abdullah hands over a drawing to the Schlagintweits, Adolph pats him on the back, but Abdullah's back remains stiff like Smitaben's limbs in the morning. I really do not mind at all that the Schlagintweit appreciates the draughtsman, I only envy Abdullah his talent. I checked to see if I also have this talent.

I do not have it. My drawing of a palki-bearer relieving himself looks like a sketch made by a drunkard. My hands are only made for writing; I can draw better with words. While working, Abdullah's head hovers close to the paper as if he were short-sighted. His eyes move back and forth between his object and the drawing. I believe this is how he lifts his objects onto the paper; his strongest muscles are his eyes. If his beard comes in the way, he blows it away, and if that does not work, he moves his chin like a cow chewing. He seems to consider his hands – the skin of which is covered by strange light-coloured, almost white spots and is as wrinkled as the skin of an elephant – too good for this. I asked him if he would also draw me. His reply was that he only works for the Schlagintweits. It sounded like the truth. But who knows? Abdullah never seems to be particularly happy or sad or angry or friendly. His voice whistles like a cowardly fart. I ask myself if all soldiers are – how should I say it? – so *mingy*. Or only soldiers who have something to hide? He is also allowed to leave the train to help the Schlagintweits with their research. He, too, would be an excellent traitor for Eleazar.

The same is true for the native doctor, Harkishen. He looks after much more than the health of the train. Harkishen also supervises the plant collectors, does magnetic tests and decides what the people in the train should eat. In this last regard he is even the master of the Schlagintweits. They abide by his guidelines. Which surprises me. Do they respect him so highly because he is a doctor? Harkishen insists on being addressed as one by everyone in the train. I am still not able to decide whether this is because he is not really a doctor and has only stolen the knowledge from someone who is. Till now we were always in the Vickys' territory where the train could use their hospitals. But now we are approaching remote regions. Soon we will cross state boundaries. There Harkishen will have to prove himself. He is a Brahmin from the Himalayas and speaks the best Hindi I have ever heard. I have never seen him without a tika. The long, red line stretches from his middle parting above the converging eyebrows till the bridge of his nose and makes it look as if he were carrying a sword on his forehead. (Or a cross – which I better not tell him.) Naturally, it is possible that Harkishen is not only not a doctor, but also not even a Brahmin. But I believe him about being a Brahmin. Something in his bearing, in the way he talks to other Hindus in the train, clearly shows that he has always been used to having more servants around him than masters. He is accustomed to people listening to him; he believes in the importance of his words. That is why the firangi get along so well with him, that is why a large part of the train obeys his orders unquestioningly, and that is why he would also be a convenient traitor for Eleazar.

The only person I can exclude is Mani Singh. He reminds me of Devinder because of his uncut hair. I wonder whether Devinder has found his way back to Bombay? Apart from the hair, he and Mani Singh have little in common. There is much more happening in this Sikh's head. The Schlagintweits hired him in Calcutta as a mountain guide. And as a translator. He speaks Tibetan. Mani Singh is very tall, even for a Sikh, and barely fits in his dhuli; his legs dangle down outside. In the night, his turban seems to be deep blue, but during the day it is green like fresh coriander chutney.

Right after we left Calcutta Mani Singh introduced himself to me and I asked for a demonstration of his Tibetan. I do not know why. Or actually, I do know why. I have spent too much time with

Adolph and have formed the habit of constantly looking into my mirror. I should have kept my mouth shut!

Mani Singh immediately said a few words, probably in Tibetan. I cannot say whether he really knows the language since I do not know it. I kept that from him. But I could not leave it at that; I had to demonstrate even greater stupidity. I praised his accent. He again said something I could not understand, and I pretended not to have heard him. He took a step towards me and said only one word which sounded like the call of a rare bird. I nodded, closed my mouth to prevent more foolishness from coming out and tried to go away.

He caught hold of me and held on to my arm with a hand as big as a thali.

You are serving more than one master, he said.

How had he found out? I considered biting his fingers. Maybe I could tear myself away and run off.

You are serving Messrs Schlagintweit, Mani Singh continued, and therefore everyone in the train. We are all your masters. As long as you serve us well, we will treat you with respect. However, if you should forget your place, then you will be a danger for the train. I will not tolerate that.

His grip became tighter.

What is your name?

I told him. I felt as if I were betraying a secret.

Bartholomew, he said, I will now ask you a question.

You are hurting me, Sir, I said.

Do you speak Tibetan? he asked.

I shook my head.

Answer! he said.

No, I said.

No, what? he asked.

I do not speak Tibetan, I said.

Why did you then claim to?

I am sorry, Sir, I will not do it again.

That is not an answer.

The pain in my arm progressed to numbness.

Why? he asked.

I do not know, Sir.

Oh, but you do, he said.

Because … I forgot my place?

Finally, he let go of me.

Since then, a few days have gone by, but I still feel his grip. My arm is blue like Krishna's skin. Mani Singh's head sits almost as far up as the crow's nest of a ship. From there he keeps an eye on everything. He has thrown palki-bearers out for not running in step. He admonished Mr Monteiro because an onward journey was being delayed so that he could preserve a red bearcat. He even urged Abdullah to draw faster by merely nodding his head. Only Doctor Harkishen can take the liberty to fall behind. As far as I know, he and Mani Singh have never spoken to each other. I cannot gauge who controls whom here. Probably they cannot either. That is why they avoid each other.

I do the same with Mani Singh. But time and again he blocks my path and says my name, nothing else; he only stands there and says my name. I wish I had not revealed it to him. Not even Father Holbein had such power over me. When Mani Singh says my name, I am terrified. It makes me believe that he knows what I am doing for Eleazar. I stand absolutely still, look at the ground and wait. After a while, he turns away from me towards some other member of the train. He cannot be a traitor. Mani Singh can never betray someone, not even himself. If he were to catch himself telling a lie, he would be the first to accuse himself. He would even be the one to swing the axe as his punishment. That is the kind of person Mani Singh is. If he discovers the page in my boot, it will mean the end of not only Smitaben. He will squash me with his thali-hands. My dreams assure me of this.

Or they send me to the paper room. There I meet Hormazd who wears his topi upside down on his head like a bowl. He fills one page after the other with the same sentence: *Serve the master*! Hormazd uses red ink. Without looking up or putting down the pen he asks me why it is red. I say I do not know. And he replies: Oh, but you do.

Remarkable Object No. 43

THE ANT MARCH

In Benares Possible-Doctor Harkishen showed the Schlagintweits around. (Mani Singh is only responsible for the mountains. It was a boon to escape his custody for a few hours.) The lanes here are even narrower than in Bombay's Blacktown, but they are cleaner. Hundreds of temples merge into thousands of houses which in turn merge into hundreds of palaces. Benares is like a single huge building with many idiosyncratic outgrowths. The entire city leans respectfully towards the Ganges. Sooner or later, all its moving parts land in the water between scores of boats and pilgrims and corpses.

To everyone's surprise Harkishen first showed the brothers the not very big Great Mosque. Abdullah was especially taken with it and set about sketching it. Harkishen said, the stones of the mosque are from a Vishnu temple destroyed by the despicable tyrant Aurangzeb. He urged us to hurry, and Abdullah had to quickly pack away his drawing materials. The Brahmin then showed us the Shiva temple. Benares is dedicated to this god, and that is why an unusually large number of bulls wander around in the city. Harkishen warned the Schlagintweits and Abdullah not to touch them. *Heilig, heilig*, he kept repeating. One of the few words he knows in German.

When we came across some fakirs smearing themselves with ash, Robert considered it remarkable enough to set up his picture machine. Adolph did not have the patience for this and took me along. We followed a group of pilgrims. Each one held on to the clothes of the person in front of him. Adolph called their antlike procession a goose march. Those are birds that taste good, he explained, before getting into the line and telling me to do the same.

You are probably not familiar with the Indian song collections, he said to me.

Indian song collections, Sir?

The Vedas.

I know them, I said.

Adolph stopped, and I almost bumped into him.

You know the Vedas?

A little, I said.

But you are not a Brahmin.

No, Sir, I am not.

Isn't it then a crime?

Will you tell Doctor Harkishen?

Adolph winked at me.

We will keep this to ourselves, he said.

I would have loved to ask him: Will you also not reveal it to anyone if I tell you that I am a traitor?

Did you memorize them? he wanted to know.

The Vedas? No, Sir. Father Fuchs has a German edition.

You have *read* them?

No Hindu is allowed to do that, I said. Not even a Brahmin.

Exactly!

But Father Fuchs read them.

He read them out to you?

No.

I don't understand, said Adolph.

He read the Vedas very loudly and clearly, I explained, and as chance would have it, I was often somewhere nearby.

As chance would have it, he repeated and turned to me. Even before I saw his grin, I had heard it in his voice.

You should talk to my brother, Adolph said. He is studying the Vedas.

Hermann or Robert?

Emil, he said.

You have another brother, Sir?

Two more brothers, he said and continued walking.

More and more people joined the ant march. Soon I could not see the end of the line.

According to the Vedas, Adolph said, the goose march is an age-old custom of Indo-Europeans. By holding on, by creating a connection with the person in front, one is unified with him. And that is what we are in a certain sense, a massive human body. Have you read Schlegel?

What is a Schlegel? I asked.

Adolph laughed.

He says India is the original homeland of the Indo-Europeans. According to him we have the same ancestors. Indians, Greeks, Germans – we were all once one people.

Everything is connected with everything else, I said.

Only, some of us are more closely connected, Adolph said and looked at me out of the corner of his eye.

I let go of his shirt then.

It is better not to be one person with the Schlagintweit. Otherwise, he might understand who I am.

Adolph also left the procession of pilgrims.

Is really everything all right with you, Bartholomew?

He again had this smile on his face which makes it difficult for me not to confide in him.

Yes, I said.

We will soon be exploring Nepal which has some of the most magnificent peaks in the world. No one has ever reached the top.

We will be the first. For the first time we will also be leaving British territory. It is important to attract as little attention as possible; our travel group will be reduced considerably. But I would like to have someone with us who looks at the world through Humboldt's eyes. Do you by any chance know someone like that?

Remarkable Object No. 44

LONELINESS

At higher altitudes, the magnetic forces decrease, says Humboldt. He has already proven this with his ascent of the highest mountain in the world, the Chimborazo in America. The Schlagintweits want to confirm this theory of their second father. They always carry out their measurements in the open or in a tent free of iron so that the data is not distorted. And thus, they enlarge their map of this invisible force. But there are so many more things one could measure! Why is there no map of loneliness? Some people may object saying that loneliness is not a stable value and it is also influenced by so many different factors. But both these objections also apply to magnetism. And loneliness is at least an equally important force. Unfortunately, the best measuring device for it is very unreliable: the human being. Everyone is lonely in a different way.

In Bombay, loneliness was not a very important factor in my life, but the more we advance into the mountains, the more it increases. It is not because one is less alone in Bombay. It is because of the mountains. They do not give me the feeling of being small, no, they show me how awfully small I always was. I am sure that on my map of loneliness the peak of the Sagarmatha would register one of the highest values. I wonder how Humboldt endured this loneliness on the Chimborazo. Perhaps he knew of someone by his side who helped him to overcome it. Someone like Smitaben or Devinder or

Hormazd. But none of them are part of the train any more. Without them, there is only loneliness by my side. It makes me tired but does not let me sleep much. It robs me of my hunger. It sharpens my hearing in order to remind me that I alone will always be with me. I hear my heart thumping all the time. I have never before heard my heart thumping so loudly. What a vulgar sound, more annoying than the cry of a tota! Sometimes it is so loud that I do not hear anything else. Not Harkishen's opinions, not Mani Singh's orders, not Adolph's braying laugh, not even Robert's brute silence. If the thumping gets too loud, I look into the depths that have been accompanying us for weeks – these friendly, sympathetic depths. They are waiting patiently just a few feet away. They, too, never leave my side.

When we had crossed the border to Nepal on remote paths, we were picked up within an hour by more than twenty sepahis. Everyone was surprised that we had been discovered so quickly. Everyone except me.

Adolph walked up to the soldiers with Mani Singh.

The havildar of the sepahis asked him in English what the purpose of their stay in Nepal was.

Hunting and collecting plants, Adolph claimed.

Robert and he had hidden the trigonometric instruments inside their luggage. They would have been exposed immediately if these instruments had been discovered.

The havildar spoke to his soldiers in Nepali. Then he turned to Adolph again.

Hunting and collecting plants?

Adolph nodded.

The havildar also nodded and told Adolph to turn back.

The Schlagintweit was astonished, at a loss for words. He protested that he and his train did not pose any threat.

The havildar did not say anything.

Adolph then asked if they could at least explore the highly acclaimed Nepal a little.

The havildar threatened to arrest our coolies and to confiscate all our rations.

Adolph wanted to object, but Mani Singh laid a paw on his shoulder.

A little later, the train turned back.

THE NEPALIS KNEW our plans. It was not the havildar, but I, who had prevented our entry. I cannot prove it, and I also would not know why Eleazar wants to keep us out of Nepal. But my instincts tell me that somehow the last message found its way from my boot to the Nepalis.

No one in the train suspects it. Only the annoying Mani Singh assumes that there is a spy in our ranks. Harkishen laughs at this assumption. Instead of justifying his failure in such an implausible manner, says the Possible-Doctor, the Sikh would have done better to take us unnoticed across the border. Most of the people in the train, especially the Hindus, are on Harkishen's side. Even if they do not show it so openly to the Sikh as the Brahmin does.

Tall people like Mani Singh have always seemed to me to be lonely. But Mani Singh makes his loneliness worse; he buries himself deeper in it. The more he looks for the person responsible, the more everyone believes that he does not want to accept responsibility, and this in turn intensifies his search for the person responsible. He questions everyone in the train, makes them describe where they grew up, what family and caste they are from, who they have served. And he checks every box, bag, pouch, and every piece of clothing, even boots.

It did not take him long to find the museum. While flipping through it he asked what was written in it.

German, I said.

He only had to look at the place on my arm that had just healed for me to provide a better answer. I explained the Museum of the World to him.

This stops now, he said.

Sir?

You will not write another word, he said, and pocketed the small book.

I went down on my knees, I wanted to touch his feet.

He climbed over me.

Please, Sir!

I will have it translated, he said.

You will do nothing of the kind, said Harkishen.

He walked up to Mani Singh and opened his hand.

Give it to me.

The Sikh did not move. His shadow swallowed the Brahmin.

But the latter was not alone. As always, a few coolies stood a little away from him. I call them Harkishen's wish-fulfillers because that is what they consider their calling. They bring him water, they wash his clothes, they massage his feet. If the Schlagintweits ask them to do something, they generally wait for Harkishen's consent before they become wish-fulfillers for the firangi. One would assume that because of them Harkishen is not as lonely as all the others in the train. But it is precisely his wish-fulfillers who remind him that he is the only Brahmin amongst us. And, as everyone knows, only a Brahmin can alleviate another Brahmin's loneliness.

Do I have to repeat myself? Harkishen asked Mani Singh.

The wish-fulfillers moved closer.

The Sikh placed my book in the hands of the Brahmin. But he did not move back.

The Brahmin thanked him and stepped away from his shadow.

Bartholomew, Harkishen said, I have a wish.

Thus, I have become Harkishen's reader. He is a peculiar listener. Harkishen does not know German, but despite that he refuses to let me translate. He simply listens to my voice. It will not be long, he says, before he learns German. To achieve this, he only needs to listen carefully. I am not sure if one can learn a language in this way. But then, I am not a Brahmin. Harkishen says he misses being with like-minded people. The train bores him. And what about the Schlagintweits? I asked him. The goras, as he calls the brothers, although in the meantime the Indian sun has burned away their whiteness, can hardly tell him what he does not already know. My German is, therefore, a welcome change. When we stop for a rest, he calls me and opens his hand as he did with Mani Singh. I place the museum in it. He leafs through it and chooses a page. Read this here, he says, and closes his eyes. While I read to him, he hums to himself and moves his head slowly. Sometimes, he opens his eyes suddenly, takes the museum from me and selects another passage. From time to time, he says that the words are now gradually coming to him, that he understands better. When I ask him what exactly it is that he has understood, he replies: the deeper meaning. His wish-fulfillers look at him in amazement. They are probably the least lonely in the train because they are similar in one regard: they are not Brahmins, and they believe they will never be able to learn a language just by listening to it. I would like to count myself with them to escape from this loneliness, but I do not know which caste I belong to. At any rate it cannot be a very low one. Otherwise, I would be much more in awe of a Brahmin like Harkishen. Most of the time, however, he only thrusts opinions about *Bharat* on me. That is his name for India. He says, we Hindus should stick together. He also says that he does not like to use the word Hindu because it comes from the Persian language. He prefers to speak of a *We* and an *Us*. And he says that *Bharat* should finally be ours again. Can someone like him work with someone like Eleazar? They would certainly have many common enemies. But they would also not be friends. A Brahmin like Harkishen lets every non-Brahmin feel that he is beneath him. Especially when this non-Brahmin is a dark-skinned, clever, influential Bania.

At any rate, I will continue to read to Harkishen. Not only because it grants me protection from Mani Singh. To read the Museum of the World alone and silently is no comparison to speaking it out. I am also reading it out to myself. And when I push sounds into the air, the museum emerges around me. It is a massive building with high boundary walls, strong walls, and thick doors. I can hide from my loneliness there for a while and spend time with Smitaben, Devinder, Hormazd and Father Fuchs. They make my heart beat more softly.

LONELINESS DOES NOT stop even at the Schlagintweits. On the contrary, they are the measuring devices that record the strongest loneliness. I had assumed that experienced mountaineers like the brothers are immune to it. But loneliness is like water; it always finds a way. It breaks in and collects. And if one is not careful, one drowns on the inside.

Even though the brothers have long since worked out a new route via Nainital, Adolph has not yet overcome the setback in Nepal. He expresses his displeasure in letters which contain an anger similar to that of Father Fuchs. Some of them are addressed to Hermann, others to James Broun-Ramsay and some to S.M.[25] But no one replies. Adolph constantly complains that even Hermann has not written for weeks. I think he needs his older brother to ward off loneliness. Robert tries. He takes off his hat, pushes more words than usual out

---

25 He actually means Frederick William IV, the king of Prussia. But S.M. is also every king after Frederick William IV. Thus, the Schlagintweit always writes to the correct king. One never knows. Letters from the Himalayas to Prussia travel slowly. The king whom Adolph is writing to may not be the king any more when the letter arrives.

of his mouth and says, perhaps the letters are just taking longer than expected. To which Adolph replies: And what if Hermann has not written any letters? What if something has happened to him?

Robert does not have an answer to these questions. He cannot be the person Adolph needs. He is, after all, not an older brother. Adolph makes this very clear when he does not smile, does not conduct measurements with him and does not warm his hands at the campfire beside him.

I feel sorry for Robert. But only to the extent one can feel sorry for a Schlagintweit. I am not unfamiliar with his loneliness. It is the loneliness of the youngest, the smallest. It makes one feel one is not enough. However fast one runs one can never catch up with the older ones. Robert has not yet understood that. Otherwise, he would turn to other tasks. But he seems to believe that he can be an older brother for Adolph. Thus, every time when his older brother rebuffs him, he is driven deeper into his loneliness.

Only Hermann could help his brothers by restoring the natural order, the trinity of the Schlagintweits. Father Fuchs would have wanted me to help them against their loneliness, to tell them that at least one postal service is working: the one between my boot and Eleazar. The other train is intact; somewhere, many miles to the east of us, Smitaben is cooking and scolding and breathing. I will not believe anything else. And for this very reason I must leave the Schlagintweits to their loneliness.

Remarkable Objects Nos. 45 & 46 & 47

ADOLPH SCHLAGINTWEIT (2) NANDA DEVI NANDA DEVI (BECAUSE NANDA DEVI ONLY ONCE IS TOO LITTLE NANDA DEVI)

Loneliness has won. Robert and Adolph have parted ways. They did not fight, they did not exchange any unkind words, they even embraced when parting. But they gave in to loneliness. After about a month in Nainital, Adolph was drawn to the mountains. For the first time on this journey the Schlagintweit wants to cross a pass in the Himalayas. A dangerous pass which leads through a sea of snow. If we do not freeze to death or get lost in a storm or plunge into a crevasse, we will need at least two weeks for this leg of the journey. Adolph says he will examine Humboldt's theory of decreasing magnetic forces and carry out numerous measurements. But I know why he really wants to cross this pass. He hopes to find an escape from loneliness.

He is being accompanied by Mani Singh, Harkishen, a few coolies, myself and the only man who appears not to be affected by loneliness. Mr Monteiro sometimes strides at the head of the train and sometimes at the end; he whistles remarkably cheerfully despite his slight build and the increasingly thinner air. Loneliness is not able to reach him because he does not live much in his head. He always puts himself in the heads of others in order to guess what is expected of him. One never needs to tell him what to do. Mr Monteiro has usually already done it. The Indo-Portuguese man is connected with all of us and is, therefore, never lonely.

Adolph, on the other hand, is sinking deeper into his loneliness. He has not shaved for weeks. His face disappears, and his eyes recede into their sockets. I tried to give him hope. Hermann is definitely well, I told him. His reply was that I could not know that. No, I said, naturally not, but I am confident. To which Adolph laughed with his lips pressed together. He seldom draws any more, but he paints watercolours of the mountains. For that he does not need a torchbearer, only daylight. The Schlagintweit puts a lot of effort into these pictures. We once had to let a whole day go by without moving on because he wanted to finish one at all costs. I am almost finished, he would say to Mani Singh each time the Sikh approached him. And then hours would go by. When Adolph has made the last brushstroke on a picture, he examines it with squinted, tired eyes. As strange as it may sound, he does not resemble himself when doing this. Harkishen says, the gora should get a pair of glasses. I doubt that is the reason why Adolph stares at the aquarelles in this way. Rather, he is looking for something in them. Or someone. Hermann, I thought at first. Robert. Alexander von Humboldt. But it is not the first time he is travelling without one of them. No, I have a much cleverer idea: I think he is looking for himself. I do not know how he expects to find himself in his pictures, yet I am certain that he is looking for a particular Adolph. The laughing, jaunty, bold Adolph who while on one journey already dreams of the next one.

When we stopped for a rest and for supplies in Khati, the last village in the Pindari valley before the decisive climb to the pass, Adolph let out a yell in the afternoon. I ran to him and saw him stabbing a painting with the pointed end of a brush. He tore out a strip, crumpled it and threw it away to be consumed by the depths.

I asked him if everything was all right.

Adolph looked up as if he had woken with a start.

Yes, he said, why?

I looked at the painting that had been destroyed.

Not my best work, he said.

Some coolies had also converged there, and they were watching him.

What is the matter? he said. Back to work!

I translated it for him, but they did not react.

They lowered their heads and retreated only when Harkishen appeared.

Schlagintweit, Sir, said the Brahmin, have you slept at all?

I have to finish the picture first, he said.

You should rest, Sir.

I am not tired, said Adolph. We will leave in an hour.

As he set about packing his painting materials, Harkishen came to stand beside me.

She is punishing him, he said softly.

Who? I asked just as softly.

The Brahmin touched his tika and raised his head. To look at Mani Singh, I thought at first. He is the only one in the train who is taller than Harkishen. But the Sikh was nowhere to be seen. Harkishen would also not have looked at him so humbly. It was Nanda Devi, the goddess of joy. She is so holy that even the Brahmin (who knows the word *holy* in at least five languages and uses it generously) does not utter her name. I better not tell him that I am sceptical about her name. For me, the goddess does not radiate joy. I try my best not to look at her. She fills me with loneliness. Never before in my life have I seen something so big. For her I am too small to be someone. I am not sure if it is a good thing when something becomes so big. Would it not be better to make small things a little greater instead of putting all greatness into the largest things? Nanda Devi could bury Bombay *and* Madras *and* Calcutta under her. We are at the mercy of her will. Harkishen has already requested Adolph several times to offer a sacrifice to her so that she lets us cross the pass unharmed. The Schlagintweit wishes to hear nothing of this. Three coolies have already deserted because they are afraid of Nanda Devi's revenge. Adolph's behaviour will drive some others away. Harkishen is convinced that the goddess is toying with the Schlagintweit, slowly robbing him of his senses till, in the end, he sacrifices himself to her. He would not be the first, the Brahmin said, Nanda Devi has already carried many wanderers to their grave in her fold. I would like to contradict the Brahmin, at least in my thoughts. But I do not see any joy any more in Adolph, the most cheerful of all the Schlagintweits. It seems as if joy is the very thing that the goddess of joy has taken away from him and left behind a hole which Adolph cannot climb out of. This puts not only him in danger, but all of us.

Mani Singh, therefore, has to take on more responsibility. The higher we climb, the stricter he is with the train. When he stops, everyone stops. If he turns around, everyone looks at him. If he calls out for something, it is brought to him. His importance for the train exceeds his height by far. Without him we would not have reached Khati. If a coolie complains, becomes obstinate or even prepares to abandon the train, the Sikh calls him by name – he makes a mental note of every individual – and touches his kirpan. He does not need to do anything else. Not one of us doubts that Mani Singh will use his sword in order to protect the train. The Sikh calls the Hindus in the train mouse-hearted. He also shouts it out to Nanda Devi. And every time he does that some coolies duck down as if at any moment, she would hurl an avalanche at the Sikh.

Mani Singh says he is not afraid of her, because for him Nanda Devi is nothing more than a heap of boulders and snow. But I have noticed that every time he provokes the goddess, he touches his kara. And thanks to Devinder who was always enthusiastic about all matters pertaining to Sikhs, I know what the bangle stands for: It reminds the Sikhs of their mortality. So, fear does indeed flow through Mani Singh's head. Even if he would not call it that. He would probably call it awe.

I am fortunate that this is what he also feels for Harkishen. As long as I am under the Brahmin's protection, the Sikh does not bother me too much. But he observes me more closely than the khansaman had done earlier. He has made it a habit to call my name. Even if I have not made myself conspicuous. Each time I freeze and wait for his reprimand or his orders. But nothing comes. If I ask him after a while why he has called me, he does not reply. On good days, when he is in a generous mood, he tells me after a long while to continue. On bad days he makes me wait for a long time till Harkishen comes to my rescue. Mani Singh has managed to make me believe that he is always nearby, even if there is no chance of him being near me.

It is not surprising that someone like him cannot make any friends. The only person in the train with whom he has something approaching a friendly relationship is Mr Monteiro. I would have assumed he would put a stop to the latter's whistling, but apparently it does not disturb him. It is possible that he even likes it. There is no evidence, absolutely none, that Mani Singh has a musical ear. However, the Indo-Portuguese man is often somewhere near him (or is the Sikh often near him?). And if anyone knows what others like and do not like, it is Mr Monteiro. I do not know his songs, and as far as I am able to judge, he does not repeat them. I asked him how he knew so many. He says he is also hearing them for the first time; they come to him while he is walking. It is as if Mr Monteiro lets us hear all the melodies that are otherwise woven in the air by birds. He translates the music in Nanda Devi's realm and is, therefore, just as valuable for the train as Mani Singh. Because music at these heights that are too high even for most of the birds is a remarkable weapon against loneliness. It does not surprise me that the train is always most compact around Mr Monteiro. With his cheerful whistling he pulls the train forward with him while Mani Singh pushes it.

Before we set off, some villagers from Khati approached the train. Harkishen spoke to them. Adolph wanted to know what was happening. He seemed impatient and said that they had no time for *these natives*. That made me miss the Schlagintweit who was always interested in new encounters. When Harkishen began to translate, Adolph interrupted him. We should use the daylight, he said. Although we had spent hours not using the daylight because he had been working on his painting. Harkishen requested the Schlagintweit to listen to him. The villagers had told him that the last firangi who had crossed this pass twenty-five years ago had lost his eyesight because he had not shown the proper respect to Nanda Devi. It was only later in Almora, after he had given her a sizeable gift, that he could see again.

Adolph laughed, but not his infectious laugh; it was a caustic laugh. The last firangi, he said, was Kumaon's Commissioner Traill. He only suffered from snow blindness for a few days because he was not prepared for the glaring light reflected by the snow. And apart from that, he had by no means given Nanda Devi a present; he had only decided in favour of a temple in a legal dispute. But such subtleties were obviously beyond the understanding of these natives.

Harkishen nodded. I do not know whether he agreed with the Schlagintweit or whether he had decided it was pointless to argue.

An old man stepped forward from among the group of natives. His skin was stretched over his bones like a worn-out cloth, and most of the hair on his head sprouted from his ears. He talked incessantly to the Schlagintweit. He moved his arms while speaking as if he were playing an invisible instrument. Of the hundred people who had accompanied Traill, Harkishen translated, he was the only one still alive. He would like to come with us as the main guide.

The natives, the coolies, Harkishen, I, even Mani Singh, looked at Adolph.

He is not young any more, the Schlagintweit said.

Harkishen translated.

The old man picked at Adolph's clothes and said something.

He is of the opinion, Sir, said Harkishen, that you are also not young any more.

Adolph looked the old man over while the latter, in turn, looked directly into Adolph's eyes. Then the old man took a step back. He looked frightened.

What is the matter with him? Adolph asked.

Harkishen talked to the old man.

Then he said: Don't pay any attention to him.

What did he say? Adolph asked.

You are right, Sir, he is not young any more.

Translate what he said!

Harkishen touched his tika.

He says, you will die.

Adolph groaned. An extremely sound statement!

That is not all, Sir, said Harkishen. He claims that you will never return home, but that you will meet your end on this journey.

Eureka! Then at least I will not have to evaluate such fiddle-faddle.

Saying this, he walked away and with arms flailing he ordered the coolies to shoulder the luggage. The prophecy appeared not to worry him in the least.

And yet, the old man had made an impression on the Schlagintweit. Adolph agreed to let him accompany us to the pass.

WE LEFT KHATI on 28 May. The old man is a great help. He is not intimidated even by Mani Singh, some of whose decisions he corrects. The Sikh allows it. This shows what an excellent leader he is. To know the way is not remarkable, but to accept when one does not know it, in that one sees the real worth of a leader. If Mani Singh and I had met under different circumstances, I would have liked to have him as a friend.

Of the thirty men who are on their way to the pass I would only call one a friend. Namely, a man who would never call me a friend. After all, he is a Brahmin and I, as far as we know, am not one. Harkishen doubts whether Adolph's methods can help against Nanda Devi's power. The Schlagintweit has given everyone in the train a piece of green gauze which is supposed to help against snow blindness. I cannot imagine how snow can be brighter than the sun. I cannot even imagine snow! I have only seen it in pictures and in the distance. (The pieces of ice I was allowed to taste in Bombay have as much in common with the snow-covered peaks of the Himalayas as a puddle does with the ocean.) And like the clouds, I have never come close to it. Although every minute brings us higher, we do not come much closer to it. The heights ahead of us seem to grow faster than the speed at which we can bring ourselves to them. Most of the time I am at the back of the train. There I am less conspicuous when I stop briefly to gather my strength. Mani Singh says I should not be a burden to the train, and if I am unable to haul even my diminutiveness, I should stay behind. I have told him I would manage it. He has replied that I would not manage it. I did not reply to that, because there is not enough air for a fight. If we were to fight it out on paper, I would have the advantage, I would triumph. My hand does not need air to write. But the Sikh will never agree to something he cannot win.

We differ in this regard. I have taken on a climb which I might not be able to do. Mani Singh is not the only one aware of it. Harkishen asked me if I would like to go back to Khati. I thought about it and then asked how long I would have to wait for the train there. He replied that the train would not be returning to Khati.

Smitaben and I will only survive if I stay with the train.

The only one who does not notice that I am slowing down is Adolph. I know I will never be a part of his family, but I miss the days when he let me ride on his horse or when he wanted to save me from a shark. The Schlagintweit strides at the head of the train. I would not have thought that someone who travels for weeks in a palki can be so good at climbing mountains. His Alps have indeed taught him a lot! Each of his steps finds firm ground, he always looks ahead, his hands are balled into fists, and he only stops when Mani Singh asks him to. But I can only guess what Nanda Devi is doing to his head.

29 May.

I was wrong! My hand does need air to write. I cannot move it steadily any more. I have to hold it with my other hand so that my words land on paper in a legible form. I do not take Humboldt's hair out any more because I cannot hold on to it. I am sure Nanda Devi would like to get the hair of the greatest scientist of our times.

We are in a meadow at the tongue of the Pindari glacier. Its bright green creates the illusion of pleasant temperatures. But I can see my breath. I lose not only air and warmth, Nanda Devi draws out life through my mouth. The meadow extends to the lower ends of rock walls which tower up to Nanda Devi's peak that is covered with snow which Adolph calls firn. (I will ask him why when I find surplus air.) A herd of goats is grazing near our camp. Harkishen went to the herdsman's tent and bought three goats as an offering to Nanda Devi. When Adolph found out, he wanted to revoke the deal. Harkishen then threatened to leave the train. The train could have coped without him, but not without his wish-fulfillers.

Adolph approved the purchase.

30 May.

Snow! You can call me stupid, but I had imagined it would be warmer. How could I have hoped to like it? If you are no friend of water, snow is your enemy. It is solid, but not solid enough to bear my weight. With every second step my feet sink in. Sometimes I sink up to my chest. The cold takes me in its embrace; it even penetrates through my boots. Mani Singh laughs at me. Mr Monteiro has to free me several times. He still whistles, though more softly and meekly. Even a Christian shows respect for Nanda Devi. Harkishen prays to her. And because he does not want to rely on the benevolence of the goddess, he makes the wish-fulfillers walk ahead of him. They seek out the best path for him. If he falls in, at least four hands are on the spot to support him.

Adolph hurries further ahead of the train. Sometimes we can barely see him in the distance.

In the morning we continue on the march, at first on the left side of the Pindari glacier. We avoid cracks in the ice that progressively become bigger. Not even the sea of snow can fill these mouths. They want to devour us. Adolph pushed on. Harkishen warned him not to provoke Nanda Devi, but the Schlagintweit pushed on nonetheless. The old man wanted us to cross the glacier, and Mani Singh agreed with him. Adolph paused for some minutes in front of a mouth that surely reaches the deepest point on earth. Then he wiped the ice from his face and followed the old man. Sharp-edged rocks obstructed our path. They jabbed at us. A coolie fell on one of them and cut his leg. I could see how the blood froze. Harkishen bandaged his leg and Mani Singh sent him with another man to Khati. After that I was even more careful about where I stepped. I have survived a khansaman and sharks and so much more; I cannot allow myself to be stopped by a stone.

According to Adolph's measurements our bearing location is at a height of 14,180 feet. Shrubs do not grow here; stones have laid claim to the place. They will not tolerate us here for long. Below us is the Pindari glacier. I do not know how we got here from there.

It should not be humanly possible. Adolph is drawing the view. It is remarkable that he is still able to use his hands to draw and to handle his instruments. His mother probably nourished him with earth and snow. He does not sleep, does not even rest, and still has the strength to grumble that the murky haze is obstructing the view. He talks about the euphoria of high altitudes. The dwindling light is replaced by another light. Lightning. But the storm is below us. We are above the clouds. Above the clouds! How can that be? I have to write it down. Only the museum is big enough to take in all of this. I interlace my fingers and move the pencil with both hands. But even the museum cannot keep out the cold. It grows inside me. We could not bring any tents since they would have been too heavy. Even the Schlagintweit has to sleep in the open. Harkishen's wish-fulfillers build a human wall to protect him from Nanda Devi's cold breath. Mani Singh holds out alone, leaning against a rock, eyes half-closed. Even his hair is not enough to keep him warm. Mr Monteiro is not whistling any more; his lips are cracked and bleeding. Only Adolph carries on. He draws a map of the glacier and of the surrounding mountains. The old man helps him. He tells him the names. He describes in what relation each of them stands to Nanda Devi. She is the centre of all existence here. The old man does not seem to realize (or care) that Adolph does not understand him. Which probably suits Adolph. He nods a lot and repeatedly points to something in the distance, whereupon the old man also nods and keeps repeating a name till the Schlagintweit writes it down. How can this old man still stand around and tell stories after such a march! Is he already so close to death that life cannot bother him any more?

31 May.

We set out in the middle of the night. Four coolies stayed back. They complained about pain in all parts of their bodies. I could no longer feel most parts of my body, especially my legs.

The snow, or firn, was now so hard that not even Mani Singh caved in. He and Adolph walked ahead and used axes to make hundreds of steps in the ice. The train followed. When the sun rose, we used the green gauze and made the snow into cold, smooth meadows that did not, in fact, harm our eyes.

When we reached the first point of transition, Adolph called out: I hereby christen this pass Traill Pass. I thought: If one says it, it is so.

Adolph began to sketch. For once, Harkishen and Mani Singh agreed that there was no time for this; the train should not stay so long at this height. Adolph did not listen to them. Five minutes went by, ten minutes, twenty minutes, forty minutes. The Schlagintweit took measurements with a barometer and a small theodolite and ignored all advice. Even Mr Monteiro was not allowed to disturb him.

One of the strongest coolies was the first to collapse. Two more followed. While I am writing this, they are writhing in the snow. Their eyes are contorted, looking into their heads. I wonder what they are seeing. They are throwing their arms and legs about in the air as if they wish to be freed of their limbs. Harkishen calls out: Nanda Devi ayi! His wish-fulfillers join in, saying Nanda Devi ayi! Nanda Devi ayi! Adolph demands a translation. Nanda Devi has come, I say and feel how something alien is growing in my head. It squirms. My legs give way. I want to leave this place. I want to be anywhere, only not here, and suddenly I am happy because I realize that this is how my parents must have felt. Father Fuchs says they brought me to the mission because they could not keep me alive. Because they could not keep even themselves alive. The Vickys had neglected the land for the sake of profits and so hunger killed many thousands of Indians. For a long time, I tried to escape it. I hid from it in the Glass House and fled miles away from it till the Himalayas. But I cannot escape it. I am my parents' son; they gave me hunger just as they gave me my laugh and my hands and my heart. It will not part from me because it is a part of me as it is of all Indians, and nothing will deter it from being my end. It is hunger which will kill me even if I have eaten. Food is not the only sustenance against it. One should also know how to feel full, when to stop, how high one should climb. One should be able to tell oneself these things. But that is a language I do not know. That is a language scarcely any Indian knows. Did my parents fall asleep in the end? Did it sweep them away with one blow? Were they swamped by pain? Were they together, did they hold one another and exchange words of love at the end? Or were they alone? Did one first have to see what happened to the other before it happened to him/her? I do not know. But I know now how it feels when one is not ready to go. In my whole life I have never been this close to them.

Still 31 May.

When the goddess came, she was not selective. She entered all of us. Mr Monteiro lay beside me. His limbs twitched, and a gentle croak came out of his mouth which I will never forget. He looked at me with one of his dark brown eyes. Nanda Devi tortured him. She drowned him in joy. He would not be able to tolerate it for long. And not only he. Everywhere coolies lay in the snow and spoke in languages never heard before. Adolph stood a few feet away from me. He asked something that I could not understand. He kept repeating it, and each time his voice became louder. Was he aware that he was speaking Bavarian? I looked around for Harkishen and discovered him at quite a distance. He was fleeing down the mountain. He kept falling, picking himself up and hurrying on. As though he could escape the goddess. I called out to him. He appeared not to hear me, even though there was no wind. I rolled onto my stomach and crawled towards Adolph. Hunger will kill me one day, but for now it was keeping me alive. I noticed the old man. He was sitting on a rock with folded hands as if he were waiting for a carriage and observing us. He seemed neither worried, nor sympathetic, nor gleeful. Something was missing in his face. His look was not that of an old man. The Schlagintweits, Humboldt and maybe even Father Fuchs would never believe me, but I swear that Nanda Devi was the old man. She can take on many forms. And it also explains how the old man could climb the pass so effortlessly. A goddess is part of our train! I looked away in order not to attract her attention; crawled on and then looked at her again. There was so much I wanted to ask her. When she noticed my movements, she turned her head towards me, and I turned away. I wanted to beg her to spare me. But I could not speak. I pressed my face into the snow. The cold enveloped me. Then I felt myself being grabbed and lifted up. I screamed, begged for forgiveness. That is when I recognized Mani Singh's stiff beard. The Sikh carried me. Away from the goddess. His steps were twice as long as usual. He held me firmly to his chest.

Please, Sir, don't do anything to me, I said. The Sikh laughed. Only a Sikh can laugh in the face of doom.

You will convince him to call everyone to order! Otherwise, this will be our end here, he said and kept running. He was already halfway to Harkishen.

He will not listen to me, I said.

Then make yourself heard, he said.

Within a few minutes he caught up with the Brahmin and put me down in front of him. Harkishen's tika was smudged and resembled a bleeding eye. He ordered us to move out of the way.

Mani Singh caught hold of his arm.

Your brothers are lying up there, he said.

Harkishen twisted his arm free of Mani Singh's grip.

It is the will of the goddess, he said.

Mani Singh drew his kirpan. The Brahmin froze. I raised a hand. The Sikh pointed his sword at Harkishen. I asked the Brahmin where he wanted to go. He did not reply. I told him we Hindus should stick together. Even that did not reach him. And so, I talked to him in the language in which I can always reach him best. I told him in German that he cannot run away from the goddess, that she will always catch up with him regardless of how far and how long he runs, and she will shatter his life and all his lives to come. I told him that none of us will survive without him, and I told him that if he does not turn around and help us, he will have killed not only us but also a cook from Gujarat because my betrayal is the only thing keeping her alive.

THAT WAS SOME hours ago. We set up a night camp in the shelter of an overhanging rock. Harkishen and Mani Singh watched over me. The Sikh does not leave my side even if Adolph asks for him. The colour of his turban is now less vibrant and tends more to green than blue. That must be the influence of the Himalayas. Or it is the muted light of the lantern.

What did you say to him? the Sikh had asked me.

Is that important? I had replied. It's more important that it had the required effect.

The Sikh bowed before me. Again. Since Traill's Pass, the smallest member of the train has seen the turban of the tallest member of the train several times from above.

We owe you our life, he said.

We owe Father Fuchs our life, I thought. If he had not taught me German, I would not have been able to get through to Harkishen and he would not have come back. Only he had succeeded in calling all the coolies to order. He chanted long prayers, he placed snow on their heads. And he threatened them with dire consequences.

Adolph says, the last was definitely the most effective. I am not so sure about that. The Schlagintweit says he cannot remember speaking Bavarian. I must not have heard him properly, he claims. But I will not allow him to dictate my memory. Only because he finds his own annoying. The Schlagintweit wants to forget his encounter with the goddess. A plan which has little chance of success. Everyone who was there will always remind him of it.

After calm had been restored in the train, Harkishen set about dividing the goats each into four parts and hurling each part in one of the four directions. Adolph wanted to object, but I prevented him from doing so. Before I could stop myself, I called him by his first name. Maybe a little of Nanda Devi was still in me. Adolph! I said loudly and expected the Schlagintweit to rebuke me at once. But he fell silent and let Harkishen continue. He did not even complain when he had to hide behind a rock and give his word of honour that he would not look so as not to desecrate the holy ritual.

Adolph is not the only one who has been assigned a new place in the train. My place is now better than it ever was before. Even though my legs can no longer be relied upon. It is as if they do not hear my commands, as if they were linked to me only with bones and flesh. Standing is only possible for a few seconds, walking is impossible. Harkishen says he cannot promise that I will ever run again. Mani Singh, on the other hand, says he is indebted to me. That is very useful. A Sikh as a personal palki – whoever heard of something like that! His shoulders afford a remarkable view. I can see so far ahead that I can make out the future in the distance. It is called Milam and is our next station. I always wished that I were not so small and now, when I can barely stand, I am taller than I had ever hoped to be.

Remarkable Objects
Nos. 48 & 49

A DASTARDLY CEILING
ROBERT SCHLAGINTWEIT (2)

I curse Milam. Even though I do not know it. In the twelve days here, I have barely left my bed. I hate the windowless walls and especially the dastardly ceiling with its gaping knotholes and gloating cracks. As soon as I turn my eyes away, it sinks deeper. On some nights I wake up and find it directly above my face. When Mani Singh is not exploring glaciers with the Schlagintweits, I ask him to carry me outside. He always points out that Harkishen has prescribed bed rest for me. Upon which I point out to the Sikh that he is in my debt. That convinces him every time. But even if I spend a whole hour breathing freely out in the open, it is never enough. After returning to my shrinking room, my body digs further into the hollow it has made in the mattress over several days. In the foreseeable future the bed will swallow me up.

How long will it be before I can walk again? I asked Harkishen when we arrived in Milam.

Not long, he replied.

How much longer? I asked him the day after we arrived.

Not much longer, he had replied.

Soon? I asked him a day after the day after we had arrived.

Since then, he has not visited me.

Instead of him, I now ask my legs every day. When I wake up, I turn to my side on the bed and pull them tightly with my arms. Then I sit up, which requires a lot of strength. I did not know how much one needs one's legs to sit. Even on a cold North Indian morning it makes me perspire. I place one leg next to the other. They hang down from the mattress, dangle impatiently. I push myself off with both arms. My toes touch the ground first. I feel that, I feel the ground. There is life in my legs. They want to carry me. I stretch them. The firmness of the ground transfers itself to my body. I stand, I am myself again. The door is my first goal; I raise a leg with the foot only a little above the ground and push it forward. Before I can put the foot down again, the other leg gives way and I fall down. I brace the impact with my hands. It does not work every time. My body is adorned with yellow and blue and violet hues as if I had played Holi. When I lie on the ground after that, I do not attempt to get up again. I do not want to go back to the bed, and I cannot go outside. (The door handle is too high, and where can I crawl to anyway?) I also do not call for help. For the simple reason that I do not want any help. So, I lie there till someone finds me. Normally Mani Singh or Mr Monteiro. They say I should not test my legs without someone there. But I cannot bear their looks when they observe me doing it. I do not want their pity; they should keep it to themselves. I cannot bear to hear them say they are confident of my recovery. They only say it to make me feel better and they manage to make me feel worse. I know what they really believe. They doubt I will ever walk again. As far as they are concerned, Bartholomew has become a cripple. And a cripple cannot be a translator, not in this train. I would rather they do not come to see me at all, like Harkishen. That would be more honest.

ROBERT IS A little too honest. His train reached Milam on a less dangerous route through the valleys. I cannot say much about his relationship with Adolph because I never see the two of them together. According to Mani Singh, they talk mostly about their glacier-observations, their glacier-explorations and their glacier-measurements. Robert uses his picture machine to document new human races in the mountain region. He has visited me twice.

The first time was shortly after our arrival in Milam. He greeted me with his characteristic stiffness. He was neither glad to see me, nor was he not glad to see me. He could have thanked me for saving his brother's life after I had already rendered him the same service. But Robert did not mention it. However, I do not hold it against him. This Schlagintweit seems to be more of a firangi than his brothers. He is probably also one in his own country. Maybe even in his family. Any dealings with another person pose a challenge for him. Even a poor observer can see it in his face. That is why he prefers the picture machine. It allows him to study the world without being disturbed. He can hide in it and take pictures of everything without ever having to give anything back.

After Robert had greeted me stiffly, he asked me to stand up. I demonstrated my inability to do so and remained lying down on the floor. I did not want to ask for help and he seemed undecided about whether to help me since I had not asked. Finally, he said: You have a serious affliction.

I will overcome it, I said, like Traill's Pass.

Unlikely, he said.

I thought about my conversation with him in Calcutta and the unbiased look.

Unlikely, Sir?

Robert nodded. He then left the room in a hurry as if he had just understood what he had said to me.

ON THE DAYS that followed I challenged my legs more often. As soon as someone lifted me onto the bed and left me alone, I got up and tried again. But my legs balked like rebellious palki-bearers. And with each fall the ceiling came menacingly closer.

Ten days went by, and I did not see Robert. Today he visited me for the second time. When he came in, I noticed something was different. It took me a minute to realize that he was not wearing his hat. Without it, Robert looks much younger, not that much older than me. His forehead is smooth like a polished tabletop.

He came to the bed and asked how I was. I replied that I was still here. Like all the others, Robert could not stop himself from looking at my legs. As if he had never seen a pair of legs before.

His silence lasted too long. In order to counteract the silence, I asked which would be our next station.

Tibet,[26] he said.

I have never been there, I said.

His forehead was now furrowed. Robert touched his head as if in search of his hat.

You are not coming with us, he said. We will be parting soon.

But, Sir, you need me!

Your condition is not good.

I can walk!

Robert paused and looked at my legs so sternly that I wanted to hide them from him.

He placed a hand on the doorknob, and before he fled the room, he said: Thank you for your services. We will praise you in our report.

---

26 Since Traill's Pass my boots were not used except to pass on this information.

He should not be allowed to say something like that and then disappear.

I stood up and fell down. I crawled to the door and banged on it.

No one opened it.

I called out to Robert, to Mani Singh, Mr Monteiro and Adolph. I even called Harkishen and Abdullah. Not one of them came.

I am writing this in a corner of the room. I am lying on my stomach, I cannot turn around, the ceiling is too close.

I curse Milam.

Remarkable Objects
Nos. 50 & 51

THE SIXTH FINGER
A PICTURE OF SOMETHING THAT DOES NOT EXIST

The goats were not our only sacrificial offerings on Traill's Pass. My legs do not obey me anymore. Mani Singh has left his pride behind. Harkishen lost the respect of many wish-fulfillers – and with it many wish-fulfillers. And Mr Monteiro has to be satisfied being able to see with only one eye. Whereby I never know which one. Both eyes roll around in his head and sometimes one, sometimes the other, is directed at me.

It is only Adolph's sacrifice that I cannot determine.

During our first days in Milam, he did not come to see me. I learnt from Mani Singh that he tried to establish contact with Hermann but was unsuccessful. (The people in the train say that the eldest Schlagintweit and his expedition have met with an accident. I prefer to believe that Smitaben and Hermann and, unfortunately, also Eleazar are well. After all, the information continues to leave my boot.)

Adolph came to see me three days after Robert had fled from my room, that is more than two weeks after we had arrived in Milam.

He entered my room without knocking and did not greet me. He also did not ask how I was feeling. Which I liked. I liked it even better that he had shaved. It felt good to see his face!

It is a matter of portraying the truth, he said.

With these words he set up an easel.

Sit up, he said.

It cost me a great deal of effort. Adolph must have noticed it, but he did not help me. That was fine with me. He moved the easel to the bed so that I could sit in front of it and mounted a sheet of white paper on it. Then he unfolded a sketch he had made on the Cheena Peak. Instead of lines, of which there were very few, it was filled with information about the view of the Himalayas from there. Adolph held out a pencil to me.

Begin, he said.

Sir?

This has to become a painting, he said.

But for that one needs a brush and colours, I said.

Adolph laughed.

I would hardly entrust my precious brushes and colours to a beginner like you!

He held the pencil in my face.

This here is your instrument, he said. You will begin with this. If you prove yourself worthy, then and only then we will see what happens.

Isn't Abdullah better suited for this?

One draughtsman alone is not enough for us, he said.

I took the pencil. It was heavier than it looked.

Sir, I said.

What is it now?

There is a problem.

Yes?

I don't have the talent for this.

Adolph looked at me, but only at my face. He had not looked at my legs even once.

Is that so?

I nodded.

My brother is of the view that I am talented, he said.

Robert?

No, he believes that painting is no longer in fashion, that it is on its deathbed. I am speaking of Hermann. He calls what I fabricate art.

It is, indeed, I said.

Nature is neither art nor adornment, it is both at once, as Goethe said.

I don't like him, I said.

You don't like Goethe?

Father Fuchs says Goethe hated our idols.

Idols?

That is a bad word for gods.

I know what idols are.

Why do you ask then?

Adolph laughed.

I don't like Goethe either, he said. He writes like someone who only wants to read his own things.

I thought of the museum.

Don't most writers write like that? I asked.

Possible, he said.

Adolph sat down beside me.

I am not an artist, he said. I use artistic techniques, yes, but my goal is only to transfer what nature shows me as precisely as possible onto paper.

Like a translator, I said.

Like a translator, he said.

Adolph gestured invitingly.

I looked at the empty sheet of paper. The longer I looked at it, the wider and higher and whiter it became.

Come on, come on! Adolph said.

I positioned the pencil and drew a line.

Stop, he said and erased the line. Once more!

I positioned the pencil again and again he stopped me soon after that.

I am telling you, I cannot draw, Sir.

Nonsense, he said.

He gripped the hand which was holding the pencil. I felt his strength and an overpowering warmth.

You only have to teach your hands the language, Bartholomew. Let us begin.

In the days following this my legs did not learn anything new. But my hands can now do things that I had never believed them capable of. When Adolph is in Milam, he visits me and teaches them a new language. And when Adolph is not there, I practise with them. I never put the pencil down. Adolph says I should make it my own, like a sixth finger. Even while sleeping I hold on to it. I have calluses on my hands and there is a silver sheen on my fingertips. Every line that I make on paper feels like a step. Even if I take more steps backwards than forwards. The view from Cheena Peak is by no means finished. As yet it only consists of a few horizontal lines that I had to translate many hundreds of times before Adolph stopped erasing them.

Once, he erased the same place so often that I threw the pencil away and cursed.

Pick it up! Adolph commanded.

I did not move.

Pick it up at once!

The pencil was under the table with the wash bowl. I had to slip off the bed and crawl for a few metres to reach it. Adolph watched me and made no move to help. Not even when I was finally holding the pencil in my hand. And so, I crawled back to the bed and pulled myself up as far as possible. Only then did Adolph help me to sit on the mattress again.

I don't deserve a brush, I said.

I will decide that, he said.

It is a very difficult language.

Don't you like it?

If it had not been Adolph, I would have said that he sounded hurt.

I do, Sir.

He turned to me.

What exactly do you like about it?

I thought about it. I did not want to tell him what I liked best about it. So long as he was teaching me, I was not alone, and the ceiling stayed in its place.

This room does not have any windows, I said.

And?

When I draw, it is as if I were building a window. I like that because I am never going to walk again. Through the window I can see things that are actually not there at all.

Adolph looked at me for a long time, and for the first time, he also looked at my legs.

After this he stayed away for two days. When he came to me today his clothes were soaking wet. It had been raining for days. The rain has found its way through a leak in the roof. Water is pooling in a puddle next to my bed. Sometimes I catch the drops with my hand and lick them. In this way I can taste the outside.

Adolph took the cloth cover off a painting and placed it on the easel. The painting depicted steep slopes, rising fog, ice.

Do you recognize that? he asked.

I looked at it more carefully. The longer I looked at it, the worse I felt. I vaguely sensed something strange in my head.

Nanda Devi, I said. Traill's Pass.

Adolph pointed to a place on the canvas.

I came closer.

There is someone there, I said.

Not just anyone, he said.

Who is it, Sir?

Look closely.

The face of the figure was not recognizable. It was covered by a piece of green gauze. The figure was bent over as if it were not going to allow Nanda Devi to bring it to its knees. The snow came up to its chest.

Is this me, Sir?

Adolph nodded.

I am dedicating this painting to you, he said.

No one has ever dedicated anything to me, Sir.

Then it is high time, he said. What does one say?

Thank you ... but Sir?

Adolph blew air out of his nose.

Is there a problem again?

The picture does not depict the truth, I said.

What do you mean?

At that point I could not walk any more. Mani Singh carried me.

Maybe, he said. But without you we would not have conquered the pass. Basically, you carried the entire train. It is as if you traversed the pass on your own. It is precisely that which I have shown.

But it is still a picture of something that never was, I said.

How can something not be if I have painted it, he said, if we can see it in front of us?

I looked at the painting once more and at the small figure in it.

Perhaps it does not depict past events, Adolph said, but is a window on the future. With its help you can see things that are not yet there. After all, it cannot be ruled out that one day you will traverse Traill's Pass again.

That is unlikely, Sir.

Let others be the judge of that.

I have a serious affliction.

He went to the door and, like Robert had done, placed a hand on the doorknob.

Are you angry, Sir?

No, he said, this time more softly.

I could not see his face, but I knew he was lying. I did not know why though.

Please don't go, I said.

A long moment passed. Water dripped loudly into the puddle.

Adolph's hand let go of the doorknob. He sat down beside me again and indicated that I should continue drawing.

LATER, WHEN MANI Singh carried me around in the rain, I asked him why Adolph was angry.

Trouble with his brother, he said. Robert Schlagintweit is urging us to leave, but Adolph Schlagintweit has been postponing our departure for days.

Why? I asked.

Mani Singh stopped.

You don't know?

No, I said.

Adolph Schlagintweit claims that they have not completed their studies. But everyone in the train knows the real reason.

The Sikh wiped water from his face.

The reason is called Bartholomew, he said.

I? The train is waiting for me?

And for your legs to recover.

The train is waiting for me.

How I would love to tell Father Fuchs.

But, I asked, what if my legs don't recover?

Mani Singh cleared his throat like someone who does not need to clear his throat.

Today, the Messrs Schlagintweit reached an agreement that they would wait till these rains end. Then we are leaving.

It is late, and I hear the rain falling on the roof. Each drop is helping me. I do not want to fall asleep and miss the last one. The puddle next to my bed drums a threatening beat. The time between two beats is increasing. Like a clock that will soon stop.

Remarkable Object No. 52

TRUSTING A SPY

The last European who reached Tibet was the missionary Abbé Krik. He is said to have been almost as scientifically inclined as Father Fuchs. The first time Krik advanced from Assam and followed the Brahmaputra which originates in Tibet. But wars in the country forced him to turn around. The second time he went through the swampy Tarai in the south, but had to retreat, again due to wars. The third time he attempted it again from Assam, accompanied this time by the missionary Auguste Boury. In Tibet they encountered the Mishimi, a tribe that occupies the upper foothills of the Himalayas. The Mishimi had received orders from the Tibetan authorities, and they carried these out to the letter. Father Krik and Father Boury were killed by Kaisha, a leader of the tribe.

This happened last year.

Mani Singh told me this soon after we embarked on our journey to the Tibetan border. He sounded cheerful. As if reaching Tibet was a cause for delight. The Sikh's grin became even broader when Mr Monteiro pointed out that Nepal and Tibet were presently at war and several thousand soldiers were camped in the regions ahead of us. He seems to be excited about confronting this challenge.

I would have preferred my first journey as a cripple to be to a less dangerous region. We are riding on small horses that resemble muscular pigs but have a steadier will. For hours they patiently carry even a giant like Mani Singh whose legs almost reach the ground while riding. I mostly sit behind the Sikh, sometimes behind Mr Monteiro and often also behind Adolph. The Schlagintweit says I carried the train, now the train must carry me. (Whether these noble words are translated into deeds will only be known when the horses are not carrying us any more.) Robert does not really agree with this. He does not contradict his older brother, at least not in my presence, but he always looks at me as if I were blocking the picture machine's view. I know he thinks that I pose an additional risk for them, and he is right.

Tibet belongs to China. Peking appoints the Dalai Lama. Only a member of a family loyal to the Chinese can become an incarnation of the Buddha. It is not for nothing that the three regions of Tibet, which the Schlagintweits want to explore, are called Gnari Khorsam. It means the three dependent circles. The Chinese do not allow any Europeans into the country and Indians only seldom get permission. The borders are heavily guarded.

That is why the train is carrying only the bare necessities: provisions, chronometers, the magnetic instruments and a barometer. The Schlagintweits took care to ensure that most of the instruments are small so that they are not conspicuous. By way of precaution Adolph and Robert also left Harkishen and all other Hindus behind. Ten tribesmen were recruited to replace them: Bhutias from Sikkim who also understand Tibetan and, as the Schlagintweits say, are more civilized than the Mishimi. Apart from them, the brothers are accompanied only by Mani Singh, Mr Monteiro, Abdullah and me. When Robert reminded his brother that one Hindu was still part of the train, Adolph replied: Bartholomew is far too small to be conspicuous.

For the first time in my life, I wish I were even smaller.

The Chinese, Mani Singh said, consider all foreigners to be spies. So, they will see the real me. And what will they make of the Schlagintweits? As a disguise, everyone in the train is dressed like a Bhutia. We all wear trousers, a scratchy cap and a completely impractical overgarment made of sheep's wool.

When Adolph helped me put on my disguise, I remembered Eleazar's words.

Are you the vanguard of the English? I asked Adolph.

He laughed.

Where did you get that idea?

I kept quiet.

We are the vanguard of science, he said.

But don't you work for the Vickys?

Vickys?

I explained it to him.

Vickys, he said and smacked his lips as if to taste the word. An appropriate name. Yes, Bartholomew, we work for them as you well know. Why don't you tell me what is really bothering you?

Sir, I said, are you a spy?

No, he said.

But you are disguising yourself …

Only as protection.

… and collecting information for the Vickys.

Adolph looked at me sternly.

I am just as little a spy as Abbé Krik was, he said.

Spies are good at telling lies, I said.

Then you will just have to trust me.

I gave that some thought.

I am not sure I can do that.

You are not sure?

No, Sir.

Well then, he said, I will have to prove that I am worthy.

That would be a possibility, I said.

He smiled.

I, at any rate, trust you.

The matter-of-fact way in which he said it sounded as splendid as Father Fuchs's cough.

I DO NOT want to betray Adolph any more. His trust makes me want to tell him the truth.

But if I do that, he will never trust me again.

And so, I must continue to betray him so that he continues to trust me.

Remarkable Object No. 53

TIBET

Father Fuchs says that Tibet belongs to India like Ceylon in the south, Dhaka in the east and Lahore in the west. He dreams of a country in which all these nations live together and rule themselves. Naturally, many rulers are averse to this dream. Especially the rulers of the Chinese and of the Russians and of the Vickys. They call this contest The Great Game. As if we were simply pawns in some game! But they are in for a surprise. Father Fuchs's dream is stronger than the grandest of games.

I can make it come true in the museum.

It is 12 July. We saw Tibet for the first time today. When we crossed the Kiungar Pass at around ten o'clock in the morning – following a lesser-known route to avoid being discovered – the gloomy mantle of the rainy season was spread behind us. But in front of us, in Tibet, the clouds were already vanishing, revealing friendly mountain meadows.

Like the Upper Engadine, said Adolph.

Is that in Bavaria? I asked.

Adolph and Robert did not reply. They have little in common, but in this moment, I could see that they are brothers. Adolph put his arm around Robert's shoulder; the latter flinched briefly but did not draw back. And so, they stood side by side for a long time and breathed in the view.

They have left their loneliness behind in Milam. Not only they. Although as a cripple I am smaller than I ever was, and the mountains around us become higher, I am not as lonely as I was before. I now have Mr Monteiro and Mani Singh and Adolph on my side, and I hear my heart thumping less often. Because I need my ears for more important things. I talk to Mr Monteiro about methods to conserve a large yellow-naped woodpecker or a rock lizard; while riding I hold on firmly to the Sikh, press my head against his back and listen to his thunderous breathing. And I continue to draw under Adolph's guidance. On my map of loneliness, the measurements on the Tibetan border are low.

WHEN WE WERE riding down the northern side of the Kiungar Pass, Mani Singh, behind whom I was sitting, suddenly stopped his horse.

Border guards, he said.

A little further down the slope there was a campsite with fires burning, yaks and eight Hunias led by a kushob. When they saw us, they picked up their weapons and came towards us.

They were expecting us, Adolph said.

Robert asked how that was possible.

Mani Singh was silent, but I knew what he was thinking: a spy in our ranks.

The information about our journey had been removed from my boot in Milam. Eleazar must have warned the Chinese.

But why?

The group of soldiers fanned out and built a semi-circle around us. Rather than seeming hostile, the men looked interested.

Mani Singh got down from his horse and went to the kushob. The Sikh towered above the chief guard. They spoke in Tibetan. The conversation ended after a few minutes and the kushob retreated with his soldiers.

Adolph and Robert looked at Mani Singh enquiringly, and I was very curious.

I told them, he said, that we are going to Niti and do not intend going to Tibet. If we go in that direction, we will not lose much time and can enter Tibet at night through another pass.

Adolph and Robert praised him for this excellent deception. Then we continued.

THE COLLECTIVE FEELING of relief in the train spurs the horses on. Or perhaps it is also the fear of what would happen if the border guards saw through our strategy.

The Hunias follow us at a distance.

13 July.

This morning, the message in which I communicated our alternative route to Eleazar was still inside my boot. For the first time since Calcutta, it has not been forwarded. Which is also a message. But this time for me. I believe, the other traitor could not pick up the message because he is no longer with the train. I believe his name is Harkishen.

16 July.

We spent three days in Laptél where Adolph collected stones which he calls fossils, and he handles them as gently as if they were the eggs of a rare bird. We have now set up camp in Shélchell. Dusk is setting in. In the distance we can see the fires lit by the Hunias.

The messages still do not leave my boot. I eat them for breakfast. That is the only way I can ensure that no one finds them. Especially not Mani Singh. He continues his search for the spy and questions all the members of the train except the Schlagintweits and me. This time, however, his anticipation holds loneliness at bay. Anticipation about what he will do with the spy when he finds him. He does not miss any opportunity to describe it. His most favoured methods include roasting the tongue, removing the eyes with his hand and plugging the ears with molten metal.

At night I was woken by Mr Monteiro. He whispered to me to get dressed quietly. Adolph, Robert and Mani Singh crept through the camp and packed up instruments and provisions. We let Abdullah and most of the Bhutias sleep. They would only have hindered a quick advance. We rode away under the cover of darkness. For the rest of the night and most of the next day we drove the horses on without stopping long to rest. It was only in the evening that Mani Singh and the brothers decided that we had put enough distance between the Hunias and us. The others began to put up the tents and unload the horses. I sat on a rock watching them and felt useless.

That is when I heard shouts. The Hunias. They galloped towards us. I held the pencil firmly in my hand – my only weapon. Mani Singh tried to block their path, but they simply rode past him. They were after our horses. The Hunias grabbed the reins and wanted to steal them. We would have been lost without them. Suddenly there was a crack and one of the Hunias fell from his horse. He held his face. Mr Monteiro then hit the next Hunia with his riding crop. This one also got it in the face and slipped from the saddle. One eye of the Indo-Portuguese man was opened menacingly wide, the other rolled wildly. The rest of the Hunias drew back. The two who had lost their horses bowed down before us. Mani Singh spoke with them. They said that they had come as friends. One of them was the kushob. He said they were only following us on the orders of their government and that Jang Bahadur, the ruler of Nepal, was responsible for this. Because of the war with Nepal travellers were in danger. We could be attacked or even murdered. Tibet did not want to be held accountable by the Vickys for such acts.

The Schlagintweits conferred with Mani Singh, and they decided to negotiate with a dzongpon. The governor of this region is in Daba, a village nearby. A Hunia was sent to fetch him.

We are waiting. Adolph uses the time to paint a view of the Himalayas. He has told me to observe him. In the middle of the picture, he draws a high peak whose white contours stand out sharply against the dark blue of the sky. I asked him the name of the peak.

Abi Gamin, Adolph replied. I will soon climb it.

He says that so confidently. The Schlagintweit seems to know with absolute certainty that he will soon find himself at the top of a mountain.

I am not sure we will even be alive tomorrow.

19 July.

The dzongpon did not come. Instead, he sent his assistant, a lama from Lhasa. A pale, delicate boy who gives off the fragrance of an unknown flower. In his presence I feel old and worn out. Mani Singh jokes that he is finally getting to see a woman again. The Sikh is convinced that the negotiations will be easy.

20 July.

The negotiations prove to be difficult. This pale, delicate boy has a marble core. He drinks brandy like water. Alcohol hardly seems to impair him. He has a strong will. He does not want to allow us to continue on our journey. Adolph is unhappy, but he is impressed by the resilience he encounters. If the lama were to lose his legs, the Schlagintweit says, he would simply continue walking on his hands.

I cannot do that. There is much that I cannot do. Walk, climb, help set up camp, get up on a horse, take measurements.[27] If I want to relieve myself, I need someone to carry me away. I do not translate

27 Even the illiterate Bhutias who can barely count to twenty are better at it than me. The Schlagintweit gave them Buddhist prayer beads with eight beads missing as pedometers. With it they can count a hundred steps and measure distances.

any more either, because I do not know any of the languages spoken in the train and in Tibet. I cannot even be a spy any more; I continue to eat the messages to Eleazar.

The only thing I can do is draw lines on paper. Thin strokes which Adolph, if he ever has time for me, mostly erases.

21 July.

It turns out that there is one thing the lama is not immune to: rupees. He gave the train permission to go till the Sutlej. However, the Schlagintweits had to sign an undertaking agreeing to pay six hundred rupees as a fine if they crossed the river.

We are now camping at the Sutlej. The Hunias are camping a little further away. They were assigned to us as guards. The men are loud; they do not talk, they only call out to each other. Their fires burn throughout the night. Their off-pitch singing which startles the horses even drowns out the river. The Hunias do this on purpose to remind us that they are there. That on no account should we dare to cross the Sutlej.

Adolph tries to persuade his brother to attempt a crossing at night. Robert objects very decidedly: he remains silent. That makes Adolph miss his older brother. He could at least argue with Hermann.

I told Adolph to draw a window to the future.

He looked at me as if I had spoken in Tibetan.

That way you can see things that are not yet there, I explained.

Adolph replied that he did not have time for such gimmicks. I should let him work in peace.

He is not only annoyed because we are stuck on this side of the river. His anger also has another source. I have noticed how he looks at me since we left Milam. In my room there it did not bother him that I was always lying down and could not walk. On the contrary, when he came to me, he made me feel I could soon walk again, and he felt good for giving me a good feeling. But that was then. When

Adolph looks at me now, he can only see what is there: a useless pair of legs, a worthless translator, an unnecessary burden.

23 July.

We have found a way. A relative of Mani Singh[28] interceded for the Schlagintweits with the dzongpon in Daba. The negotiations were reportedly so intensive that all of Daba could hear them. The train now has permission to advance to the Chakola Pass. Mani Singh strokes his beard contentedly. He says that thanks to Bara Mani he has averted the greatest disgrace. The Sikh still feels responsible for the train being discovered at the border. He advises me to sleep with my eyes open. The traitor, he says, is among us.

26 July.

I have an important task for you, Adolph had said. I can only assign it to you.

And I, I said yes at once like a hairless, toothless, tailless ape. Yes, Schlagintweit, Sir, what is the task?

You must guard the train, he said.

The Hunias are already doing that.

That is the reason why I need someone to look after the train. You, Bartholomew, are now a khansaman.

That is impossible, I said.

I am serious: you are a khansaman.

I am a cripple, Sir, I cannot look after the train. Mani Singh is much more suitable for the task.

Robert and I need him for our excursion, he said.

Where are you going?

We will not stay away long. Only a few days.

---

28 He is called Bara Mani. Unlike our Mani, however, he is considered big because of his wealth as a trader.

Are you leaving me behind because I am a cripple?

No one is being left behind, he said.

THAT WAS THE last time we spoke to each other before he rode away with Robert, Mani Singh and Mr Monteiro. Not even an hour later the Hunias came to our camp and helped themselves to our provisions. I ordered them not to do it as loudly and authoritatively as I could. Even if we do not speak the same language, I did not need a translator to make myself understood. But I am not surprised that this did not stop them. I am, after all, no khansaman. The three Bhutias Adolph had left behind were also no help. They ran away and only came back when the Hunias had left with their loot. At that moment I was glad that even they could not understand me. I called them cowards in five languages.

27 July.

The Bhutias are as useful as a blunt knife. They lie around and chew grass. I told them to gather firewood. They pointed to me and laughed as only mean-spirited people would. I threw a stick at them. They ignored it. So, I threw stones at them. A largish stone hit one of them in the shoulder. After that he finally stopped laughing and got up. He came to me, grabbed my legs, and dragged me outside the camp. I screamed at him, threatened him with punishment. He stopped. I stretched out my arms to him so that he would carry me back to the camp. He grabbed my hand, pulled me up and brought me to a standing position. For a moment I stood. Then my legs gave way, and I fell down hard on my head. All the Bhutias laughed. I jabbed the Bhutia on the leg with Adolph's pencil. He took it from me, broke it in two and flung the pieces away. Then he kicked me down a slope, and my fall was broken only by a rock a few metres away. I tasted dirt and shame and blood.

Now I have one tooth less. I have crawled up the slope and back into the camp. In the meantime, dusk has arrived and the Bhutias have gone into the tent. They do not let me in. I am now lying at the edge of the camp; the warmth of the fire does not reach me. But one thought warms me: what Mani Singh will do to the Bhutias when he returns.

28 July.

I have not eaten for two days. The Bhutias do not share their provisions with me. But if one of the Hunias comes to the camp they give him whatever he demands. The smell of roasted meat and hot, rich milk wafts towards me. My stomach feels as if I had swallowed shards. I would like to crawl to the Bhutias and ask them to give me something. But I know they will not do it. And so, I stay here under my fur. These men with the mind of debauched sheep will not break Khansaman Bartholomew.

I HAVE CRAWLED to the Bhutias. As I came closer to them, their backs, which were turned to me, became broader and higher. I called out to them. They did not react. I crawled even closer and indicated that I wanted something to eat. They talked among themselves. One of them made a gesture as if to chase away a dog. I was afraid they would drag me off again. The pain in my stomach gave me courage. I kept indicating that I wanted to eat. Finally, one of them threw me a bone. Almost all the meat had been gnawed off. I did not touch it and pointed instead to the charred animal on the fire. The Bhutia cut off a piece of its meat and held it out to me. I could not identify what animal they were eating, but it was all the same to me. I reached out for it and the Bhutia stepped back, put it in his mouth and chewed like a haughty buffalo. The other Bhutias laughed. You are the fathers of the Others! I called out in German; I curse you even more than Milam! The Bhutias all looked at me blankly. I would have loved to place even more curses on them but I was losing my strength. I took the bone and crawled back to my place at the edge of the camp.

I devoured every scrap of meat I found on the bone and then started sucking on it. The stabbing pain in my stomach became sharper.

How long did my parents live like this before their end came?

29 July.

I woke up in the night to find a Bhutia rummaging through my things. I tried to stop him, but he pushed me aside. When he found the museum, he tore some pages out. Fortunately, they were blank. He used them to ignite their fire again.

I have to protect the museum. After this entry I will bury it and only take it out when Adolph and the others return.

I SHOULD NOT be writing. But I cannot be without the museum. It is the only place where I can walk and never feel pain. In the museum I am the Bartholomew I want to be. The Bhutias will never be able to understand that. Two of them came to me at daybreak and wanted to take the book from me. I hid it under my shirt. They tore at my clothes. I screamed for help. The first name that came from my mouth was Adolph. That surprised me. I would have thought it would have been Mani Singh. Naturally, I also called out to him. And also, to Mr Monteiro. And to Smitaben. And even to Father Fuchs. The Bhutias exchanged a few words. They appeared to disagree about something. I used the opportunity and held out the drawing of the Cheena Peak with its horizontal lines. One of them took it happily and lit a fire with it. The other one seemed to be thinking. Even if I do not believe this intellectual flea is capable of stringing two thoughts together. He bent over me; his breath smelt of sour milk. The Bhutia seized my shirt collar and tore it in order to get to the museum. Then he stopped and reached for something. Father Fuchs's handkerchief. He held it up and called out to the others as if he had just shot a panther. I demanded that the handkerchief be returned. He pocketed it and went away. I crawled after him and held on to one of his legs. He tried to shake me off, kicked me, but I did not let go. The others found this amusing. The Bhutia grabbed my hair, but I still did not let go. Then he said something angrily and hit me in the face.

When I woke up, the sun was shining. But it could not dispel the haze around the camp. I ran my fingers over my face. My nose was swollen; it might be broken. I do not know how to find out. I was still lying in the place where the Bhutia had struck me unconscious. It took me a moment to sit up. The first thing I checked was that the museum was still there. But Father Fuchs's handkerchief! I have to get it back. At least that. Humboldt's hair is lost forever. The Bhutias are lounging around in front of the tent and are not doing anything. I have never seen so much idleness. Not even Devinder was so good at doing nothing. I want to crawl to them and get the handkerchief back. But they would only hit me again. It is better to wait for the night.

The night is taking its time.

Although the sun is shining on my fur, I am freezing.

One of the Bhutias stood in front of me and smelt the handkerchief.

I will get back at you, I said to him.

Even though he does not know German, I will help him understand.

30 July.

When the Bhutias finally slept, late at night, I crawled up to them. It took a long time because I was trying not to make a sound. The fire was very accommodating. Its crackling concealed the noise of my lame legs. The Bhutias were sleeping in the tent. I crawled inside. The fire helped me again by providing sufficient light for my eyes. I was surprised that these useless men were not snoring. They slept as silently as newborn babies. Inside the tent it smelt of sheep's wool, wood and old sweat. The Bhutia I was looking for was lying at the back of the tent. I had to weave my way through the two other Bhutias to reach him. Every centimetre required a lot of time. My recalcitrant legs wanted to kick the Bhutias in the face. I had to use both hands to prevent them from doing so. When I reached the Bhutia I wanted, I could not see the handkerchief. I patted him down carefully. His pockets only contained a curly tress and a few copper coins with a Chinese stamp strung on a leather cord. I wanted to break his nose too and demand that the handkerchief be returned. But I decided to do something else.

When I had filled his waterskin, I heard voices outside. I looked out through the tent opening. The Hunias were roaming through the camp. I decided the tent was the safest place and pretended to be asleep. Someone entered the tent. I kept my eyes closed. The Hunia was breathing loudly. All of a sudden, my legs began to itch. It felt as if invisible cockroaches were scampering over my bare skin from my feet to my stomach. I felt thousands of feelers and many thousands of legs. I had to scratch. Slowly, carefully. But the more I pressed my clawed fingers into my skin the more cockroaches there were. The Hunia did not seem to notice. He left the tent. I waited for a while and fought against the cockroaches as much as I could. When the fire died down and I could not hear the Hunias any more, I left the tent and returned to my fur.

The cockroaches do not let me sleep.

It is snowing.

I WOKE UP under a layer of snow. But I was not cold. I am still not feeling cold. The snow is warming, and it soothes the cockroaches.

In my white cocoon I watched the sun rise. I will not get many more opportunities to do this. Some rays pushed through the fog. One of them warmed my skin. Soon after, the Bhutia emerged from the tent. I observed him carefully. He scratched his neck, coughed, drank from his waterskin. Stopped. I smiled. He can taste it, I thought, but he does not know what it is that he is tasting. The Bhutia lifted the waterskin again and took a big gulp. Then he spit it out. Hurled the waterskin away and screamed. His voice broke as it sometimes happens with the Others. It was the sound of fear. My liquid juice in his mouth reminded him that even he has to fear the world. It does not let anyone get away. Because he stole my handkerchief, he thought he was powerful. But he does not have any power. Much less over me. He is only a small man with an even smaller brain. Roaring loudly, he rushed back into the tent and started quarrelling with the other Bhutias. My laughter melted the snow in front of my face. Isn't *Schadenfreude* one of the best words in German? It warms my heart. I am happy that I can experience it once more. If Adolph does not come back soon, or if he has indeed decided to leave someone behind, I will die. It is difficult to say how this will happen. I will freeze to death, or die of starvation, or the Bhutias will take care of it. When one is dead, does one then know of what one died? I am not sad that soon I will not exist any more. After all, I am much older than many people in Blacktown when they die. But I am sad that I cannot protect Smitaben any more and cannot complete the museum. I hope Father Fuchs and Smitaben forgive me. I hope I am reborn as an elephant. Elephants are the most beautiful animals in the world. They are big even when they are small. And their family always stays together and protects them.

The Bhutias came, this time all three of them. They trampled on my warm snow-cover and threw my fur to the side, searched through my things, removed my boots, took off my clothes. In turns they all called out the same word. Whatever it means, I know they mean the museum. I had hidden it long ago. They could have me, but not the museum.

One of them grabbed hold of me and stood me up as they had done before. For a moment I stood. And for another moment. And for yet another. My legs did not give way. The cockroaches were in an uproar. They pierced through my skin. But I stood. The Bhutias were no less surprised than I was. They fell silent and did not move. As though they had only now seen a person in me. It was too much for their shrivelled minds. They pushed me and I fell. When I was on the ground, they kicked me. I rolled myself up and protected my head with my arms. The kicks became stronger, harder. The pain drove the cockroaches away. I saw the sole of my boot in front of me. Snow and mud and yellow moss hung to it. And Humboldt's hair.

I knew at once that it was his. Not only do none of the Bhutias have silver hair, but I have also looked at Humboldt's hair so often that I would never mistake it for someone else's hair. My breath made it dance cheerfully. It had been with me this whole time. I stretched out an arm towards it, even though it left my head unprotected, and concentrated solely on the hair. I plucked it from the sole and closed my fist around it.

Then the kicking stopped.

Humboldt's hair has saved me. I know that is unscientific thinking, but there is no other explanation for the fact that I saw the Hunias when I looked up. They fanned out as they came towards us with their swords drawn. Humboldt's hair had called the guards of the train to help me. The three Bhutias stretched out their arms in entreaty. The kushob spoke very loudly; his spittle flew through the air. The Bhutias went down on their knees. The kushob knocked them over, one after the other. They lay on the ground stunned. A Hunia placed the fur around my shoulders and wanted to take me away. I fended him off. My body ached inside and outside, but I could not leave; I still had something to do. The

Hunia let me go. The kushob gave some orders, and the Bhutias took off their clothes. With each piece of clothing their movements became slower. The Hunias raised their swords as a warning to hurry. When they were naked, the kushob went to the fire and took out the iron rod on which the carcass of the charred animal was still speared. He removed the carcass, held out the iron rod to me and said: Schlagintweit. I shook my head. Indian, I said, and placed a hand on my heart. He blinked and repeated: Schlagintweit. Do I look so foreign to the Tibetan that he thinks I am European? Or have all these months with the brothers made me somewhat Schlagintweit-ish?

The kushob placed the rod in my hand and pointed to the Bhutias. They now bowed so low that I could see bald patches on the backs of two heads. I had never seen such hairy backs. Their bodies were trembling. I wanted to let them feel the iron to remind them that I am the khansaman. But I had more important things to do. I gave the iron rod back to the kushob, fetched the museum and drew the handkerchief for him – remarkably detailed despite only a few lines. I indicated to him that it was made of cloth, and I was looking for it. He addressed some questions to the Bhutias. They replied in high-pitched voices. The three men had become quivering sacks of flesh. A Hunia went behind the tent and returned with the handkerchief dangling from the tip of his sword. It was so dirty that one could not see the roses on it any more. The Bhutias had cleaned themselves with it. The handkerchief stank like a latrine in Blacktown. The smell of Father Fuchs was forever extinguished.

I turned to the kushob and asked for the iron rod.

I HAVE BID farewell to Father Fuchs's handkerchief with a big fire. The Bhutias obediently brought me, their khansaman, as much firewood as I asked for, and the flames danced festively. I know that objects are not reborn, but this handkerchief is more than a mere object. It is an important part of Father Fuchs. Maybe he will return one day in a different form. The least I can do is ensure that his red roses continue to bloom. They now decorate the skin of the Bhutias.

ADOLPH AND THE others arrived at the camp in the evening. The Schlagintweit jumped down from his horse and called out to me that their expedition had been perilous, and they had almost not made it back.

I did not react, and so he came closer.

When he saw me, the bruises and scratches and the dried blood, he stopped and asked: What the devil happened?

I did not say anything.

He demanded an explanation.

But I was as formidable as Robert in my silence. I kept sitting at the fire, a little too close, and breathed in its warmth.

Adolph learnt much of what had happened from the kushob whose report Mani Singh translated. Then the Schlagintweit came to me again. He sat down very carefully beside me as if he were moving over a glacier. There was no sign of cheerfulness left on his face. He repeatedly drew a breath as if to say something. But no words came. I was grateful for that. The most beautiful languages do not need words. In order to hear them one must sit quietly together.

7 **August.**

I slept for a long time, for many days. I do not remember how I got from the camp to Mangnang. Mani Singh says, Adolph did not leave my side the entire time. The Schlagintweit insisted on carrying me on his horse. He fed me soup, washed me and treated my wounds. In long negotiations with the Hunias he persuaded them to allow us to enter Mangnang. He claims he wants to study the place. But it is only so that I can recover, says Mani Singh.

I should be furious with the Schlagintweit for not returning sooner, but I am only happy that he is here. He kept his word. (If one disregards the three Bhutias whom he chased away with a gunshot into the sky and left behind in the wilderness.)

I wish Adolph would ask me once again if I trust him.

I would like to know what my reply would be.

Since our arrival in Mangnang I feel so remarkably well again that I was able to accompany the Schlagintweit when he went to see a temple. He carried me on his shoulders. The side walls held books, music instruments and these strange prayer machines. An aged lama was turning an especially large one. However, it could also be said that the machine was turning him.

A saffron-coloured light fell through a square hole in the roof. Adolph stepped into this pillar of light and looked up into the sky. I followed his gaze. A cloud above us had taken on the shape of a mango. The last time I tasted a mango was so long ago. So many months and miles separate me from Mazagaon. I seldom think of Bombay now; I do not even know if I want to go back there. Father Fuchs and Hormazd and Smitaben are no longer there. Can Bombay be my home without them?

Remarkable Object No. 54

THE HIGHEST PLACE IN THE WORLD

I am the highest point of the world.

Everyone else is below me.

Naturally, I am not there any more, because no one can write so far at the top; most people cannot even walk or breathe. But I only have to close my eyes, and I am there on the Abi Gamin again on Adolph's shoulders where I set a record.

22,600 feet.

The last foot is the difference between Adolph's head and mine. One of the smallest Indians has reached the hitherto highest points in the world.

We attempted the Abi Gamin on our return journey from Tibet. While climbing, Adolph insisted on carrying me almost the entire time. Mani Singh took over only rarely when the Schlagintweit stopped for a longish interval to gather his strength and suck in air, and so could not object if the Sikh placed me on his own shoulders. Adolph carried me like Jesus carried the cross. I am, of course, lighter, more manageable, and no Roman was forcing him, but he did it with a similar devotion. He had to do it. I think it was his way of apologizing for having left me alone with the devious Bhutias.

It was fine with me. Otherwise, I would have been thwarted by the Abi Gamin like so many others in the train. The pain hammered away at our heads with each step that we took. Blood ran from everyone's nose, for some it ran out of the ears, and one had blood running from his eyes. Only half of the fourteen people managed to reach the highest point. Adolph called the Abi Gamin a nasty mountain and tried to grin but only managed a smile. Robert told Adolph that he had never seen him so exhausted. He was criticizing me for being on his brother's shoulders. When we were at 22,259 feet according to Adolph, a raging north wind set in, and the brothers decided not to venture to the peak. Robert's look said that the wind, too, was my fault. But I did not let him spoil this grand moment for me. There was hardly any view. Clouds and fog closed in on us; it was almost fifty degrees below zero, our eyes hurt from the snow powder, and yet, I had seldom experienced something so remarkable.

A narrow line in the snow marked our path here to the top. Adolph stood at the end of this path. His strength pushed me into the sky.

No one has ever been where we were.

Remarkable Object No. 55

THE SUDDEN WARMTH OF BADRINATH

We are finally on Indian territory. Therefore, on Vicky-territory. In Badrinath Abdullah and Harkishen joined the train again. The Brahmin still makes me read to him from the museum. According to me he has made no progress in German, even though he claims each time that he has already heard one or the other passage. He also says that about passages that I wrote in his absence.

I know now that he is the other traitor. On the morning after he returned to the train my message for Eleazar left my right boot again.

I am keeping this discovery to myself for now. It might come in useful at some point in time.

In Badrinath Adolph took me to the thermal spring. Other pilgrims, men and women, had trouble removing the wet clothes, with which they had covered themselves, from under their dry clothes. Adolph was not ashamed of his nudity. His skin is whiter than ivory. He wanted to help me undress. I refused and kept my kurta on. But I allowed myself to be carried on his shoulders through the hot water spring. It was almost like swimming. Father Fuchs would have been happy.

Adolph asked me if I would go with him to Tibet again; he had not completed his research there. I was silent because I never want to go there again. And also, because I do not want him to go. After we had waded for a while in silence through the steaming water, he promised not to leave me alone this time. That filled me with a sudden warmth. I had last felt that warmth when Father Fuchs let me lead him through the museum.

Remarkable Objects
Nos. 56 & 57 & 58

FALSE THEORIES
LAUGHING ON ADOLPH'S SHOULDERS
HARKISHEN

The greatest scientist of the world is wrong. While I am writing this, Humboldt's hair trembles with chagrin. (I keep it safe between the pages of the museum.) Adolph is measuring the invisible dimensions of earth's magnetism: the horizontal and vertical intensity, the magnetic declination and inclination; but his instruments are not telling him what he wants to confirm. Humboldt's theory is wrong. The intensity does not decrease with altitude. Despite this, Adolph continues with his measurements. At first, I thought: because his belief in his second father is so strong. But no. He says that the importance of a new point for a general theory is greater the further away it is from the others that are in our possession. These are not his words; they belong to a certain Gauss who, according to Adolph, is also a great scientist of our times. If Gauss is right, then it is not only the points which the Schlagintweits collect that are of great importance, but also my points.

It is true that I do not possess anything in Bombay. But if one assumes that my life there is in my possession because it only belongs to me and to no one else, then the Himalayas are conceivably far removed from it.

I went to Tibet a second time. Adolph is my palki. Maybe it was a stupid idea to accompany him. A part of me wishes that he breaks his promise so that I have a reason not to trust him.

But what if he keeps his promise?

Robert, Mr Monteiro and the coolies did not come with us. From the time we reached the border, everyone in the train, which consists only of Mani Singh, Abdullah and Harkishen, is dressed like a spy. Robert had not wanted the Brahmin to accompany us because he is a Hindu and Hindus are not welcome there. But once again Adolph did not listen to his little brother.

I know why. Even if he does not say it. Adolph hopes that Harkishen can cure me. Every time we stop to rest, he calls the doctor and tells him to examine me. The doctor does as he is told, palpates my legs, and asks me if I feel this or that. I say yes and yes and yes. Harkishen does not know why my legs, which seem to have sensation in them, do not want to carry me any more. That makes Adolph think. With the same conviction with which he had spoken about climbing the Abi Gamin, he announces that I will soon recover. If my silence speaks louder than words, or if I avoid looking at him, he repeats his words as if that would make them true. In the beginning I had to ask him to pick me up, but now I do not even need to stretch out my arms. He sees when I no longer want to be where I am and lifts me each time onto his shoulders without the slightest objection. Although I can see further from Mani Singh's shoulders, I prefer the Schlagintweit to my friend. When Adolph carries me, the feeling of being a burden on another's body is not as bad. The Schlagintweit holds my legs in a way that seems to make them adhere to his body. Jerks are absorbed before they reach me. Sometimes it also seems as if I were determining his movements. If the East India Company were to only know that the leader of their costly expedition is being directed by a cripple from Bombay!

A laughing cripple. In Tibet there is less air to breathe than in India. And on Adolph's shoulders the air is even thinner. And yet we use most of it to laugh.

Mani Singh admonishes us to use the air as sparingly as water in a desert, and Harkishen says that the arrogance of laughing wanderers in the Himalayas is punished by the gods with avalanches. But Adolph says he prefers to die laughing than in silence.

I, too.

The Schlagintweit tells me how when he and Hermann were children, they once baked a cake filled with crisp bees and gave it to their art teacher, Dillis, and how the latter devoured three slices one after the other. How they stole their neighbour Rosa Salz's underwear and dressed their cat in it. How they fell from the roof and Hermann broke his left arm while Adolph broke his right one, so that they now had to help each other to get dressed, to eat, to wash and to beat up the other.

The stories are not substantially different from those he had told me in South India when I had considered him my brother. They are not remarkable.

What is remarkable is what they do to us.

If the greatest scientist of the world can be wrong, then so can I. My theory was wrong. Adolph's mirror is not particularly large. In fact, of all the Schlagintweits, he has the smallest mirror. He mostly sees Hermann in it and occasionally Robert. Both appear more often in his stories than he himself does. He misses his brothers, especially Hermann, who he believes is dead. I still cannot help him in this regard. But I can laugh with him. When we laugh together, it almost feels as if I had been there with them; with each laugh I weave myself into his past. It has not even been a year since we met, but it seems to me as if I have known him much longer than that. Our laughter bursts out, but actually it permeates deep into me and often I cannot determine which laughter is his and which is mine.

I want to continue sharing this new language with him.

Late at night or at the crack of dawn, when everyone is sleeping, I see what my legs can do. I crawl to a rock or a tree, pull myself up and stand. And stand. And stand. My legs cannot take me anywhere, at least not yet, but they support me as long as I stay in the same place. If the strength in my legs continues to increase, Adolph will be right after all. I will recover. That should cheer me up, but instead it makes me sad. As soon as Adolph finds out that my legs are working again, he will not carry me any more and feed our laughter with his stories.

Does Harkishen suspect something?

Each time he examines me, he pinches my skin more tightly. I do not take it amiss. Because of me he has to travel through a country where he is not welcome. His wish-fulfillers were not allowed to accompany him. Without them he is quieter, more acquiescent and, if I am not mistaken, a few centimetres shorter.

When I read to him now, he occasionally repeats individual words: *Dattelpalme*? *Fühlen*? *Bräunlich*? *Toga Virilis*? *Totenwärter*? *Holistisch*?

I am happy to explain them to him. Harkishen is the first Indian to enter my museum. It has grown considerably. Father Fuchs would be proud of me.

Unfortunately, Harkishen does not seem to like the museum. When I explain a word to him, he says almost every time: I knew that. The further we venture into the museum, the less he lets me finish speaking. By now he has started correcting me; he even contradicts me. He claims a *Schwarm* is a feeling and *rasch* a colour and *Husten* a word for the time of the year in which most weddings take place.

In the beginning, I did not allow this to deter me. On the evening of 9 September, when we had set up camp on the south face of the Phoko-La Pass, he insisted that a *Taschentuch* was a German insult. I could not tolerate it any more and suggested he ask Adolph.

To which he replied immediately, almost as if he had been waiting for this opportunity, that I was obviously not sure about it myself.

Of course, I am, I said.

Yes, he said derisively, but you need the gora's help.

I reminded Harkishen that I am a translator.

He laughed and added: For the goras! You only say what they want to hear. You are more at home in their language than in yours!

Rage made him spit the words out.

I will not read to you any more, I said.

You will never be healed, he said. Even if you can walk again, you will remain a cripple.

I wanted to know what he meant, but instead of asking him I let myself be infected by his anger and called him a traitor.

What do you mean by that? he asked.

You know what I mean, I said.

He avoided looking at me and touched his tika.

Before either of us could say anything else, Mani Singh came to fetch me to help him look for water and wood. It was a long time before we returned to the camp. The Sikh was carrying me on his shoulders, and he had to be careful. The darkness hid steep chasms. And even though I could not help him much, I was looking for something. I needed an answer for Harkishen. And for myself.

I found it at the edge of a scree slope. I will give him the answer tomorrow. I will tell him: You are wrong. Although I am at home in many languages, that does not mean I could ever forget which is my real home.

Abdullah woke me up. The light was hazy, as if we were looking through a thick veil. We were alone in the camp. I asked where Adolph and Mani Singh and Harkishen were. The draughtsman was silent.

He left me alone, I thought.

I called out to Adolph.

Abdullah placed a wrinkled forefinger on his lips.

I called out to Adolph again.

This time he replied. I was relieved to hear my name. The Schlagintweit approached slowly. His steps were heavier than when he carries me. I looked at him the way I do when I want to be lifted up.

But Adolph sat down beside me. He seemed tired.

Something has happened, he said and took my hand.

He has never held my hand.

Should I show him, Sir? Abdullah asked.

No, said Adolph.

I asked what they were talking about.

Sir, it is sometimes better if one sees it, said Abdullah. Not as bad as imagining it.

He is just a boy, said Adolph.

I refrained from saying: But what about the Toga Virilis? I sensed it was not the moment for that.

Abdullah looked at Adolph.

Sir, what should we do?

Adolph was still holding my hand.

The unfortunate man, he said.

Who? I asked.

Adolph advised me against seeing him. Some images, he said, can never be forgotten. I wish I had listened to him.

He lay on the bank of a half-frozen stream. Blood had seeped through the snow around him and congealed into a red puddle. His bones impaled his body, only his face seemed untouched. He looked surprised. Because he had not seen death coming? Or because he had imagined it would be different? Mani Singh placed a cloth over Harkishen and murmured a prayer. Adolph pressed me to him, or perhaps he pressed himself to me. Abdullah did not display any emotion. The water in the stream flowed quickly as if to get away from this place. Abdullah says the Brahmin must have plunged into the depths in the dark.

Mani Singh says Harkishen grew up in the Himalayas. How could he have been so careless?

Adolph says perhaps he was not himself tonight.

And I do not say how close the Schlagintweit is to the truth.

If Harkishen had been himself, the Himalayas would have spared him. But I showed him who he also was, namely a traitor.

That did something to him. He wanted to run away from himself, and he fled so far that he can never come back.

I did not mean for that to happen.

Before we continued on our journey, I made Mani Singh carry me to him again. I opened the museum to a random page and read to him a last time. I did not get very far for I was crying too much. I told him how sorry I am. But I think he could not hear me.

Remarkable Object No. 59

AN OMINOUS PACKAGE

After Harkishen's accident this part of our journey came to an end. Although we continued to explore Tibet for another month, seeing yak-herds, golden monasteries, large families of snow-covered mountains, crossing singing iron bridges, the shared journey between Adolph and me was over.

I mourn that. And I ask myself: If our laughter had not died with Harkishen, where would it have carried us? To a place no one has been before?

He will never be my brother, yes, I understand that. But I imagine that maybe we would have discovered that he could have been something much better.

As things were, however, Harkishen's image accompanied us. I saw it in quiet moments, in every abyss and at nights when I could not see anything else. Whenever an avalanche thundered in the distance, I heard him call my name.

Because I had lost my link with Eleazar I did not write any more messages and tried not to think about what that meant for Smitaben. But I was never good at not thinking about something. On our long, silent paths she died many deaths in my head. And I was responsible for each one of them.

Then, when we had left Tibet behind us and had met up with Robert's train on 21 October in Mussoorie, I found a package in my boot the very next morning. It was no bigger than a small book, but it was heavier. When I shook it, something rustled inside.

A message had been attached to it:

Guard this with your life. Do not open it under any circumstances. Someone will come for it.

Do not hold off too long with your next report.

I knew the handwriting. Once it had pretended to be Hormazd's and had lured me to see his end.

THE CORNERS OF the package jab me. I hide it in my pocket or under my sheet; I have to spend each day and each night with it. The Schlagintweits should not discover it. I want to know what is in it, but I also do not want to know.

One thing is certain: this package is dangerous. Just like the person who brought it to me. I should have exposed him long ago.

Harkishen was always loyal to the train, more faithful than most of us. Adolph and Robert talked about Harkishen for a long time. That is how I discovered that Harkishen had another name, an alias: Explorer No. 9. He worked as a Native Surveyor for the Schlagintweits. That he called them goras and often waxed lyrical about Bharat was part of his cover. He made maps and took measurements for the Schlagintweits in those regions that were difficult for white men to access. The Schlagintweits say that Harkishen risked his life for science once too often.

When I called the Brahmin a traitor, it must have hit him very hard; so hard that he fell.

I owe it to him to find the real traitor. If I had exposed him earlier, Harkishen would still be alive. My legs have not only paralysed my body, but also my mind. I have looked too long into my mirror, in love with my suffering and drunk on the laughter on Adolph's shoulders.

But that ends now.

PART V

Central India 1855–56

Remarkable Object No. 60

THE MOST LIKELY TRAITOR

Every evening Adolph says good night to me. He has not failed to do so even once since our second Tibet journey. Sometimes, while doing so, he taps me on the shoulder or quickly pulls my nose or nods to me. He never touches my legs.

I believe he needs this ritual. His 'Good Night' is also directed at himself. Adolph says he often dreams of Harkishen. He does not want to tell me what happens in these dreams. But he does not need to tell me. I can imagine it. Although the Brahmin does not appear in my dreams, I continue to see his image.

Father Fuchs also often whispered a Good Night to me on his last round in the evenings. At that time, I thought it was meant for me alone. Now I am no longer sure about it. Perhaps he directed it at himself as well, perhaps he murmured it again and again when he lay in the khana and struggled with his cough.

In the Glass House, however, Father Fuchs's Good Night was also a signal for the Others that they could now pounce on me because I was at their mercy for the duration of the night. Adolph's Good Night is exclusively a signal for him and me. As soon as he retires and the camp settles down for the night, my night begins.

I learn how to walk. I can already take seven steps without falling. In the process the cockroaches march up to my hips and penetrate my lower back. Every step takes a lot of strength, as if I were battling against Nanda Devi's stormy winds. My legs are as heavy as those of an elephant. I raise one, stretch the other and press it into the ground as if to entrench it. Then my body follows the raised leg and swooshes ahead so eagerly that the entrenched leg is carried along. Now comes the most difficult part. I lean back a little so that I do not fall forward, but not too much because otherwise I would fall backwards; I control the momentum and land with one foot beside the other. I stand and gasp for breath, remain standing and smile, but not too proudly because that destroys my balance, and my smile kisses the dust. For each step I need as long as it takes to write the following sentence: I took a step.

I TOOK THE first step the day I received the package. I immediately wanted to call Adolph and tell him about it. But something kept me from doing it. Instead, I tried to take a second step.

Till now no one in the train knows that I am again teaching my legs their language. I take care to ensure that no one sees me learning.

Everyone in the train has secrets. And it seems fitting that my secret is being able to walk although everyone thinks I cannot. After all, it is only a matter of time before one has to run away from something or someone. Blacktown has taught me this.

Robert is the only one who has not failed to notice the change in my body.

Are your legs better? he asked me when we were passing through a gorge and Mani Singh was carrying me.

I pretended I had not heard him.

Mani Singh did not pretend.

What do you mean, Sir? he asked.

The boy is sitting differently, more upright.

Is he now? asked Mani Singh.

I can now sit better, I said.

The Sikh laughed.

Robert did not. He only looked at me.

I would prefer if he would direct his rigorous look at more scientific objects. My secret should remain a secret.

But there is another reason why my nights are long. I lie in wait for the traitor.

As soon as I leave a message in my boot, I lie down and wait. I am patient, attentive and quiet. Only, to pretend one is sleeping without actually falling asleep proves to be more difficult than taking seven steps. I must become better at staying awake. Even if I close my eyes briefly, the night has suddenly disappeared and, with it, my message.

Apparently, Abdullah's talent is not limited only to drawing.

I consulted the museum, and it showed me who was part of the train at which point. Since I can exclude Harkishen, the draughtsman is the most likely traitor.

A soldier has the necessary contacts to send messages around the country. In Tibet, he did not have these contacts and he was also separated from me most of the time, which is why the messages did not leave my boot.

Furthermore, Abdullah is a master at remaining inconspicuous. When I observe him, my gaze always slides away. He is an unmanageable object, extraordinary in his ordinary way of walking, talking, combing his beard, scratching his neck, praying, spitting, listening, pissing, bathing, and acknowledging the Schlagintweits' orders with a nod.

The only things extraordinary about him are his drawings. If pictures depict the truth, then Abdullah's drawings should reveal something about him. I keep him company while he draws. But not too often, so as not to make him suspicious. His hand dances over the paper like Adolph's does. I cannot learn any significant truths from Abdullah and his drawings. As opposed to the Schlagintweit, however, the act of drawing does not appear to engender any feelings in him. He sketches a view of the valley or fading clouds or the haziness of sand-filled air without any expression, as if he were staring into emptiness.

Does he guess that I suspect him?

I have to penetrate deeper into him. Fortunately, the most popular man in all of Bombay showed me how that can be done.

WHERE ARE YOU from? I asked Abdullah.

From Pushpapura, he said.

I waited to see whether he would add any more details.

Abdullah only continued to draw.

Do you miss Pushpapura? I asked.

What? he said.

Your hometown.

Abdullah paused for a moment.

No, he said.

Why not?

You ask a lot of questions, he said.

I told him about the museum and that he is a part of it.

He said: I don't want to be a part of your book.

Why not?

Don't make me a part of your book.

Fine, I won't put you in my book.

Do I have your word of honour?

I gave it to him.[29]

He nodded and continued drawing.

I decided it was not the day to penetrate further and started to crawl away.

That is when Abdullah said: I know who has sent you.

I am here of my own free will.

It was the Sikh, am I right?

---

29 It is fine to lie to a traitor. It is possibly even honourable.

I looked towards Mani Singh who was talking to Robert, and he raised a hand in greeting.

I know you are close to one another, Abdullah said, but if I were you, I would not trust him.

Why?

Abdullah finally put his pencil down and turned to me. His eyes shone like the leaves of a banyan tree when the sun shines on them. I could clearly see that they were burning with a strong emotion.

There is only one thing worse than an Angrez, he said.

And what would that be?

Naturally, a Sikh!

ONE OF THE most famous Sikhs aroused this emotion in Abdullah: Maharaja Ranjit Singh,[30] the lion of Punjab. When he conquered Pushpapura, he had many mosques in the city destroyed, including the one where Abdullah offered prayers every day at his father's side. During the Friday prayers the Sikhs closed the doors of the mosque and set it on fire. Before long, the flames surrounded the men. Many of them called out for Allah's help. Abdullah's father did not want to depend on him alone. He carried his son into the washroom and ordered him to climb into the large stone basin that was filled with clean water. Abdullah had never defied his father (except once, secretly, after the latter had forbidden him to make images of people in his drawings). But this time he refused. He pulled at his father and begged him to dive with him into the water that would save them. However, the basin was too small for a grown man. Although Abdullah was only nine years old, he could see that; he had a talent for precisely estimating the size, the volume and the dimensions of things. And he could guess what would happen if his father did not come with him. The father did not allow himself to be deterred. He grabbed his son and embraced him as no father has ever embraced

30 No relative of Mani Singh.

a son. In that one moment he wanted to give him all the embraces that he would never be able to give him in the coming years. Then he pushed him into the basin. Abdullah resisted, but his father was stronger, and he held Abdullah's body down in the water. Even when the flames enveloped him, he did not give up. Abdullah stretched out his arms to him. His father did not scream; the fire had not yet got a firm grip on him. Abdullah reached out for his father, but the latter pushed him for a last time under water and then fell backwards into the arms of the fire. Abdullah wanted to follow him, but he could not see his father anywhere. The dense smoke made it difficult for him to see, and soon afterwards he became unconscious.

When he regained consciousness, he was a boy without a father. His hands were bandaged. But even after the wounds had healed, he had no feeling in his hands. He could bend his fingers, clench his hands into fists and press them flat on the prayer mat. But he could barely feel anything with them. Months passed, before he could hold a pencil, years before he could load, aim and shoot a gun.

When he had mastered this to some extent, he signed on as a sepahi with the Vickys. He did not particularly like the new rulers of Pushpapura; they prayed to another god, they wore uniforms the colour of deadly flames and they thought Hindi and Urdu were the same language. In fact, they forced their barbaric language onto everyone who wished to speak with them. Nevertheless, Abdullah was grateful to them. They had driven the Sikhs out of Pushpapura and had repaired some mosques. By joining the army Abdullah hoped to carry on the war against the Sikhs. But his superiors soon discovered that his talent lay in drawing rather than in shooting. They replaced his Brown Bess with a pencil and trained him as a draughtsman. Abdullah would have preferred to shoot down the Sikhs, but it was not difficult to convince him. Till today, drawing is the only activity which makes his hands feel again. But he does not feel the pencil, not even the paper. No, he feels what he felt last before his hands were burned: his father's touch.

THUS, ABDULLAH BECAME the man with two emotions. He carries the hate in his eyes and the love in his hands.

Why didn't you tell me this earlier? I asked Abdullah.

He said: You didn't ask me.

That is true. I never even asked myself who the draughtsman could be. And now that I have heard one possibility from him, I do not know what to do with it. His story demands that I understand him, that I like him. But I do not let myself be influenced so easily by stories. In order to not be exposed, every likely traitor can reinvent himself.

And not only himself.

He has cast Mani Singh, especially, in a new light. Abdullah claims the Sikh is the traitor who revealed our travel routes to the Nepalis and Tibetans. When Abdullah first said it, I only laughed. When he said it a second time, I crawled away. When he said it for the third, fourth, fifth, sixth, seventh time, I did not pay attention to the groundless accusations; I know that they stem from his two emotions. When he said it for the eighth time, I contradicted him. I did that again the next four or five times. I told him that more than anyone else Mani Singh had looked for the traitor in the train. In fact, when we advanced into Nepal and Tibet, he even suffered under the traitor's doing and, according to me, he is not at all capable of betraying anyone, not even himself. Abdullah replied: That is precisely why Mani Singh is the perfect traitor, because no one considers him to be one. Abdullah went on to describe in detail how Mani Singh eliminated his biggest adversary in the train, Native Doctor Harkishen, in the Himalayas. This story was so … I would like to ask Father Fuchs whether there is a word for something that is false and yet convincing. While listening to the story I did not once feel the need to laugh, to crawl away or to contradict. It was so wrong, so unlike my friend. It would be an understatement to call it a lie. Never, never could Mani Singh have done the things Abdullah accuses him of. The draughtsman should let his hands speak, then there would be more love in what he says, and the drawing would be clearer. His stories strengthen my belief in Mani Singh and in the truth of our friendship. They wipe away every doubt. Yes, every doubt. Mani Singh is the man who saved me from Nanda Devi, and who I saved from Nanda Devi. We are joined together by gratitude and obligation and trust. All of this far outweighs the words of a draughtsman. But I do not tell Abdullah any of this. Who is he that I must explain myself to him! I do not need to defend Mani Singh. Not to Abdullah, not to anyone. Especially not to myself. That would make me think too much about him. The Sikh is a vast object. One has to distance oneself considerably in order to see all of him. But at that distance one cannot see him properly. When I am with him, I am mostly on his shoulders, and from there I see less of him than from every other angle. When he is carrying me, we hardly speak. Till now, I thought that was a good thing, that we do not need to translate our friendship into words in order to live it. I want to think more about that.

But why can I still not determine the colour of his turban?

Remarkable Object No. 61

THE WAY HOME

We have reached Mirath.

Adolph has already wished me (and himself) a good night.

Today I only managed five steps.

Now I am lying in wait again. In the museum I can keep sleep at bay. As long as I am writing, I do not succumb to tiredness. I only hope my candle does not keep the traitor away.

I hear footsteps approaching.

Everything, really everything is connected! Even Alexander von Humboldt would have been surprised to know *how* holistic the world is.

I should explain that.

When I heard the footsteps at night, I put out the candle and put the museum aside. I breathed deeply as if I were sleeping and ignored the cockroaches in my legs and back. The footsteps stopped at my boots. I saw dusty black shoes and the rolled-up cuff of white pants. When the owner of the pants turned in my direction, I closed my eyes. I heard him searching through my boots. It lasted a long time. Had he picked up the wrong boot? He breathed too loudly for a spy. I risked another look. The traitor's hand was in my boot. His back was turned to me, and he was wearing a sepahi's tunic. His hand seemed to be stuck. He grunted, which was most unlike a spy. He yanked his hand out and the boot fell to the ground near my head. I need not have made such an effort to stay awake; the traitor would have woken me up. He was now crawling on all fours, searching and breathing heavily.

That is when it struck me: I knew this breathing. Earlier, it used to reverberate under the fig tree in the Glass House.

Devinder? I said.

He picked himself up, turned around to go, stopped, turned back to me, and pointed a knobbly forefinger at me.

That is not my name, he said.

Of course, it is, I said.

His arm came down.

This man was slimmer around the hips and broader around the shoulders than Devinder and, most notably, was much more shaven. Neatly cut whiskers adorned his face. The hair on his head was so short that it could hardly be seen under his long and ridiculous hat.

And yet, this man was Devinder. I would never forget this tired-looking face!

What are you doing here, Devinder?

He moved quickly, which was unusual for him, and pressed both hands on my mouth.

Who are you? he asked. How do you know my name?

I wanted to reply, but his hands on my mouth did not allow me to speak. I pointed to them.

Don't call for help, he said.

I shook my head.

Does that mean you will not call? he asked.

I said I would not call.

Devinder's hands translated my words into muffled sounds.

I cannot let go if you call, he said.

By now I was sure that the sepahi was Devinder.

I bit his fingers.

He pulled his hands away and looked at me reproachfully.

It is I, I said, Bartholomew!

His expression changed as beautifully and slowly as a flower blossoming. From annoyance to incomprehension, to hesitation, to a glimmer of recognition, to more recognition, to recognition, to delight.

Devinder took me in his arms and hugged my roughly. He smelt strongly of salt and sweat.

I had not realized how much I had missed his hugs.

Why didn't you say at once that it is you? he asked.

I looked at his uniform, the intense red, the severe white lines and the shiny buttons. The uniform looked a little too big for him, but I had never seen him so well-groomed. He was no longer the Devinder who lives with his family in one room.

Why aren't you in Bombay? I asked him.

Devinder avoided my eyes.

He said: I am on the way to Bombay.

DEVINDER TOLD ME that he had lost his way. He added: a little. After the Schlagintweits had dismissed him from their service over a year ago in South India, he had set out for Bombay on foot. Sometimes he woke up in the morning and did not know which direction he had come from and in which direction he had wanted to go. After a few days he finally reached a place which looked familiar.

It was the place where the Schlagintweits had dismissed him. He stayed there for a while. If he could not find the right way, he hoped that the right way would perhaps come to him. But Devinder did not remember. What he remembered was the fragrance of the fig tree in the Glass House. How he missed it! And naturally also his family, he said. But the memory of the fig tree was so much stronger. (He also spent more hours there.) The longing for it, says Devinder, or too much time without food and scarcely any water, I say, made him sleep for longer periods of time. If he did not find the way back to Bombay while awake, he told himself, then at least he would in his dreams. The more he slept, the more tired he felt. Who knows what would have happened if a friendly man had not woken him up and brought him back into a state of wakefulness with the help of idlis and coconut water?

The man promised Devinder that he would get him back to Bombay. In return, he only asked for time. That made Devinder happy. He is poor in every respect, but time is something he possesses in large quantities; if he were able to fill his time in Battliwala's bottles and sell it, he would be richer than Jeejeebhoy.

Devinder agreed, and the pact was sealed. A day became a week, a week became a month, a month became half a year, and Devinder became a sepahi. Ever since the man, an Indian soldier in the army of the Vickys, had enrolled him in military service, they had not encountered each other again. But Devinder waited patiently for the man as he had been told to do. Devinder is more faithful than a dutiful dog. He did not find it difficult to wait. A little time did not seem to be a high price for the way to Bombay.

Moreover, he felt more at home in the army than in the Glass House. Most of the soldiers did not appear to act or think any faster than he did. His regiment consisted largely of Punjabis who came from the same region as he did. They took him in like a brother, ate parathas with dal every day and taught him how to shoot and how to march. Devinder said he learnt quickly. So, at least he was not slow to learn.

I was always a good gardener, he said to me, but you should see me as a soldier!

I remembered his desolate garden, but I kept quiet so as not to interrupt his flow of words. Like earlier, he had to search so long for some words as if they had to be invented first.

After Devinder had served in the army for some time, the friendly fellow came back. He promised Devinder that he would take him home soon. It would only be a little longer.

How long ago was that? I asked Devinder.

He thought about it.

Then he said: Not very long.

A week? I asked.

A few months, he said.

I buried my face in my hands. Father Fuchs would have wanted me to help Devinder.

You don't have to rely on his help, I told Devinder. I can tell you the way to Bombay. And I am not the only one who can do that. Why didn't you ask someone else all this time?

I promised him I would wait, said Devinder.

How do you know that he will keep his promise?

Devinder was silent for a moment.

I don't know, he said.

But? I said.

But, he said, he will keep it.

You cannot depend on that, I said.

I can, Devinder said, this time remarkably quickly. He is my friend.

A friend does not keep you waiting so long, I said.

It will be worth it, Devinder said. Afterwards everything will be better.

What do you mean by *afterwards*?

I am not allowed to tell anyone.

What are you not allowed to tell?

I am not allowed to say that ...

Devinder paused and smiled.

Bartholomew, he said, I am not the dumb Punjabi you think I am.

Devinder ...

I am a valuable ally!

For whom? I asked.

Devinder rolled his eyes as if he had already explained it all to me.

For us!

I don't understand, I said.

India, he said.

At that moment he saw the package that was jutting out from under my blanket and he took it. He ran his hand gently over it as if he were holding one of his children in his arms.

Thank you, Bartholomew, for keeping it safe.

Now I understood.

Your friend, I said. His name is Eleazar, right?

Devinder lifted his head. He pressed his lips tightly together and stared past me. He could just as well have said yes.

What is in the package? Why did Eleazar want me to bring it to Mirath?

Devinder hid the package silently in his tunic.

Don't look so dejected, he said. We will soon be free, then we can all go home.

For the rest of the night, he left me alone. I could not sleep. Maybe I will never sleep again. It pained me to see what Eleazar had made of Devinder. If he could mould even the rough Punjabi, what would the Bania then make of me?

Will I also soon call the traitor a friend?

On the following day, Devinder showed me the military cantonment in Mirath. When he came to fetch me and told me to follow him, I asked him about Smitaben. Whether he knew how she was. He shook his head and said his friend had never mentioned her name. I believe him. Devinder is as incapable of telling lies as he is of making plants grow. I raised myself awkwardly into a standing position. Devinder observed me. His eyes were fixed on my legs.

I am not as fast as I used to be, I said.

That is not a problem, he said.

Apart from this he said nothing. He lifted me onto his back as if he had done it often, and we started out. He said as little about my legs as he did about the previous night. We walked around and were simply Devinder and Bartholomew, two old friends.

The barracks of the Vickys are cleaner than some of the rest-houses on our journey. There is even a barrack for white women. They belong to the soldiers from Europe. Devinder says that because of them the firangi drink less. He laughs about it. He would never let his wife stop him from drinking!

Other, not so clean buildings house the servants. They help the firangi against the weather. The higher the temperatures rise, the less the firangi move. Their servants sprinkle water on the dusty ground, sew uniforms, polish boots and blink in the heat, as if by doing so they could produce a cooling breeze. The sight of them makes Devinder snarl. He says, every firangi in Mirath has power over many bodies, and many Indians did not have control even over their own hands.

The sepahis are accommodated in even less clean mud huts. Devinder says he would like to be in a large barrack where the hot air would not make his blood boil. But then, he would have to share the space with lower castes or, even worse, with Muslims. In that case, he prefers that his blood boils.

DEVINDER WAS ALLOWED to join us at lunch. I sat between him and Adolph who was talking about a theatrical performance he had seen the previous evening in which only officers of the Vickys had acted. Despite this, according to Adolph, the performance could be compared with those he had seen in London.

With one exception, he said. I missed the youthful element.

I translated for Devinder. He wanted to know what a youthful element is.

I asked the Schlagintweit.

With both his forefingers Adolph drew a figure in the air.

Devinder laughed. So did Adolph.

I did not understand what they found so funny. But I was too proud to ask. Never before has the Punjabi understood something more quickly than I have. And now he had even understood one of Adolph's drawings more quickly!

Robert, who sat opposite us, said: He means women.

Robert looked at me and, if I am not mistaken, his look said that at this moment he did not think very highly of his brother. Strangely enough, this made me feel closer to Robert. Devinder and Adolph communicated in a language that I do not know, at least not yet. But Robert and I communicated in the language of the youngest, the smallest. The language of those who have come later and who always have to make a greater effort than the others.

In the evening, I sat with Devinder in front of his mud hut. The last rays of the sun lent the sand a red shimmer. We did not talk. Devinder had never been one to talk much, and I was silent because in this silence I hoped to find the old Devinder who gathers hope in the shade of the fig tree (or at least of the mud hut).

Abdullah approached and reminded me that we would be leaving for Agra early the next morning. He and Devinder exchanged a military greeting before the draughtsman left. I did not discover any signs that there was anything more than a military link between them.

Is he an ally? I asked Devinder.

He is a Muslim, he said.

Is that a yes or a no?

Ah, Bartholomew!

I straightened up and made myself as big as I could while sitting. Which was fairly small.

You should come with us, I said. Don't you want to go home?

Devinder did not reply.

I will show you the way to Bombay, I said. You could be there in a month.

The Punjabi stood up and carried me into his mud hut. He made sure that no one was watching us, then he moved a cover to the side, dug a hole in the ground with his hands and took the package out of the hole. He handed it to me.

That is my way home, he said. Open it!

I am not supposed to.

The Bartholomew I knew never let himself be deterred by what was allowed and what wasn't.

Who would have thought that the slowest Punjabi would one day have to remind me of the fastest orphan!

I took the package and opened the wooden lid.

In it I saw small containers made of paper, barely bigger than cocoons.

I looked at Devinder.

He nodded invitingly.

I examined one of the containers. It held something granular.

The gunpowder for the new Enfield rifle, Devinder said. With it we will defeat the Angrez.

But there isn't much of it, I said.

There is enough, he said.

Never, Devinder, never!

We will not use it to shoot.

That doesn't make any sense, I said.

You are really not as quick as you used to be, he said. But you will understand soon. *Afterwards*. Come, I will take you to your bed.

Devinder wanted to lift me up.

I resisted.

He killed Hormazd, I said.

I know, said Devinder.

You know it? And you still call him a friend?

Hormazd was a traitor, Devinder said soberly. He deserved it.

I looked at him once again, but I saw nothing of the good-natured gardener in him and so I did not say any final words to him before I crawled away. I had, after all, taken leave of Devinder a long time ago.

Remarkable Objects

Nos. 62 & 63

ADOLPH SCHLAGINTWEIT (3)
JAHANNAM

Adolph breaks his promise. This should not surprise me. I never trusted this German word, *Versprechen.* How can it instil confidence and a feeling of safety, when it also means that one did not say what one wanted to?

When we reached Agra on 21 November, I did not suspect what Adolph would soon reveal to me. We stayed longer in the city than we had originally intended, a little more than a week. I believe it was because Adolph did not want to let go. He held on – to his brother and to Agra, but also, undoubtedly, to me.

Perhaps this is what made these days with the Schlagintweit particularly nice. He spent more time with me than with any of the others in the train. I reaped cold looks from Robert because of this. It did not bother me. Together Adolph and I explored Agra. He shared his strength, his food and his knowledge with me. He praised almost all the lines I drew.

During one of our explorations Robert said that the rough structures of the natives could not be compared with the aesthetics of Muslim architecture.

Abdullah agreed completely. Muslims, he said, were not appreciated enough in India although they were an important part of it.

It was strange to hear Father Fuchs's words from the mouth of a probable traitor.

Adolph looked at Agra as his brother did. But he did not only observe the city. At every opportunity he touched the red sandstone used for most of the buildings here. I noticed that he never washed his hands or even dusted them off afterwards. As if he did not want to lose the connection to this place. He applauded the Vickys for having demolished many of the broken walls between the Taj Mahal and the city.

That way it is easier for the people to find the way to the mausoleum, he said.

Not everyone wishes to be reminded of death, I said.

They should consider themselves lucky, he replied. Death has a beautiful face in Agra.

Robert took many measurements of this face. He noted down: A sandstone wall 960 feet long and 330 feet wide encloses the main area. From the garden surrounding it, a flight of steps 60 feet high leads to the Taj Mahal. Its large dome is 70 feet in diameter and soars 260 feet into the dusty heights.

Inside, with the help of a coolie who could climb buildings better than him, Robert had an ostrich egg hung halfway down on a thin thread from the top of the arched ceiling for his measurements. He looked up to the egg which dangled from the ceiling like a tiny inaccessible fruit and said that most European churches would fit into the space along with their spires. The Schlagintweit also found that the inner and outer walls covered with white marble from Jaipur and decorated with inlay work of ornamental flowers made of semi-precious gemstones as well as with Koran passages in black marble were fairly decently executed. Coming from Robert it was high praise indeed. However, he could not resist pointing out how much more splendid Arab art could be if their faith did not prohibit them from depicting humans and animals.

Adolph saw the Taj Mahal, as already mentioned, with different eyes. He spent a long time inside at the sarcophagi. Something happened there to the light that came in from outside. It appeared precious, as if there were only a limited amount of it. We were in a place where many had been before us and yet I had the feeling that no one like us had ever been there before.

Did you notice that Shah Jahan's sarcophagus is placed higher? he asked me.

But Mumtaz Mahal's is more remarkable, I said.

She was his third wife, said Adolph.

Second wife, I corrected.

Are you sure?

Which one of us is the Indian?

Adolph cuffed me playfully and I had to smile.

I tried to remember what else I had learnt about Agra from Father Fuchs.

When they got engaged, she was fourteen and he was fifteen years old.

Almost your age, he said. I have never asked you if you are engaged.

No, Sir.

Do you love someone?

Adolph looked at me.

Not yet, Sir.

Don't ever let the opportunity slip by Bartholomew.

I will see to it, I said.

Shah Jahan must have loved her a lot, he said. I don't think I have ever loved someone so much.

Did you know, Sir, that Shah Jahan spent his last years as a prisoner of his own son? He was imprisoned in the Agra Fort.

At least with a view of the Taj, Adolph said.

It is said that it was as hot as Jahannam there, I said. For the Muslims that is ...

... hell, Adolph added.

The Schlagintweit was still able to impress me.

At least Shah Jahan always had paradise in sight, he said.

But he knew he would never reach it. That must have made hell even more terrible.

I would always prefer to be in hell if it meant I would be able to see paradise in exchange.

Even if you could never enter it, Sir?

He did not reply. Adolph sat down on the ground beside me. While sitting he was not much taller than me. He massaged his neck while talking, making his words smooth.

I lied to you Bartholomew. And to myself.

The light disappeared. Some of the stone flowers on the walls seemed to close slowly.

Adolph said that in the Himalayas, when we defied Nanda Devi, a boundless sorrow had taken hold of him, a sorrow that had pervaded him to such an extent that he did not know how to escape it except to move forward, further and further through the ice. It had undoubtedly been stupid, he said, to run away from something that he carried within him. He had not expected this; he had assumed that the absence of sorrow all these months was proof that he and his father had never been close. But that was not true. When, in the Himalayas, the fear that Hermann had met with an accident changed into a certainty, the pain at the loss of his father broke out. Adolph could not stop thinking about him. He saw him in his pictures and his dreams; it felt as if he were watching paradise from hell. There were no bad memories. He missed even the dark moments. The worst one was when he told his father that he would not be taking over his medical practice but would be following his great love, geography. Old Schlagintweit had not said much; he had cleared his throat and looked at Adolph's younger brothers (who in the years that followed would also take different paths). But Adolph clearly felt his father's disappointment. It took away something from both of them which never returned. Adolph does not know what to call it. Something intimate, something warm and protective. He had denied his father his greatest wish, and with this his father became less his father. Adolph felt this at that time and still feels it. With Adolph's decision, a part of his father that he carried inside him also died. The worst thing was that his father was not particularly surprised; in fact, as it turned out, he had been expecting it as one does an illness whose symptoms have been apparent for a long time. That hurt Adolph the most: when it became clear to him that his father had foreseen his son's decision but had still hoped that his intuition would prove wrong. His death shortly before their departure, said Adolph, had not been a coincidence. The old Schlagintweit must have arrived at the conclusion that his sons were turning away from him completely, that they did not need or want him, and so he gave up.

Adolph turned his head away. But I had already seen his tears. The Schlagintweit was silent. I did not know if he was expecting something from me. I do not know how to console someone. Normally it is I who is being consoled. I decided to put my hand on his shoulder and to pat him like Father Fuchs sometimes did to me.

Adolph felt soft.

Night had set in, and our voices were the only sounds in the tomb. How many such stories have Shah Jahan and Mumtaz Mahal had to listen to in their sarcophagi?

It must be galling to create so much out of love and people only seeing death in it.

I expressed my condolences to Adolph. I did not say that I had only just understood how weak the Schlagintweit is. His father's disappointment is the worst moment they ever shared? Adolph should consider himself lucky. In India, many fathers express their affection only through disappointment. Or through blows. Compared to most of the Indians I know Adolph's Jahannam is paradise. He had been blessed with an excellent father.

But what is more important: he had one.

After Adolph had composed himself again, he hid his weakness behind a smile and carried me out. The darkness forced him to go slowly. Even the otherwise dazzling white of the Taj Mahal looked dirty. A wind began to blow. Above us the shrill calls of bats. Suddenly, flashes of lightning illuminated the sky. When we had gone a little distance away from the Taj Mahal, Adolph stopped and turned around. The four minarets no longer grew upwards; they were bent, and their tips moved towards a common point above the Taj. Adolph gave a detailed scientific explanation for this phenomenon.[31] He wanted to talk himself back out of the role of a son into that of a scientist. But I could not allow that just yet. First, I had to know why he had told me about himself and his father. When I asked him, he became silent. The flashes of lightning looked like luminous cracks in the night sky. There was no thunder. It was an incomplete storm. Adolph formulated his explanation in general terms and in a long-winded manner. He began each sentence in the same way: one should, one thinks, one realizes, one never knows. But I saw through him. He was talking about himself. Actually, he only wanted to say that he was breaking his promise.

---

31 In one breath he said almost exactly the following: Viewed calmly, such objects, if each of them is vertical, are all parallel, and one sees them as vertical because we unwittingly examine each of these momentarily on its own and then, through abstraction, think of them as being parallel, unless these objects were, by way of exception, high and narrow, and the visual angle were, through close proximity, unusually large, but the reason why in contrast to their usual impression on us vertical objects like these four minarets appear to converge when there is lightning is because the length of time is extremely small and the impression for each of the lines is absolutely simultaneous.

Remarkable Object No. 64

THE WALKING STICK

The walking stick is bigger than I am. Its dark wood is not from India; it belonged to a tree that Adolph calls an ash tree. It is so firm and hard that it could even take Mani Singh's weight. There is an iron tip at the lower end of the walking stick. It would be useful if one wanted to make unfaithful Bhutias obedient again. But it can do more than that. It embeds itself like a claw into the ground which is very useful while hiking through the mountains or while crossing rivers and fields of ice. It not only gives strength to its owner, but it also marks his way. It tells the earth and all who come after him that he was here.

This is perhaps its most important feature, Adolph had said when he handed me the walking stick on 19 December in Sager, on the day he left.

But, Sir, you will need it, I said.

It will be more useful for you than for me, he said, and added in a lowered voice: especially during your nightly undertakings.

I lifted my head in surprise and looked at the Schlagintweit.

It is possible, he said, that I might have sometimes secretly observed you.

The idea that during many nights the Schlagintweit had watched me at each step unleashed an unfamiliar feeling in me, warm and prickly.

I do not know whether I like this feeling.

You know about it? I asked. Why didn't you say something?

You are doing very well, Bartholomew. When we meet again, you will be able to run.

I know why he did not give me an answer. If he had responded to my question, he would have shown me his weakness; he would have had to tell me how much it had meant to him to be able to carry me on his shoulders. It made him feel strong and useful.

I hugged him, or rather, his legs and held him tight just as Smitaben had held me when we had last seen each other. In this way I gave him strength for the coming months. Adolph will be travelling to the south again with Mr Monteiro to complete his investigations. I am of little help to his train since I do not know any of the languages there. But, in the uncertain North-West Provinces, which Robert will explore with Mani Singh and Abdullah, my knowledge of Hindi, Punjabi, Gujarati could make a difference between life and death.

Don't you worry, Sir, I said to Adolph. We will meet again soon.

Adolph laughed raucously and deeply – his most honest laugh. It is also the laugh I like to hear the most. Perhaps because it reminds me of Father Fuchs's cough. He can do nothing about it; it bursts out of him before he can translate it into something that his counterpart would perhaps prefer to hear.

I took the walking stick, leaned on it, and pulled myself up.

When Adolph left with his train, I was standing and following him with my eyes.

Maybe I should have reminded him that he is breaking a promise. But that would have put too great a burden on him. It would have deterred him from his decision to part company with me for several months.

No Remarkable Object

How is it possible that someone who sees so much has so little to say? Robert's silence envelops the train; it envelops all of India. Around him the sky is less blue, each roti is chewy and an hour is as long as a day.

It seems to me as if we have been travelling for months and yet we are still caught in December.

Robert generally walks at the back of the train, often even as the last person, in order to observe everyone and everything and also in order to avoid being dragged into a conversation.

Mani Singh leads the train with me perched on his shoulders. Every time I complain about the uncommunicative Schlagintweit he shakes his green or blue turban. The Sikh is not even afraid of boredom.

Abdullah is generally in the middle of the train so that he can quickly get to wherever he is needed. This man makes no mistakes; not while drawing, and not even otherwise. Without my even noticing, he had stolen the information about the new route of the train that I had left in my boot.

Perhaps I should lurk less and exercise more. Every night I win more steps. With the walking stick I manage at least thirty. I can now move so far away from the camp that I chance upon something surprising in the dark: I miss a Schlagintweit.

Remarkable Objects

Nos. 65 & 66 & 67 & 68 & 69 & 70

EVIL MUSIC
TRAP AND DIORITE
A LETTER TO HIS MAJESTY
HERMANN SCHLAGINTWEIT
THE BLUE OF AN INDIAN RUMAL

In Jabalpur we made the arrangements for the most dangerous part of the journey. We will penetrate deeper into the jungle and the ragged hills of the Gondwana plateau, the home of Nitu from Calcutta. Robert calls it an unhealthy area. Many Indian rivers originate there. Every year Hindus make a pilgrimage to the holiest ones.

But not all of them return, Mani Singh told me. Some are ripped apart by tigers. But even more become victims of fevers and epidemics. Most of them, however, are killed by thugs. The Vickys are doing their best to eradicate these gangs. They are bad for trade. Thug Behram, one of their leaders, has supposedly murdered more than 125 people. It is said that the thugs consist of lower-caste Hindus who are commanded by Muslims. It is all the more astounding,

Mani Singh says, that they all worship Kali. When Abdullah heard that, he clicked his tongue. There is only one god, he said. Mani Singh continued: Not for the Muslims among the thugs. Legend has it that Kali once fought against the demon Raktabija. Although the goddess fought relentlessly, every drop of Raktabija's blood gave birth to another demon. Kali was losing strength, becoming tired. So, she created two men from her sweat and gave each of them a rumal: at first glance a nondescript cummerbund twisted into a strong belt. Kali told the men to strangle all the demons with it. Thus, Kali defeated Raktabija. Then she made it the life's work of these men to pass on the rumals from one generation to the next and to destroy every man who is not one of them.

An encounter with thugs is not improbable on a journey through the Gondwana plateau. They pretend to be your friends, accompany you for a while, share their campfire and many laughs with you. If you are a woman, a fakir, a travelling musician, a leper or simply a European, you can laugh with them in a carefree manner. They will not harm you; their tradition forbids it. Other than that, you have to be careful because they are only waiting for a favourable moment. As soon as this moment arrives, they pull out their rumal. Some thugs sew a coin into it. The rumal is looped around your neck in such a way that the coin is pressing directly on your larynx. This stops air from going in and any cries for help from coming out. It is over quickly. The thug buries you. From the loot he keeps only what is necessary for himself. The rest he gives away to a Kali temple.

Even otherwise Robert does not count on a friendly reception during our survey of the plateau. He claims that the people there are rough and wild. Therefore, he has arranged everything in such a way that he can travel independently of the people there. (It seems to me that he arranges his whole life in this manner.) In Jabalpur we equipped the train with horses, tents, fifteen camels and an elephant. Many coolies wanted to be dismissed after they heard about the dangers ahead. Robert complained that he had to increase their wages in order to make them stay. And yet, it was mainly my arguments that convinced them to stay. It is a pleasure to be needed as a translator again. I had missed it so much! Suddenly I feel so agile again. And although I know that I belong at Adolph's side rather than at Robert's, I know that with Robert I am in the right place. He made me tell the coolies that they were not allowed to go to the bazaar without his express permission. This was to prevent them from losing courage by hearing even more terrifying stories. He also equipped them with weapons. Some were given muskets, and everyone was handed either a talwar or a barcha. Most of them have never held a sword or a lance in their hands. They swung the weapons around enthusiastically and aimlessly in the air. Looking at them I was reminded of Devinder when Father Holbein once tried to make him eat with a knife and fork.

9 January.

We have been travelling for four days. I have never seen Robert this gloomy before. He only talks when it is unavoidable. Where does he put all the words that his head produces? The way he pulls his hat low on his forehead tells me that he is angry with our slow progress. It proves difficult to find local guides. Every time we approach a group of bamboo huts, the natives flee into the jungle. Then we always have to wait. They come back only after a few hours. We are seldom able to convince them to accompany us for more than a day. Which does not surprise me. Our group consists of firangi, Sikhs, Muslims, Hindus who look different, speak different languages and pray to different gods. I would also not trust us.

10 January.

The camels are being adversely affected by the rough-edged stones which, according to Robert, are called trap and diorite. Their hooves are bleeding. The elephant moves sharp stones out of the way with its trunk as if it wants to create order in nature.

11 January.

A tiger! We cannot see it, but its roar keeps us awake. Abdullah estimates that it is less than 100 feet away. The camels and horses are agitated. In their fear some coolies feed the fire that is always lit all around the camp in the evenings to keep predators away. Most of the coolies hold on firmly to their barchas and talwars. With one hand I clutch my pencil and with the other my walking stick. I have never before heard a tiger. Its roar cannot be translated into words. It penetrates deep into you and makes your fear swing like evil music. No one is immune to it. Not even Mani Singh. With each roar he takes a step back or to the side as if he were losing his balance. His eyes are trained on the darkness beyond the fire. I call out to him. He does not hear me. So, there is something after all which he is afraid of. That reassures me, but it also feeds my fear.

No one in the camp is sleeping. The tiger is circling us. The roar always comes from another direction. The coolies fire shots aimlessly into the dark and make a noise: shouting, rattling, stamping on the ground. But the tiger is not intimidated by that. Robert climbed onto the elephant and shot each time in the direction from which the roar came.

We are waiting for daylight.

12 January.

Robert sent the elephant back. Trap and diorite have made it too sore. It refused to walk any further. But we have to move on. Robert says that before him there has rarely been a European in this region.

Perhaps, I think to myself, there is a reason for that. Is it really necessary to penetrate into those regions where no one has been before?

What a foolish thought! Father Fuchs and the Schlagintweits and even Alexander von Humboldt would laugh at me. Naturally, the map of the world has to be filled in. Just like the museum.

14 January.

I now know where Robert puts his words. I saw him writing a letter to His Majesty. When Mani Singh called the Schlagintweit because a river was holding up the train again, I crawled to the letter, but I did not read it secretly. I only looked to where it was lying. And everyone knows it is impossible not to read something when the letters are staring you in the face.

The first impression is not a favourable one, and even subsequent meetings do very little to mitigate the impression of a people that are rough and wild.

Despite everything, the traveller is also confronted with the question whether what he has seen can be called satisfactory. His Majesty can decide this more easily and favourably, not only because the discomforts of the journey do not impair the pleasure – and not because the account is laudatory and full of praise – but because impressions are generated more quickly through narration and one forgets those long stretches which offer little of interest or of novelty with respect to landscape, architecture and customs of the people.

Robert returned, and I had to look away. I would like to ask him what he would find interesting, and why all the novelty around us is not new enough for him. But his reply would definitely not contain more than five words. And he would certainly not be happy that I have read his thoughts by chance.

16 January.

The plateau tries its best to stop us. Mani Singh and some coolies have to cut down some creepers and vines, otherwise the camels would not be able to pass even if they were not carrying a load. The streams are even more of a hindrance. It is not so much the water which makes the crossing difficult, but the riverbed: broad, flat stones covered with algae. We need a full two or three hours to lead twenty camels across a stream that is barely a hundred feet wide and two metres deep. Everyone in the train has already fallen several times on the slippery surface under the water. But such a fall is perilous for the camels. They injure themselves more seriously. Robert has already had to shoot two of them after they broke their legs. Robert had one of them gutted and laden on another camel despite a brief protest by the coolies. When Mani Singh asked him why he was doing this, Robert replied that the camel belonged to an unusually large species of the dromedary camel; he wanted to have it stuffed for the zoological museum in Munich. I do not think the Sikh knows what a zoological museum is, or where Munich is. He only nodded and busied himself with the loading of the camels. The Schlagintweits really want to take everything out of India. If they could have transported the Taj Mahal, they would have taken it to their country and set it up again there.

18 January.

Tonight, the evil music sounded again. Is it another tiger? Or did the same tiger follow us?

19 January.

Why should the tiger follow us?
When will it leave us in peace?

20 January.

Amarkantak. That is Sanskrit and means: the place where the immortal gods meet. When we arrived there, the Hindus in the train asked Robert for time off. He did not have any choice. If he had refused, they would have left him. Robert pulled on the brim of his hat and let them go. They carried out their ablutions at the source of the Narmada near the Hindu temple. Mani Singh asked if I also wanted to be carried there. I declined the offer with thanks. At this time of the year even holy water is too cold for me; I did not want to catch a cold. Instead, I accompanied Mani Singh and Robert on a long ride. We explored the plateau and looked for a good place to set up camp. Robert intends to stay in Amarkantak for several days. We soon discovered a remarkable spot. Scattered in small groups were the most beautiful mango trees I have seen since we left Bombay. We set up camp under their thick branches. The sweet juice of its fruit forced even Robert to smile. I ate so many mangoes that my stomach was bloated. Mani Singh farted loudly. Robert fanned away the smell with his hat. Abdullah approached and handed Robert a thick packet of letters. Some of them were dirty and torn. Robert took them and went away before I could even make out the sender's name.

I asked Abdullah from whom the post was.

Hermann, he said.

He is alive? asked Mani Singh.

Abdullah did not reply. Sometimes he provokes the Sikh by pretending not to understand him.

I asked you something, said Mani Singh.

What did you ask me, Mani Sahab?

Sometimes he provokes the Sikh by calling him Sir or Sahab although they are equals in the train.

The Sikh got up and took a step towards Abdullah.

The Schlagintweit is alive? said Mani Singh emphasizing each syllable as if he were counting to seven.

Sometimes the Sikh lets himself be provoked too easily.

Abdullah nodded.

Amazing! Mani Singh said. I had long since counted him among the dead.

He turned to me.

You don't seem very surprised, he said.

He and Abdullah looked at me.

Of course, I lied, of course I am.

A 'POSTAL EXPEDITER in West Bengal, too clever by half' as Robert called him, had severed the connection between the brothers. The expediter had not paid attention to the Christian name and had sent Hermann's letters to Hermann's last official address in Calcutta. Hermann had discovered this only recently. This 'only recently' was, in the meantime, several weeks ago. From now on, Hermann wrote in his last letter, he would have to address all letters to Adolph, for example, in the following way: *Adolph Schlagintweit, not Robert or Hermann Schlagintweit.*

Robert was so happy about this new development that he, who normally spends most of his evenings alone in his tent, joined us at the campfire, took off his hat and read out parts of the many letters. At first, I only listened. But Robert then told me to translate for Abdullah and Mani Singh. So, on this night, we travelled with Hermann first in Sikkim, where the Nepalis forced him to turn back (I suspected Eleazar), then along the Khassia hills and in Bhutan, and finally through Assam.

We saw how Hermann filled an elephant's skull with plaster and then stripped off the bones piece by piece in order to get the form and the size of the brain.[32] We sailed with Hermann in heavily laden boats over large stretches of Bengal which, in another season, produces a rich harvest. Not all of us agreed with Hermann when he speculated that the spicy food of the natives not only made the eyes water but also caused abdominal diseases. We disagreed with Hermann even more when he stated that Indian cities have a uniform appearance and that it is difficult to distinguish between the races as well as the individuals. Together with Hermann we drank the reportedly excellent Assamese tea which, at least in the Schlagintweit's view, the Hindus and Muslims do not use.[33] We took part in boar-hunting in Hindostan and speared Indian wild boars in a competition with Hermann and officers of the Vickys. When I translated that the natives everywhere in India had no appreciation for sport which they seemed to find too strenuous, Mani Singh harrumphed so loudly and indignantly that Robert laid the letter aside and opened another one. We and Hermann realized in Assam that the chieftains of the *hordes*, as Hermann calls the natives, had no interest in trading in gold and silver; they were far more interested in the Schlagintweit's silk hat and especially in alcohol made from sugar cane. We heard from Hermann that when a man in the Khassia-tribe leaves his wife for another woman, he not only changes his wife, but he becomes the property of the next wife and a new member of her family. With Hermann we smelt the rotting yolks of eggs thrown on the ground which the Khassias use for predictions. And with Hermann we looked for objects for the Schlagintweits' collection in a gorge into which a large number of victims of a cholera epidemic had been thrown. And in this, as Hermann wrote, horrifying dump of corpses

32 It should be mentioned, as Hermann writes, that the absolute size of the brain as well as its proportion to the body weight of the animal is to be considered favourable as far as animals are concerned.

33 Why should they? Such putrid water in which old dry leaves are boiled can only be savoured by a firangi.

which was overgrown with plants and where traces of predatory animals could be seen, we found several well-preserved skulls, but also the entire skeleton of a male corpse.

I have never seen Robert so happy. He sat surrounded by the letters, leaning back more than usual without even folding his arms across his chest, and with his head raised. He now held proof in his hands that his big brother was alive … the big brother who is the true big brother for him. When I saw him like this, I regretted not being with Adolph. He will also hear from Hermann soon. I would have liked to share that moment with him.

24 January.

For some days now the Schlagintweit has undertaken excursions from Amarkantak. He is getting a general idea of the orography[34] of the plateau. Mani Singh says that as a result of Hermann's letters Robert no longer hides his face in his backside. I agree with the Sikh. Robert shares his thoughts with us more than he did earlier. Even if we do not want to hear these thoughts. The Schlagintweit is not really taken with the landscape. He calls it monotonous. I can hardly contradict him there. The forests extend as far as we can see. Because of the proliferating plants and the mist that rises from the jungle even the outlines of the mountains look more like green clouds than rocks. It is, says Robert, the picture not of a desert, but of a wild zone where the climate and the vegetation appear to exclude humans as inhabitants.

Once, when I was alone with Robert while he set up his picture machine on a rock, he spoke the longest sentence that I have ever heard him say: While in bright sunshine an Indian landscape

---

34 A word that taciturn Bavarians use to sound scientific. Robert says orography is a special field within geography which deals with the face of the earth's surface.

resembles a faded photograph with sharp outer contours but blurred in the centre, by the light of the moon the long, deep shadows show all the details, and instead of looking limpid, nature gains a strong exterior which makes a person feel exalted and centred.

Are you also such a person, Sir? I asked.

I would always prefer night to the day, he said. If only it had more light!

You need it for photography, Sir.

Of course! Photography is nothing other than capturing light in a particular moment at a particular place, he said.

Your picture machine is then also a light catcher? I asked.

One which is all too limited in its means, he said.

When one talks to Robert about his favourite science, he can be as generous with words as Hermann. In this way I learnt a few things. I know now how costly it is to procure the required chemicals in India, how carefully the delicate glass containers must be handled, and how difficult it is to control the process for developing pictures in a tropical climate. In particular, Robert is grappling with the problem of reproducing colours. This is the reason, he says, why painting is still superior to photography. The grey of his pictures alienates us from the objects photographed. Our eyes do not see like the picture machine.

Maybe your light catcher is not all that limited, I said, while Robert positioned his picture machine on the rock. Maybe every eye sees differently, and blue for Mani Singh is quite different from what it is for Abdullah and something else completely for me. That would mean that the picture machine lets us all see the same thing.

You mean, he said, my Voigtländer connects us with one another? It allows me to see your blue, the blue of an Indian?

I nodded.

My grey is your grey, Sir.

A remarkable idea, he said.

Since it is very rare for him to be friendly, or even to praise me, I asked him what I have been wanting to ask him for a long time but have not asked since Bombay: Would you also take a picture of me, Sir?

His reply was the same as in Bombay: Why should I?

This time I gave him a better reason.

I have remarkable ideas, I said.

And you think, said Robert, that this will show in the photograph?

I thought about it.

Yes, I said.

Bartholomew, he said, and took off his hat. We should test that.

25 January.

I did not feel anything. When Robert took my picture, he took something from me, but as far as I can tell I am not missing anything. I do not look like myself in the picture. I look like someone who is trying to look like a boy. Someone, who in fact is actually older. In Father Fuchs's mirror I always found so much of myself. In Robert's picture I am sitting on a rock, and only Adolph's walking stick which I am clutching with both hands seems to hold my arms in the air. My back is stretched to make myself as big as possible, and yet I am terribly small. My gaze has been reproduced falsely. There is not a single remarkable thought shining in it.

After Robert had, as he said, *developed* the picture, he handed it to me. I looked at it for a long time and then held it out to him again.

You can keep it, he said.

No, thank you, Sir.

You are one of the few Indians whose photograph exists, probably the first Indian orphan at all, he said, and you refuse this gift?

Yes, Sir.

Robert shook his head and took the picture from me.

Even if you do not wish to see it, Bartholomew, it is you.

Says your machine, Sir. But you should see me once with my eyes!

I am already doing that.

Impossible, I said.

I know, said Robert, what you did that time with the khansaman.

Sir?

Don't pretend to be stupid; that does not suit you. You put the letter in his pocket so that he would be thrown out of the train.

I tried to hide my astonishment. Sometimes, in rare cases, a firangi can apparently see what an Indian sees.

Why didn't you say anything, Sir?

Because I see you. I understand what it means when people think you are weak. One should put up a fight.

After a brief moment he added: Moreover, I wasn't against it.

That the khansaman was thrown out of the train?

That the letter was destroyed, said Robert. Humboldt did not even make the effort to address it also to me. As if I didn't exist.

Robert wanted to pack my picture away, but I held out my hand.

May I, Sir?

I thought you didn't want it.

Maybe there is in fact something of me in it, I said.

26 January.

I managed fifty steps with my walking stick! Slowly, but surely, I am walking back to my earlier briskness. In a sense Robert carries me a part of the way. Naturally not with his body, he is not even aware of my – what did Adolph call them? – nightly ventures. But, with the picture he also gave me a piece of advice which makes me go on. I include the advice and the picture in the museum. It may well be that the boy in the picture does not resemble me. But he reminds me of who I am.

Robert says that I must accept that I will never be respected[35] in the way that I need. That is why I should take care of it on my own, look more into myself and less to the outer world for respect.[36]

Fortunately, I am and have always been remarkably good at just that! After all, one cannot rely on the love of others. Either they give you none, or they want to give you some but cannot do it.

An unforeseeable twist: by showing me how well he sees me, the youngest Schlagintweit has made me see him. There is a pain blazing in him which is fed by his brothers. They are like my picture. They remind him of who he is: the Schlagintweit who will always receive less love than his brothers.

I WOKE UP in the night. The museum was still lying in front of me. I must have dozed off. When I looked in my boot, I realized that the traitor had outwitted me once again. But the ground in India can also be treacherous. I discovered footprints that led to my boot and away from it. I took my walking stick and followed them. After taking a few steps I stopped. Something was coming towards me out of the dark. Something that was trying not to make a noise. The tiger. It had come back. This time it crept up without the evil music. I took a deep breath to call out for help, but no sound came out. I was pulled back; the walking stick fell from my hand. A hard, flat object pressed down on my throat. In the semidarkness I saw bearded men. They did not belong to the train. They rolled me onto my stomach. I thrashed around, but two of them held down my arms and legs. A third man pressed his knee into my back and pulled on the rumal. I could not breathe. I turned my head so that the pressure would ease. I could now see Robert's tent. His guards had been overpowered, but the Schlagintweit slept undisturbed. Where was Mani Singh? I did not want to die. I gathered all the strength I had conjured up every

35 With which the Schlagintweit actually means to say: loved.

36 Love.

night in the past weeks and pushed myself off the ground. A man fell on the ground next to me and stayed there without moving. The other two let go of me, moved back and ran off into the night. I was impressed with myself. Then I saw Abdullah. Blood shone on his barcha. He helped me get up. While doing this a piece of paper fell out of his coat and landed in the dust between us. My information for Eleazar. A moment passed; we did not move. Then Abdullah pocketed the piece of paper, said: Thugs, and then: go where it is safe. When I hesitated, he pointed to Robert. There, he said, run! And I ran. I ran so quickly as I had not run since Bombay.

Remarkable Object No. 71

THE ABILITY TO NOT THINK OF SOMETHING

Simla. I think only of Simla.

And I try not to think of the fact that the train thinks I am an imposter. Too many eyes saw me running to Robert's tent on the night of the attack. And the mouths talk about the boy who pretended to be lame in order not to have to walk. I asked Mani Singh if he, too, considers me an imposter. He denied it. But he does not carry me as much any more. Occasionally he asks me if I would like to walk part of the way. Each time I say I would like to but cannot do it for long. He does not comment on that.

Even the Sikh is not good at not thinking of something. He calls it a disgrace that he did not save me from the thugs. I call it coincidence. Mani Singh does not wish to hear that. What angers him especially is that Abdullah of all people saved me. I saw Mani Singh making scratches on his lower arm with his kirpan. He did it with such calm and concentration, as if he were noting down something. And that is what he is doing in a way. Mani Singh wants to record his disgrace. He says he is not a good Sikh. Regardless of how often I contradict him, he adds new wounds to the ones on his arms. There is only one thing that helps him to Not-Think-of-Something: if I sing with him. 18 March is approaching, so I teach

Mani Singh Father Fuchs's song. He already knows the melody and hums it. We still have to practise the words. I say them to him: *Froh zu sein bedarf es wenig*. And Mani Singh murmurs something into his beard. I continue: *Und wer froh ist*. Mani Singh's voice becomes softer, almost diffident. I finish: *Ist ein Köenig*. And Mani Singh falters. The strongest man I have ever met clears his throat helplessly. Although he towers above me, he looks at me from below. His eyes tremble. He is afraid of my verdict. I tell him it does not matter; German is a cruel language, and he must wear it down patiently. Then we start again from the beginning.

Robert is better than the Sikh and me and all others in the train at not thinking of something. He does not believe that we were attacked by thugs. He ascribes his strangled guard and the robber Abdullah had stabbed to what he calls the *quarrels among groups of Indians*. When Mani Singh and Abdullah (without whose efforts the thugs would never have been driven away) reported the events of the night to him, Robert said it was *nothing worth mentioning*. The Sikh and the Muslim stood there with open mouths. It was the first time they were on common ground. Robert's reaction does not surprise me. He finds most things not worth mentioning. The Schlagintweit had also managed to sleep through this remarkably silent attack. Robert ordered Mani Singh and Abdullah not to speak of the thugs any more. They should not create unnecessary panic in the train. One can see how both of them would like to rant against the Schlagintweit to each other. But that could bring them together. And that is a risk which even these brave men do not like to take. They prefer to obey the Schlagintweit who has retreated even more into himself since the attack. With each passing day I find it more difficult to see in him the person who gifted me a picture and a piece of advice. Robert's silence falls on us again. He looks more into himself than to the outer world for love.

Some of the coolies must envy him his ability to so successfully not think of something. They desert the train fearing another attack by the thugs.

But half of February has already passed, and the thugs have not returned. They probably also do not have the ability to not think of something. Especially not of Abdullah's barcha.

I wonder what the draughtsman is trying not to think of.

That I now know who he is actually working for?

I follow Robert's example and do not talk about it to Abdullah. He has also not once mentioned our encounter during the attack. Mani Singh would call him the enemy and Eleazar would consider him an ally. But my relationship with the draughtsman is more complicated. What does one call a traitor who risks his life for you?

I try not to think about it.

Simla. I concentrate my thoughts on Simla. In two months at the latest we are supposed to join up with Hermann's and Adolph's trains there. Simla will finally unite me with the people who mean something to me. (And, unfortunately, also with those who mean less than nothing to me.) I do not know how I am going to do it, but I will embrace Smitaben and Adolph, hold on to them and never let go.

Remarkable Objects
Nos. 72 & 73 & 74 & 75 & 76

GERMAN
GAUDI
DIVINE JUDGMENT
DESASTER
FATHER FUCHS (2)

I found Father Fuchs!

Someone like Robert who only believes what he sees cannot understand this. But someone who like most of us also believes in what he has never seen, like in Lord Ganesha or Allah or Jesus, will understand me.

WE REACHED SIMLA on 25 March. Robert rented a handsome house with outhouses which could accommodate the entire train, set up his meteorological and magnetic instruments and waited for his brothers. There was still a whole month before they would arrive. During this time, we got to know Simla better.

It is the oldest *health station* as the firangi call it. Not only pines and cedars grow on the green hills, but also the villas of the Vickys. They proliferate along the crest of the mountain like a tenacious fungus. The mall in Simla is especially popular with the Vickys, a pedestrian mile where no Indians are allowed. From March till September the Vickys retreat to Simla to escape the Indian heat at cooler heights. They even come from Calcutta, over a thousand miles away. Firangi from other European countries also join them. This is what the Vickys call *the season*. When we arrived there, the place was bustling. There were concerts and balls and picnics[37] and theatre performances. Robert spent a lot of time with the firangi, in an observatory for magnetic and meteorological readings as well as in non-scientific spaces. None of us were allowed to accompany him. Each time the Schlagintweit left the house in a different suit and always came back smiling. The firangi gave him something he could not get from us Indians.

I asked him once what that was.

He replied: After being deprived of the company of Europeans for so long, I enjoy their stimulating charm.

But you have to dress up like a spy, I said, because I knew how reluctantly he had worn suits in Calcutta.

These small shackles of fashion and etiquette are but a small price to pay, he said.

Could I come with you once, Sir? I asked.

No Indians on the mall, Bartholomew, you know that.

I could be your translator at a ball, I said.

Why? he said. I know all the languages spoken there. Besides, to participate in such festivities even Indian princes require much more in the way of higher education.

And that coming from a man who without my help cannot even tell his servants to bring him tea! Actually, I was glad that he did

37 For the first time I saw Vickys sitting on the ground and eating. Some were not even able to bend their legs. They are as stiff as the chairs they normally sit on.

not take me along. I would not want to accompany such a lowly educated man.

On 25 April, when I heard that a train had arrived in Simla, I ran – yes, I ran – outside. I wanted to keep the last moments of this long separation as brief as possible. On the winding road I looked in the direction from which the train would come and caught myself looking out for a well-built Bavarian. When I saw Hermann, I felt a stab of disappointment. But it did not last very long in Smitaben's arms.

You have grown, she said. And you are limping.

I wanted to tell her everything that had happened in this last year. I wanted to tell her what form Nanda Devi had taken on, what firn is, what evil music sounds like, where Harkishen is, who reached the highest point in the world, why pictures sometimes show something that is not there and, especially, yes, I especially wanted to tell her how often, fearing for her life, I had forced myself to put a sordid message in my boot.

But first I had to catch up on every embrace that we had missed.

Smitaben was alive, more alive than ever before. The Gujarati woman had become slimmer; my arms almost reached around her hips. There was a thick, shining black strand in her hair. The travels had made an almost pretty woman of her. And she had learnt Hindi! She was not particularly fluent in it, but it was enough to order around the servants assigned to her the moment they arrived.

Hermann came to me.

God's greetings to you, Bartholomew, he said.

I did not ask him which god because I was shocked at how haggard he looked. The pink had gone out of his cheeks and his beard was blotchy. His eyes seemed to be smaller than they had been a year ago. The Schlagintweit looked like Father Fuchs when the cough did not let him sleep for nights on end.

You have grown, said Hermann.

Robert appeared. He strode quickly towards his brother. Like someone who is trying not to run. Robert touched Hermann's shoulders. As if to make sure that his brother was really standing in front of him. Both of them said the other's name several times. Then they shared a loud laugh that had waited a long time to leave their throats. It was not nearly as glorious as Adolph's laugh. But I took it in almost as gladly as the handvo which Smitaben made for us that same evening and which tasted better than everything I had eaten since her last handvo. It was not only joy that quickened my appetite, but also relief. Because Eleazar had not returned with the train. Hermann had sent him via a different route to Simla, and the Schlagintweits expected him only after a few days. And so, I ate and ate. Not even Hermann's lengthy descriptions bothered me. It seemed as if he wanted to catch up on a whole year in one evening. Robert listened to him in silence with his arm around him. Now that he had his big brother again, he did not want to let him go. I would never have thought that one day I would write: Robert and I had similar feelings. I became aware that I, too, had missed Hermann. His German is more sophisticated than that of his brothers. What a joy it was to listen to him! Although Hermann only talked about his scientific observations and studies, he did it with so much feeling as if he were telling us a love story. He could do that only in German. No other language brings such disparate things together. The heartfelt and the practical, the uncanny and the factual, the pleasant and the proper.

The next day I was woken up by voices that came from the ground floor. I did not understand the words, but the sound of the voices took me back to Bombay, to the consul's residence. Then I had thought only every fourth Bavarian is nice; in the meantime, it is at least every second one. And one of them was now in Simla, in this house.

It was not at all easy to get dressed more slowly than usual, although I wanted to be quicker than usual. The moment I had longed for had arrived. I wanted to give it a little more time. It had to become a good moment.

When I came down the stairs, Adolph and Hermann were sitting next to each other like they had done in Madras, only this time without a punkah. I again approached them from behind. But this time Adolph noticed me and turned around.

Bartholomew! he said, you have grown.

Yes, Sir, I said.

The Schlagintweit looked me over.

Won't you greet me? he asked.

I held out my hand.

Adolph jumped up and hugged me.

I hope you have missed me a lot, he said.

I hugged him back.

He pulled me with him to sit between him and his brother. For a moment we just sat there quietly. As if we had reached a high point on the Abi Gamin and were taking in the view.

Adolph, Hermann then said.

What? said Adolph.

Get a grip on yourself, said Hermann.

Adolph wiped a tear from his eyes. And yet another.

Hermann stretched out his arm and laid a hand on Adolph's head till his brother did not have to wipe away any more tears.

Over the following days the brothers were busy calculating their observations and writing their reports. They compared their chronometers, barometers, thermometers. Many of the instruments are subject to changes over time which make the measurements imprecise. Like a clock that stops briefly once and then always shows the wrong time. The Schlagintweits corrected all this as precisely as possible. But not only the instruments, even the brothers were adjusted precisely after this long separation. When they were together each of them knew better who he was. Robert, the silent one.

Hermann, the not so silent one. And Adolph, the most remarkable one. But unlike his brothers he needed yet another person in order to be precisely adjusted. I ask myself what would have happened to Adolph if we had never met. Or maybe I should ask instead: what would not have happened to him?

At any rate, the Schlagintweit seldom left my side in Simla. He is like his walking stick. As long as he has to be strong for your sake, he will carry you. But if you do not need him, he seems to be lonely and lost. That is why I never had the heart to refuse him anything. I even accompanied him to the mall. Many firangi turned to look at us. Adolph looked each of them in the eye. I whispered to him that we should probably not stay there too long. Adolph said: *Schmarrn*. That is Bavarian and means that he has set his mind on doing something and even an army of two thousand men will not stop him from doing it. Some firangi harrumphed or told Adolph to send his servant away; others pulled their children away or stood protectively in front of their wives.

Adolph ignored all of them.

Don't all goras look alike? he said to me and laid his arm around me. That is when I knew that nothing could happen to me. I belonged to Adolph like an object to the museum.

Two days later we went to a reception of the Vickys. Adolph first persuaded the Vickys to let me come because I had saved his life, then he persuaded me to come because apparently, he could not survive a party given by Vickys without me. Lord Hay, the most senior Vicky in Simla, had organized it in honour of the Schlagintweits. According to Adolph, Lord Hay was one of the better Vickys since he supported their research generously and gave them all the help they needed.

As soon as we arrived, an army of women swooped down on us. I have never seen so many female Vickys gathered together. From all sides they went on and on at the brothers, praised their courage, their spirit, their will and, although the women did not look foolish at all, they asked stupid questions that were meant to make the men feel clever when replying. They emphasized their words by touching the shoulders and the hands of the Schlagintweits. I was in the middle of a veritable battle.

Adolph says that a war is being fought in Simla. On one side are the so-called grass widows, older, more experienced women who are on a visit to Simla without their husbands. On the other are young girls who are looking for a husband. Mostly, the grass widows win.

On this evening, however, the battle had an unexpected ending. Adolph pulled me along with him through the battle and told his brothers to stay with him. The women took up pursuit. But before they caught up with us, we reached Lord Hay who greeted the Schlagintweits most cordially. The women kept their distance. Lord Hay was stooped. His hands were interlaced on his chest and could not be used to gesture, as if he did not want to take up too much space. His nose and ears were untypically fine boned for a Vicky. He, too, praised the courage, spirit and will of the Schlagintweits. But his admiration sounded more sincere. Lord Hay does indeed seem to be one of the better Vickys. He even noticed me. The lord called me by my name – someone must have whispered it to him – and held out his hand. It was soft, like my earlobe. When I pressed it, I was afraid I might hurt him. Adolph began to talk about how we had braved Nanda Devi. With his words the Schlagintweit drew the army of women closer to us and left Lord Hay wide-eyed. What was even more astonishing was that he succeeded in making his older brother listen silently, and that his younger brother became curious enough to interrupt him several times: And then? I sensed that soon all of Adolph's listeners were asking themselves the same thing. How was it possible that despite these mortal dangers the Schlagintweit lived to talk about it now in Simla? Adolph laid a hand on my head and replied, this young man saved my life and saved the entire train. I had not expected this conclusion even though it was true. I had thought that Adolph would grow larger than life in the story. Instead, he let me grow. The grass widows and the girls examined me as if to try and assess my age. Lord Hay applauded softly. Robert nodded, clearly impressed, and Hermann patted me on the back. It was their way of saying thank you. Naturally, I care little for what firangi, especially Vickys, think of me and yet I must admit to feeling proud. Without me two of the Schlagintweits would not be alive. And what is far more important is that they not only know it, but they are also willing to admit it. This is what distinguishes them from most of the firangi. This evening here was the most improbable place for what Adolph calls *Gaudi*, fun, but he was full of it. The Schlagintweits and I told each other and our female audience, as also Lord Hay, stories about our travels, and not once did the brothers make me feel as if I were not one of them. And surely that meant that I was one of them?

If November is the worst month of the year, then April and May are the most beautiful months.

But I was afraid of this beauty. After all, I come from Blacktown. I learnt early on that all good things carry the promise of bad things. The longer these months lasted, the stronger was the threat of their end. Eleazar could arrive in Simla any day now. I had to do something.

But I did not do anything. I wanted to hold on to this beauty, if only for a little while.

On 15 May Mani Singh asked me, no, he ordered me to follow him. I had not seen him for many days. The Sikh was all wrought up, as if he had encountered a tiger. I thought it might be because of the Christ Church in Simla. Its chimes reminded him every day that the bells were cast from cannons looted in the war against the Sikhs. At any rate, Mani Singh did not want to tell me where we were going. We soon reached a shed in which a dozen members of the train stood around and waited, among them also Abdullah and Mr Monteiro. Mani Singh told me to translate for him, and he announced that he had finally found a way to expose the traitor. I looked at Abdullah, but Abdullah did not look at me. Mani Singh went to a sack full of rice and slit it open with his kirpan. Grains of rice trickled to the ground. He made each member of the train step forward individually and gave each one of them an exact amount of rice grains measured with a set of scales. While doing this, the Sikh explained that this would be so-called divine judgment. Each of those present had to chew the rice grains as much as possible; god would prevent the masticatory muscles of the culprit from working. He did not give me any rice. When I asked him, why not, Mani Singh laughed as if he thought I was not capable of betrayal. And so, I also demanded rice. This time, I believe, Abdullah looked at me. But I did not look at Abdullah. Yes, the Sikh had insulted me, but there was a better reason for what I did; I understand it only now. A part of me wanted to be exposed. Mani Singh was my friend, and I was tired of hiding from him. I wanted to relieve him of his constant search for the traitor. The Sikh huffed and handed me a tablespoon of rice grains. Mani Singh gave us three minutes. We chewed our way through the silence. After a few seconds already, I came to my senses. What would happen to me if he discovered who I was? I could not allow that to happen! I tried very hard. Chewed as I had never chewed before. The rice was hard. But no one else in the train has as many fresh teeth as I do. When the time was over, each one of us had to spit the chewed mass onto a table. Single grains could be seen in every heap. Except in mine. I had mashed up the rice completely. Mani Singh nodded and dismissed the train. When we were alone, I asked him if it meant that everyone apart from me was a traitor. The Sikh braced himself on my shoulder. Without the walking stick I would not have been able to support his weight. His disappointment is profound, I thought. And I was correct. Only, it was not the disappointment I assumed it to be. I helped the Sikh stand up again. Mani Singh bowed to me and, before he left, he wished me a long and bright life.

On that same evening he left the train and Simla. I only discovered this the next day and so, I could not convince him to change his mind. I underestimated his shrewdness one last time. I understood his disappointment too late. God's judgment had indeed revealed the traitor, but he was disappointed to find out who this traitor was. A stupid boy who out of fear turns uncooked rice into pulp and gives himself away.

I thank you honourable Mani Singh for sparing me. Your debt has been paid. We are not friends any more. But you will have a place in the museum as a friend.

I HAD VERY little time to mourn the loss of Mani Singh. On 17 May, Mr Monteiro came to me with a message. Eleazar had returned and wished to speak to me immediately. One of this Indo-Portuguese man's eyes was looking at me, the other was looking at a point directly behind me. I should tell him who Eleazar really is, I thought, that would cause both his eyes to blink in surprise. But first I had to do something I should have done a long time ago.

I ran off, but not to Eleazar. Fortunately, I found Smitaben in the kitchen cutting coriander. I asked her to follow me at once. She must have seen something in my face. It is virtually impossible to stop the maasi from cooking. She came without any protest. I brought her to a secluded lookout point where I had been with Adolph several times. There I told her everything. I was aware how difficult it would be to convince a remarkably stubborn person like Maasi. But I had to at least try. I told her I am a traitor, that Eleazar was a threat to her life and that she should run away.

When I had finished, Smitaben said: What a *Desaster*!

You mean *disaster*.

No, *Desaster*. The most important German word.

Maasi, do you also speak German now?

No, but Hermann talks a lot, and a little of that sticks even to me.

Smitaben did not appear to be particularly unhappy. She simply shook her head as if she had let food burn in the pan.

I am going to Calcutta to become a female doctor, she said finally. In any case, the Schlagintweits want to go to Leh very soon. And even further north on the other side of the mountains. I am an old Gujarati woman. That is too far, too high, and much too cold for me.

I was relieved. Her story was taking a happier turn than that of Father Fuchs, Hormazd, Harkishen, Devinder or Mani Singh.

Come with me, she said.

I thought about it. In a year's time the Schlagintweits would be going back to Berlin. There was nothing waiting for me in Bombay. Why not begin a new life in Calcutta with Smitaben?

A crack rent the air. Mr Monteiro came towards us. In one hand he held a riding crop.

I cannot allow that to happen, he said.

WE CLIMBED SIMLA's highest peak. Mr Monteiro walked behind us. Every time we slowed down, he cracked his whip. Smitaben wheezed; the dark strand of hair stuck to her damp forehead. I supported the maasi; the walking stick supported us.

How can you work for a man like him? I asked Mr Monteiro.

I don't work for him, he said. We work together for a greater cause. That is what distinguishes us from the firangi.

Finally, we reached the Jhakoo temple. According to legend, it goes back to the time of the Ramayana. It is dedicated to Hanuman. His descendants are also aware of this. Two dozen monkeys sat on the roof. Their suspicious looks that followed us greatly resembled the looks of the Vickys at the mall.

Eleazar came out of the building with Abdullah. The Bania had not changed. Whereas the strain of the journey had aged Hermann by years, Eleazar appeared rested, even cheerful.

You have grown, he said to me. And you walk differently.

I limp, I said.

No, your walk is different. Like a firangi.

How does a firangi walk?

Like you, he said.

I had almost forgotten how even his insults sound friendly.

How many more traitors are there? I asked and pointed to Mr Monteiro and Abdullah.

We are an entire country, he said. But that is not what you should be asking yourself. You should ask: If most of us are traitors, what does that make of the remaining few? Are they then not the real traitors?

What do you want from me? I asked.

To thank you, he said. You were a valuable support, my friend.

He held out his hand.

I raised the walking stick, pointed the iron tip at him.

Smitaben came to stand in front of me.

Leave the boy alone, she said.

The short, pointed knife she always carries with her appeared in her hand. It is her sixth finger. With it she can cut a mango faster than anyone else. Or cut other things.

Eleazar took a step back.

Abdullah reached for his barcha and Mr Monteiro for his riding crop.

All three men were linked by something they were not accustomed to: uncertainty. They had bargained for everything, but not for a woman. Especially not for a Gujarati woman who can defend herself against good men.

Bartholomew, Smitaben said, run!

Wait, said Eleazar.

Smitaben cried out: Now, Bartholomew!

But I could not leave her alone.

No one is stopping both of you, said Eleazar.

He is a traitor, she said to me, don't listen to him.

The Bania looked at Abdullah and Mr Monteiro. They lowered their weapons and stepped back.

It wasn't easy finding it, said Eleazar.

Slowly and carefully, he pulled an opened letter from his breast pocket and put it on the ground in front of him.

For you, he said. Even if it is not addressed to you.

It's a trap, said Smitaben. Don't touch it.

But I had to. The handwriting on the envelope demanded it. It was Father Fuchs's.

MANY MONTHS AGO, when I was still living in the Glass House and walking like an Indian, I helped Father Fuchs to see the museum. Since then, the museum has helped me to see Father Fuchs better. But I found him only in a letter on Simla's highest peak.

And yet I miss him. At least the side of Father Fuchs that he had always shown to me.

But, after everything I have learnt in the past months, I now know that this Father Fuchs never existed. Eleazar is right. The real Father Fuchs never smiled honestly; he fed me only lies.

I wish I had never found him.

PART VI

The Overland Route to Europe 1856–57

Remarkable Object No. 77

THE GREEN OF LEH

It is 24 August 1856. I have not opened the museum for months. I am in Leh, the capital of Ladakh, which became part of Jammu and Kashmir a few years ago. Adolph is studying glaciers and mountains in the Himalayas. As the first Europeans to do so, Hermann and Robert will cross the mountain chains of the Kuenluen and the Karakorum. If they do not perish in the attempt, they will return to Leh. It was the brothers' idea that I wait here for them where it is safer. But I had also wanted to be alone.

I have collected so many remarkable objects; India's first museum is bulkier than Hermann's notebook, and yet I am no smarter than I was before. It seems to me that the more I learn the less I understand. Earlier, in the Glass House, I knew what I hated and loved and what I was afraid of. Now I do not see clearly any more.

I hope to change this in Leh. Without the train I have more time to get to know Bartholomew. Each day begins by waking up over the roofs of Leh. I pitched my tent at the top of the house rented by the Schlagintweits because I get more air there. The summer heat in Leh is more unbearable than the Vickys' accent.

I walk in the walled-in garden of the house where we have set up their magnetic and meteorological instruments. I make sure they are intact and note the values in a table.

After that I go to the western part of the city. I continue to use the walking stick even though I do not really need it. I feel more confident with it. I cross the huge bazaar. Adolph measured it: 1030 feet long and 170 feet wide. There is more trade in Leh than in every other city I have seen so far. Caravans set off in all directions, or they arrive from distant regions. The most important article of trade is opium. But, for the Vickys, Leh is also a key military base. Russia and China, their great rivals in the Great Game, are not far. The ruler of Kashmir, Maharaja Gulab Singh, calls himself a friend of the Vickys. But in these times, everyone who does not want to be considered an enemy, claims to be their friend. The Schlagintweits presented him with a photograph of himself in order to win his favour. He showed his gratitude by ordering a guard of honour to accompany the brothers. Only, these soldiers have little to do with honour. They follow every movement of the train. Gulab Singh probably also calls himself a friend of the Chinese.

In this case, it is an advantage being a small Indian cripple. The guard of honour does not pay any attention to me. I can cross through Leh to reach a rocky ridge unchallenged, lie down on the gompas, abandoned Buddhist temples. I climb up to the main tower. It is split in two, only one half is standing. I wait on the meadow bordering it. Its green fills me with something. Not hope, but the feeling is strong enough to carry me through to the next day till I can see the green again. Because apart from this there are no bright colours in Tibet. Windblown sand obscures every view.

I always notice Eleazar only when he greets me. I never reciprocate his greeting. He asks whether he may sit down with me; I do not reply, and he remains standing.

I wrote that I was in Leh in order to be alone. And I am alone. The Bania does not change that. Whoever he is, or claims to be, someone like him can never make me not alone. But for the time being I have to share the green of Leh with him. He is the only one who can help me understand who I probably am.

Remarkable Object No. 78

HANOVERIANS

In the previous century, when America was still part of the empire of the Vickys, the American colonies, as every Indian knows, went to war against the Vickys. (Eleazar says India will be the next America for the Vickys.) The Americans were supported by the French who are also no friends of the Vickys. But the French did not fight against the Vickys only in America. In an alliance with Hyder Ali, the Sultan of Mysore and, as Eleazar says, the heroic adversary of the Vickys, they fought against the East India Company. It was a remarkable *Desaster* for the Vickys. They had sent too many of their soldiers to America. They needed more. How convenient then that George III, the ruler of a German country called Hanover, was also the ruler of the Vickys! Soon, two new regiments were created. The soldiers who had been recruited through an announcement were artists, preachers, monks, deserters, Jews. Hundreds of them were not even sixteen years old. Father Fuchs never told me about them. And he had lied. The Germans are no different from the Vickys, or the French, or the Danes, or the Dutch, or the Portuguese. They are equally bound more to the sword than the pen.

In the years following their recruitment, quite a few of these two thousand soldiers sent letters and travelogues home. Some of them were published in the *Hannoverische Magazin.*[38] Their wives accompanied them. Together they sailed from Hanover to England, to Rio de Janeiro (Eleazar says that is a city in the Americas) and finally to Madras; together more than one hundred died on the way – in storms, in a naval battle and in a mutiny. When they arrived, the Hanoverian troops were incorporated into the army of the Company. In one of the first letters one of them writes: *The servants here are not Europeans, but people from the local population who unfortunately are almost all thieves and cheats. One has to maintain a good number of them at a large cost, because the people here are divided into certain families or castes, and according to the religion and politics of this country every caste can only carry out a particular task. The one who cuts hair does not do the shaving; and the person who feeds the horse does not saddle it; the person who brings water for washing will not take the dirty water away. That has to be done by someone else from a lower caste.* Eleazar says this is further proof that the perception of German firangi is not much different from that of the Vickys. But I say that the Hanoverian could not have found all this out himself so soon after arriving. I recognize a translation when I see one. This report is an opinion of the Vickys translated into German; they tried to poison the Hanoverians with their politics.

Most of the Germans appear to have been immune to it. Many of their letters prove this. The voices of these firangi surprise me. What they say is respectful, friendly, correct. They write about Hyder Ali: *The rumour that is being spread in Europe that prisoners of war are being treated cruelly is completely false. I have heard many officers who became his prisoners tell that all European prisoners are immediately handed over to the French.* And also: *Hyder's economic rule is to improve something in the beginning so that everything is well maintained, saving a great deal of expenditure. The Europeans in India let everything fall apart.* About

38 Eleazar got much of his information from this magazine, and he let me read the articles so that I would doubt his words less.

Indian soldiers they write: *There are no troops in Europe better trained than the sepoy battalions. They carry out large manoeuvres very precisely and twice as fast as German troops in Europe.* And also: *The sepoys are the most essential part of our army. They man the outposts, they are the guards, the patrols, the escorts, in brief: everything. The Europeans have nothing to do but to march and fight. But the brave sepoys have to do that too. Their bravery is the best example for the Europeans.* And last but not least: *Our black regiments are beautiful, courageous, well-mounted, well-trained, respectably turned out and obedient to a fault.*

I particularly remember the letter in which a soldier wrote: *A sepoy's wife prepares the meal for her loved one, and amidst the hail of bullets, she cooks his well-spiced rice behind a hedge not knowing if the throat that is meant to enjoy it has not already been slit. She looks for him in the battlefield. Carrying three pots one on top of the other on her head, clothes pulled up above the knees and the breast veil abandoned to the wind, she flies through the ranks and looks for the battalion, the company in which her bearded loved one serves, barely seems to notice the bullets which bring down, here a son of Mars, there a co-sister, an unlucky victim of her love.*

The Hanoverians took part in the Battle of Cuddalore. They were placed in the centre. For many of them it was their last day, 13 June 1783. One of the survivors of this battle later wrote: *I forgot the danger when I saw my brave compatriots fall on both sides, and I called out: Aim children, and hit the enemy!* Some of these enemies were also Germans recruited by the French. (Eleazar says one can always choose which side to be on.) Neither side emerged victorious in the battle. Therefore, the French and the Vickys were relieved when both countries signed a peace treaty a few days later.

But for the Hanoverians, their time in India had by no means come to an end. Tipu Sultan, Hyder Ali's son, continued the war against the Company. They had to fight in dense forests, they helped in the siege of Mangalore, and they were deployed against smaller rebel groups after Mysore and the Vickys made peace.

Many of them did not die in the battle against Indians, but against the many diseases in India. The rest had to continue fighting for the Company. The third war with Mysore broke out; this led to the fourth war in which Tipu Sultan died and Mysore's power with him. After that most of the Hanoverians wanted to return home. In 1792, 614 of them sailed to Europe. Only 217 remained. This group is particularly interesting for me. Some deserted. The most famous of this group became an officer in the army of the Marathas. (Eleazar says once more that one can always choose which side to be on.) It is very possible that this was the Hanoverian who warned in a letter: *The natives secretly hate all Europeans. I believe it will require a great deal of judiciousness if the latter want to maintain their territories here. Because the former are so abundant in number that there are perhaps 1000 of them to one of the latter. The Blacks are also becoming cleverer and seem to be aware of the ploys and the open deceit they are facing. Therefore, it is to be feared that sooner or later a revolution is in store for this peninsula.*

From the letters of the rest of the Hanoverians we see how they helped the Company to capture more of India, but also how they were captured by India. Their German withered away. They complained about how often the expressions of their mother tongue were no longer available to them. This probably happened because they did not marry German women. They were not available. But Christian Indians were. With them they spoke a miserable English. Or they did not speak with each other at all, which the Hanoverians, unwilling to learn an Indian language, preferred.

Apart from these marriages, there were seven illegal alliances that produced children who were baptized at birth – but none with the name Bartholomew. In the letters, however, another name appears which I know very well. It belongs to the firangi who carried out the baptisms.

Remarkable Object No. 79

FATHER FUCHS'S LETTER

To Rector Fuchs in Munich

Respected Brother,

In my last letter I had mentioned that I was bedridden for one and a half months. After that, my health seemed to get better, and I also began to preach on the holy days, but it did not last. Now things are as they were before, and none of the medicines seem to help. The root of this illness is in the mind. Because, for some years now, struggle, grief and worry on account of my work have made my heart heavy. These have continuously increased through the many events that take place on this strange continent, especially the wounds inflicted on it by the English. This worry and grief of the mind has led to constant physical distress. Moreover, I have had to endure a great deal of fatigue linked with my work. I have shortness of breath, a strong pressure in my entire body, pain in my sides, a severe cough which causes convulsions in my chest and does not allow me to sleep. Meanwhile, I have freed myself of all worries and have handed everything over to Mr Holbein. I bear such trials patiently and trust that God will help me to become useful to this work again. May His divine will prevail! The only medicine that does any good is the boy I have often talked about. His remarkable, bright spirit strengthens and refreshes your ailing brother. Bartholomew is thriving better than all my other little black sheep in St. Helena, even though I have to still count him among the heathens. But my belief gives me hope; may God have mercy on him. It would be a great relief for me if I could leave this world knowing that the boy is walking on the path of the Lord. I have cared for him ever since his mother left him behind on this earth at his birth. As my spiritual brothers on the east coast have reported, his father, one of the last Hanoverians in India, has entered God's kingdom. I do not wish to waste ink or thoughts on this man; you know in what low esteem I hold the degenerate behaviour of soldiers everywhere. Far too often it meant that I had to take in the unwanted, innocent souls that were the outcome of such behaviour. I had to baptize them and shelter them in St. Helena in order to protect them from the worst. Therefore, if the Lord should call me to Him soon, it is my dearest wish that Bartholomew remain under the mercy of Jesus Christ when I am no longer there to protect him. I sometimes indulge in wanton dreams of wondering what would have become of him if his life had begun in our wonderful Bavaria. I would like to be so presumptuous as to state that he would today be one of the brightest pupils of your school. But enough about my entanglements! How is your health, your work, your family? Please write me a long letter, because knowing I will receive a reply, I find the strength not to leave this world all too soon.

Bound in prayer and love
To my brother and dear friend
Johann Ernst Fuchs
Servant of the Divine Word in India
Written in Bombay, 7 August 1854

Remarkable Object No. 80

ETERNITY

While I was reading Father Fuchs's miserable letter on Simla's highest peak, the three traitors, and even I myself, were observing me. The letter created two Bartholomews in my head. One of them had not yet arrived where the other had tarried for a long time. One of them read the letter again and again, and although he could understand it, he could not comprehend it. The other comprehended it only too well. So many emotions coursed through him and if there had been an instrument to measure them, its indicator would have been knocked out. Sympathy, sorrow, bafflement, anger. And, naturally, loneliness. I cannot remember everything I felt while reading the letter. But I still know every question the one Bartholomew asked the other: Your father was still alive? Why did Father Fuchs not bring you together? Why did he keep you in the dark about him? Why did he keep you in the dark about the Hanoverians in India? Why did he feed you lies for at least twelve years? You are an Indo-European? An Indo-European? Which side are you on then?

While reading the letter I could also feel Father Fuchs's approaching death.

With that I mean not only his first death in Bombay. I mean also his second, when he died for me.

Eleazar took a step towards me as if he knew in this moment that a place beside me had become free.

Sometimes, our truths are only the lies of others, he said. But don't forget that India is your mother.

How could I forget that? I said.

Excellent, Eleazar said.

But he did not understand. I did not want to be neither one thing nor the other; I wanted to forget it. And I would only be able to do that, I thought, if I closed the museum.

In the weeks that followed I kept it at the bottom of my luggage. If by chance I happened to see it, I felt as if Father Fuchs was looking at me in the mirror reproachfully. How was that possible? I have many reasons to reproach him. He does not have a single one.

For the time being I stayed with the Schlagintweits. I had decided not to return to Bombay. There was no future for me in that city. And I do not want to be reminded of my past there.

Naturally, I could have gone with Smitaben. I should have! She left the train after Simla. I said goodbye to her (and failed in the attempt not to cry).

I had to stay with the train. I knew that only Eleazar could help me find the answers to my questions. He did not force me to spy for him any more and assured me that nothing would happen to Smitaben.

I did not trust him. The maasi and I made an arrangement.

Since then, a letter arrives for me every few weeks – despite the addressee's name given as *B. Schlagtwein* – written each time in a different hand by a helpful soul who has taken pity on Smitaben. But each letter speaks unmistakably in Smitaben's voice. Even, or rather, precisely, a devious person like Eleazar could not pass off as her.

When we arrived in Leh, I had already been suffering for some days from what Hermann called a *persistent constipation*. The Schlagintweit examined my swollen stomach and said it must be because of the low barometric level of the climate and the barely digestible food in Tibet. I was not the first such case in the train, and so he told me regretfully that the laxatives had long since been used up. But I did not need any. Because Hermann's diagnosis was wrong. It was not because of the climate or the food. I certainly felt the urge. But I did not want to. Every time my body urged me to, when it forced me to stop and squat down, when it shook me up, I kept it inside. The Schlagintweits thought my exertions, my groans and the sweat on my flushed face were an indication that I was trying to get it out. But it was the exact opposite.

These scientists comprehend less than they think they do. They have no idea which forces are working around them. If I were to tell them everything about Eleazar, Abdullah and Mr Monteiro, and about Devinder and Hormazd, they would laugh at me. And the Bania would probably kill me.

After Simla, he behaved as if he were merely an assistant and I merely a translator. He only spoke to me when it was absolutely necessary.

Then he came to me in Leh after the Schlagintweits had left for their mountain explorations, and he told me the following story:

When Alexander the Great came to India hundreds of years ago, he met a naked, wise man whom he called a gymnosophist.[39] This man was sitting on a rock and staring at the sky.

What are you doing? Alexander the Great asked.

I am experiencing the void, said the yogi. What are you doing?

I am conquering the world, said Alexander the Great.

Then they both laughed.

Is that supposed to be a metaphor? I asked. Alexander the Great represents the firangi and the yogi us Indians?

Eleazar's smile reminded me of the time when I had told him about the museum. It reached his eyes.

---

39 That is long-winded Greek for a yogi.

It is a joke, said Eleazar. Each one thought the other is a fool and is wasting his life.

A pathetic joke, I said.

That may be, he said. I was never particularly good at joking.

Was that all? Can I be alone now?

Never, never will I open myself up to him.

There is little which comes so close to the truth as a joke, Eleazar said. Eternity was born in India. There is an age-old temple in Gwalior on which a zero has been engraved. When the Greeks stopped counting at ten thousand, we were already playing with billions. Did your Father Fuchs not teach you that?

He had not. But I said: Of course.

Eleazar looked at me.

I can teach you so much more, my friend. I know how lost you are feeling.

I am not feeling lost, I said.

Eleazar was silent.

I am not lost!

The Bania nodded as if I had agreed with him.

Eternity is also always a beginning, he said. Let me help you. I am sure you want to know who you really are.

Before I could say I am everything he is not, he handed me a newspaper. The *Hannoverische Magazin*. The article on the first page was titled: 'About East India'.

Eleazar did not tell me to read it. Maybe because he knew that then I would not have read it. He simply left me alone with the paper.

On the same evening, I shat like an ox. I shat as if I had to fill eternity. The words of the Hanoverian were a remarkable laxative. I felt as if I were shitting out what had been dammed up in me for years.

WEEKS HAVE GONE by since that evening. Almost every day Eleazar brings me a new article. He does not tell me to read any of them.

I read each and every one.

Eleazar's only condition is that he gives me the articles where Leh's brightest green thrives – and where neither a Schlagintweit nor an honour guard can see us.

I swore to myself that I would not tell the Schlagintweits any of this, especially not Adolph.

He would listen to me. He would hold my hand. He would help me to understand. He would rob me of my anger at Father Fuchs.

Eleazar does not say much while handing me the newspapers. Occasionally, I ask him a question if I want to know more about something in particular. He always has an answer. Whereby I am aware that the replies of a traitor are mainly self-serving. If he says anything without being asked, then it is mostly this: Do not forget that India is your mother.

I asked him if he can find out more about my real mother, and he has promised to try. But both of us know he will not find anything. My mother was poor. So poor, that a firangi could make her his wife. So poor, that her caste would not have mattered. So poor, that she had to pay for my life with her own. So poor, that there is nothing left of her, no name, no picture, no property, no memory. Only me. So poor, that she most certainly could not write her own name, let alone articles for a magazine.

The more I read what the Hanoverians wrote, the stronger is my desire to hear my mother's voice.

What would she have said about all this?

This thought made me open the museum again. I am the last living part of her; I can speak with her voice better than anyone else. Maybe it is not entirely an Indian voice. But it is certainly also not entirely a German one. I doubt whether as an Indo-European I am the right person to create a museum for India, and I will never forgive Father Fuchs. But that should not stop me from giving my mother a voice. We have an eternity of things to say.

Remarkable Object No. 81

THE DISCOVERY OF A NON-EXISTENT THING

It took some effort for our train to cross the Suru Pass in October which was already covered in snow so early in the year. Robert and Adolph were waiting for us in Srinagger. Many Europeans stay in the city; a church was even built for them. Most of them come for the *Sommerfrische*. I learnt this word from Adolph. It describes a longish period of time when one does not work. Only Germans can have a word like that. Most of the inhabitants of Srinagger can neither pronounce it nor comprehend it. They are Muslims and have to work much harder than the few top officials, most of whom are Hindus. Gulab Singh appoints Hindus in most of the jobs because he himself is one. Otherwise, he would be isolated in his kingdom. Eleazar says that the maharaja is risking peace in Kashmir by doing this. For once, the Schlagintweits say the same.

We are all living in the Shekh-Bagh, a *Palais* as Hermann calls it, on the banks of the Jhelum. The Schlagintweits have spread out their maps, drawings, collections in the large rooms. They review everything. It seems to me as if the brothers see many things properly only now when they talk about it.

They gather every day at Dal Lake to celebrate their successes. And how do these three scientists celebrate? By imprisoning this landscape in pictures with their pencils and brushes and their machine. But the beauty of the lake does not allow this. The wide opening of the two valleys on the side, the Shalimar Gardens, an old alley of cottonwood trees, the dam, the Rahds and the Panjal range in the background – they copy all of it and, despite their best efforts, it comes out more blurred, smaller, paler.

Even the Schlagintweits are not satisfied with the result. But that does not stop them from lauding their attempts. I respect what they know and what they have achieved, yes, but their pride and joy about what they like to call their *achievements* make them look like boastful children. Hermann gave Adolph and me a detailed account of how he and Robert – never Robert and he – outmanoeuvred the guard of honour in Leh and secretly explored Turkestan on the other side of the mountains.

Eleazar says the guard of honour was thrown into prison for this, and that the Chinese are now convinced that the Schlagintweits are spying for the Vickys.

I do not ask Eleazar how he knows that.

But I ask myself whether the Schlagintweits are also convinced that they are spies.

They are convinced of one thing at any rate. That they are the first Europeans to have crossed the mountain ranges of the Karakorum and the Kuenluen. Hermann says that not even Marco Polo[40] advanced to these heights. He speaks at length about danger as if it were a beloved who treats him badly. This danger took on the most diverse forms: cold, spitting up blood, lack of food, lack of water, eye infections, loss of orientation. The longer his German words become, the smaller the dangers in his story seem to be. Hermann thinks he has shown a lot of courage on his journey.

He should journey into the truth once, like me.

---

40 A merchant from Venice who dared to go to China.

Their greatest discovery, as he calls it, is something they did not find: the Kuenluen is not, as many scientists in Europe have assumed till now, a watershed between Central Asia and India.

I do not understand why the discovery of a non-existent thing should be so important. How can one be happy at not finding something one has looked for? And how will the brothers prove to others that they did not find something? With sketches and measurements and pictures? These are hardly more credible than their words. The Schlagintweits will return home and state: The Kuenluen is not a watershed. And then? Will people simply believe them? And even if people believe them, what will the Vickys and other Europeans do with the information? Record it in books and study it? Teach it to their children? How many subsequent generations will believe they know that something does not exist because once a small group of men did not find it?

All this ran through my head when Adolph took me aside on one of these afternoons sitting on the banks of the lake and said that I was unusually quiet.

Wouldn't it be better, I said, to concentrate on something one has found?

Adolph's eyes reflected the intricate blue of the lake.

I have found a lot, I said, and my voice broke. I handed him Father Fuchs's letter so that it would continue to speak for me. I had not wanted to tell Adolph anything, but I had forgotten to put myself into the equation. Since Simla, the Schlagintweit and I had not been together. Without him, it was easy to keep my vow. With him, it was impossible.

Adolph read the letter carefully and then I told him that I still miss the parents I never had. And that I feel nothing when I think of the parents I had.

Adolph looked at me as if I had more to say.

And I realized that I did.

Which side am I on now, Sir? Am I Indian or German?

Adolph took my hand.

That is easy: You are an Indian through and through.

He smiled.

I did not.

Father Fuchs wanted to protect you, said Adolph. He did not want you asking yourself whether you are Indian or German. It is simpler to be just one thing. He would have probably told you about this at some point.

You cannot know that, I said.

No, said Adolph. But I know what he told me.

You spoke to him?

We corresponded, long before India. He always spoke highly of a very talented young translator. He strongly recommended that we take you with us on our travels.

He wanted to send me away!

He wrote more than once that he wanted you to get to know India. So that you know where you belong.

THIS MORNING THE anger had disappeared.

But that does not change the fact that I know I am not an Indian through and through.

Otherwise, I would not ask myself who I am. Father Fuchs was mistaken. He did not protect me. He should have told me the truth. Then, I would have had at least fourteen years to get to know it, to study it like a brutal, difficult language. We would have grown up together and grown together. I could have been a boy with an unpleasant but familiar truth. One who could have been an Indian through and through, because he knows that he is not.

I JOINED HERMANN, Robert and Adolph on the banks of the Dal Lake and observed them drawing for a while. What they produced was still quite unremarkable. I could not bear to watch them fail any longer and told them what they must do. If one picture cannot capture reality, then several pictures must work together to do it.

After I had explained how this was to be done, the brothers exchanged glances.

No one contradicted me. And contrary to my expectations, they even followed my instructions.

First, Robert produced a photograph. Because of the stark lighting of our Indian sun, one could not distinguish what was close by and what was further away.

Therefore, Hermann cut out the individual objects and pasted them on newspaper.

Then, Adolph incorporated them in the surroundings painted in the watercolour.

The result was still far from perfect. But it was better than all their previous attempts.

Hermann shook my hand delightedly as if we were meeting for the first time. Robert said in his loudest voice: Bravo! And Adolph conferred a title on me – the discoverer of non-existent techniques.

Remarkable Object No. 82

RESULTS

The discoverer of non-existent techniques accompanied Adolph and Hermann on the short route from Srinagger to Rawalpindi. They have never travelled together in India without their younger brother. On the evening before we arrived in Marri, they spent the night deep in conversation inside the tent with lamps and warm covers. So much so that I had to remind them about our early departure in the morning.

Adolph invited me to join them. The brothers were discussing the book they wanted to write about their research. The English version would be titled *Results*; it would comprise nine volumes and contain all their observations.

Will you require my help, Sir? I asked.

We will begin the analysis only in Berlin, Hermann said.

There was a long silence.

We are all aware that we will be parting soon. But none of us talks about it.

Will I also appear in the *Results*? I asked.

Certainly, said Adolph.

We will see, said Hermann.

Both cleared their throats.

I could share some findings from my own work, I said.

In this way, I thought, something about me would definitely be in the *Results*.

Your work? said Adolph.

The Museum of the World, I said.

Is that what you call your notebook? Hermann asked.

I, too, am surprised that I have never told them about the museum although we have been travelling together for so long. I made up for it that evening. The Schlagintweits listened to me and did not laugh; they did not correct me even once.

When I had finished, Hermann said: A noble enterprise.

May we see it? asked Adolph.

I went to fetch it at once.

The brothers bent over the little notebook. Hermann opened it and leafed through it.

It was only then that I realized how stupid I had been. In the discoverer of non-existent techniques, the Schlagintweits could discover the traitor!

You may not read it, I said, and took the book back.

What a pity, said Hermann and looked at me: Maybe one day?

No, I thought, and said: Perhaps.

I knew from the beginning that you are extraordinary, Adolph said to me.

You were against taking him along, said Hermann.

Is that so? said Adolph.

That is so, I said.

Hermann and I looked at him in silence.

Then all three of us laughed.

Bartholomew, said Hermann, may I write something in your museum?

Our laughter died down.

It would be an honour for me, said Hermann.

I was not sure whether I could allow it. Hermann has always been an object. Is an object allowed to write? Would it mean that the object now observes me? And what will it make of me?

Remarkable Object No. 83

BARTHOLOMEW SCHLAGINTWEIT

Scientific data would diminish greatly in value if one had to reflect on it and examine it on one's own. A great deal of the discomforts of travel arises because the country and the people are not varied enough to mitigate boredom which can lead to a longing for home. It was therefore a great and rare joy for me to travel with Bartholomew.

The ideas of a philosopher of the previous century, his name is Immanuel Kant, have increasingly gained favour in German countries. They serve the efforts of those people who dream of having German colonies. Under the disguise of the Enlightenment Mr Kant proclaimed that mankind has reached its greatest perfection in the white race. He is of the opinion that the yellow race is less talented. The Negroes are even lower than that. And some of the American peoples are at the lowest end of his chart. After spending many months among this so-called yellow race, I would have to challenge Mr Kant's ideas. Yes, I, too, believe that civilization prospers most in the white race. In the political system and in the sciences our pre-eminence is decidedly greater than in the quality of our classical literature. But our condition loses some of its aura when we realize that our circumstances have not been like this for very long. In the fifteenth, and even in the seventeenth century, the conditions in Europe were quite different from what they are today – namely worse. Not in India. There had been progress till what were our Middle Ages. The present shows only a few changes. Travellers would have found many things in the moral conditions better than in Europe. The seeds of civilization are spread throughout the world.

Instead of judging foreign races from a distance, Mr Kant would have done better to embark on a discovery of distant regions. Then, like me, he would have personally encountered numerous inconsistencies with regard to his ideas. Bartholomew not only saved the lives of my brothers, but his bright mind has also impressed me just as much, indeed even more. I cannot find any notable differences between the talents of a Bartholomew and those of a younger Hermann. We could both be called Schlagintweit, so help me God!

Remarkable Object No. 84

THE FIRST INDIAN MUSEUM

Before I could stop him, Hermann grabbed a pen and wrote me – and somehow also himself – into the museum. BARTHOLOMEW SCHLAGINTWEIT. I had to read his entry several times to believe it. Not because it told me something new.[41] I have always known that his talent and mine are on par. But I would not have thought that he knows this and is even willing to admit it.

I thanked him and made him a promise.

I will never tell anyone, Sir, what you did on the palm tree.

The monocotyledon? he asked. The one I climbed in the south?

I nodded.

That should remain our secret, Hermann said, and winked at me.

ON 17 NOVEMBER, almost two years after leaving Bombay, we arrived in Rawalpindi. A restlessness has taken hold of the Schlagintweits. They are packing and checking their collections. Hundreds of boxes have to be sent to Berlin. Soon, the brothers will part for a last time and reunite again only in Berlin. Robert will travel with a major portion of the collections and a massive train through the Salt Range and via Karachi to Bombay, where he will board a ship to Alexandria.

---

41 I did not know Mr Kant. But it seems he is a gentleman I do not wish to know at all.

Hermann's next destination is Lahore, then Nepal (he finally received permission), and his last one before Europe is Alexandria. He and Robert will travel home together by ship.

Adolph will take a different route. It leads to Attok and Peshawar, towards the northwest and much further. Like Alexander von Humboldt he wants to go to Europe on the overland route through Central Asia and Russia. He says, Constantinople and Damascus and Kashgar and Isfahan and Kabul and Samarkand and so on once constituted the central nervous system of the world. Just as anatomy explains how the body works, the study of this system of cities allows us to understand how the world works.

And I?

In Rawalpindi I again helped the Schlagintweits to collect racial types. They were very taken up with the many different kinds of people they saw in the vast bazaars. We achieved a yield of almost two hundred racial types. Have so many faces of the world ever been collected before?

One night I was woken by a coolie. The Schlagintweits wanted to see me. I was to bring the museum with me. The coolie was carrying a sword.

I took the museum and accompanied him to one of the tents in which the brothers were checking their collections. The coolie remained standing in front of the tent. I went in.

Only three candles lit the interior of the tent and the serious faces of the Schlagintweits.

It was quiet except for the wind, which, coming from all directions, pushed against the sides of the tent from outside.

Hermann said: Good evening, Bartholomew.

Then he paused as if he had said something remarkable.

We have spoken at great length about you.

Don't make it so dramatic, said Adolph.

It is important that he realizes the significance of our decision, Robert said.

And, Hermann continued in a raised voice, we have arrived at a conclusion.

Again, he paused.

Not unanimously, I would like to say.

And he glanced briefly at Robert.

But, on the basis of certain experiences and observations in the previous weeks, the majority of us is for it.

I wanted to ask for what when Hermann said: However, you must take an oath.

Why? I asked.

Some of us don't trust you completely, said Hermann.

Some of us still haven't forgotten your scheming in Bombay, said Robert.

Scheming! Adolph protested.

Before Robert could reply, Hermann said: Swear that you will never betray us.

All three of them looked at me.

Hermann nodded encouragingly.

Robert did nothing.

Adolph placed my hand on the museum and let his hand rest on mine.

I swear it, I said, and although I immediately feared that I would not be able to keep this vow, I meant it honestly.

Good, said Hermann.

Excellent, said Adolph.

Both of them looked at Robert. It seemed as if he had to fetch his next word from a great distance.

Agreed, he said finally.

Then, I would now like to inform you of our decision, said Hermann. We have decided …

Do you want to come to Berlin with us? Adolph interrupted.

The wind hit against the side of the tent behind me.

I was so surprised that I did not know what to say.

Did you understand me? asked Hermann.

Yes, I said.

Then? said Adolph.

I looked for the right words.

Thank you for this offer, I said.

It is not an offer, said Robert, it is a great honour!

Thank you for this honour, I said.

This time I paused as if I had said something remarkable.

Together we will set up the first Indian museum, said Adolph. His Majesty was enthusiastic about India even when he was Crown Prince and devised a secret script based on Sanskrit. He is making the Monbijou Palace in Berlin available to us. All the different disciplines of our collections will be exhibited there. Geology, geography, botany, zoology, ethnography. The museum will unite our numerous objects into something splendid. Like the British Museum.

An organism entirely in the spirit of Humboldt, Hermann added.

Adolph corrected him: A museum of the world.

That is why we are asking for your help, both of them said simultaneously.

But I know the real reason.

You don't want to miss me, I said.

Hermann and Adolph exchanged looks.

That … cannot be ruled out, said Hermann.

Will you take us up on this? Adolph asked.

He sounded almost diffident.

How long would I be in Berlin? I asked.

As long as you want, said Adolph, and added: If you want, forever.

So, said Robert, what is your decision?

The wind skimmed the side of the tent like a tentative hand.

I looked at the brothers. Maybe it was the dim light which made them appear smaller than they were. I barely had to raise my head to return their looks.

I will think about it, I said.

Adolph laughed, and after a brief pause, so did Hermann. Only Robert's lips remained in a thin, straight line.

You will *think about it*? he said.

Yes, I said and left the tent quickly.

Hermann called out after me: Don't take too much time!

THAT SAME NIGHT Abdullah woke me up. He took me to a tent in which again only three candles were burning. Eleazar and Mr Monteiro were waiting for us. Abdullah pushed me down to my knees. Mr Monteiro took my hand and placed it on the dry earth.

Before we talk, Eleazar said, you must swear not to abandon or betray us.

Never, I said.

Eleazar and Abdullah exchanged looks.

You will take a vow, said Abdullah.

Will you kill me otherwise?

We will not do anything so barbaric, said Eleazar.

Abdullah caught me by the collar to drag me outside.

Wait, said Eleazar.

Abdullah stopped.

We are accompanying Adolph Schlagintweit to Kashgar, said Eleazar.

I know, I said.

But do you also know why?

Eleazar, Abdullah called out and went to him.

We can trust him, Eleazar said to him.

You cannot, I said.

I don't know what Eleazar sees in me.

We are meeting with a Chinese delegation in Kashgar, Eleazar said.

Abdullah muttered something under his breath and left the tent. One of the candles flickered and went out.

You will help us, Eleazar continued.

With what? I asked.

Freedom, he said. The enemy of my enemy is my friend.

I thought of Jeejeebhoy's assistant.

You are working for the Chinese, I said. That is why you prevented the Schlagintweits from advancing northwards several times.

I work *with them*, said Eleazar. Friends help one another.

Why are you telling me this now?

In Cochin I saw that all the peoples of India can live together peacefully. We do not need the firangi. We need you. You always say everything is connected with everything else. Your father helped to rob India of its freedom, and his son must now help to get it back. You cannot go to Berlin, my friend; there you will only be a firangi. This is your home.

I left the tent so that Eleazar would not continue saying what I was thinking.

He and I, we have nothing in common.

Early on the morning of 13 December – Hermann's watch showed three o'clock – Adolph's train set out. In the light of the torches held by our massalchis we parted from his brothers. Robert stood a little further away; he had pulled his hat down on his face. His protruding ears reminded me, as at our first meeting, of a bat. Since then, he has not changed much. Or he has hidden this change well. Even after all these months, he has remained for me a product of his picture machine: flat, blurred and grey. The youngest Schlagintweit only raised a hand in farewell. I reciprocated the gesture. I would have really liked to give him a piece of advice for life: in future, he should be less himself and more his brothers. But he has probably already received this advice from many others.

Hermann's tuft of hair has thinned out. It no longer flounces around when he talks; it dances. He still loves to talk. But his thoughts no longer originate only in his head. I get the impression that many of them have arisen on this journey. Some of them are mine.

While taking leave, Hermann caressed my shoulder. It felt like praise. Verbose as ever, he stressed the need to be careful. It has always been difficult for Europeans to advance across the border, and the antipathy of Chinese authorities against all foreigners was even greater now. The train's advance into the Chinese province Gnari Khorsum had alarmed China's commanders. There would now be hundreds of official reports in Peking against the brothers. The Chinese government had sent an order to its officials in Turkestan: *If any European advances into a district controlled by you, his property is yours, but his head belongs to Peking.*

It is good to know that I have Bartholomew Schlagintweit on my side, said Adolph.

The brothers embraced.

When I held out my hand to Hermann, he took it in both of his and said: I am sure we will meet again in Berlin. A glorious future awaits you.

Remarkable Objects
Nos. 85 & 86
VASCO AND VENKATESH

Every day I remind myself that Eleazar is a bad man, as bad as Smitaben's good man. He took another man's life. Even if Hormazd was not a particularly good man and had threatened Eleazar's life, even if he has helped me discover my past, Eleazar is a bad man. I know that.

But why do I have to remind myself of it every day?

Not even the museum helps me understand it. Normally, it provides clarity. It is a tidy house which controls even the disorder of space and time. The meagre happenings of many weeks – in which the train moves through the northernmost and westernmost parts of the Punjab; in which Adolph, with me as a translator by his side, even attends an important meeting with Dost Mohammed, the Emir of Kabul, and his military entourage of ten thousand men, where the Vickys and the Afghans renewed their alliances (which, so that they are upheld, apparently has to be done more often with Kabul than with other neighbours of India) – are reduced to a single sentence.

This does not work with Eleazar. For the first time, an object does not allow itself to be made an object. The Bania does not allow himself to be studied. He does it on purpose. Because he wants me to be closer to him. But I do not fall for this trick.

There is a better way. It is paved with Mr Monteiro's knowledge. Of the three traitors in the train the Indo-Portuguese seems to me to be the least traitorous. At least, as far as I know, he has not yet committed a murder.

Since I wanted to be sure, I asked him.

Why do you want to know that? he asked.

A murderer cannot be trusted.

To that Mr Monteiro gave a strange reply: You are mistaken, Bartholomew. It is precisely a murderer who can be trusted. One knows after all what he has done. Where he stands. There is no going back for him. He will always remain a murderer. But a man who has not yet committed a murder … one should be careful of such a man. He could become a murderer at any time.

When you met Eleazar for the first time, was he already one?

That was not a very elegant transition, said Mr Monteiro.

I tried to decide which of his eyes was the healthy one. Definitely, the left eye.

If you want to know more about him, why don't you ask him? said Mr Monteiro. He will gladly give you the information.

Or no, it was the right eye.

You are more than his ally, I said.

His oldest friend, he said.

And as such you have nothing to say about him?

Oh, I could tell you a lot. But I think you wouldn't hear me.

Try me, I said.

Mr Monteiro took the whip from his belt and let it swirl around gently as if he were still undecided what or whom it should grab next.

I cannot tell you who he is, he said. Only Eleazar can do that. But I can tell you something about myself. Maybe that will help you to see him as I do.

With his one eye he gave me a more penetrating look than other people with two eyes. I was quite sure it was the right eye – and then he winked at me with the left eye.

Mr Monteiro said that before he joined up with Eleazar, the most important person in his life was a boy called Venkatesh. Their story began many years ago in the south, in Cochin. At that time Mr Monteiro was an orphan who only had a first name: Vasco. He had lost his parents in a tidal wave and grew up in St. Stanislaus, a Catholic home run by the Portuguese, which the people of Cochin called the Dream House. Because most of the children there – many of them former slaves from Africa or the result of an illicit affair between firangi and Indians – lived in a dreamlike condition. The four Fathers who managed St. Stanislaus bought the weakest children at the port, gave them enough to eat so that they could sleep through the night, taught them to read and write, and they beat a child only if it ill-treated other children. Their care of the orphans gave rise to the saying in Cochin: One who enters the Dream House as a worm, leaves it as a butterfly.

Vasco got to know Venkatesh when both of them, as he says, were at least fourteen years old. The Vickys had caught him stealing and handed him over to the Fathers. Everyone in the Dream House noticed that he was darker skinned than all the others. Venkatesh was so dark skinned that he stood out in the dark. Although the Fathers baptized the Bania and gave him a Christian name, it did not stop the other children from calling him O Negro. During his first weeks in the Dream House all of them, including Vasco, stayed away from him. They were neither hostile nor friendly. They were afraid that his blackness could befall them like an infectious disease. Some children were darker than others, but no one wanted to be so dark. A blackness like this was considered a curse. All the children agreed that Venkatesh would never find a family, a job, or even a dream of his own. Moreover, he was small and slender. Smaller and slenderer than even the younger children. No one could understand how he had survived on Cochin's streets. After his father had died of cholera, Venkatesh's mother had burned herself on his funeral pyre. Nothing more was known about Venkatesh's earlier life. The Bania kept his past to himself; he hardly spoke. Vasco, at any rate, seldom saw him talking to anyone.

Venkatesh only spoke for others. As it turned out, his strength lay in this. The Fathers often took his help when they were negotiating in the port, or in the offices, or in the Jewish spice market. Venkatesh spoke Malayalam, Hindi, English, Portuguese, Dutch, Chinese and even a little Hebrew. Vasco, who only knew Malayalam and a little Portuguese, was fascinated by this.

When he approached O Negro for the first time since his arrival in the Dream House, he asked him how he had learnt all these languages.

Venkatesh replied: I am a child of Cochin.

Vasco found out only later what he had meant by it. Venkatesh had learnt Dutch from the sailors who anchored in Cochin on their way from Europe to the Dutch East Indies. He learnt Chinese from the fishermen who empty the sea with their giant nets and boast that they are the descendants of merchants at the court of a famous Khan. English he learnt from the occupying force, Portuguese from the clerics of the firangi, Hindi from a translator who had been thrown out of the royal palace in Mattancherry, Hebrew from a Jewish spice merchant called Eleazar who had sometimes given Venkatesh a bowl of rice. And he had been brought up with Malayalam instead of breast milk.

Venkatesh had learnt to speak all these languages because his appearance did not speak for him. Once Vasco understood this, he no longer wondered how Venkatesh had survived all these years on the streets of Cochin. He asked himself rather why he had come to the Dream House voluntarily.

Venkatesh answered this question without Vasco having asked it.

Like every child in the Dream House, they were assigned tasks. Both the boys were made punkah-wallahs. By pulling evenly on ropes they kept large fans made of framed cloth in motion. These hung from the ceiling of the St. Francis Church, and their breeze made it easier for the perspiring congregation to pray. Vasco liked this task. The church was the oldest in India. Once, Vasco da Gama, after whom the Fathers had named him, had been buried here. And even though the Portuguese later took his mortal remains home, Vasco always felt at home and safe in the church. Venkatesh changed that.

I am here to save all of you, he whispered to Vasco once when they were operating the punkah.

From what? Vasco asked.

From your dreams.

Venkatesh told him that the four Fathers were not as good and fair as everyone assumed. They mixed something in the food of some children. Men paid to come to these children at night and do unspeakable things to them. The children would remember these nights, if at all, only as strange dreams.

Vasco did not believe a word of this. It was true that some children occasionally mentioned some peculiar dreams. Dreams that were so intense that the children fell from their beds and got scratches and bruises. But everyone dreamt a lot in the Dream House. One could not blame the Fathers for that. Rather, it was because of the disturbing song of the surf washing up on the shore.

That is what Vasco explained to Venkatesh.

The latter nodded in silence and Vasco assumed that the matter had ended there.

How mistaken he was!

Every time they operated the fans in the church together O Negro fed him more thoughts. He insisted he knew danger better than most. He had studied it extensively and talked at length with Eleazar in Jew Town about danger. The Jews were long acquainted with it. Because of it, the ancestors of the Jews, he said, had fled from their home, Jerusalem, when a king named Nebuchadnezzar had laid siege to it, and they had settled down on the west coast of India. When the Portuguese came, many of them were burned at the stake. They had to flee again, to the south. It was only in Cochin that the raja gave them land near the royal palace. The synagogue was built. Jew Town was established. But none of them ever forgot the danger. They remained alert because they knew that danger could catch up with them at any time.

Eleazar has taught me how to become a compass for danger, Venkatesh said to Vasco.

Vasco still did not believe that the Fathers also represented danger, the same four Fathers who had brought him up and protected him for years. But he had to admit that Venkatesh's exciting stories offered a whiff of change. O Negro was in a certain way also his punkah-wallah, but with words instead of air.

The other orphans to whom O Negro whispered his truth about the Fathers did not accept his stories. Even his sophisticated language did not convince them. They warned him several times to stop spreading lies.

But Venkatesh did not stop. And so, they began to show him how little they thought of his stories. Often enough Vasco saw how, when the Fathers were not nearby, Venkatesh was pushed, spat upon, kicked. Vasco never intervened. He was far too afraid of being considered O Negro's friend. The wounds on Venkatesh's face only made him suspect how many more the Bania must have in places he could not see. He was surprised that O Negro did not betray anyone. Although the Fathers demanded, under threat of punishment, that he name the culprits, he did not speak.

The children showed their gratitude by forcing him to eat fish that was off.

The four Fathers, who had heard his stories, also told Venkatesh to stop spreading lies. They treated his wounds, gave him more to eat than the others and swore to him that they were not bad people. They almost begged him to believe them.

Venkatesh replied, even if the other orphans resisted, he would free them of their dreams. He would show them that the honey they loved to swallow was poisoned.

The Fathers asserted that they were only concerned with the children's well-being.

O Negro heard them out in silence, but he did not listen to them. That same day he continued to talk.

The children set his hair on fire, and he had to shave off the rest, but the smell still lingered on for some days. While working the fans Vasco asked him why he was doing all this to himself.

Venkatesh replied: Because no one else will do it.

If it hasn't happened to you, Vasco said, how can you be so sure that the Fathers are guilty?

Venkatesh looked at him.

While moving the fan, Vasco added: Don't say because you talked with the Jew. That is not enough for me.

How do you know, Venkatesh asked, that hell exists?

From the Bible, said Vasco.

Have you been there? Did you see it with your own eyes?

While Vasco moved the fan, Venkatesh added: No. That means it is a matter of faith. We know some things because we believe other people. And everyone in the Dream House can decide for himself whom he believes – the Fathers or me.

You did not answer my question, said Vasco.

No, he said, smiling, I did not. But the men who wrote the Bible also never saw hell. And yet you don't doubt that it exists.

Vasco admired Venkatesh. His faith was on par with that of the Fathers. Although Vasco still did not believe the Bania, he now believed that the Bania fully believed his own truth.

He wanted to tell him that when they next met.

But it never happened.

O Negro did not turn up for work. He was replaced by another boy. After mass, Vasco looked for Venkatesh and found him in his bed. The Bania was still sleeping. Vasco wanted to wake him up, but one of the Fathers stopped him. Venkatesh must rest, he said, he has suffered a lot. Vasco agreed and left Venkatesh alone. When the

Bania woke up later, he still seemed tired. His face looked unusually dull. He did not want to get up, wished only to eat something and to sleep again. But what disturbed Vasco: O Negro did not talk about the Dream House. He was no longer interested in it. Vasco asked him if he had finally realized his mistake. Venkatesh nodded. Vasco asked if he was feeling well. Venkatesh nodded again. Vasco asked if he was really feeling well. Venkatesh lay down to sleep. Vasco shook him, but Venkatesh fended him off and shooed him away. It was as if he really wanted to find a wonderful dream again.

Vasco did not know how to handle this. With each passing day that Venkatesh slept, Vasco's fear of sleep grew.

In the St. Francis church, he prayed to the infant Jesus, a small wooden figure that he felt a greater connection to than to the half-naked bleeding man on the cross. The right hand of the infant Jesus was raised with the forefinger, the middle finger and the thumb stretched out in blessing. His eyes were only half-open and looked dreamy. Vasco particularly liked his smile. It was as if he did not take all these religious carryings-on very seriously, or as if he were aware that he was standing naked and without genitals in a church. Vasco told him about Venkatesh. He whispered to him that he would like to help the Bania. And the infant Jesus blessed his plan.

After Venkatesh had not left his bed for two weeks, Vasco crept up to him in the night and woke him up. Venkatesh did not seem very pleased at this. Vasco offered to help him escape. The Dream House, he said, was not good for him.

I am staying here, said Venkatesh.

The wounds on his face had healed. Since he had stopped telling his stories, the other orphans left him in peace. But, instead, there were dark circles around his eyes. The long hours of sleeping seemed to make him even more tired.

You have changed, said Vasco.

Yes, said Venkatesh.

You have to leave this place.

He dragged the Bania out of his bed.

Venkatesh called loudly for help.

Vasco begged him to be quiet. But it was too late. Lights came closer and with them the Fathers. They pulled Vasco away and rebuked him for not letting Venkatesh sleep. They threatened him with consequences if he were to continue with this and sent him to bed.

On the following day, Vasco took the blessings of the infant Jesus for his decision not to eat. The first few hours were easy. The next day was horrible. He became dull and his thoughts centred only around fresh idlis with coconut chutney. He became dizzy while working the punkahs. But he held out. Two days later, the dullness cleared, and he felt as if he could see more clearly. He also slept a lot. But not like he had before. Deeper, yet not as deep as before. In the mornings he felt more rested. Vasco could not say whether it was because of the fasting or because he did not eat what the Fathers allegedly mixed in the food.

Four days later, he became unconscious while working the punkahs. The Fathers carried him to his bed in the dormitory. He had kept it a secret from them and from all the others that he had stopped eating. They brought him fish moley, his favourite dish. The steaming bowl gave off a wonderful fragrance. He tore off a piece of appam and dipped it in the curry; he could not help himself.

Then he saw Venkatesh a few beds away. He was in the process of devouring his food.

Vasco let the piece of appam fall. Later, he secretly threw away his favourite food.

That night he woke up when he felt himself being lifted up. He was carried out of the dormitory. Vasco kept his eyes closed and pretended to be asleep. Whatever was going to happen, he thought, cannot be as bad as O Negro had said.

They went down many stairs. Doors were opened and closed again, the last one was latched. Vasco was placed on soft cushions.

The air in the room was thick and warm and full of whisperings. A hand touched his forehead. It did not belong to the Fathers. The fingers were too soft and had rings on them. The hand caressed his face. It gently pulled his hair. Rattled breathing grazed Vasco's cheek. An unknown male voice said he was beautiful.

It was then that Vasco realized something bad was going to happen, and he also understood that it would be worse if they saw he was not asleep. And so, he continued to breathe evenly and deeply; he kept his eyes closed and his arms and legs slack. But he found it difficult to do this; in fact, he only wanted to run away.

He was undressed. When he was naked, the hands returned. There seemed to be more than two. They were now not so friendly any more. The rattled breathing grew louder. It was almost worse than the touches. He could not bear it any longer. Vasco winced.

The hands disappeared. Voices whispered in confusion. One voice hissed angrily: he is awake. There was movement all around him. The door was unlatched and opened. He was hastily carried to his bed.

The rest of the night Vasco was afraid that they would come for him again. But they stayed away.

Despite this he could not sleep. For the first time he had encountered the unspeakable about which Venkatesh had warned him. The most awful part of it was not the hours of this night; it was all the hours he did not remember. How often had he been carried to this place in the depths of the Dream House? How often had other hands touched him? How often had they made his body their own?

Vasco thought about this the whole night. Even the next morning at breakfast, which he did not touch, he thought about it. He thought about it every time he saw Venkatesh, who now emptied his plate at every meal and was full of praise for the Dream House. Vasco thought about it especially when one of the Fathers smiled at him, patted him lovingly on the shoulder or hugged him and told him what a good child of God he was.

His hatred did not grow gradually. It was there all of a sudden. Vasco no longer went to the infant Jesus so that he would not take away his hatred. Vasco wanted to hold on to it. He needed it. It alone gave him strength. Hatred filled him with strength and courage.

It was not difficult for Vasco to find out how the Fathers made all the children dream. He discovered that on certain evenings the Fathers mixed a white powder in the food of those children who had to sleep especially deeply. It was only in Venkatesh's food that the powder was mixed every evening. They kept this ingredient in a small room behind the altar otherwise meant only for the musty register of marriages and funerals in Cochin. Vasco did not know what kind of powder it was, but Mr Monteiro is convinced that it was opium.

Vasco mixed it in the Fathers' food and waited for the night.

Long before the fire reached the Fathers' bedrooms, Vasco had woken up the children and driven them out of the Dream House. With tears in their eyes, they saw how their home collapsed. Vasco also cried. He was surprised at how sad he felt. But another emotion was even stronger. Satisfaction. He imagined that the Fathers were now caught forever in a burning nightmare. At his side, Venkatesh screamed in desperation. He wanted to run back into the burning Dream House. Vasco could only stop him by holding him close. O Negro calmed down when the fire began to die out. The people of Cochin stood in a chain down to the beach and put out the fire with buckets of water. Many of them wondered later why none of the Fathers had woken up in time.

Vasco and Venkatesh found refuge in Jew Town. Eleazar, the spice merchant, took them in. The boys helped to wash the ginger and coriander, they looked for worms in containers of curry leaves and cardamom, and they ground the fenugreek seeds into powder.

It took a few days for the real Venkatesh to return. The sluggishness left him, and he started to talk. Vasco bowed down in front of him and asked to be forgiven for not having believed him. He told him what he had done. Venkatesh looked at him dumbfounded. The Bania said he had never wanted to hurt the Fathers; he had only wanted to save the orphans. Vasco did not know what to say.

Neither did Venkatesh.

They soon learnt that the authorities were looking for the arsonist. They had to leave Cochin immediately, before they were found. With Eleazar's help they fled the city in a crate full of curry leaves and found shelter in an abandoned hut without a roof. There, Vasco took leave of Venkatesh. He did not want to expose his friend to any further risks; after all, the authorities were looking for him. They embraced.

But neither one could let go of the other.

And so, together, they left the punkahs, O Negro, the infant Jesus, and all false dreams behind them. It was not going to be the last time that they saved each other. In the years that followed, Mr Monteiro would not always see what his friend saw, but the Indo-Portuguese man never doubted him. They chose new names so that they would not be connected with the fire. Vasco became Mr Monteiro. And Venkatesh called himself Eleazar out of gratitude and in memory of the Jew. For each other, however, they remained Vasco and Venkatesh, two boys from Cochin.

Remarkable Object No. 87

TRUTH AND BEAUTY
OR
TRUTH
OR
BEAUTY

Mr Monteiro says he and Eleazar want to wake me up. And not only me. The entire country! They think even Indians who have fathers and mothers are orphans who are caught up in dreams. We must, he says, be a large family for one another.

I told Mr Monteiro that I do not want to be a part of his family.

He asked me whether I had listened to him at all.

Of course, I had. But I will never believe a word a traitor says. Mr Monteiro's past is definitely as fake as his stuffed bird skins.

Venkatesh, I said to Eleazar, was that your name before?

Yes, he said.

Did, what Mr Monteiro claims, really happen?

Why should he lie?

So that I see the good in the bad.

For that he does not need any lies, my friend. The truth is enough for that.

The train has left the Punjab behind along with its sandstorms and salt lakes. To celebrate what would be at least my fifteenth birthday, Adolph and I polished off a bottle of Old Monk. I was drunk for the first time. Unfortunately, I do not remember anything. Adolph says I will become *a fine figure of a man*. I asked him what that is. He said, someone like him.

The Schlagintweit does not mention Berlin any more. (Or, Old Monk has made me forget this, too.) He probably thinks that as long as we do not talk about it, I cannot decide against it. With each mile that we cover his wish comes closer to reality. When he looks at me, I clearly feel how happy he is about it. Especially when he thinks I do not notice him looking.

I will arrive at a decision soon; I only need a little more time.

In Lahore we had to get wool and silk as well as Turkestani clothes for ourselves, and we had to have our heads shaved so that if we encountered someone in the mountains, they would think we were merchants.

Before our departure, Abdullah, our khansaman for the journey to Turkestan, asked Adolph for his official papers. The Schlagintweit gave him his Indian travel documents. Abdullah said these would be of no use to the Schlagintweit in the north. The draughtsman was in an unusually bad mood, even for him. I cannot say whether it was because we were surrounded in Lahore by the ruins of mosques and other remarkable Islamic buildings which Ranjit Singh had ordered to be torn down. Or because the Vickys of all people had rebuilt some of them. At any rate, Abdullah was in a sullen frame of mind. When Adolph showed him his documents from Bavaria and Prussia, he returned them to the Schlagintweit without kissing them as he usually did. These are also not the right papers, he said, since the bird on them only has one head. Did he not have a Russian pass with him?

When Adolph laughed, Abdullah advised him against taking scientific instruments along. If they were discovered, they would betray us immediately. This time, Adolph did not laugh. The region ahead of us has not yet been studied. He considers himself honour-bound, he said, to carry out his measurements.

I CONSIDER MYSELF honour-bound to spend as much time as possible with him. But Eleazar always appears in my thoughts or in front of me. Each time he points out to me what Adolph is noting down: access ways, food for the animals in the transport, distances, natural resources, human settlements. The Bania calls this *Intelligence*. He says, the Schlagintweits are spying for the Angrez.

That is not true, I say.

And Eleazar says, the price for truth is beauty. If we open ourselves up to truth, if we really admit to it, we see that there is no beauty.

Yet Adolph says that beauty comes from truth.

He is teaching me to paint the truth. I have finally proved myself worthy! Adolph trusts me with his valuable brushes and paints. The most important things are an accurate eye and the correct standpoint, he says. Although we are using paper from the trigonometric offices of the dishonest East India Company in Calcutta, it disappears under true and beautiful colours and forms. Adolph sets a lot of store by accuracy. The portrayal of every gorge, snow deposit, cloud formation, crestline and shadow spread had to be exactly right down to the last detail.

But sometimes, Adolph allows me to change some things. Once, I had to add a goat, which was not there, in the foreground of the picture. I pointed out that the painting would then not be completely true. He explained to me that the goat is a visual aid. It allows the viewer to get a better feel for depth and height, and thus brings the truth closer to him. Another time he told me to remove a human settlement from the picture. At first, I asked myself how this could lead to greater truth. But once I had removed the houses, I had to agree with him. The deserted wilderness in the picture gives a better feeling for the loneliness here. Pictures of this part of the world have never been made, said Adolph. We must help the Europeans to feel the difficult nature of this expedition.

The firangi will never be able to feel all this. We are moving through the remotest regions and crossing the highest mountain ranges. Even General George Everest, who supervised magnetic studies long before the Schlagintweits, had not come so far. I am glad I have the walking stick. It is only because of my three legs that I can keep up with the train. The higher we climb, the more I feel the weight of my bones. Even Mr Monteiro's whistling does not provide any relief. I know too many ugly things about him which make me incapable of hearing the beauty of his music. Every time I fall far back in the train, Adolph wants to carry me. I allow it only when I am too exhausted.

I can forget my body only when I am painting. The watercolours are like painted entries in the museum. I like it most when Adolph teaches me new techniques. He never does it with words. He always uses his hand. While I guide the brush, he guides me. Sometimes I make a mistake so that he will help me. As long as we are painting together, my joints and my ears do not ache, I am not freezing cold, I am not tired, I am not afraid of our parting and of everything that will follow after it.

If one must really decide between truth and beauty, what is there to be said against beauty?

Remarkable Object No. 88

THE BEAUTY OF BERLIN

WATERCOLOUR OVER PENCIL ON PAPER

A room in the Monbijou Palace. Hundreds of wooden chests are stacked in the background. Objects are scattered everywhere. Racial types, a yatagan, a jug made from the lining of a camel's stomach and filled with palm wine, fossils, black-spined toads preserved in spirit, a tree trunk, barchas, a Tibetan rosary made of snake vertebrae, ivory, stuffed Psittacidae, a double-tongued riding crop and many, many stones. Three white men stand lost among all this. One of them has bat-like ears, one has chubby cheeks, and one is holding a hand to his mouth as if to stop himself from talking. Their distrustful and benevolent and envious looks are directed at the central motif of the picture that allows the viewer to get a better feel of depth and height: a small Indian boy is pointing to a globe on which his country is shining gloriously. He appears to be proclaiming something important. Directly beside him: an old man with his head weighed down heavily by time. But his eyes shine with curiosity like those of the small Indian boy to whom he is listening attentively. In one hand he is holding a single, silver hair. He is smiling a smile of heartfelt respect.

Remarkable Object No. 89

INDECISION

For some time now, I have been trying to write a farewell letter. But I cannot decide whom to address it to. Indecision is one of the heaviest objects in the world, and I have to carry it all the time. No one, not Eleazar, not Adolph, and not even Smitaben can relieve me of this burden.

Remarkable Object No. 90

WHAT BURNS IN THE HEART

On 31 May, the train was able to enter Tibet undiscovered. We stayed away from Leh so that Gulab Singh would not hear about us. Otherwise, a guard of honour would definitely have been ordered to accompany us, and we would not have been able to travel further.

Now we are resting for a few days in Pangmig, the last inhabited place before the border to Turkestan. Adolph sees to it that provisions are organized for the long journey into uncertainty. The animals have to be taken along. But we could barely ensure sufficient fodder for them; the supplies of barley are scarce, and the train has thinned out. Till recently we were between forty and sixty men. Some of them are from Turkestan and Bukhara. They know the language of the country and are experienced mountain climbers. Adolph has sent the others, especially the Indians who are less useful in the north, back to India with parts of his collections in order not to endanger them – the collections, that is. In the meantime, the train comprises just about twenty people.

Adolph has not yet decided which route we will follow. No one knows this part of the high mountain range. And, even if we succeed in overcoming the Karakorum Range as well as the far steeper Kuenluen without being discovered by the border guards, we then have to face the uninhabited high-altitude desert.

In Pangmig we learnt that the caravan traffic between Turkestan and Tibet has been interrupted. This does not worry either Adolph or Eleazar. Fallen rocks are said to be the cause.

NEAR PANGMIG THERE are three hot springs. I wandered off there alone. In the shade of poplars and apricot trees, I once again pulled out the farewell letter. Having stared at the blank page for a while, I threw it into the water and the paper disintegrated. The pieces were carried away in a small canal built by the people living there.

Eleazar appeared. I told him to go away, but he remained standing in front of me and smiled.

Something wonderful has happened, he said.

Even a spy could not have received information about events in India on our remote route. But now! While our train had turned its back on our home, the country had awakened.

For months now, news had spread in the sepahis' barracks: the small paper cartridges which contained the ammunition for the new Enfield rifle were said to be greased with tallow from beef and lard derived from pork. To use them, the soldiers had to bite down on the cartridge to open it. A Hindu thus had to eat his holy cow, and a Muslim unclean pork. Eleazar says, he had foreseen that our country could only be united in this way: through faith and food.

During a drill at the end of April, a certain Colonel Carmichael Smith in Mirath ordered his sepahis to bite open the cartridges. Eighty-five of ninety men refused. The colonel, therefore, had the proud soldiers, many of whom belonged to higher castes, divested of their uniforms, laid in chains and sentenced to ten years' imprisonment. There was one thing, however, said Eleazar, which the colonel could not lock up: the Indian will to be free.

This treatment burnt in the hearts of the sepahis. It reminded them of harsh taxes. It reminded them of famines caused by the Angrez. It reminded them of the factory-made textiles with which the Angrez had destroyed the value of Indian handwoven cloth. It reminded them of lost battles against the firangi and lost battles for the firangi. It reminded them of maharajas and Mughals kneeling down, of destroyed mosques and temples. It reminded them of the Doctrine of Lapse. It reminded them of Catholic missionaries who lock Indian children up in dreams. It reminded them of family members who had been put to death. And it reminded them that Colonel Carmichael Smith had humiliated them.

A few days later, on 10 May, some Angrez were in the Sadar Bazaar in Mirath buying beer. A large group of sepahis came towards them. The Angrez demanded that they explain why they were not at their posts. The sepahis replied by striking them. Then, some of them rushed to the parade ground where the armoury was, others went to the prison. The sepahis who had been freed went to Colonel Carmichael Smith's house and shot him repeatedly, as if they wanted to kill him many times over.

On the same day, the sepahis marched to Delhi and joined the regiments there. The royal cannon gave a 21-gun salute. Bahadur Shah was proclaimed the new emperor of India. Delhi belongs to Indians again. All the firangi have either been captured, or are dead, or they have fled the city. Even women and children are said to have died.

I am very sorry about that, said Eleazar.

His evident joy said something else.

He continued talking about the rebellion in Lucknow, about fighting in Agra, about unrest in Barrackpore, but I could only think of Mirath.

Where is Devinder? I asked.

He will go down in history as a hero, said Eleazar. Just like you. Without both of you, the ammunition would never have reached its destination. The Angrez did not want to reveal what it was greased with. But thanks to both of you, the proof of their ignorance could reach the sepahis. By transporting the package, you, Bartholomew, sparked off the rebellion.

Where is he? I asked again.

I had to repeat the question two more times before he replied.

The Vickys tied Devinder in front of a cannon for, as they called it, his mutiny, and fired it.

I thought of the Punjabi in the shade of the Ficus tree, of how he slept there as if he never had to wake up again.

Eleazar was saying that he had underestimated this rapid development of events; that his mission had now become all the more significant, namely, to attack the Angrez from all sides with the help of China.

Because of you, thousands will die, I said.

Thanks to me, less people will die than without me. Think of your mother. If the firangi had not come to India, she would still be alive.

But not I! I called out and wanted to leave.

Eleazar held me back.

Bartholomew is not your real name, he said. At least not the one your mother gave you. Father Fuchs wanted to make you one of them. That is why he changed your name, just like the firangi change all the names in the country.

Eleazar let go of me.

But now I did not want to go.

What name did she give me? I asked.

I am sorry, he said before leaving me alone, only she knows that.

I stepped up to the steaming water and looked for my reflection while listening to my heart.

Remarkable Object No. 91

A WORD OF LOVE

This is a letter of farewell. I have struggled with it for a long time. Now I can see more clearly. It is not only the air that is clear so high up in the mountains.

Today is 5 August 1857. We are on the Kilian Pass; we will have soon crossed the Kuenluen. Kashgar is only a few days away on the other side of the high-altitude deserts.

Would you have ever imagined that I would one day travel so far?

The past weeks were as merciless as rebellious sepahis. Most of the time I was too tired to think. My thoughts moved as sluggishly as the train. Adolph had strong stone slabs placed on the hillslopes so that the pack animals could climb more easily. The sun either burned in our faces at such a high angle that we had to squint our way along gorges, or it denied us light in the dusk, which forced us to feel our way with hands, feet and faith. Several times, members of the train sneaked away secretly. One of them stole not only provisions and a horse, but also a thermometer and a geological hammer. When Adolph discovered this, he cursed loudly. Never before have such Bavarian curses resounded in the Kuenluen.

However, the greatest challenge lies ahead of us.

Thanks to a caravan – the first people in six weeks – we got the news about a rebellion against the Chinese in Turkestan. We were strongly advised against travelling any further. But we cannot hold out in the deserts for long, our supplies are scarce. Abdullah was sent out as a scout by Adolph (actually by Eleazar). To our relief, the draughtsman later reported that the rebellion had not yet spread very far. Adolph hopes to reach the Russian-dominated part of Turkestan without encountering militant forces. Eleazar hopes that the Chinese have not been driven out of Kashgar.

Despite the danger that faces the train we have been resting for a few hours on the Kilian Pass. Adolph and I are working on an aquarelle: *The Kilian Range and Its Northern Branches.*

The Schlagintweit is unusually quiet and serious. Not because he is afraid. No. I believe he senses, as I do, that a great change is about to take place. If only I could convince him to stay in India! Adolph eats with his hands almost as fast as I do. When he sits down, he squats; his *O-asch* never touches the ground. And he speaks almost fluent Hindi; he hardly needs his brilliant translator any more. The Schlagintweit has not made me more of a firangi, rather I have made him more Indian. For me, he is not a Bavarian. Adolphji belongs to us.

That is why I feel even more dejected at the thought of leaving him. I have not told him yet, but this aquarelle will probably be our last. I will not go with him to Berlin, I will not get to meet the greatest scientist of the world, and I will not set up an Indian museum with the brothers.

Eleazar will be pleased about this. It means everything to him that I do not leave my country. He sees a lot of himself in me. I struggled against that for a long time. After all, Eleazar is a bad man, and even if India now needs bad men on its side to fight and win our country back, I have always considered myself to be good. But I am not. I have not murdered anyone, but I am no better than Eleazar, Abdullah or Mr Monteiro. I deceived Mani Singh and the Schlagintweits, I delivered Hormazd to his fate, I did not save Devinder. And I now also know why. Despite all the ordeals I have overcome in the last three years I am still a cowardly small boy who trembles at the thought of the dare in Bori Bunder. I am useless for a rebellion.

But I also cannot turn away from my country.

What should I do?

For the first time in a long time, this question has led me to you again. What would you have advised me to do, I thought; what solution would the wise Father Fuchs have revealed to me? That is when I understood the mistake I had been making since the worst month. I act as if you were still here. Smitaben would smack me on the mouth for saying this, but I believe Adolph and Eleazar are nothing other than your reincarnations. So much of you has come back into my life with the firangi and the Bania. I stay close to these men because I do not want to let you go.

But that is exactly what I must do now. You told me once that one can only be free when one knows who one is. That may be true. But the opposite is also true. I can only know who I am if I am free.

That is why I will not travel with Adolph into the centre of his great love, and not with Eleazar either into the heart of the rebellion. As soon as we reach Kashgar I will tell them this and will join a caravan going to India. I am at least fifteen years old, and I can find my own way. If I do not make any stupid mistakes, my way will lead me to Calcutta. I do not know whether I will go there as a firangi or as an Indian. But I will go. To live with the only person who has never fed me lies but has always given love. Smitaben is my true family.

In the night you left us, my kind, precious Father, I did not have the time to send you one word of love, of remembrance, of my heartfelt esteem and of eternal farewell. Among all the things I have been instrumental in doing, this expedition, which began with my first day in the Glass House so many years ago and which is now coming to an end, remains one of the most important. It will gladden me even on my deathbed. May you be well.

Yours
Bartholomew

Remarkable Object No. 92

THE END OF OUR ROUTE

Today, on 5 August, our train reached the first inhabited place north of the Kuenluen range. It is called, if I have understood correctly, Chisganlik. A rough settlement, no more than a service place for caravans. There is fodder for the animals here. And fresh mutton, which most people in the train are willing to eat.

8 August.

We are still going down the Kuenluen. Adolph has divided the train into two parts: into a smaller group that comprises only him, Eleazar, Abdullah, Mr Monteiro, me and a groom, posing as a caravan from Turkestan; and into a bigger group with the rest of the Indians, Tibetans and the goods. This group will maintain a distance of a day's march from us. We are following byways and camping in secluded villages in order, as far as possible, to avoid the *wild hordes*, as Adolph calls them.

10 August.

Yesterday we arrived in Kargalik. Adolph has dispensed with all unnecessary items, has dismissed the Indians and Tibetans, and has told them to hand over his notes to the authorities of the Vickys in

India. Would it not be better to hire more men? They could protect us if something were to happen. Adolph and Eleazar do not share this view. They say we would never be able to find (and pay) so many men. It would be better to travel on without attracting attention. Our train can hardly be called a train any more.

A few days before we had arrived, Kargalik was plundered by the rebels. As we now learnt, a certain Vali Khan has risen up against the Chinese. (I wonder what Abdullah thinks of the fact that a Muslim brother is acting against his ally.) The people of Kargalik had no means of withstanding a rebel attack. Most of them are peasants. Many were seriously injured, and even their chieftain suffered a slash wound. Adolph is treating the wound. In return, the chieftain is offering us a good price for our three camels from Ladakh. We got a lot of provisions for our journey through the desert.

11 August.

Departure from Kargalik. Our next destination is Yarkant, the only city on our route to Kashgar.

13 August.

Villagers have told us that Yarkant has been besieged by the rebels. The Chinese are hemmed in. Adolph and Eleazar want to avoid Yarkant. They are both of the same opinion again. That scares me.

15 August.

We encountered the wild hordes. Outside Yarkant, they surrounded our small train on their horses. The chief was Dil Khan, a vassal of Vali Khan. One would not expect wild men to know so much about textiles. Adolph gave him silk from the Punjab. Dil Khan barely had to touch the material to judge its quality. He called out something, and the silk changed hands.

In the evening we were guests of the wild hordes. They may not smell very friendly, but in fact they are. We have not eaten so much in a long time. Horseflesh was served in our honour. The slice with the most fat was handed to Adolph. He put it in his mouth and chewed on it for a long time. Just when I thought he would never stop, he swallowed it and laughed. Abdullah, the only one who knew the language of the not-so-wild hordes, warned him that this could be construed as an insult. But the draughtsman underestimated Adolph's laugh. It is his most extraordinary weapon, and it works in every language. When Adolph laughed, the wild hordes also laughed and handed him another piece of horseflesh.

16 August.

The Chinese, or as Adolph calls them, the *Katais* risked a sortie and routed the rebels. Now, the Katais are proceeding brutally against all non-Katais. Eleazar and Adolph agree that we should wait, hide in the vicinity of Yarkant and travel on later.

18 August.

We continue on our journey to Kashgar.

19 August.

The train has very little merchandise or silver left. I do not know how Adolph will reach Europe with so few means. He says the Russians will help him. I asked him if he speaks Russian. He said, no, but after all, he is accompanied by a brilliant translator who will definitely learn Russian quickly.

23 August.

To the east and west of our route the surrounding area is devastated. Isolated settlements have been abandoned and burned down. The debris is still hot. We find it difficult to get provisions. In the few populated villages, the people have barricaded themselves. We are not let in.

25 August.

We approach Kashgar cautiously. With each step forward we become slower. About two miles south of the city we came to a bazaar. It has come up there because travellers and caravans do not dare to go to Kashgar. It has been captured by Vali Khan.

When we heard this, neither Adolph nor Eleazar said anything. I asked them what they planned to do now. Adolph replied that under these circumstances one would, unfortunately, have to avoid Kashgar.

Eleazar did not reply.

We set up camp near the bazaar. It seems to be safer there than in the open. I lay down next to Adolph. Even though I do not want to sleep. These are my last hours at his side; this is the end of our route. Tomorrow, in the bazaar, I will hire myself out to a caravan that is going to India. The Schlagintweit has to find his way home without me.

Eleazar is lying down not far from us. His back is turned towards me, and he is not moving, but I know he is awake. The Bania cannot fool me any more. I can see that he is deep in thought, that he is trying to overcome his disappointment. Has Vali Khan thwarted his alliance with the Chinese? I am sure Eleazar is already hatching new plans. I presume, he, Abdullah and Mr Monteiro will part company with Adolph and go back to Yarkant. If they can get through to the Chinese, they might have another chance.

While everyone, even Eleazar, slept, I crept up to Adolph. I wanted to wake him up gently to say goodbye, but I only looked at him. The chubby cheeks had been thinned down by the journey. But there is more of him that remains here. One cannot take away so much from a country without leaving something of oneself behind. The greatest part of that is what I carry of him within me. I will tell everyone the remarkable story of Adolph Schlagintweit. It is about a firangi who became a friend. And about a scientist who understood that his people and ours belong to the same world.

I did not wake him up. One cannot say goodbye to someone like Adolph. One must either stay with him or leave him. I whispered a Bavarian salutation and crept away.

In the bazaar I negotiated with a broad-shouldered and thin-lipped Muslim whose caravan was leaving for Leh that same day. I told him in six languages that I am a brilliant translator. Since he knew three of them himself, I was able to convince him to take me along.

While the camels were being loaded, Vali Khan's soldiers rode into the caravanserai. They stole provisions and replied to pleas with blows. One of them approached me. He asked me something in his language which I did not understand. I looked down. The soldier caught hold of my chin and forced me to look him in the eyes. They were the most beautiful eyes I have ever seen in a man. I would have liked to look at them a little longer in order to discover what made them so beautiful. But the soldier caught hold of me. I hit him with my walking stick. The soldier broke it and threw me onto his horse like a sack of meat. Before he could mount the horse, someone called out something to him. I knew the voice. It belonged to Abdullah. I had never been so happy to see the draughtsman. His eyes were not particularly beautiful, but the dawn shimmered in them. He had come for me. Not only he. Mr Monteiro, directly behind him, had taken out his riding crop which moved like a nervous snake. Even Eleazar was there. None of his knives were visible, but I knew they would be as fast as Adolph's rifle. The Schlagintweit, standing next to him, held it in his hands as if it were only an oar. But if someone who means something to him is threatened, he can, as I have seen for myself, slash you to shreds with it.

I will never forget the sight of these four men. I do not like most of them, but I liked how they stood there together.

Abdullah and the soldier called out to each other in short sentences. Neither moved. The tumult in the caravanserai now spread to the bazaar. Merchants hurriedly packed up their goods. A macaque screamed in its cage, coughed and continued to scream; tents collapsed, sand rose in the air, a camel trotted off riderless into the desert. Abdullah now called out in longer sentences, the soldier in even shorter ones. The draughtsman and the others came closer. But not Eleazar. The Bania moved away. Abdullah's sentences became longer and longer, they surrounded the soldier's sentences till the latter fell silent and drew his sword. By then Eleazar, who had come up directly from behind, had already reached him and held one of his knives to the man's throat. The soldier gave up and threw himself face down in the sand. Adolph lifted me from the horse onto his shoulders. At first, we hurried, looking around us carefully, then we ran.

We are riding. I am sitting behind Adolph, holding on to him tightly. Our four horses are breathing heavily. Their hoofbeats dictate my heartbeats. We cannot see or hear anyone chasing us. But we know that they are coming. We have to reach Russian territory before they do. The direct route forces us to ride past Gul-Bagh, the fort at Kashgar which the rebels have captured. The fortress is quiet. Its gates are closed. We leave it behind and follow the flow of a river. It gives us cover. Soon we will reach safety.

Remarkable Object No. 93

ADOLPH SCHLAGINTWEIT (4)

They were lying in wait for us behind a bend in the river; they took away all our weapons, even the museum. They separated Mr Monteiro from us, took us into the courtyard of the governor's house in Kashgar and put us in chains. They spat out unintelligible words at us and warned us with threatening gestures not to talk. But they did not forbid us from writing in the museum. I do not need pencil and paper for that. I am recording everything in my head and will write it down later.

Their rules do not apply to Adolph. As a European, he can talk as much as he wants. The soldiers allow it. He tells me that in the previous century, the Bavarian legal code had placed the death penalty on a large number of crimes. I ask myself what that has to do with our situation, but I do not ask the Schlagintweit because I prefer to do without the blows. Adolph says, at that time five executions took place every Saturday in Munich, and in a single district of the city, 1100 people were executed in twenty-eight years, whereas in India it was much less common to inflict such drastic punishments for robbery, or even for murder, as befitted a high level of development.

Upon hearing this, Eleazar, who had been listening quietly the entire time, said: But we are no longer in India.

Immediately, a guard steps up to him and holds his weapon in the air. Eleazar nods, presses his lips together.

No one steps up to Adolph.

What is the date today? he asks.

He looks at me as if it were an obvious question.

26 August 1857, I whisper.

Start of the summer holidays! he cries out.

Keep quiet, I tell him with my eyes.

It has always been my favourite day, says Adolph, now things can only get better.

Do you really believe that, Sir? I ask with my mouth.

Adolph replies by sitting up. He gazes at me steadily and smiles. I wish he would show some fear. It must be somewhere inside him. The fact that he does not let it show, scares me even more. I feel his fear for him, and I want to tell the Schlagintweit that I could gladly do without it. Not because it is too much for me, no, an orphan from Blacktown can never have enough of it. Fear keeps me alive more than water or air; without fear I would not be here today. A firangi so far from his home also needs some of it. Even a firangi working for the Vickys. The Schlagintweit has still not understood this.

The door opens. A Turk of average height and breadth enters. His beard draws a triangle around his mouth. He examines us briefly and then turns to Adolph. Abdullah translates. The Turk is in the service of Vali Khan. He wants to know whether we are spies. Adolph says, we are not. The Turk is silent for a moment, then he says, he knows that we are spies for the Russians or the Chinese or the Angrez. But Adolph insists that we are not spies. The Turk calls out something and the door opens again. A soldier hands him the Museum of the World. He holds it with both hands in front of Adolph's face. The Turks could not have read it, it is impossible that they know German. Adolph pretends not to recognize the museum. The Turk clearly believes that only a firangi could have filled so many pages. He asks for a torch and holds it close to the museum. Adolph says nothing, Eleazar says nothing, Abdullah says nothing. I cry out to him not to do that, and the Turk turns to me. He asks me if I know something. I look down and shake my head and hear Eleazar. In his friendliest voice he tells the Turk he is right, there were indeed spies in the train, but they had been executed long ago. Eleazar is then dragged away. The Turk drops the museum down in front of me. Talk! he says. But I remain silent. And then he sets fire to the museum. The Turk waits for my reaction; he looks at me hungrily. I concentrate on not letting the tears fall from my eyes. Before these very eyes, the Museum of the World disintegrates into its smallest pieces. The smoke is acrid. When the fire dies down, the Turk steps on the ashes, continues to look at Adolph and holds out his hand for mine. I hesitate for a moment, as if I had a choice, then I stretch out my hand to him and finally see fear in Adolph's eyes. While I am still thinking that this fear will protect us from the worst, the Turk grabs my thumb with the other hand and breaks it. I scream. Adolph screams. The Turk has also seen Adolph's fear. He takes my hand again and asks once more whether we are spies, and Adolph protests that I am his servant and he, the subject of the honourable East India Company. The Turk then clutches my hand more tightly and looks at Adolph. I try not to look at Adolph because I know that he cannot deal with so much fear. But then I do look at him and Adolph looks at me and I understand that I have to save him one last time, otherwise he will never reach Berlin. I tell the Turk that I am the spy, and I tell Adolph that I had to do it to protect Smitaben, and I tell him that I am very, very sorry, and then I look away so that I do not have to see Adolph's disappointment. Abdullah does not translate any of my words, he only tells me to keep my mouth shut, otherwise that will be the end of me, and the Turk breaks my little finger and the ring finger, first one, then the other, and I scream, but the pain does not go away from screaming; it stays, as if my fingers were breaking again and again. The Turk takes my hand a third time and does not become louder; he does not speak politely, but also not in a hostile manner; he speaks as if he were reading out scientific measurements. He claims that Adolph is an ally of their enemies. But this time Adolph does not reply immediately. He is thinking, and I can see how my words seep into him, and I use the moment to tell Abdullah that he should translate the truth. But the draughtsman is silent. And Adolph, who should also keep quiet, now tells the Turk in remarkable Hindi that he is right, he, Adolph Schlagintweit, leader of this research expedition, is a spy in the service of the East India Company. I cry out to Abdullah not to translate this, but the draughtsman does not listen to me, and when he is done, the Turk lets go of my hand. I look at Adolph. All fear has left him. I tell him he should not have done that, and he replies that he had to do it, otherwise they would execute me, but the Turks would spare him, they had no other choice, they would certainly not wish to invite the wrath of the powerful Company on themselves. Adolph stands up now. He is taller than the Turk. The Schlagintweit demands to speak to Vali Khan.

The Turk looks at him, longer than before, then he nods.

Adolph, Abdullah and I are led out of the governor's house. I do not look at my broken fingers, as if that would alleviate the pain. We follow the not so tall Turk. Soldiers guide us with the pointed ends of their weapons. We cross the marketplace which borders on a mosque. Many people stop and look at us. Most of the looks are trained on Adolph, the gora with the dirty clothes of a caravan merchant, the unwashed hair and the unkempt beard. Our group leaves Kashgar through a gate. Perhaps they will put us on horses and send us away, perhaps the fear of the Vickys is already widespread, I think. But then I see the pyramids. They are made up of heads, hundreds of heads neatly piled up, a new head growing out of two others. Some of them are sun-bleached bones; the birds satiate themselves from others. The Turk stops. An executioner steps up to us. Adolph looks at me, and I can now clearly sense his fear, I want to say something to lessen this fear, I want to help him, just then the Turk stabs him in the chest with a dagger, Adolph falls and is caught by the executioner and dragged to a bloody scaffold and beheaded.

The Last Object

We share a cell with the night. Since many weeks or more. It is so dark here that one cannot see even shades of darkness. Sometimes I touch my eyes to make sure they are really open.

The cell of our Jahannam has four corners. In one of the corners, we relieve ourselves, Eleazar sits in one, I sit in another, and we move around in the fourth when we cannot tolerate our corner any more, when the walls bear down on us and slowly crush us.

The problem with darkness is not the dark. It hardly bothers me, I am sure it even protects me from seeing things I would not want to see: the dirt, the rats, my broken fingers, Eleazar, and my reflection in his eyes. But I curse the darkness because it contains a void which is sucking me in, which is dousing me out, making me forget that I am here. I blink into the darkness. I try to see the difference between black and blacker. But I am unable to do this.

When the darkness becomes too large and powerful, I creep up to Eleazar and feel for his hand with my uninjured one. He does not hold me as tightly as he did a few days ago. But I do not tell him this. I do not want to remind him of his condition. He needs light and stuffed rotis and hot milk with haldi, and perhaps also a little opium. But here he gets only water that tastes brackish and is full of sand. Eleazar's cough is as constant as his breathing. And it sounds exactly like Father Fuchs's cough. I told him that, and it made both of us laugh (and then made Eleazar cough). This laugh tasted better than fresh water. It was our first since Adolph's end.

I think of him constantly. In my dreams I am the executioner who chops off his head. These dreams keep me in their grip for a long time; I rarely wake out of them with a start, and if that does happen, I immediately sink into them again.

That is only fair. It will not be very long before I die. Till then these dreams are my punishment. If I had not left the train, all this would not have happened.

When the Turks found out that Mr Monteiro was a Christian, they cut open his throat in front of us. They did not give Eleazar time to bid farewell to his oldest friend. At least not with words. Venkatesh returned Vasco's look till we were led away. Since then, he has not talked about it even once. But I know that he cannot forget it. Eleazar says often: At least Abdullah got away with his life.

But this life will not be very worth living. Because he is an Indian, he was sold into slavery. The dealers were not interested in Eleazar and me. That is why the Turks wanted to execute us too. We only managed to save our lives by converting to Islam. Eleazar said, he always envied the Muslims their heaven; now he had something to look forward to. With that he gifted us our second laugh since Adolph's end.

We had to wait a long time for our third laugh, even longer than a reply from the firangi. Before the Turks locked us away, Eleazar convinced them to let us send some letters. He promised them that the Angrez would pay a big reward for our release. And so, we wrote: to the Court of Directors of the East India Company in London. To Lord Hay in Simla. To Governor-General James Broun-Ramsay in Calcutta. To Lord Elphinstone in Bombay. To Consul Ventz and Consul Schiller. To Friedrich Wilhelm IV. To Alexander von Humboldt. To Hermann and Robert Schlagintweit.

Then we moved into the darkness and the wait began.

In the early days of our imprisonment, the Turks still brought us food. It did not look very impressive; Smitaben would not even have called it food. Soaked nuts and flat bread full of holes. Sometimes a handful of dried, fermented fruits. At least it was enough to fill me and to combat Eleazar's cough. The Turks kept us and their hopes alive for a reward. But after some time had passed and no reply had come, less food was brought and soon afterwards they stopped bringing us anything at all. I doubted that our letters had even reached their destinations. Could the Schlagintweits have received our news at all? Had they reached Berlin already, or were they still on the way home? Would the addressees be able to read our shaky handwriting? Was the postal service between Turkestan and India functioning again?

On a day that was as dark as all the others, they brought us a letter. It had the seal of the Company. It took a long time till our eyes got used to the light of the torches and we could read it. It did not take long for us to understand the message which consisted only of two lines written by some official in the offices of the Company. Your matter will certainly be taken up, he wrote, the honourable East India Company does not neglect any of its subjects, nevertheless we should be patient.

That was all. He did not say any more, we did not receive any more letters.

I would like to believe that Hermann and Robert have no inkling of our predicament and have, therefore, not written. But I cannot rule out that they know what happened to their brother and who caused his death. In their place I would not help me either. And as far as all the other firangi are concerned: I thank them for their silence. It shows me clearly which side I am on.

Ever since we know that no one is going to help us, Eleazar is dying faster.

He coughs more and talks less. His voice in the dark, the voice that is friendly even now, reminds me of how I had heard it the first time. It was three years ago, when I was sitting in the box. I find it difficult to remember who I was then.

I wish I had a handkerchief for Eleazar. Sometimes his coughing wakes me up, and for a brief moment I think I am in the Glass House and this journey was only a dream. But the more I come awake, the more the Glass House seems to be a distant dream.

It is amazing how much Eleazar's cough sounds like Father Fuchs's cough. An exquisite sound. The fact that it belongs to the Bania does not change anything. When he coughs, my thoughts don't bother me. When he coughs, I can fall asleep easily and wake up quickly. When he coughs, I know that I will soon know a little more.

Eleazar held my hand, and, in his friendly voice, he described the synagogue in Cochin. He had never been allowed to enter it, but he had often peered inside through a window. Gold crowns of allied maharajas are kept in the synagogue as well as four scrolls of the Bible edged in silver and gold which the Jews call the Torah. But this splendour never impressed Eleazar. He always admired the floor of the synagogue. It is made of hand-painted blue and white tiles produced in Canton. They tell the love story of the daughter of a Mandarin and a commoner.

I asked Eleazar how the story ends.

He replied: Go to Cochin and find out.

The Bania believes that Kashgar is only another station on my journey. He insists that I drink his water. I refuse. My life can no longer be paid for with the death of others. I explained that to Eleazar. I even confessed that I had wanted to leave him and Adolph. That did not make him angry. Eleazar was silent for a moment, and then he told me again to drink his water. My thirst wanted to do as he said, but I remained firm. If only I had the museum! Then I could write how remarkably firm I am. That would make it a little easier.

An hour, or several days later, Eleazar asked me what I was thinking about since I was painfully quiet.

My museum, I said.

He asked where it was.

I told him about the ash.

A moment passed. I was grateful that he did not ask why I had not defended it with my life.

That is India's first museum, he said.

That was India's first museum, I said.

He asked for a tour of the museum.

It has been burned down, I said.

But not in your head, right? They can never burn what is in your head.

No, I said, they cannot.

Then show it to me, he said and – I am quite certain – closed his eyes, lead me through your museum.

I hesitated.

I am waiting, he said.

And so, I began.

It does not seem to me as if I were narrating the museum to Eleazar. It is also not a description, or a report. Rather, I translate it for him. He does not know German. I do this last translation of my life for the first reader of my museum. All at once, everything I have observed, experienced and written down sounds so true in Hindi, truer than ever before. It was never false, but the first museum of India sounds the way it should only now. Naturally, I do not translate everything. Eleazar does not need to hear what he has also experienced, or what I sometimes thought of him. And I cannot remember many things exactly. But I translate everything that I still know and that he should know. First, the bamboo cane and the Bavarian handkerchief. Then I translate bubble-free ice and the khana and the kingdom of evil. Then, Lord Ganesha's true head and Moby Dick and the Toga Virilis, the ant march, loneliness and Tibet. Then, Jahannam, the blue of an Indian, Gaudi. Then, infinity.

The entire time Eleazar holds my hand. When his touch slackens, or when his hand slips out of mine, I stop and wait till he wakes up again and asks me to continue.

But it is not only his weakness that interrupts me.

We laughed for the third and fourth and fifth and sixth and seventh and eighth and ninth and tenth and eleventh time. That may not be much, but for two traitors in a dark dungeon waiting for their end, it is a lot.

AFTER I HAD finished, Eleazar did not stir for a long time, as if he were I facing the dare. Then – of this I am again certain – he opened his eyes and applauded. He clapped his hands so long and so loudly that the guards came to our cell and prodded us with their cursing and swearing.

I congratulate you, said Eleazar, your entire museum is a remarkable object. But, he added, Father Fuchs was wrong. The objects in the museum do not tell you who you are. They only tell you who you were.

I wanted to let go of his hand. He did not allow it. I was surprised that he still had so much strength.

The firangi invented museums, because without them they would forget themselves. But you do not need a museum. You are one yourself. *You* are India's first museum. The firangi cannot take your objects away from us and hoard them in their countries. Your existence here ensures that all Indian objects remain in the country.

Eleazar pulled me closer.

I have never before met someone who knows so clearly who he was. However, it is far more important that you find out who you want to be.

I did not need to think about that.

An Indian, I said.

An Indian, he said.

I heard the smile in his voice.

Now Eleazar was not holding me firmly any more. He did not have to. I was holding him firmly.

Then you should choose a new name, he said. A strong name that contains all the contradictions that go into being an Indian.

I thought about it. But no such name occurred to me.

Can you give me one? I asked.

Eleazar let go of my hand.

Can you? I asked again.

He proposed a deal: if I drank his water immediately, he would tell me the perfect name.

That made us laugh a twelfth time.

I THOUGHT ABOUT Eleazar's deal. After some minutes, or hours, I finally picked up his water bowl and drank it. Then I crept up to him, took his hand and told him to tell me the perfect name.

But Eleazar was no longer there.

I hold his cold hand and curse him, again and again, that he left without saying goodbye. I had wanted to tell him that he was not such a bad man after all.

THEY HAVE NOT taken away Eleazar's body. I call the guards in every language I know. They do not come; they do not even bring me water. That does not worry me; it will hasten my death. At least I hope so. I do not want to drag out this last step. If only I had a sharp object! I would make it the most remarkable object.

In the dark I hear water dripping. I do not look for it. Every drop will only delay my death. But the constant noise undermines my will.

SINCE I AM now a Muslim, I will probably not be cremated. Hormazd would have approved; it will not please Lord Ganesha so much.

I hope they at least bury me with Eleazar and Adolph.

THE DOOR TO my cell opens. The light blinds me. Hands catch hold of me and carry me out. The voices that belong to these hands do not speak the language of the Turks, and even though I do not know this language either, I remember it. Eleazar and Jeejeebhoy's assistant spoke it in Calcutta.

I AM FREE. The Chinese recaptured Kashgar and freed all the prisoners of the Turks from the dungeon. Vali Khan is on the run to Kokand in the Fergana valley. Most of the people of Kashgar have joined him; they fear the reprisals of the Chinese. The city is deserted except for Chinese soldiers. They take no notice of me. I would like to tell them that their ally died in Vali Khan's dungeon. But they do not speak any of my languages, and I speak none of theirs. And how would that change anything? Eleazar is dead. India must liberate itself without his and China's help.

I sleep in a stately house because no one stops me from doing so. The owners must have left in a hurry; the pantry is full. With each bite and each sip, I find myself returning to life. At dusk I walk through the streets but stay away from the place where Adolph took his last breath.

My eyes are still sensitive to the light.

But now I am finally awake.

I managed to enter the abandoned governor's house in Kashgar and to find the place where the museum had been burned. A black spot on the ground is all that remains of it.

It does not matter. I have found something much better: my perfect name. It is definitely not what Father Fuchs had in mind for the museum, and I cannot imagine that Eleazar or my mother would have chosen it for me. But it is the only right one, and far more remarkable than all the remarkable objects taken together. It is the name of a Hindu, but also of a baptized Christian and of a converted Muslim. And it is a Jewish name. It is a strong name that contains all the contradictions that go into being an Indian.

As soon as I have found my way back home, I will remind my country of who we were. Many stories will be written about the Schlagintweit brothers; after all, they are firangi. But I will speak of the life and death of invisible forces; I will be the measuring device that proves their work. Smitaben and Hormazd, Devinder and Mani Singh, Harkishen and Abdullah, Mr Monteiro and Eleazar, Adolphji and Father Fuchs. And all the others. They were the true invisible forces of this research expedition. They were all around us, but they were never seen, not truly seen. I will change that.

First, I must deal with one thing. I climb onto the roof of the stately house. From there I can see beyond the city walls. The high-altitude desert extends in all directions and all possibilities. I take the last object out of my kurta pocket. I had hidden it there before the Turks took the museum away from me. In the dungeon I had not dared to take it out for fear that the darkness would swallow it up. Now I hold Humboldt's silver hair in the wind and see it tremble excitedly. I thank it for accompanying me so faithfully for so long.

Then I let it go.

From this hour on, I will never speak, write or think in German, Bavarian or English.

My name is Eleazar, I am at least fifteen years old, and today, on 20 October 1857, I have joined the rebellion.

Author's Note

In the notes and publications of the Schlagintweits, an orphan boy from Bombay is not mentioned.

After returning home, Hermann wrote numerous volumes about their journey with Robert's help. For their achievements, the brothers were elevated to the ranks of Bavarian aristocracy, and as the conqueror of the Kuenluen, Hermann was given the honour of the name *von Schlagintweit-Sakünlünski*. From then on, two Bengal tigers graced the new family coat of arms. Robert went on extensive lecture tours to Russia, France, America and, especially, to German-speaking countries, where he always advocated the colonization of the Himalayas while emphasizing his brother's tragic end in the same breath.

In a passage in Humboldt's *Kosmos*, which deals with the new findings of the brothers about the Karakorum Range, Adolph is mentioned as an 'excellent friend'. The Schlagintweits are also named in five novels by Jules Verne. Later, when German colonialism began, their *Reisen in Indien und Hochasien* was reprinted. A Prussian advocate of German colonies wrote as early as in 1867: 'Humboldt, Leichhardt, Schlagintweit are names for which the greatest seafaring and colonial countries envy us, and we can justifiably call every undertaking aimed at German colonization an act of piety towards our martyrs of science who rest in foreign soil.'

Despite all this, the Schlagintweits were never able to establish an Indian museum. Firstly, because Adolph was not there to help with the analysis of the extensive data that had been collected. Secondly, they lost their most influential supporters very quickly. At the end of 1857, Frederick William IV gave up the duties of government. Alexander von Humboldt died in 1859. Doubts about the worth of the expedition also increased. Heinrich August Jäschke, an acknowledged mission director and linguist, is said to have stated about the brothers: 'The Schlagintweits have the wrong name; they should be called Schlagaufsmaul.' And in the Berlin satire magazine *Kladderadatsch*, the brothers were called 'Schnabelweit'.

The brothers also did not get much support from England. The leading London scientific journal *Athenaeum* wrote about them:

> Well, the Messrs Schlagintweit have come back, and have told the world their secret. They have been, it seems, on a voyage of discovery, and if we understand their report correctly, they claim to have found a range of mountains in Upper India called the Himalaya, and to have crossed the country between Bombay and Madras. Their travels in well-worn roads are styled 'a careful exploration of Asia'. The Prussian gentlemen, we find, have opened up Tibet, and are about to make India known to Europe. We in England fancied that we knew a little about India, and that we had done something towards laying open its physical and geographical features. But we were labouring, it would now appear, under strange illusions. [...] We have no hesitation in saying that the facts claimed as discoveries by the Schlagintweits were *all* known to English scientific men. [...] Our scientific corps in India consists of men unequalled in their own studies. Their Trigonometrical Survey is one of the noblest scientific labours of our generation. Is this the way to impress the native mind with the superiority of the English intellect and with the legitimacy of English rule?

In the empire, this emphasis on 'legitimacy' became particularly significant against the background of the Indian rebellion. Fearing a loss of power in South Asia, one's own importance had to be magnified, and all others disparaged. Most of the results of the studies conducted by the Schlagintweits – these German firangi – were declared irrelevant. The brothers were buried in oblivion. Even the East India Company did not survive the changed times. As a result of the rebellion, it was dissolved, and its privileges were transferred to the British Crown. The British dealt severely with the bloody 'mutiny'. More than a hundred thousand people died. In the end, the empire was able to regain control. The Raj was born, and with it the darkest era of colonial history. India would gain its independence only in 1947, eighty-nine years later.

C.K.

Acknowledgements

At the outset, I would like to express my gratitude to Jutta Jain-Neubauer. She was the one who told me about the Schlagintweits, which gave rise to my wish to write about the expedition. Without her inspiration I would never have set out on this adventure.

I would also like to thank everyone who collaborated on the volume *Über den Himalaya*; first and foremost, the editors Friederike Kaiser, Stephanie Kleidt and Moritz von Brescius. Their knowledge was my compass on this journey into a long-forgotten time.

My thanks also go out to the Robert Bosch Foundation and the Goethe Institute. With their help I was able to follow the trail of the Schlagintweits in many corners of the world.

I especially thank Saskya, who introduced me to Bartholomew. Both of them have been my dearest, most precious friends and they often saved me during this long venture.

Last, but not least, I owe a debt of gratitude to my editor Günther Opitz. In one of his first emails to me he wrote: 'In one of our last meetings I had said, one should sometimes take a risk. And I remembered this while reading your novel. I think one, i.e., dtv, should risk publishing your novel. And if you should like to risk it too, it would make me happy.' Since then, more than twelve years have gone by. *The Museum of the World* is the fifth book that we have done together. Günther is, as Bartholomew would say, a remarkable person. One may not be able to prove it scientifically, but I am convinced that Günther is the best editor an author could wish for. Our journey now comes to an end. I will miss him a lot.

About the Author and Translator

Christopher Kloeble is an award-winning scriptwriter and the author of three novels, a short-story collection and a memoir. He has taught at Dartmouth College, Georgetown University, Cambridge University and Hong Kong University, among others. His books have been translated into nine languages. He lives in Berlin and New Delhi.

Rekha Kamath Rajan spent the better part of her life reading, studying and teaching German literature at Elphinstone College in Mumbai and at the Centre of German Studies, Jawaharlal Nehru University, in Delhi. Her research focuses on representations of India in the German literary and missionary discourse.

30 Years *of*

HarperCollins *Publishers* India

At HarperCollins, we believe in telling the best stories and finding the widest possible readership for our books in every format possible. We started publishing 30 years ago; a great deal has changed since then, but what has remained constant is the passion with which our authors write their books, the love with which readers receive them, and the sheer joy and excitement that we as publishers feel in being a part of the publishing process.

Over the years, we've had the pleasure of publishing some of the finest writing from the subcontinent and around the world, and some of the biggest bestsellers in India's publishing history. Our books and authors have won a phenomenal range of awards, and we ourselves have been named Publisher of the Year the greatest number of times. But nothing has meant more to us than the fact that millions of people have read the books we published, and somewhere, a book of ours might have made a difference.

As we step into our fourth decade, we go back to that one word – a word which has been a driving force for us all these years.

Read.